and if you're a fan of writers like Lars Kepler, Stefan Ahnhem, and/or Søren Sveistrup, you won't want to miss this thrilling crime-fiction series' Crime by the Book

'*Stigma* surprises on many levels, ... a completely nerve-wracking story' *Tvedestrandsposten*

'Great entertainment! *Stigma* is a perfectly poised suspense' *Verdens Gang*

'The series offers everything you would expect from Scandinavian suspense literature ... An absolute must for thriller fans' *Krimi Couch*

'Horst and Enger simply write wonderful detective stories and *Stigma* is living proof of that' Thriller Zone

'The collaboration between the two authors has resulted in some excellent books, and that level is absolutely maintained in this unusually angled crime novel' *KrimiFan*

'A fast-moving, punchy, serial killer investigative novel with a whammy of an ending. If this is the first in the Blix & Ramm series, then here's to many more!' LoveReading

'One of those jaw-dropping "what did you just do" kind of conclusions that will leave fans of the series reeling' Jen Med's Book Reviews

'Intense, dark, emotional and utterly outstanding!' Karen Cole

ABOUT THE AUTHORS

Jørn Lier Horst and Thomas Enger are both internationally bestselling Norwegian authors. Jørn Lier Horst first rose to literary fame with his no. 1 bestselling William Wisting series. A former investigator in the Norwegian police, Horst imbues all his works with an unparalleled realism and suspense. Thomas Enger is the journalist-turned-author behind the internationally acclaimed Henning Juul series. Enger's trademark is his dark, gritty voice paired with key social messages and tight plotting. Besides writing fiction for both adults and young adults, Enger also works as a music composer.

Death Deserved, the first book in the bestselling Blix and Ramm series, was Jørn Lier Horst and Thomas Enger's first co-written thriller and was followed by *Smoke Screen* and *Unhinged*.

Follow Jørn Lier and Thomas on Twitter @LierHorst and @EngerThomas; Instagram @lierhorst and @author_thomas_enger; Facebook: facebook.com/thomas.enger.77 and facebook.com/jlhorst; and their websites: jlhorst.com and thomasenger.com.

ABOUT THE TRANSLATOR

Megan Turney is a literary and commercial translator and editor, working from Norwegian and Danish into English. She was the recipient of the National Centre for Writing's 2019 Emerging Translator Mentorship, and holds an MA (Hons) in Scandinavian Studies and English Literature from the University of Edinburgh, and an MA in Translation and Interpreting Studies from the University of Manchester. She has previously translated the Blix and Ramm Series by Jørn Lier Horst and Thomas Enger and *Thirty Days of Darkness* by Jenny Lund Madsen for Orenda Books. You can find a list of her other translations and work at www.meganeturney.com.

The Blix and Ramm Series – available from Orenda Books:
Death Deserved
Smoke Screen
Unhinged
Stigma

STIGMA

THOMAS ENGER & JØRN LIER HORST

TRANSLATED BY MEGAN TURNEY

ORENDA
BOOKS

Orenda Books
16 Carson Road
West Dulwich
London SE21 8HU
www.orendabooks.co.uk

First published in the United Kingdom by Orenda Books, 2023
First published in Norwegian as *Arr* by Bonnier Norsk Forlag, 2022
Copyright © Jørn Lier Horst & Thomas Enger, 2022
English translation copyright © Megan Turney, 2023

A catalogue record for this book is available from the British Library.

ISBN 978-1-914585-76-0
eISBN 978-1-914585-77-7

This book has been translated with financial support from NORLA

Typeset in Garamond by www.typesetter.org.uk

Printed and bound by CPI Group (UK) Ltd, Croydon CR0 4YY

For sales and distribution, please contact *info@orendabooks.co.uk* or visit
www.orendabooks.co.uk.

PROLOGUE

Walter Kroos looked down at his watch.

01:14.

The house was silent.

His mother had gone to bed hours ago, but he hadn't heard his father come in from the shed. So he must've fallen asleep out there. Again.

This was just the opportunity Walter had been waiting for.

It was time.

His hatred had stewed for long enough.

After they had returned home from Norway, he had started hearing voices in his head, yelling, barking at him, and they'd only grown louder. Now they were screaming.

Walter pushed himself up from the bed and lowered his feet to the cold floor. He swiftly headed into the kitchen and opened the drawer where they kept the knives. Took out the sharpest one he could find.

It felt heavy in his hand.

And suddenly, everything felt foreign. His hands, legs, heart. As if he had taken up residence in another body.

Walter didn't bother putting on his coat, even though it was cold and snowing outside. He simply shoved his feet into a pair of tatty old trainers. The rubber soles squeaked as they crossed the stark white yard, over to the shed. His breath hung in the cold air like a cloud. The voices urged him forward.

The door to his father's woodworking shed was stuck in the frame as always. For a moment, Walter was afraid that the jerk it took to open it would wake his father, but he found him sitting there in the chair, fast asleep, his head slumped to one side, chin resting on his chest.

As always, the cramped little room smelled of sawdust and alcohol. But there was another scent this time, one Walter couldn't quite put his finger on.

He didn't close the door behind him, just pulled it to. He stood there for a few moments, in the shed, staring down at his father's greying hair, his bulging stomach. His clothes were filthy. Shoes coated in white sawdust. A sad excuse for a human being. You'd actually be doing him a favour, Walter thought. And that was almost reason enough *not* to go through with it.

On the table next to his father were sheets of fine sandpaper and a butter knife he had almost finished carving, as well as a small bottle of gun oil.

That was what he could smell.

His father would often take out his service weapons, polish them, oil them. The rifle was propped up behind him. His pistol on the workbench. Walter tightened his grip around the kitchen knife.

Then again, it was possible to shoot yourself. And suicide was such a pitiful way out. His father deserved to be humiliated – he who had always been *a man,* a soldier, always so proud and strong.

Walter went to take a step round him, but one of the floorboards creaked, so he stopped. His father let out a snort. Made some movements with his mouth, but his eyes remained closed.

Walter waited a long time before moving again. He put the knife on the workbench. Grabbed the gun instead. Felt the weight of it.

A few years ago he had asked if he could try it. His father had just scoffed at him and laughed. 'You'll only end up shooting yourself,' he had said.

Walter now turned to his father, face to face, raised the gun, and slowly moved his index finger to the trigger.

Aimed the barrel at his head. Closed one eye and focused.

His hands began to tremble.

Walter pressed down a little more firmly, but the trigger refused to budge. He studied the weapon more closely. Realised that he had to take the safety off first. He had no idea if the gun was even loaded, but there was an open box of cartridges on the table.

Maybe the bastard had actually intended to take his own life, Walter thought, and aimed the gun at his head again. Took a step closer this time and held the muzzle almost right up to his forehead. Closer now, he could see how his father's beard was speckled black and grey. How his flabby skin sat in folds under his chin.

Walter gritted his teeth, tried to get his heartbeat and his hands under control. Pulled even harder on the trigger, and felt it start to obey. His whole body shook, his hands shook, and in that moment, he felt the rage erupt like an inferno inside him.

And then, his father opened his eyes.

✳

He needed to take a moment. He had never spoken about this to anyone before.

'And then...?'

The voice on the other end was impatient.

'And then ... it went off.'

'You shot him?'

Walter raised his head. Heard someone knocking on a cell door further down the hallway.

'Yes,' he answered.

'Wow,' she said.

Walter thought that was a strange thing to say, but didn't comment on it.

'How did it feel?'

'At the time?' Walter said, thinking about it. 'A bit ... weird. I mean, just before I pulled the trigger I felt...' He couldn't find the right words.

'Powerful?' she suggested.

Walter considered the word. Powerful was probably about right.

'What happened after that?'

Walter took a deep breath in.

'He just slid off the chair and crumpled into a heap on the floor. His eyes were open, as if he were still alive. It was like ... I couldn't quite believe what I'd done. And the bang ... it was so loud. So, so loud. Inside that tiny shed ... My ears were ringing.'

He had to pause again.

'Did it help?' she asked.

'Huh?'

'Killing him. Did you feel better, afterwards?'

Walter wasn't sure how to answer that. He thought for a moment.

'No. They didn't stop. In my head. But it's not like someone's in there now, talking to me, like, on a daily basis. There's just more ... noise.'

'And you didn't try to make the police believe he'd just shot himself instead?'

'No. I didn't care enough to bother. At that point I'd just thought, like, come and get me. I wanted people to know what a piece of shit Kurt Kroos was. I didn't say anything about what he did to *you* though. Mentioning that felt unnecessary, but—'

'Wait, what do you mean?'

'Hm?'

'What he did to me, you said. What are you talking about?'

Walter swallowed.

'That summer,' he said. 'When you...'

He couldn't finish the sentence.

It took a long time before she said:

'Walter, it wasn't *your father* who—' She stopped herself.

'What are you saying?' he asked.

As she continued, the nausea rose from the depths of his stomach. It felt like a tight fist had its grip around his chest.

'Oh my God,' he heard in his ear. 'Did you think ... is *that* why you killed your father?'

Walter didn't answer.

Just hung up.

1

Blix put his head in his hands and listened as the door to the visiting room slammed shut.

It was over for today.

The footsteps disappeared down the corridor. He waited until it was all quiet, then he stood up, walked over to the window and leant his forehead against the plexiglass. The visiting room faced out onto the rear courtyard. There was a newly planted tree in the yard, frail with feeble branches and a thin trunk. Grey, almost leafless. He wondered how tall it would be in twelve years.

Sounds reached him from somewhere in the large building: shouting, in a foreign language. The man persisted for a short while, repeating the same thing over and over. Then there was silence.

A bird landed on one of the tree's young branches. It cocked its head to the side and jumped onto another branch. A new set of footsteps could be heard out in the corridor. Keys rattling in sync with the steps.

Blix turned his back to the window and stood waiting in the middle of the room. The door opened. It was Kathrin. Young, insecure. She walked into the room, and glanced around to make sure everything was as it should be, then beckoned Blix out of the room.

He walked ahead of her, down the underground passage that connected the administrative building with the rest of the prison. The sound of shoes scuffing against the worn linoleum. At every door they approached, he had to step aside and wait until it was unlocked. Five, in total.

The other prisoners looked up as Blix entered the common room. One of them made a snorting sound, mimicking the grunting of a pig. The others laughed and returned to whatever card game they were playing.

'Don't go straight to your cell,' Kathrin ordered. 'Do as the principal officer said. Try spending at least half an hour out in circulation today.'

Blix didn't answer.

Jakobsen was clearly on shift. He usually brought a copy of *Aftenposten* with him to work and left it out for the inmates. It had been a long time since Blix cared about what was going on in the news, but reading the daily newspaper was just about the only thing that reminded him of the life he had had on the outside.

The newspaper was on the table closest to the TV. He tried not to get in the way of those watching. The man who had grunted when Blix came in now followed him with his gaze. He put his hands together as if to make a gun with his fingers and imitated the sound of gunshots. Four in quick succession. The others laughed, drowning out the sound of the TV. Blix remained standing where he was, attempting to appear unfazed.

The news anchor was reporting on a story from Germany, something about how the German police had launched a major manhunt for an escaped prisoner who had been serving time for the murder of his father, and who had now also killed his mother. Blix pretended to follow along, standing there, watching the TV until the bulletin ended. He then bent down to pick up the newspaper.

The sound of a chair suddenly scraping back. The man on the other side of the table had quickly launched himself at him, and now had a firm grasp of his arm.

The room went silent. Only the reporter on the TV continued to speak.

Blix lowered his gaze. On the front page of the newspaper: a headline about a wave of youth robberies across Oslo. The grip around his wrist tightened.

'I didn't hear you say please,' a voice said.

Jarl Inge Ree had positioned himself at the top of the prison hierarchy, dominating everyday life within its walls. He had snarled the words, just low enough for none of the officers to catch them.

Blix looked up, fixed his eyes on Ree's. The eyes that met his were dark and showed no signs of backing down. Physically, Jarl Inge Ree had the upper hand, but unfortunately for him, he was sitting in a chair; he'd simply lurched forward to grab hold of Blix's arm, and was now teetering on the edge of the seat. Blix stood over him and so had the advantage.

He could easily wriggle free, grab Ree's arm with both hands, yank him out of the chair, hurl him on the floor and twist his arms behind his back, shove his knee into his neck. He felt his heart beat faster at the thought.

The consequences – being excluded by the inmates or put in isolation – meant nothing to him. Blix clenched his fist, but immediately released it again.

'Sorry,' he said, just loud enough for only those around the nearby tables to hear.

Jarl Inge Ree slowly let go.

Mortgage interest rates were on the way up, Blix read. It wasn't even that interesting. He left the newspaper and went to his cell.

2

The late-afternoon sun soaked the tired apartment buildings in a bright light, which also bore down on the people waiting for the city-centre tram at Holbergs Plass. On the rare occasions they looked up from their mobile phones, they had to shield their eyes and squint around at their surroundings.

Emma Ramm jogged on the spot, wondering whether her lungs and legs would do as they were told today. Yesterday, she almost made it all the way up to Blindern, but unlike today, she hadn't eaten before that run, nor had she been to the prison beforehand.

Blix had become even thinner. Paler. Had lost some hair too. When she asked about his life behind bars, what it was like to be a former police officer among that many criminals, he had answered evasively. The only thing she had managed to get out of him was something about someone called Jarl Inge Ree, who'd been paying him a little 'extra attention'. She knew him well enough now to realise that he internalised the concerns he didn't want to share, or, at least, he kept to himself anything he thought she couldn't help him with.

Regardless, the visits always had an effect on her. The sight of his tortured expression, the heavy silence. She could only imagine what it was like for Blix, having to carry the loss of his own daughter in addition to the prison sentence for taking the life of the man who killed her.

Emma felt her chest tighten.

She was not without blame for what had happened, even if Blix insisted otherwise. Emma felt like she owed him ... well, what, exactly? She just wished there was something she could do to make his life better. A little easier.

Emma pulled one of her earbuds out for a moment. Amid the noise of the passing cars, she had heard, and felt through her feet, the approaching rumble of the light-blue tram now gliding up from the city centre.

She put her earbud back in, pulled the zipper of her running jacket up her neck a little further, and took a few deep breaths. She adjusted her leggings slightly and checked that her phone was secure on her upper arm. The tram stopped. People got off, others got on.

Emma pressed play.

All Shall Fall. Immortal's best album – ever so slightly better than *Sons of Northern Darkness*. If she was going to work out, there was nothing better to do it to than Norwegian black metal. The tram slid away as the intro to the title track ended. The pale-blue colossus gradually picked up speed.

As did Emma.

She jogged right behind it, in the middle of the track, matching its speed until, eventually, it was too fast, and she watched it gradually put metres and metres between them. She knew she didn't have to push too hard at this point, however, as it wasn't that far up to Dalsbergstien, where the tram would stop for at least twenty seconds – enough time for her to catch up with it again.

She thought about Jarl Inge Ree.

Who was he, exactly?

The passengers poured out. Emma jogged on the spot until the doors eased shut and the tram continued onward. She concentrated on keeping her forefoot running form, landing on the ball of each foot and maintaining minimal contact with the ground. The tram ended up trundling behind a few cars this time, so it was easy to keep up. It drifted calmly across the roundabout outside Bislett Stadium.

Information was power, she thought. Maybe she could find out more about Ree? Something Blix could take advantage of?

Thereses Gate was a long road, all uphill. The tram sailed ten metres ahead, then twenty, evading her even though she was running almost at maximum speed. At the entrance to the next intersection, she took a moment to catch her breath, getting seven, maybe eight seconds of rest on Stensgata before continuing up towards Adamstuen. It was impossible to maintain that high a speed over a long distance. The lactic acid burned her calves, making her muscles tense up. Emma started lifting her shoulders as high as she could to create more room for oxygen in her lungs.

The traffic wasn't on her side though – at the intersection on Ullevålsveien she had to stop and wait for passing cars. She barely managed to catch up with the tram before it continued up towards Ullevål Hospital, but very quickly realised that she wouldn't be setting any kind of personal best today. She simply didn't have the same burst of energy as yesterday.

At John Colletts Plass, she stopped and bent over, resting her hands on her knees. Breathing hard as the enormous rectangle rattled ahead. Almost nine minutes, she registered on her sports watch.

Not good enough. She turned and calmly jogged home.

Instead of showering straight away, she sat down with her laptop and commenced a few online searches on Jarl Inge Ree. Soon found a photo of him in a local newspaper from when he turned thirty. A fair-haired man with close-set eyes.

He was from Osen, which turned out to be a small inland village about two hundred kilometres or so north of Oslo, and a favourite destination – apparently – among camping tourists, Norwegian and foreign alike. All Blix had said about him was that he was in jail for attempted murder after hitting a man on the head with a bat. In an article about the case, it was stated that he had previously been convicted of three other instances of violence, including against a policeman who had arrested him outside a nightclub in Grünerløkka. On top of that, he had a conviction for drug trafficking.

Emma returned to the photo from the local newspaper and examined it more closely. The picture was accompanied by a simple message, just a statement that he had turned thirty, with congratulations from his mother, father, Boffa and the rest of the family. Almost as if those closest to him didn't want their full names published.

There was something about his expression that she didn't like. As if he had some unfinished business with the photographer, or the world itself. She stood up and took off her sweaty running clothes. Before turning on the shower, she removed her wig and ran a hand over her completely smooth scalp.

She needed to find out more about Ree. She needed something else.

3

The numbers on the digital clock on his bookshelf ticked over to 07:14. Blix counted the seconds that followed. He closed his eyes and forced himself to lie still for at least one more minute.

Footsteps approached in the corridor. They stopped outside.

He glanced at the clock again.

07:14.

He listened as the key was inserted into the lock and rotated firmly, before the door was pulled open.

The bright light from the prison block flooded the room.

Nyberget stood in the doorway in his wrinkled uniform and dirty shoes.

'Urine test,' he said.

Blix sat up. It was the third time in a relatively short period that he'd been randomly selected. He grabbed his T-shirt from the back of the chair and pulled it over his head. Yanked on his trousers, slid his feet into the rubber sandals by the bed and followed the officer out into the hall.

Two others from his wing had also been selected. The large Polish man known as Grubben, staggered out of his cell, squinting at the light. Further down the hall, another officer was waiting outside cell six. Ree appeared in the doorway. His hair stood on end, sticking out in every direction. He tightened the drawstring at the waist of his joggers and then looked over at Grubben, then at Blix.

Nyberget led them down the tunnel and across the long corridor. Blix walked in the middle, with Ree shuffling along behind him.

Grubben was taken in first. Blix raised his head towards the surveillance camera outside the testing room. Ree leant back against the wall.

'S'been a long time since there were any rats down here,' he said.

Blix didn't respond, but understood what he was implying: that it was Blix who must have notified the officers about drug use on the wing, and he'd only been brought along for a sample so the others wouldn't suspect him of ratting them out. A kind of reverse psychology that had long since been sussed out by the inmates.

Grubben came out. Blix was called in.

He took one of the test tubes from the box on the table, went behind the shower curtain and positioned himself in front of the urinal. He filled the glass and corked it without spilling a drop, then let the rest of the stream hit the porcelain, before heading back round the curtain with the vial. Nyberget marked it with his name and number, and gave Blix a nod as a sign that he could go.

The rest of the wing had sprung to life. Eighteen men, all needing their breakfast. Blix headed to the kitchen but hung back until there was space, before taking out a bowl and filling it with cereal and milk.

His place was at the end of one long table, with his back to the rest of the room. It was uncomfortable not knowing what was going on behind him. Over his many years in the police, he had developed a habit of always sitting with his back to a wall, so he'd have an overview of who came and went. In here, he had no choice. Or rather, he could try, but it wouldn't be particularly wise.

Blix sat down. Around him, low, mumbling chatter in a number of different languages.

A short man from the Netherlands would usually sit across from him. Blix took it for granted that he was serving a drug sentence. Most inmates from the Netherlands were.

This time, however, Jarl Inge Ree cut in front of the little Dutchman and took his place. A large stack of toast swayed perilously as he dropped the overloaded plate on the table.

The chatter around the table died down. Everyone turned their attention to them.

Blix took a spoonful from his bowl and calmly chewed the cereal. Clenched his jaw with each chew, trying to prepare himself mentally for whatever was about to come.

Jarl Inge Ree just stared at him, a wide grin on his face. He leant back a little in his chair, digging his right hand into his pocket.

'I've got something for you,' he said.

Blix swallowed the mouthful.

Ree fished out a test tube full of urine, unscrewed the cap and leant across the table. Waited until he was sure he had everyone's attention, then poured the pungent contents into Blix's breakfast.

Laughter erupted around them. Applause and whistling.

Blix's gut instinct was to just get up and go. Empty the bowl into the sink, put it in the dishwasher and retire to his cell. But he'd been challenged so many times now – and still hadn't retaliated in any way.

He took the spoon and stirred the yellow liquid into the milk and cereal before helping himself to another mouthful.

The laughter stopped.

Blix chewed. The salty addition to his breakfast was overpowering.

He fixed his gaze on Ree, slowly pushed his chair away from the table and stood up.

Then he leant forward and spat the contents into Ree's face.

The reaction was instantaneous. Ree threw himself across the table, like a spring that had been stretched and stretched, just waiting to recoil. Plates, glasses and cutlery flew off the table. Blix took advantage of the momentum and power of the attack. He dodged to the side, grabbed hold of Ree's wrist with one hand and grasped onto his shoulder with the other, hurling him in the same direction as his attack, then slammed him onto the floor. Twisted his arm behind his back and knelt over him, as he would if he were handcuffing him.

He felt a kick in his back. A boot hit him square between the shoulder blades. The blow sent him into an overturned chair. Ree scrambled up and lunged at Blix, hammering his fists into his face before seizing hold of a chair leg and pressing it against his throat.

The man above Blix snarled. Ree's lip had burst, and blood-stained saliva ran down his chin. Blix managed to get a hand in between his throat and the chair leg to prevent his larynx from being crushed.

The prison officers were on their way. Blix could hear them close by, but none of the inmates who had now formed a ring around them did anything to let the officers through.

The pressure bearing down on his throat increased. Ree had now placed his left forearm on the chair leg, putting the full weight of his body on top of him. With his right hand he had managed to get hold of a fork. He grinned as he let Blix see it. He then rammed the four prongs into his cheek. Blix felt his skin puncture.

And then the officers were there, dragging Jarl Inge Ree off him. Blix was helped to his feet. He took a few deep breaths and scowled at Ree, who was now wiping the bloody saliva off his chin with the sleeve of his jumper as he was hauled away, a smile on his face. His teeth were stained red with blood.

More officers arrived, running through from the other wings. A cacophony of rattling keys. The inmates were all ordered into their cells.

Blix touched his cheek, felt the warm blood.

'What the hell was all that?' Nyberget asked.

Blix shrugged. There was no point explaining.

4

The wing went into lockdown.

After an hour, some of the inmates started banging on the doors. Some shouted, some complained that they hadn't finished their breakfast.

Blix was sitting on the edge of the bed when his cell door was unlocked. Nyberget beckoned him over.

'The doctor wants to give you the once-over,' he said.

Blix stood up and checked his face in the mirror. The blood around the wounds from the fork had congealed. His throat was swollen. It hurt when he swallowed.

'That won't be necessary,' he said.

'Now,' Nyberget commanded and turned, ready to go.

Blix sighed and followed, through the tunnel and over to the medical wing.

The female doctor was in her thirties. Blix liked her but couldn't remember her name. She told him to sit and pulled her chair close to his. It stung as she washed the wounds.

'I thought you usually stayed out of trouble,' she said.

'Usually,' Blix replied.

'I suppose you'll be sent to isolation?'

Blix wasn't actually sure what would happen next, but reckoned that either he or Ree would be transferred to another wing.

The doctor gently felt around his neck.

'If you could take your top off, please,' she said, as she inserted the tips of a stethoscope into her ears. Blix unbuttoned his shirt and pulled it off. He knew she was looking for internal bleeding or signs of any other injuries. Then she listened to his breathing.

'It probably looks worse than it is,' she commented. 'I'll just take a photo and then you can put your shirt back on.'

Blix closed his eyes as she took the photographs.

It suddenly came to him that her name was Mette.

'I think we'll be fine just putting a bandage on this one,' she said, examining the fork wounds again. 'But it'll probably leave a scar.'

She applied some ointment and covered the laceration with a small wound closure strip. Blix put his shirt back on.

'Could you step on the scales for me as well?' the doctor asked, pointing towards the corner of the examination room.

She followed him and watched the arrow on the display move as he stepped on.

78.2 kilograms.

'Still within the normal range,' she said and sat back down in front of the computer screen. 'But you need to make sure you're eating. You've lost almost five kilos since your last weigh-in.'

Blix had noticed that his clothes were looser.

'How are things otherwise?' the doctor continued. 'Have the medicines been helping? Have you been able to sleep?'

'Yes, thank you,' Blix replied. 'Things are fine.'

The doctor finished updating his file and said he was good to go.

Nyberget was waiting for him outside.

'I've been told you need to pack,' he said.

'So what does that mean?' Blix asked.

'Not sure,' Nyberget replied. 'But it seems like your time's up on this wing.'

When they reached the end of the tunnel, Nyberget's radio crackled.

He stopped in front of the door, removed the radio from his belt and responded. The echo from the radio reverberating around the brick walls meant that Blix wasn't able to catch any of what was being said.

'Now?' Nyberget asked.

He seemed surprised.

'Yes,' Blix heard through a crackle of the radio. 'You can go straight there.'

'Copy,' Nyberget confirmed.

He turned and pointed back in the same direction they came from.

'Where are we going?' Blix asked.

'You've got a visitor,' Nyberget answered.

'Who?'

Nyberget shrugged and led him back through the two sets of metal doors. Stopped outside the visiting room.

Blix only had two names on his visitor list. Merete and Emma. Merete had visited him three times. The first two times had mainly been to discuss practical things in connection with Iselin's death. Papers for various public agencies that had to be signed. The third time, Blix had learned that it was over with the man she had met after their divorce, and that she had found herself an apartment in Majorstua.

Part of him hoped that she was the one who had come to visit unannounced, even though he knew it was unlikely.

Nyberget fiddled with the keys and pulled the door open. A man was standing on the right-hand side of the room, his back to them, looking out the window. Blix recognised the man before he'd even turned round.

Gard Fosse. Once Blix's fellow student and best friend, later head of the department and Blix's immediate superior in the Oslo police. It was unusual seeing him in civilian clothes.

'Ring the intercom when you're done,' Nyberget said to Fosse, pointing to the device on the wall.

Then the door slammed shut, and they were alone.

Fosse lowered his gaze. Went to say something, as if he had already planned out how he was going to start the conversation, but stopped mid sentence.

'What happened?' he asked instead, moving his hand up to touch his own cheek.

Blix ran two fingers over his bandage.

'Nothing,' he replied.

They stood on either side of the low table, on which a plastic folder lay; Fosse had clearly placed it there in advance.

He cleared his throat and said: 'Abelvik and Wibe send their regards.'

Blix nodded, not bothering to ask Fosse to send his back.

'Shall we sit?' Fosse suggested.

Blix took his seat.

'How are things going with the appeal?' Fosse asked.

'I'm seeing my lawyer on Friday,' Blix answered.

'You'll have a better chance in the Court of Appeal,' Fosse stated. 'A greater number of judges, so there's a better chance of someone assessing the case differently.'

'I killed a man,' Blix said. 'Because he killed Iselin.'

'You acted in self-defence,' Fosse tried to argue. 'He would have killed Emma Ramm too. It was him or her. You know that.'

Blix didn't answer, but knew Fosse would never have done the same.

'What are you doing here?' Blix asked instead, looking at the folder on the table.

Fosse pulled it back towards him, but didn't open it.

'Have you heard of Walter Kroos?' he asked.

Blix shook his head.

'A German citizen who shot and killed his father a number of years ago,' Fosse began. 'He was serving a custodial sentence at the Billwerder correctional facility in Hamburg, until two days ago when he escaped during a dental appointment, went home and killed his mother. Then fled with her car and some cash.'

Fosse opened the folder and took out Kroos's prisoner ID photos. A young face seen from the front and side, with dark-blond hair, cut in military style, blue eyes and a severe gash across one cheek.

'It's an old picture,' he said. 'Taken right after he was arrested.'

Blix recognised him. The manhunt for Walter Kroos had been covered on the news the day before.

'Seems as if the escape had been planned,' Fosse continued. 'Looks like he'd been chewing on a soup spoon in prison and broke a molar, likely on purpose.'

He looked inside the folder and referred to what looked like a note with a list of key words.

'Before the police realised what was going on, he had managed to get across the border to Denmark. His mother's car was then found abandoned outside Copenhagen.'

Blix shifted in his seat slightly. 'And what does any of this have to do with me?' he asked.

'German police believe he may be on his way to Norway,' Fosse said, choosing not to acknowledge the question. 'By bus, train, or a stolen car.'

'Why do they think that?'

'Scraps of paper were found in the toilet in his cell. A document that had been torn to pieces. The police put it together and managed to decipher a Norwegian name.'

Fosse pulled out another piece of paper and showed him a photocopy of the torn-up sheet. The pieces appeared to have been crumpled up, then smoothed out again. Some of the ink had run, and a few pieces were missing. But it wasn't difficult making out the name written there.

Jarl Inge Ree.

5

His father kept an eye on him in the rear-view mirror. Walter stared out of the side window. Hopefully, this was the last summer he would have to spend on holiday with his parents. Next year he would be seventeen, soon eighteen.

Walter readjusted his headphones so they sat over his ears more comfortably. Rammstein's heavy riff drowned out the noise coming from the car. It also meant he could avoid listening to his parents' idle chit-chat.

After far too a long a drive through the mountains and forest and sheep, his father finally pointed to a road sign that read: *OSEN*. Only a few hundred metres further down the road, they pulled into a campsite where the grass was brown. A sign outside the reception building welcomed them in Norwegian, German and English. Beyond that were caravans, tents and small cabins, all packed in one beside the other.

His father headed into the building.

It took forever for him to come back out. He shook his head as he got in the car and slammed the door shut so hard behind him that Walter heard it even through the bass drums of *Reise, Reise*. His father waved and gesticulated towards the campsite reception. Not long after, the car lurched off in the opposite direction.

Walter changed the song.

Within a few minutes, they were parked up at a small cabin right next to the edge of the forest. It began to dawn on Walter what the problem must have been – they couldn't see the water from there. Father always had to see the water when they were on holiday. If he didn't, it wasn't a proper holiday.

Walter felt stiff after the long journey. He followed his parents into the tiny wooden cabin. Without any warning, he felt a smack on the back of his head – his father had knocked off his headphones. He barely managed to grab them before they fell to the floor.

'And you,' his father began. 'Just clocking out with your damn headphones on.'

He turned to his wife, who was setting down a cool-box next to the fridge. 'Stupidest thing we ever did giving him those,' his father continued. 'Besides becoming parents.' He turned to Walter. 'Have you done your reading today?'

Walter lowered his gaze.

His father snorted. 'No shit,' he scoffed. 'Go help your mother unpack, then you'll read.'

'We have to eat first,' his mother said, with her back to them. 'Walter must be hungry.'

'*After* we eat then,' he barked at her. 'You'll sit down and read,' he demanded, turning back to Walter. 'Half an hour. Minimum.'

They ate dinner at a plastic table set up on the dry grass outside the cabin. Walter poked at the food. Tinned stew. The air was warm, close. The sun burned.

'We must remember to wear our sunscreen,' his mother said. She had changed into a bikini. One leg crossed over the other.

'Sunscreen,' his father repeated contemptuously. 'A little sun never hurt anyone.'

Walter thought his father was looking a little red already, at the top of his chest. Fortunately, he had calmed down. He usually did after some food and a few cans of beer.

After dinner, his mother cleared away the plates and went back into the cabin. His father followed her with his gaze.

He took a sip of his beer and slurped. 'Go for a walk, boy.'

'Huh?' Walter responded.

'Go and explore the area a bit.'

'Shouldn't I be reading?'

'Didn't you hear what I said?'

His father's stern gaze shot right through him. He thrust his hand deep into his shorts pocket. 'Your mother and I need to ... relax a bit.'

His father stared at his mother as she emerged from the cabin and started collecting the jars and spices. Walter had seen that look in his eyes before.

'Go on,' his father commanded. 'Get out of here. And take your time.'

Walter didn't feel like going for a walk, but did it anyway. He followed a trail that turned into a path, that wove into the forest. It was warm, everything smelled dry. Walter regretted not changing into his shorts first.

There was an abundance of bird activity in the forest. Walter liked birds. Maybe because he had dreamed of flying once. Becoming a pilot. But that was before they found out that the letters got all jumbled up in his head. You couldn't fly a plane if you couldn't keep your words from jumping around the page.

Walter cried the day he realised his dream had been crushed. His father had come into his room, wondering why he was bawling like that. 'You never would have made it anyway. You should follow in your father's footsteps. Become a soldier.'

A little further on, he could see the glistening of water just beyond the trees. There were people along the water's edge. A jetty stretched out into the lake. At the far end, a group of young people. The girls lay on their stomachs, the boys resting on their elbows. Walter heard music coming from somewhere.

He moved a little closer and followed a girl with his eyes as she jumped in the water with a squeal. The smile spread across her face made Walter smile too, on the inside. The girl turned onto her back and swam out.

Emerging from the lake, she walked over to a long-haired boy who was lying on his back with his eyes closed, and squeezed a few drops of water from her ponytail so that they landed on his stomach. The boy howled and jumped up. Everyone laughed.

The girl fetched a towel and dried herself off. As she did, she met Walter's gaze, and held it. Then she smiled. Smiled at *him*. It was a smile that made Walter smile too. For real this time.

❋

Walter remembered that hot summer day as if it were yesterday. That's when this all started. That summer. That day.

He closed his eyes and took a deep breath. Without realising it, he had clenched his fists.

The bus veered round a bend. Walter let his body follow the movement. According to the bus timetable, he was supposed to arrive at 20:15. He regretted having not sat further forward, so he could keep a better eye on the road.

The Osen sign suddenly came into view, illuminated by the bus headlights. Walter pressed the stop button and grabbed the small backpack and shopping bag from the seat beside him. Six beers, a loaf of bread, butter and some sliced meat. Only what was absolutely necessary. A minute later the driver pulled into the side of the road. Walter got off and was left on the pavement in a hot cloud of oil and diesel.

He could see the Osen campsite diagonally across from the bus stop on the other side of the road, just as he remembered. The reception building and the small kiosk lay in darkness. There were a couple of cars parked outside. The lights were on inside one of the cabins, but he couldn't see anyone.

Walter looked around. Caravan after caravan. Some nice little fences had been erected outside some of them. The cabins stood in a row, stretching down the length of the campsite.

He walked towards the edge of the forest.

The same cabin as the one back in 2004. The sign by the door – K1492 – was the only thing that was new.

Walter took another quick look around and walked over to the deck. He lowered one knee to the ground and fumbled around with his hand underneath. It didn't take long until he found the nail. With the key.

6

'Enjoy yourselves.'

Emma hadn't seen this officer before. A man with a big moustache. His eyes darted over to the sofa, where someone had placed a clean bed-sheet and towel.

'He'll be here soon,' he added with a wink.

Emma felt like making it clear that this certainly was not a conjugal visit. She was half Blix's age, and more importantly, she saw him as a father figure. But she said nothing.

The heavy door locked shut behind the officer.

It was the second time in two days she had been here. She did not like being in the visiting room. She saw that some attempts had been made to create a pleasant atmosphere – a tablecloth draped over the table, a green plant in the corner, a box of toys for children – but the walls around her were metres thick. It was impossible to shake off the feeling of being trapped.

Emma, who hadn't even done anything illegal, felt uncomfortable here. It was as if the walls edged closer and closer with every minute she sat there, waiting.

Then the door opened. Blix was escorted inside.

Emma gasped.

He had a bandage on one cheek. His neck was swollen, covered in bruises.

'What happened?' she exclaimed.

Blix smiled, as if to say that it wasn't anything to worry about.

She wasn't sure if she could or should give him a hug. Ended up doing it anyway, carefully, on the non-bandaged side. He smelled strongly of sweat. His hair seemed unwashed.

She pushed herself away from him and surveyed the damage.

'Tell me what happened,' she pleaded.

The officer retreated from the room.

'Got into a fight,' Blix replied when they were alone.

'With Jarl Inge Ree?' she asked.

They sat down. Blix nodded.

'Did you know that he was convicted of having sex with a minor?' Emma asked.

Blix raised his eyebrows slightly.

'I got hold of his court documents a few hours ago,' she continued, retrieving the print-outs she'd brought. 'See for yourself.' She slid the old district court verdict over the table to him.

Blix began to read as she recited the contents:

'Ree was nineteen years old at the time. Lived in Oslo, where he was selling drugs and had amassed a circle of regular customers. A girl who had escaped child welfare ended up in his clutches. Nina. Fifteen years old. She'd run away from one foster family after another. Ree kept her hidden and had sex with her.'

Blix didn't seem convinced.

'The other inmates should know that he's a paedophile.'

'This isn't paedophilia,' Blix responded. 'It is a legal technicality. She was just a couple of weeks away from turning sixteen.'

Emma felt a wave of disappointment. She had thought Blix would've appreciated what she'd dug up.

'But you get the point?' she asked. 'This is hardly something he's bragging about in public, is it?' She pointed to the nearest wall, unsure whereabouts the prison's common room was. 'You can use it,' she said, her voice now raised slightly.

Blix put the papers down. 'I understand that you're trying to help,' he said with a meek smile. 'But the problem will sort itself out soon enough. Ree's being released on Monday. If I'm going to use that time for anything, it'll be in trying to find out more about him. Get closer to him.'

Emma shook her head, gesturing as if she didn't understand.

'I had a visitor yesterday,' Blix said with a nod to the chair Emma was sitting in. 'Came to talk to me about that German killer currently on the run.'

Emma had been following the news story.

'All signs indicate that he is probably on his way to Norway, and that he has some connection to Jarl Inge Ree. Gard Fosse...' Blix hesitated a moment and then shook his head '...wants me to try to figure out what that is. But there's no point even trying. Ree would rather pull his own teeth out than open up to me.'

'Why can't Fosse just question him himself?'

'Ree isn't exactly a fan of the police,' Blix explained. 'According to Fosse, he's never said a thing when he's been questioned. Not a peep. Never confessed or admitted to anything. There's no reason why he would start now.'

Emma grabbed a pen and started fiddling with it.

'But can't you try?'

'It's got nothing to do with whether I can or want to try or not. It simply won't work.'

'But the German might be dangerous,' Emma objected. 'He's killed before. Who's to say he won't kill again when he gets to Norway? What if you could have prevented it?'

Blix lowered his gaze, but didn't have an answer.

They sat in silence until they heard footsteps outside. Keys rattling. A new officer appeared.

'Time's almost up,' he said, locking eyes with Blix. 'You're wanted elsewhere.'

7

Jakobsen was one of the more pleasant prison officers. A northerner of Blix's age who trained horses for harness racing in his spare time. He didn't want to say what Blix had been sent for, just that he was taking him over to the medical wing. Once there, he let him into a sparsely furnished meeting room and then left. Light streamed in through a barred window that couldn't be opened. The air was clammy, stagnant.

A man in a checked flannel shirt with long, curly hair tied back in a ponytail stood up from a chair and adjusted his glasses. He met Blix with a dry, outstretched hand. 'Otto Myran,' he said. 'Nice to meet you.'

Blix estimated that Myran was in his mid-thirties. With a wave of his hand, he gestured for Blix to sit in one of the three chairs in the room, two of which were placed far apart, both facing the third, which Myran now sat back down on.

Myran placed one leg over the other. Folded his hands on his lap but otherwise said nothing, just stared at Blix with a gentle, friendly smile.

'Are we waiting for someone?' Blix asked.

'He should be here any minute,' Myran replied.

Blix felt a throbbing in his temples. The wounds had slowly begun to heal, but it still felt like someone had inflated his cheek. In fact, his whole face felt numb.

The door opened.

Jakobsen had returned. He remained standing out in the hall, however, and made a motion with his hand to usher someone else into the room.

Jarl Inge Ree appeared around the doorframe. He took in the sight that met him for a moment or two, then stopped abruptly.

'What the hell...?'

Blix returned the same surprised and contemptuous look. Under the bandage, the wound twinged.

Jakobsen followed Ree inside and led him over to the vacant chair, positioning himself between Ree and Blix.

'What the hell is this?' Ree barked.

Myran said nothing, just motioned for Ree to sit in the chair.

Jakobsen leant against the nearest wall, not too close, but not so far away that he couldn't, if necessary, react quickly and intervene.

Ree squirmed, seemingly unable to find a comfortable position in his seat. Blix was waiting for Myran to get started. Finally, Ree seemed to settle down.

'I'm a social worker,' Myran began. 'You may have already seen me around the corridors here.'

Neither Blix nor Ree answered.

'As you know, the aim of correctional services is to rehabilitate convicts and prepare them for a future life of freedom. We – social workers – like to act as a link between correctional services and the outside world. Our aim is for you to feel a sense of belonging in society, for you to want to partake in activities that are for the greater good of the community.'

Ree snorted.

Blix said nothing.

'And that,' continued Myran, 'is always difficult when...' He weighed his words carefully. 'When there are elements in your everyday life that challenge that willingness to contribute. Elements that introduce unfavourable conditions for your successful rehabilitation. And you two—' Myran looked from one to the other. 'Well, it doesn't exactly seem like you bring out the best in each other. And that's just how it is sometimes. You don't get along. And there can be plenty of reasons why that is.' Myran brought his hands together. 'So, rather than separating the two of you in isolation, we here at Ullersmo felt that ... *we* – the three of us – should sit down and see what we can do to improve the situation.'

Ree moved his gaze to Jakobsen, who placed his thumbs on the inside of his belt.

'Improve the situation,' Ree mimicked, a big grin on his face. 'You mean, like, sit here and talk about our feelings and stuff?'

Myran said nothing.

'What the fuck is this – some kumbaya, mindfulness bullshit?' The smile disappeared. 'I'm out of here in five days.'

'The way I see it, that's all the more reason to do this,' Myran said. 'Give yourself the best possible start in your new life out there.'

'But I won't have anything to do with him on the outside,' Ree continued. 'He's here for years.'

Blix spoke up. 'I can just stay in my cell until he's out. It's fine.'

'That is some constructive input, Alexander,' Myran said, addressing Blix. 'And thank you for that. But see it as an exercise in being less conflict-oriented.'

Ree scoffed again. 'I'm not conflict-oriented in the slightest.' He stood up. 'Nah, I'm not doing this.'

Jakobsen removed his thumbs from his belt.

Ree noticed and stopped. 'We're meant to be here for another...?'

Myran conferred with his wristwatch. 'Hour and twenty-five minutes.'

'You're shitting me.'

The social worker shook his head. A bead of sweat broke loose from his forehead and slid down his cheek.

Ree groaned. 'Jesus Christ.'

Blix said nothing. He looked over to Jakobsen and back at the social worker. It felt like he was taking part in some absurd performance.

'Of course, we could just sit here,' Myran insisted. 'And stare into space. But that would be terribly boring.'

'What are you on about?' Ree barked.

'This,' Myran answered. 'This process. Ordered by the management. It's mandatory.'

'Jesus H. Christ.' Ree sat back down and crossed his arms.

After a long, heavy silence, Myran started:

'I want you to think of three questions to ask each other.'

Blix barely lifted his head.

'Three questions that aren't related to your lives in here,' Myran elaborated.

Ree snorted.

'It could be anything,' the social worker continued. 'Something private, if you're curious about something of a more personal nature, and if the other is comfortable answering it. Or it could be about the first thing you're planning on doing when you get out of here, for example. Anything,' he repeated. 'But try to avoid disrespectful questions or hate speech.'

Ree leant back. 'I'd rather keep my mouth shut.'

Myran adjusted his glasses a little. 'What about you, Alexander? Do you perhaps have a question you would like to ask Jarl Inge?'

Blix was not used to being addressed by his first name. 'Me? No.'

He did the same as Ree and leant back in his chair. Crossed one leg over the other and put one hand on top of the other on his lap. The room went silent.

It stayed silent.

Jakobsen shuffled a little, his shoes rubbing against the floor. Myran moved his gaze from Ree to Blix, and back to Ree again. One minute turned into two, which turned into four. Blix turned to look at Ree, who seemed to be staring at something on the ceiling, occasionally moving his gaze to something or other on the wall.

'Jarl Inge, what do *you* plan on doing when you get out?' Myran asked.

'Get to fuck.'

'What about you, Alexander?'

Blix met his gaze. 'Me? No idea. Can't bear to think about it.'

Again, silence.

'I have a question,' Ree said, smiling. He turned to Blix. 'How old were you the first time you got spanked?' He laughed to himself, a raw laugh.

Blix didn't answer.

Ree seemed to suddenly be enjoying himself.

Myran looked at him rather sternly and then said to Blix: 'You don't have to answer that.'

'But that counts as a question, right?' Ree said, surprisingly eager. 'It has to. That was a question.'

'If you can ask a slightly more serious one next time, I'll consider it.'

'How kind of you,' Ree said ironically. 'Because I really do feel like I have to do everything you say.'

Myran did not respond.

Ree continued to chuckle a little to himself.

Blix just stared ahead. 'How old were *you*?'

Ree stopped smiling. The next moment, he was out of the chair and standing up as if to launch himself on Blix, but Jakobsen was beside him before Ree could do anything. Blix just stared straight ahead. Barely bat an eyelid.

Ree took a moment to compose himself. 'Alright, alright,' he said to Jakobsen. 'I'll sit down.'

'Great idea, this,' Blix said to Myran.

The social worker did not answer this time either.

Ree dropped heavily back into his chair. Stared sullenly ahead for the next few minutes. Jakobsen, who never said anything just for the sake of saying something, cleared his throat.

'Well, that's one all,' he said. 'Two more questions from each of you, then I'm sure the social worker will be so kind as to end class a little earlier than planned?'

Myran returned Jakobsen's gaze with one of disapproval.

'Who wants to start?' the social worker asked, carrying on regardless, looking from one to the other again.

Neither answered. Ree scoffed, shook his head. Myran kept his eyes fixed on him. Ree took a deep breath and exhaled hard. Then it was like he just gave up, to end it, get it over and done with.

'Where...?' He stopped himself, as if he hated even having to open his mouth and talk to Blix. 'Where are you from?'

The words seemed to leave a bad taste in his mouth.

'Oslo,' Blix answered. 'You?'

'Osen,' he answered immediately.

'Almost the same,' Myran interjected. 'Oslo, Osen.' He was the only one laughing. 'But there are certainly some rather large differences between the two. Jarl Inge – what was it like growing up there?'

'Get to fuck.'

Myran ignored him. 'That was two questions anyway. Let's try one more – preferably one that encourages you to talk a bit more, say something about yourselves a little more freely, and then I think that'll be good enough for this time.'

'This time?' Ree bristled. 'Are you saying we have to come back here more than once?'

'Like I said, it's a priority project ordered from the higher-ups.'

'Project...' Ree shook his head.

'And it's a process where we'll work on understanding, relationships and curiosity. The faster we make progress, the sooner we can finish.'

Ree grimaced.

Again, silence.

'I have a question,' Blix said, after a while, still staring straight ahead. 'Who's your best friend and why?'

'That's *two* questions,' Ree argued.

'That doesn't matter,' Myran said. 'But those are two good questions, thank you for that, Alexander.'

Myran shifted his gaze to Ree and held it there.

Ree snorted and shook his head again. 'No one in here, that's for sure,' he began, contempt in his voice. 'There are only losers in here.'

Blix saw that Myran was itching to ask what he meant by that, but didn't.

Ree sighed. 'She – yes, *she* – is called Samantha.' Again he exhaled hard. 'I've known her since I was little. We ... we always stuck together. Had fun together. Kept each other's secrets. That's why she's my best friend. My other mates ... none of them come close.'

Myran nodded approvingly. 'Good,' he said. 'Very good, thank you, Jarl Inge.' The social worker smiled, satisfied.

'Do you have a final question for Alexander?'

'Yes,' Ree said, turning his head toward Blix. 'And please do speak freely, including lots of details.'

Mimicking Myran's voice, Ree sent Blix a faint smile and asked: 'How would you like to die?'

8

The coffee machine let out one last spurt. Emma removed the cup. She had sat in front of her computer screen throughout the evening and well into the night, collecting information about Walter Kroos. The German newspapers were full of material about his escape.

She still had a week and a half of leave before she was supposed to start back at news.no, but the fact that a feared murderer was on the run and could be heading to Norway was a big deal. And she could be first to publish anything on it.

She called Gard Fosse.

As always, he parried Emma's small talk with short, measured answers. He clearly wanted her to get to the point.

Emma took the hint. 'A German murderer is on the run,' she began. 'Are the Norwegian police acting on this at all?'

A few seconds of silence followed.

'Why would we do that?'

'In case he was heading to Norway,' Emma replied. 'Or in the event that he was already here?'

Again, the investigator stayed silent. It was almost as if she could hear the cogs turning, thinking through how he should answer.

'We, like every other police agency across Europe, are of course aware that the German police are hunting for an escaped prisoner. As always, our lines of communication with our foreign colleagues are open, but as thing currently stand we are not directly cooperating on this particular matter.'

'But you'll be keeping a look out?'

'We always do.'

'So, are you doing anything extra in terms of monitoring the borders?'

'Our border control is as solid as ever.'

He's well versed, Emma thought. Police speculation must be its own subject at the Police University College.

'Are you at all concerned that Kroos is on his way to Norway?'

'No.'

'There's no reason for Norwegian citizens to be concerned about it either, then?'

'I wouldn't say so, no.'

She could hear that Fosse was getting impatient.

'Okay. One last question: do you know if Walter Kroos has ever been to Norway before?'

Fosse cleared his throat and said: 'There is nothing to suggest that.'

Which means they were investigating the possibility.

Emma smiled. 'Thank you, Fosse. It was nice talking to you again.'

Fosse didn't respond. It seemed like he was about to say something, but changed his mind and hung up.

Emma immediately called Anita Grønvold, the head of news.no.

'Well, well,' said Anita. 'Couldn't stay away?'

Emma recounted what Blix had told her, and what she herself had learned from the information she'd collected. She finished by summing up Gard Fosse's short answers.

Anita whistled, as she often did when they landed on a good story. 'Well, sounds like your holiday's over.' It sounded like Anita had a smile on her face.

The truth was that Emma didn't know if she even wanted to go back to her everyday life as a news journalist. There had been a little too much drama in recent years. She had spent the last six months writing and completing a book about some of the most brutal and talked-about criminal cases in Norway's history. The process had been somewhat cathartic, and yet simultaneously a little tedious. But she did miss having a finger on the pulse of the daily goings-on of the country.

'Try to find out if anyone in Ree's inner circle knows if he's acquainted with Walter Kroos,' Anita added when Emma didn't answer.

'I should go to Osen, you mean?'

'Maybe. But didn't you say that Ree lived here in Oslo for several years?'

'I did.'

'Right, well, start in Oslo. And keep me posted.'

9

Blix had spent the last fortnight making wooden boxes. They were made in sets of one large and two small. Before lunch, he would cut and prepare the materials, and after lunch he would join them together. The boxes were to be sold at the prison's Christmas fair in early December. They could be used for storage or decoration. Merete had a similar one on her balcony with flowers in it.

A radio droned on in the background as he worked. Radio P4. Small talk and music with commercials in between. Once an hour, Blix would put down his tools and listen to the news. The escaped German prisoner was not mentioned. It couldn't be known publicly that there was a possibility he intended to flee to Norway. No other news reports caught his interest. No serious incidents that could be linked to Walter Kroos.

At half-two, the working day was over and they were taken back to the wing. Blix went straight to his cell and found his shower soap and towel.

The prison was built in 1970. Wing K was the only one that still hadn't been upgraded to modern standards. They had three communal toilets and two showers. Only one of the showers actually worked properly. Blix had not yet settled into any routine for when he used it. He no longer showered every day, and never in the morning when there was a queue. He liked to shower immediately after work, while the others were lying in bed, waiting for dinner.

He threw the towel over his shoulder, slipped his feet into his sandals and left the cell. The shower was at the far end of the corridor. The door was closed, which meant it was probably occupied. He walked over and just as his hand touched the door handle he heard the sound of the shower turning on.

The Dutchman strolled by with an apple in his hand. He nodded towards the shower door and smiled. 'Jarl Inge,' he said, with his Dutch pronunciation. 'Long shower.'

Blix turned and walked back to his cell. He could wait. Although the shower room would likely be steamed up for hours yet.

Ree's cell was number six, in the middle of the corridor. The door stood ajar, with the key still in the top lock. From half past eight in the evening through to the next morning, all of the inmates were locked in their cells. During the day, they were employed in some form of work or were enrolled in study programmes, but in the afternoon and evening, they could move around freely, letting themselves in and out of their cells with their own keys.

Few actually locked their cells unless they were leaving the wing to exercise or had a visitor. Things were stolen all the time. Food from the communal kitchen, tobacco left unattended or lighters someone had dropped somewhere. But the inmates never entered each other's cells without permission. That was like boarding a ship without asking the captain's permission first.

The Dutchman had disappeared into his own cell. Blix turned and looked back at the cell he had just passed – cell six. Without further thought, as if acting on impulse, he turned, pulled open the door and slipped inside.

The cell was pretty similar to his own. Narrow, with a window at the end. A bed on one side and a desk with floating shelves above it on the other. A sink, mirror and a cupboard. A TV at the foot of the bed.

Blix estimated that he had no more than five minutes, but he was trained in this. He knew how to conduct a search.

He started with a pile of comic books on the bottom shelf. Between the two bottom comics he found an envelope, addressed to Jarl Inge Ree, written in clumsy handwriting. The sender was listed on the back. Tom Erik Ree, with an address in Osen.

The envelope was relatively thick. Blix fished out the contents. There was a pile of old photos and a letter. In fact it was more akin to a note, and was signed *Dad*. He wrote that he'd had a visit from Aunt Maren: 'She brought some old photos with her, from the first summer she was here – of both you and Samantha. I thought you would want to see them.'

The pictures showed children in their swimwear on a beach, children in a playground, in front of a kiosk. It wasn't difficult picking Jarl Inge out of the little crowd of children. A light-haired boy with a narrow face. In the photos, he was around ten years old. Another boy stood out too, the one beside him with his tongue poking out of his half-open mouth, not looking particularly alert. His fringe was crooked, and he was paler than the others. In one of the pictures, a girl of the same age looked as if she was trying to get him to join them in the water.

A collection of photographs was taped to the wall above Jarl Inge's bed. The same girl appeared in the pictures there too. A photo of her in a bikini, from around the same time the photos from the envelope were taken. In the next photo along, she was a few years older and had grown up. She was standing with a microphone, singing as she stared straight into the camera. Blue eyes and a charming smile. In the most recent photos, she had become a woman, probably about thirty or so. It looked like she had lost some of her youthful radiance, but she was still beautiful.

Samantha, Blix thought.

The woman Jarl Inge had mentioned to the social worker.

The bottom piece of tape on one of the pictures had come loose from the wall. Blix lifted the picture and turned it over. There was nothing on the back. The other pictures he could not examine without it being obvious that someone had been in there.

He put the photos back in the envelope and placed it back between the covers of the comic books.

The top drawer of the desk was empty aside from some stationery and a blank notebook.

In the next drawer down were two thick brown envelopes. The top one contained various correspondence with public offices. The most recent document was a rejection of an application for council housing in Osen.

The second envelope contained similar correspondence with the prison. Jarl Inge Ree's application for parole had been denied as a result of his various previous convictions. The end of his sentence was set for Monday, 27th September.

A sound from the corridor made Blix stiffen. Footsteps – approaching the cell, but then carrying on past, followed by the sound of a cell door slamming shut. Blix put the envelopes back and examined the rest of the contents of the drawers without finding anything that proved any connection to Walter Kroos or what Jarl Inge Ree was planning upon his release.

Blix presumed he had a minute or two left to wrap up.

At the bottom of the cupboard he found a box containing several letters. Some of them were from Samantha, mostly sent for Ree's birthday and Christmas. Blix skimmed through one of the most recent letters. She had written that she was thinking about him and said something about how things would have to change in the future.

A couple of the other letters were from a former inmate with whom he had obviously served time. He had also received letters from friends who were incarcerated in other prisons. The content was difficult to read. Blix shuffled through the crumpled and clumsily written pages, finding nothing of significant interest.

Out in the corridor: someone shouted something or other about food. Another answered from inside their cell. Blix was running out of time. This was a terrible idea.

He rummaged around quickly in a drawer of socks and underwear without finding anything, but as he went to close it, he found that he couldn't. He pushed down a pair of thick woollen socks and tried again, but was struck by a thought. Blix opened the drawer, took out the socks and felt them to see if anything might be hidden inside. Nothing there, but the drawer still wouldn't fully close. One of the socks must have ended up getting stuck behind the drawer. It had happened in his own.

He reached his hand in, confirmed his suspicions and fished out the sock that had fallen back there. But then he felt something else brush the top of his hand. Something fixed to the shelf above the drawer. It felt like a square box, wrapped in a thin sock. He recognised the sound of Velcro as he yanked it out.

His first thought was that it would be drugs – a box of pills or powder of some kind – so it took him a while to realise that he was looking at a phone. A fairly old one, with a small screen and keyboard under a sliding cover.

Blix took a step towards the door and tried to listen for the sound of the shower, but it was too far away. He briefly considered taking the phone with him, but found a button to turn it on, and the screen immediately lit up. A battery indicator glowed red, but otherwise the display was blank. No code required to unlock it.

His towel slid off of his shoulder. He left it on the floor and explored the functions of the phone. After a little trial and error, he found the call log. Empty. The same for the inbox. Two numbers were stored in its memory, but without names, only designated as A and B. Blix concentrated on memorising the first. It started with 92, the same first two digits as his own former number, and was therefore the easier to remember.

His pulse was now racing. He switched off the phone, wrapped it back in its sock and slid it back into its hiding place. Pushed the drawer all the way in and closed the cupboard behind him. He then grabbed the towel from the floor, listened closely to the sounds of the corridor, and slid out of the room.

It had been a long time since Blix had felt any similar kind of fervour. A long time since he had felt anything.

Behind him the door to the shower room swung open. Blix continued on to his cell and sat on the edge of the bed. Having a hidden phone in your cell was risky, Blix thought. Jarl Inge Ree must have really needed to contact someone on the outside.

10

A woman in a navy trouser-suit pushed open the door. With a steady gaze, she scanned the café.

Emma recognised Nina Bach Hansen from the newspaper articles she'd read and made herself known with a wave.

'Sorry I'm late,' Nina Bach Hansen said, moving an expensive bag from one hand to the other so as to greet Emma. There was nothing that indicated that she had been on the run from child welfare services over twenty years ago.

Despite a difficult childhood, Nina Bach Hansen had become a successful businesswoman. At the age of twenty-eight, she had come up with the idea of creating a digital platform to recycle used clothes. An idea that, just a few months ago, was acquired by a Danish company for several million kroner – exactly how many was unknown.

'Thank you for making the time to meet with me,' Emma said. 'Do you want something to eat? Drink?'

'Water will be just fine, thank you.'

She helped herself from the jug on the table.

After a bit of polite, introductory chit-chat, Emma cleared her throat and said: 'As I wrote in my email, I'm primarily looking for a bit of background information. You've been quite open about your upbringing before.'

'Yes, it can be quite good, free therapy, talking to journalists such as yourself,' Nina said, smiling. 'Fire away.'

Emma held her glass with both hands. 'I'm doing some research into someone who's currently incarcerated, and your name came up in connection with an old case.'

Emma didn't continue straight away.

Nina stared at her for a moment, before she said: 'You're referring to Jarl Inge Ree.'

'I am,' Emma replied. 'Can you tell me about your relationship with him?'

Nina took a sip from her glass of water and then began: 'There's not much to say, really. There wasn't really a relationship to speak of. I was young and stupid. Jarl Inge was older. He was tall, he was *a man*, you know? I remember thinking that he was exciting. He gave me what I needed and I gave him what he needed. Everything was consensual. There was no more to it than that. But legally, I was too young.'

Emma said nothing, just waited for Nina to elaborate.

'It wasn't *love* in any way. And I wasn't looking for that.'

'But what you're saying is that he generally treated you well?'

'Yes, but he wasn't a good guy. I realised that eventually. Probably even more so after the fact.'

Nina paused.

'There was this guy he would hang out with – I can't remember his name – who I think fancied me a bit; he flirted quite openly anyway. Jarl Inge didn't like that. One night he smashed his face into a coffee table.' Nina demonstrated with a gesture. 'Broke his nose in several places, I think. Threw him out.'

'Jealousy?'

'Oh, definitely.'

'Even though, as you say, there weren't really any feelings involved?'

'Jarl Inge was rather possessive.'

Nina then continued, telling stories about both her childhood and her life since she'd left Jarl Inge. Emma let her speak. She was fascinated – Nina was the perfect interviewee – outgoing, funny, reflective, timed every inhale and exhale. No detail was too private.

Emma decided to steer the conversation back on track. 'I'm looking for someone else who might have information about Jarl Inge's friendships over the years. Someone who knows him well. Can you think of anyone he maybe had more contact with than anyone else, while you knew him?'

Nina thought back.

'There was this girl,' she began. 'Sara, or something. No. Wait. Samantha.' She snapped her fingers. 'Definitely Samantha. He talked about her a lot. I think she was the love of his life or something.

Regardless, something happened there that kind of sent him off the rails.'
Nina made a spiralling motion with her finger, down towards the table.
'She was his weak spot – if she called and needed something or other,
well then there he was, straight away. But she wasn't quite right either,
or so it seemed – I wasn't really invested enough to dig into it. And I
didn't really care.'

'But what gave you that impression?'

'The way he talked about her,' Nina said. 'Like he genuinely cared, I
think. There weren't many people he seemed to actually care for. They
were all a bit fucked up, his friends.'

'Do you remember anything else about her?'

Again, she had to pause as she thought back.

'I remember she was fairly well known at the time,' Nina said. 'She'd
taken part in a singing competition on TV and a bunch of other stuff,
but I don't know anything more about her than that. Like I said, I just
didn't care. I'm not even sure what her last name is.'

Emma hadn't even started covering celebrity stories back then, let
alone working as a news journalist, but she knew that TV singing com-
petitions had always been popular. It had to be possible to find out who
this Samantha was.

'Did Jarl Inge ever talk about a German guy at all? Maybe a friend of
his?'

Nina lifted her gaze obliquely up to the ceiling as she thought.

'This was many years ago,' she started, 'but there was a guy, yeah. He
may very well have been from Germany. Jarl Inge spoke about something
really messed up that he'd done.'

'Messed up how?'

'I don't remember the details, but I think he went to jail.'

'Could this have been Walter Kroos?'

'Walter Kroos,' Nina murmured to herself, as if searching through her
memories.

Nina clearly hadn't caught wind of the German prisoner on the loose,
Emma thought.

'That *might* have been his name, yeah. But I can't say for sure.'

'I don't expect you to know this,' Emma carried on, 'but do you have any idea where Jarl Inge might have met this German?'

'I'd imagine back home?' Nina offered. 'Fosen or Fjøsen, or something like that.'

'Osen?'

Nina snapped her fingers again. 'That was it, yes. Jarl Inge more or less grew up on a campsite there. And if there's anything Germans like,' she said with a wink, 'it's Norway. And camping.'

11

Walter was lying on the sofa in the living room – the largest room in the cabin. That was where he felt least confined. The room smelled of dust. The wind whistled through the window frame. The ceiling, floor, walls and furniture were all made of pine.

He swung his legs off the sofa and sat up. It was getting dark out. He was used to time passing slowly, but he needed to move.

The air had turned colder. Damp. He looked around. There were lights on in some of the other cabins, but not in those closest to his. From the road, a few hundred metres away, he heard the tell-tale sound of car tyres whooshing past the campsite on the autumn-wet asphalt. It must have rained.

He could not shake the memories away. It was through his thoughts that she had lived with him all these years. The look she had given him from the beach that time, the smile, how she'd tossed her hair and looked in his direction now and then, maybe just to see if he was still watching her. And every time – a new, wide, warm smile, which he had felt deep, deep within himself.

The same night he had seen her for the first time, she had performed a song on the stage at the campsite. The audience loved her. Walter had realised straight away that she had *something*, that there was a star up there on that stage, a girl whose life was on track and who loved having everyone's eyes on her. There were even TV cameras there.

She seemed to live through her songs. She believed in them, she felt them – which made Walter and all the others believe in her too. Every time she finished a song, she waved to the audience, smiled and called out two words that were not difficult to understand, even for Walter, who didn't know a word of Norwegian. He, like everyone else, was completely mesmerised.

The next day, Walter was again told to 'go for a walk'. Without having planned it, he ended up outside the campsite shop, which also happened to be a meeting point for the children and young people in the area.

And there she was.

Hanging out with some friends, probably the same ones she was with down by the lake the day before. They were eating ice cream – it was sweltering hot outside. Again she met Walter's eyes with a smile as he passed. He was unsure where to look. Walking by on legs that suddenly felt like jelly, he continued into the shop, even though he had no money. At the magazine section, he stood there and flipped the pages back and forth, without any of the words or pictures making sense or even registering in his brain.

'Hi.'

Walter span round.

And swallowed.

The singing girl had pushed her sunglasses onto the top of her head. She was dressed in a skirt and tight-fitting top, both white. She was golden brown and her skin glistened with sunscreen. She smelled sweet, good.

She scrutinised him for a moment, before asking: *'Hvem er du egentlig?'*

Walter didn't understand a word she just said.

She carried on: *'Jeg har ikke sett deg her før?'*

Walter just stood there, gaping at her, unable to say anything himself. Until he finally stuttered: *'Entschuldingen Sie...'*

'Ah, du bist aus Deutschland.'

Which made him light up. *'Ja. Ja.'*

Walter smiled and laughed nervously. Immediately felt how clammy his hands had suddenly become and how little saliva was left in his mouth.

She switched to English:

'That's all the German I know,' she said, grinning to herself. 'That and *durch, für, gegen, ohne, um*.'

Walter laughed again.

'My name's Samantha,' she said.

'I ... know,' Walter said. 'I saw you on stage last night.' He pointed out the window, although he couldn't remember exactly where the stage was.

'You are ... good,' he said, feeling himself blush all the way up to his hairline.

'Thank you,' she said, smiling. 'I'm competing in a national singing contest.'

'Oh, are you?'

'That's why we had the concert. But, actually, I've done plenty of concerts before. Here, I mean. I live here.'

Walter couldn't think of anything to say.

'So, what's your name?'

'Er, Walter.'

'Hello, Walter.'

She held out her hand. He took it – slight, warm – and hoped she didn't notice how sweaty his was.

'Is your name just Samantha?'

'Is your name just Walter?'

They both laughed. It made him breathe easier. Relax a little.

'Samantha is just my stage name,' she said. 'My full name is Samantha Kasin. My father' – she nodded toward a burly, bearded man who was standing behind the cash register serving a customer – 'had a crush on some singer years ago whose name was Samantha. Samantha Fox.' She rolled her eyes. 'And that's how I ended up with my name.'

Walter liked the name. It sounded like some sort of gem. 'My name is Walter Kroos...' he started. 'My dad...'

He didn't know why he'd mentioned his own father, because there really wasn't a story there to tell. He looked down. Tensed and untensed his hand.

'We're all heading down to the beach tonight,' she said. 'Light a fire, grill some food, go for a swim, that kind of thing. Maybe you'd like to join us?'

Again, that smile. That beautiful, welcoming smile that somehow touched him so intrinsically, so deep within him.

Walter thought of his father, the fact he would have to ask first. That he might not be allowed to go, but that didn't stop him from saying:

'Definitely.'

*

Walter remembered how happy he had been afterwards, how light and springy his legs had felt on the way back to his parents. He had looked forward to the evening. At that time, he hadn't been in the habit of looking forward to *anything*.

It amazed him how clear his memories of that time were. Perhaps because he had replayed them to himself over and over. Now, as he walked along the road in the direction of the centre of the village, it was like travelling back in time. Everywhere he looked, more memories popped up.

After a couple of minutes, he turned off towards a residential area, moving in and out of the light from the streetlamps. He passed large houses with high hedges. The gardens were all well kept with mature fruit trees.

Through an illuminated window he saw a plump, blonde woman cooking. It seemed that she was talking to someone, as she would turn her head slightly every now and then, her lips moving. Walter couldn't see anyone else in the room.

The next house was dark, with the exception of an outside light. At the house one along from that, a small Volkswagen was parked in the driveway. Alternating colours from a TV took turns lighting up the back of the living-room curtains.

A cat dashed across the road in front of him. Walter turned onto a path between two houses. There were trees lining the back of one. He stepped in between them and stopped. The curtains weren't even drawn. Three candles were lit inside. He saw a chest of drawers and a display cabinet with glass panels. Pictures hanging on the walls.

The memories flooded back.

Last time he had been there, he had spoken to her through the bedroom window. He had come here in such turmoil, with a pain in his heart that he had never before experienced. Now, so many years later, he could easily invoke that very same despair. Those were memories he didn't want to relive.

His thoughts were interrupted by movement inside.

Walter gasped.

Samantha was too far away for him to see her properly, but there was no doubt – it was her. Her face was the same. It looked like she was talking on the phone. She walked into the living room, turned and walked back the other way. Gesturing with her hands.

He crept closer and stood in the shadow of a large conifer tree. Followed the movements inside the house. Moved closer, behind an old apple tree, as Samantha walked from the living room into the kitchen. She opened a cupboard, standing on her tiptoes to reach for something on the top shelf. Her jumper rose to reveal a strip of her bare stomach. Smooth, white skin.

He swallowed.

It still hurt.

And there was no doubt. He was still angry.

12

Even on the evening before, a rumour had been doing the rounds that a new inmate was moving onto the wing. One of the cells had been empty since last weekend.

After breakfast, the suspicion was confirmed. Outside cell seven were two black plastic bags. Blix went into his own, but left the door open. The other inmates buzzed around the common area, waiting for the new man to come up from registration.

As always, there was plenty of speculation before he arrived. Some had acquaintances who had applied for a transfer, but the discussions mostly focused on whether the new prisoner had been in the news. Whether a celebrity criminal would be joining their ranks. The hottest tip-off was that it could be a fifty-year-old from Fredrikstad who had raped and killed a Swedish man. Presumably doing the latter before the former. After his arrest, the case received rolling coverage on the TV and in the papers, and during the trial saw yet more engagement. According to the calculations Blix heard around the breakfast table, his sentence would be coming into force any day now, and he would be transferred from custody to prison.

When he realised that something was happening out in the corridor, Blix moved over to his cell door. It wasn't the killer from Fredrikstad after all. The officers were escorting Valdemar Hjorth.

He walked with a somewhat rolling gait, his chest up and forward, his neck straight and his head raised. A large tattoo stretched up the right side of his neck, all the way to his temple. His expression transformed as he passed the cell door and caught sight of Blix. Hateful and hostile, as he had been the last time they saw each other.

For a moment it looked like he was going to stop and say or do something, but he carried on, picking up the plastic bags from the hallway and heading into his assigned cell.

Blix pulled back and sank onto the bed.

It had been seven, maybe eight years since he had arrested Valdemar

Hjorth. A case of attempted murder – a young man had been shot three times in what appeared to be a dispute over drugs, but was purely about gaining power, moving up the hierarchy. They had little to go on in the investigation, but Blix had received a tip-off from an informant who told them about Hjorth and led them to the weapon, hidden in a garage in Alna. Later, Blix led an operation in which they faked a burglary in the garage to lure Valdemar Hjorth back to check if his gun had gone astray. Which meant they ended up catching him with the murder weapon in his hands.

The operation had been criticised by the suspect's defence during the trial, but in his testimony Blix had explained both the legal and practical reasons behind the approach. He seemed to recall that Hjorth was given four years. He must have been out for a few, but now he was back. In a few hours, they would have to sit at the same table for dinner.

Blix stood up again and went to the window. A plane was on its way to Gardermoen. He could always request a transfer. It would save the prison trouble and be in everyone's best interest. Anyway, it made sense that he would be the one who wanted to be moved out of the wing.

But that would stop him from getting closer to Jarl Inge Ree.

He hadn't promised Gard Fosse anything, neither did he owe the police at all, but he did, reluctantly, have to admit that the case had started to pique his interest. Besides, it was just four days. He could manage that.

13

There was a doorbell on the wall and a cast-iron knocker on the door. Emma tried both, but no one appeared.

She stepped back and squinted at the windows. There was light shining through one of them, but no movement behind the curtains. Emma walked over to the mail box and double-checked that she had come to the right place.

Karina and Samantha Kasin, Osenløkka 24.

The drive had taken a little under two and a half hours. She could have called first, but if she'd learned anything from her years working as a journalist, it was that it was best not to forewarn people of her arrival.

Karina was Samantha's mother. She had a father too – Kenneth – but Emma hadn't been able to find an address for him. Information about Samantha online, however, was abundant. As a fifteen-year-old, she had taken Norway by storm on a televised singing contest. Emma had clicked through various old articles and watched some of the videos on YouTube. Samantha had undoubtedly been a future superstar. She had it all: the voice, the charisma, the stage presence. And everything seemed to indicate that she loved the attention that came with that. But then, during the semi-final, something seemed off. She looked uncomfortable, nervous, and was more sobbing than singing. Under normal circumstances, Samantha's performance wouldn't have been good enough to keep her in the competition, but the viewers still voted to send her through to the final, from which she later withdrew. Samantha disappeared from the limelight, never to return.

Emma walked back to her car, but didn't get in. An elderly lady was walking towards her along the street, a stubby-legged terrier by her side.

'Excuse me,' Emma said, taking a step out onto the pavement. 'You wouldn't happen to know if Karina or Samantha were home, would you?'

The woman tugged on the dog's lead, stopped and smiled kindly.

'I know Karina is in Spain at the moment – she always is at this time of year. She has Bekhterev's disease. The warmth helps. Samantha is probably at the campsite. That's where she usually is.'

'Thank you for your help.'

Emma drove over to the Osen campsite. Outside the reception building faded flags from various countries hung limply, each from its own flagpole. Emma parked up and went inside.

There was no one at the reception desk, but she could hear someone rustling about a little further inside, in what looked to be the campsite's shop-cum-kiosk. Emma followed the sounds.

A woman with white earbuds in her ears and work gloves on her hands was busy painting a wall. The back of her clothes were also coated in paint, as if she'd leant against a wall where the paint wasn't yet dry. Emma tried to catch the woman's attention. And only then did she realise she had company.

She turned and took off her gloves. She had a dust mask on her face, which she also removed. There wasn't a shadow of a doubt: this was Samantha, almost twenty years after she had stood on the stage of Oslo Spektrum and captivated a packed audience of *Hit of the Summer* spectators.

The years had treated her well – she was still strikingly beautiful. Her hair was currently tied back under a red-and-blue polka dot bandana. She was thin, which meant her painter's trousers were baggy, perching on her hips, and Emma was convinced that Samantha had had something done to her breasts. They were far too big for her otherwise slender body. She reminded Emma of a bare-faced Marilyn Monroe.

'We're closed for the season, as you can probably tell,' was the first thing Samantha said, before Emma could introduce herself. 'The campsite, that is. But you can still rent one of the cabins. They're 690 kroner a night.'

'Thanks, but that's not actually why I'm here. Not this time, at least.' Emma smiled then continued: 'My name is Emma Ramm. I work at news.no. I'm just looking for some information.'

'Okay?' Samantha put her gloves down on the workbench.

'I tried calling you a few times,' Emma continued, an inquiring tone to her voice.

'Ah, you should've called the office phone,' Samantha replied, glancing into a back room. 'I rarely pick up calls from unknown numbers.'

Emma returned her smile and looked around, taking in the room. 'Do you run the campsite alone?'

'My dad died three years ago,' said Samantha. 'It was his business, but what do you do when you don't have anything else going on?' She shrugged, raising her palms.

'Is there a lot of work?'

Samantha pointed at all the mess and sighed. 'There is when you've got a tonne of renovating to do and can't afford to hire anyone to help.'

'Aha, yes, I understand that too well.'

'But I'm guessing that's not why you're here – for advice about renovating on a budget?'

Emma laughed and shook her head. She took a few steps closer and said. 'Jarl Inge Ree. You know him, is that right?'

Samantha frowned. 'Why do you ask?'

Emma thought for a moment.

'I work as a crime reporter. A German killer is on the run, and there are signs that he might be on his way here.'

'Here?'

'Yes. I mean to Norway. I don't know if he would come *here*, exactly, but he does have some connection to Jarl Inge Ree. I'm just trying to figure out what that might be.'

Emma could see that she had piqued Samantha's curiosity.

'What did you say his name was?'

'Who, the German? Walter Kroos.'

Samantha looked like she was searching her memory for the name. 'Never heard of him.'

Emma glanced at the German welcome sign in the window.

'Is it possible to find out if he ever came here, stayed at the campsite?' she asked.

'Maybe,' Samantha replied. 'But we got a new computer system around ten years ago. So anything from before then will have been deleted.'

Emma did the maths, and came to the conclusion that if Walter Kroos had been to Osen, then it would it have been before then.

'I've known Jarl Inge most of my life, ever since we were little,' Samantha added. 'We're still in touch. It would come as a huge surprise if he had any sort of connection to a German murderer.'

'He would tell you though, if he did?'

'Oh yeah, for sure.'

Emma scrutinised her for a few moments before saying: 'Okay. Well, thank you for your time.'

Samantha didn't say anything else, just went back to the workbench and picked up her gloves.

'It was a shame you stopped singing,' Emma added.

'Hm?' Samantha turned around.

'You had, and probably still have, an incredible singing voice. It's too bad you don't use it anymore.'

'Who says I don't use it?'

'Oh, I mean ... I just thought...'

Samantha smiled. 'I'm just messing with you. But thank you. It just doesn't appeal to me anymore. But it was fun while it lasted.'

14

It was getting late.

Walter crept over to the window and pushed the curtain aside. Two men had walked by, each with a fishing rod in hand, but otherwise, he hadn't seen a single other person.

The forest was full of autumnal colours, dazzling variations of yellow, orange and red, now muted by the evening light. A large bird took off from one of the treetops. Walter followed it with his eyes until it disappeared from sight.

He walked back over to the kitchenette, turned on the stove and warmed up the remains of something or other from a tin. After it had simmered for a while, he took the pot and a tablespoon over to the sofa.

Various landscape paintings hung on the walls. Mountain peaks, fishing lakes and forest paths. Next to them: an aerial photo over Osen. Walter's gaze drifted from one picture to the next as he chewed. One of the paintings was of a Norwegian midsummer festival. Old and young alike were gathered around the big traditional bonfire.

The orange and blue of the flames pulled his mind back into his memories, back in time. He closed his eyes.

❋

He stood at a distance.

Had been standing there for a while, watching the flames as they danced, the colour of the fire lighting up Samantha's face as she sat in the middle of a group of ten or fifteen teenagers. She laughed the whole time. Her skin looked like it was glowing.

He spotted a chubby boy down by the water's edge – he was walking back and forth along the beach, talking to himself. Walter thought he was drunk at first, but then decided it looked more like he wasn't quite *all there.* The boy had caught a toad. It slipped from his hands, and he lunged after it.

The moon disappeared behind a cloud. Walter wasn't sure if he could, or even should, approach them. There had been no mistaking the invitation; she had even placed her hand on his arm and squeezed it, a sensation he could still feel hours later.

Someone was playing the guitar. One of the boys was really going for it, singing the chorus. They seemed okay. What they were drinking, Walter wasn't sure, but it must have been something strong. Some of them danced. Another boy emerged from the water, soaking wet. He shook his hair and tugged a little on his swimming shorts.

Walter decided to do something he had never done before: go out of his way to speak to strangers. He was actually going to do it, right here, right now. Slowly, he put one foot in front of the other. With each step he grew more and more nervous. What if she didn't recognise him? It was dark. She might feel different about him when there were so many others around. But he just had to let what happens, happen.

Samantha was in the middle of a conversation when she turned her head and noticed Walter walking over. She stopped talking and smiled broadly, as if she were both surprised and happy.

Hot and cold surged through his body.

Samantha jumped up and came running to meet him.

'You came!' she cried, throwing her arms around his neck. Walter, who had never known a girl like her to be happy to see a boy like him, didn't know what to do with his hands, but he caught her and returned the hug. She still smelled of sunscreen, but now with a hint of perfume, a sweet scent of something floral.

'Come,' she said loudly. 'Come meet the others.'

Samantha pulled him along. Walter let himself be led. When they arrived at the circle of teenagers, she released him and clapped her hands.

'Everyone,' she shouted. 'This is Walter. Walter is from Germany.'

'Deutschland!' someone yelled, as if it was something to cheer about. Walter nodded nervously and looked out over the faces of everyone sitting around the fire. Didn't register what any of them looked like. All he felt was something crawling around in his stomach and chest.

'And these are my best friends,' Samantha said, leading Walter over to the boy who, until just a few seconds ago, had been playing a nylon-string guitar with impressive skill. 'This is Markus.'

'Hi Walter,' Markus said. 'Markus Hadeland. D'you want a beer or anything?'

'I'm good, thanks,' Walter stammered, but then worried that he might have said something stupid. He wanted to be cool, too. It looked like everyone else was drinking.

'Oh come on,' one of the girls sitting on the grass piped up. 'Loosen up, you're not in Deutschland now.'

Walter was about to give in and take a beer when Samantha interjected:

'Hey now, no one's going to force anyone to drink anything if they don't want to.' She looked at him and rolled her eyes. 'That idiot over there is Trygve.'

She pointed to a boy with military-short hair, who was sitting on the grass. He flexed his biceps by way of a greeting. He did a military salute as well, which made Walter think of his father, but he smiled anyway.

'That one over there.' She pointed to the boy sitting by the water's edge; he had caught another toad and laughed as it tried to escape. 'That's my cousin, Fred. Pay no attention to him.'

Fred didn't seem to notice that Samantha was talking about him.

'And this here is Jarl Inge.'

A tall, thin boy with a can of beer in hand contented himself with a brief wave and a nod. Walter heard more names, and he mumbled his own back.

Samantha sat down on the grass and motioned for Walter to follow suit. He didn't quite know where to put his hands, so he sat forward a little and wrapped his arms around his knees. Walter tried to hear what they were talking about, but everything was in Norwegian. It didn't matter. He was as happy as he could possibly be. Everything was new. Different.

A boy stripped off almost all of his clothes and ran into the water. One of the girls jumped up, ran over, stopped and took off her bra, ready to join him.

'*Blir du med?*' she said to Samantha, placing an arm in front of her breasts. Walter guessed she had asked if Samantha was going in too.

Samantha replied in English. 'Not now, Rita,' she said. 'I don't want to leave Walter alone with so many weirdos.'

The topless girl now turned to him: 'Come along too, then. The temperature's perfect.'

She stood directly in front of them, almost completely naked, completely unfazed. Walter didn't know where to look.

'Thanks, but I'm good,' he said, which made the others laugh. He didn't like that. But Samantha was still sitting next to him, smiling. That was all that mattered. The friend shrugged her shoulders, took off at a sprint and jumped in.

'She's crazy,' Samantha said, laughing.

And practically naked, Walter thought, with a fascination that almost overwhelmed him. He had never met such people before.

He was handed a sausage from the barbeque that tasted more like charcoal than ketchup. Someone passed him a plastic cup of Coca-Cola. Walter said thank you, in Norwegian, and felt like he was part of something very special, something he couldn't put into words. But one thing he did know for sure: this was the best summer vacation he had ever had. How could it end?

Something was happening on the other side of the fire. Loud voices. Samantha stood up. Walter did the same, squinting through the flames. A man in a police uniform stood talking to the boy Samantha had introduced as Jarl Inge.

'That's Borvik,' Samantha explained. 'He's always giving us grief.'

The discussion between the two became more heated.

'He wants us to go,' Samantha translated. 'Bonfires aren't allowed in the summer. Something about the risk of forest fires.'

Walter looked around, unable to understand how there could be any danger of the flames from the fire spreading to the forest.

The girl who had been bathing half naked was now trying to calm the boy who had been arguing with the policeman. Markus poured water on the fire. The flames hissed. The smoke thickened and drifted up into the dark night.

The policeman turned his back. Jarl Inge shouted something after him, without getting any reaction. The other teenagers packed up their blankets and mats, threw on their backpacks and grabbed what drinks they had left.

They left the rubbish.

'Walk with me?' Samantha asked.

Walter nodded. Happy.

They formed the rear guard. It didn't take long before a wide gap appeared between them and the others.

'I've lived here my whole life,' Samantha began. 'Dad's the one who runs the campsite. He does it alone, really. Mum's involved in the management and admin and stuff, but she has so many problems with her health that Dad ends up doing all the physical jobs. I contribute a bit when I can. But I have school and everything, and friends. And now, of course, all this *Hit of the Summer* stuff. It takes up a lot of time.'

'Do you enjoy it?' Walter asked.

'Enjoy what?'

'Singing and being on stage and all that?'

'I love it,' she answered.

'Is that what you want to do?'

'When I grow up, you mean?' She laughed. 'Yeah. Yeah, definitely. That's the dream.'

They walked on a little.

'What about you? What's your dream?'

Walter wanted to say that he wanted to learn to play the guitar too, and play in a band like Rammstein, but he wasn't sure if she knew who they were, so he just said:

'I don't know. I guess I haven't dreamed much about ... anything.'

That wasn't true – he had dreamed of becoming a pilot, but he didn't want to tell her why he couldn't be one.

'Having a dream is important,' Samantha said. 'I'd quite like to move to Oslo. My uncle lives there. He's said I can stay with him if I want. But I don't know if that *is* what I want. I don't really want to live under the same roof as Fred. He ... he can be a bit weird.' She made a circular motion with her finger up by her temple. 'They're just visiting for a few days,' Samantha explained. 'And I'm always the one who has to take care of him.' She rolled her eyes.

Walter could see Fred ahead, almost at the front of the group. He was walking a little away from the others, apparently lost in his own thoughts.

'Shit,' Samantha said suddenly. She nodded towards a figure standing on the path further ahead. 'My dad,' she explained.

The others in the gang acknowledged him, but just continued past. As Walter and Samantha arrived in front of him, her father said something Walter didn't understand, and it wasn't long before he and Samantha were arguing. Her father had a forbidding voice. A forbidding look as well, which he sent in Walter's direction before stomping off.

When they were alone again, Samantha sighed. 'I was supposed to be back with Fred an hour ago,' she explained. 'Dad's strict about curfew. He has a little trouble understanding that I'm not six years old anymore. Is your father like that too?'

My father is quite a bit more than that, Walter wanted to say, but he just nodded.

Walter hoped the walk back would never end. He loved hearing her talk. Being beside her.

It was a clear night. It had started to get a little chilly. Walter fantasised about putting an arm around her. Pulling her close. Keeping her warm.

'See you tomorrow?' she asked as they emerged from the forest.

'You will,' Walter responded.

That made her laugh. They stopped for a few seconds.

Samantha came towards him and gave him another hug.

'Sleep well,' she whispered.

'You too.'

Walter stood and watched her leave, right until she disappeared out of the campsite. He caught himself staring at her legs, how her white skirt brushed her skin. How her muscles moved. He dreamed of touching her. Knowing her intimately.

When she was completely out of sight, he turned and walked back towards the cabin. He could see his parents were sitting outside. There were beer cans on the table in front of them, peanuts in a bowl. Soft music streamed from a portable radio.

'Hi,' Walter said before they spotted him.

He saw at once that his father was drunk.

'Where have you been?' he barked.

'Around,' Walter retorted, waiting for a bucket of water that never came. 'How long are we going to be here?'

'Five more days,' his father answered.

Five days, Walter thought to himself. So little time.

※

Walter drained the beer can and cracked open another. Sat down again and thought about what had happened the day after that wonderful evening. It was a thought that excited him – he felt the start of an erection.

Accompanied by a wave of fury.

Certain things were impossible to forget.

15

For each of the large wooden boxes, thirty-two planks of wood were needed; for the small ones, twenty-two. A post was then required for each corner. Every plank was secured with a staple at each end. Sixty-four staples for the large boxes, forty-four for the small.

The staple gun ran on compressed air. It was an inmate from Wing B who had taught Blix how to use it. Some guy from a motorbike gang serving an eight-year sentence for violence and narcotics. On his first day at the carpentry workshop, he had grinned through his bushy beard and given Blix a thumbs-up. It was meant as a warning. On the inside of his thumb he had a crater-like wound caused by being careless. The staple had gone all the way through. On the other side, it had split the nail. The thumb nail had never grown back and resembled the cloven hoof of an animal.

The staples came in strips of one hundred. They kept separating, much like with a stapler in an office.

It had come as a surprise to Blix that the inmates had access to every tool imaginable. He'd worked on a case once where a gang's enforcer had stapled a man to a table, shooting one through each palm. The guy had been stuck there for seven hours before a friend turned up with the money he owed. But that was outside the walls of a prison: even though the workshop was full of violent convicts, they wouldn't turn on each other without reason.

Valdemar Hjorth had been escorted into the workshop after lunch. Every inmate had an activity or work duty. It was where they got their money to shop at the prison kiosk. Seventy-four kroner a day. Blix had hoped that Hjorth would choose a study programme or be placed in one of the other workshops, but here he was, standing at the other end of the room, making bins.

Blix put away a finished box and started on a new one. The third staple hit a snag. The entire plank cracked down the middle. He threw the pieces into a pile and pulled out the staple with a pair of pliers. Started again.

One of the officers came over and said something.

Blix took off his hearing protectors and let them hang around his neck.

'You have a visitor,' the officer repeated.

The clock on the wall at the end of the workshop showed that it was only half-one.

The compressor in the staple gun sputtered, releasing air as he put it down. He brushed off his clothes, pulled off his work gloves and hung the hearing protectors back in place on the wall.

Gard Fosse was sitting in the visitors' room. He stood up as soon as Blix was brought in. Both of them remained standing until the door was locked behind them.

Blix pulled the chair out and sat opposite Fosse.

'How are you?' Fosse asked, studying the scar on Blix's cheek.

'It's only been two days since you were here last,' Blix replied. 'Same as I was then.'

Fosse sat down and cleared his throat. 'Have you given any more thought to what we spoke about?'

Blix plucked out a wood chip that had become lodged in the fabric of his shirt sleeve.

'I hope you've managed to build some kind of rapport,' Fosse said. 'The counselling programme didn't seem to work out.'

The corner of Fosse's mouth turned up slightly, as it was wont to do when he was embarrassed.

'It was an attempt to get the two of you to talk,' he explained.

Hardly Fosse's idea, Blix thought to himself. Sounded more like Wibe's or one of the younger investigators.

'We have another session at two,' he responded. 'I doubt we'll get anything from it.'

Gard Fosse leant forward, as if he wanted to say something confidential. 'He's here,' he said.

'Who?' Blix asked. 'The German?'

Fosse nodded, taking out a plastic folder and placing a picture on the table. Blix recognised it. Oslo Central Station. He'd retrieved images from the surveillance system there plenty of times himself and knew where the cameras were located.

The photo was taken at the Jernbanetorget exit. There were six people in the picture. Two teenage girls, a red-haired man carrying a guitar case, a woman with a child in her arms and a man wearing a dark cap with a red emblem on the front. He walked with his head down, so only his mouth and chin were visible under the brim.

'The man with the cap,' Fosse announced.

Blix was about to object that that could be anyone, but didn't. Fosse had more. He took out another photo. A man in a cap filling up a Golf, an old model. Same cap, same jacket, same trousers.

Same man.

'We got this one from Germany,' Fosse explained. 'His mother's car. Fills up in Flensburg. Pays in cash. Ten minutes later, the licence plate is registered crossing the border into Denmark. Now he's here.'

And on Monday Jarl Inge Ree would be out, Blix thought.

'I searched his cell,' he said.

Fosse put the pictures away. 'So did we,' he said. 'Nicolai Wibe was there on Wednesday.'

Blix sighed. Of course they did. A secret search.

'You could've told me,' he said. 'It wasn't exactly risk free.'

The corner of Fosse's mouth tugged upward again as he gave Blix another embarrassed smile.

Blix frowned at the folder with the pictures of Walter Kroos.

'Do you intend to make it public that he's here in Norway?' he asked.

Fosse shook his head. 'Not yet,' he replied.

'Emma Ramm is looking into it,' Blix said.

'I know. She called me yesterday. Wasn't exactly difficult to figure out where she'd got her information from.'

Blix saw no reason to deny it. 'She's probably gone up to Osen,' he said.

'Osen?' Fosse repeated. 'Why?'

'Maths and statistics,' Blix replied. 'Jarl Inge Ree grew up there. Walter Kroos has been in prison for the last ten years. If their paths ever crossed, the most likely place it would've happened is there.'

He could see that Fosse was thinking it through.

'Do you have people up there too?' Blix asked.

'We're keeping a low profile for now,' Fosse replied.

'You should talk to the local police anyway,' Blix said.

Fosse didn't seem to appreciate his investigative advice. In one swift movement, he pulled back the file with the photos in it and placed it in his bag.

'I've arranged with the prison to lift the restrictions on your calls,' he said. 'You can ask to make calls whenever you want, and receive calls anytime, from anyone.'

He stood up and remained standing for a moment before adding:

'Call me. If you find anything out from either Jarl Inge Ree or Emma Ramm.'

Blix didn't answer   said nothing and did nothing to indicate what he was thinking.

Fosse pressed the call button on the intercom and announced that the visit was over.

'*Coming*,' came a crackle in response.

'Did you get anything from his phone?' Blix asked.

It was clear that Fosse didn't understand what he meant. Blix had taken it for granted that they had found Ree's phone, and instead of taking it with them, they'd wiretapped it then left it behind.

'You didn't find it?' he asked. 'In the sock drawer?'

Fosse sat back down. Blix told him about the burner phone he found, and gave him the one contact number he had memorised, repeating it twice so Fosse could write it down.

'Thank you,' he said.

On the other side of the door came the sound of keys rattling in the lock.

'We're going to need you to keep helping us with this,' Fosse said finally. 'You'll hear from us.'

He stood up again.

'And call me when you know more.'

16

It took Emma less than half a minute to drive through what could be called, with some benevolence, the centre of Osen. She noticed a few shops, a café, a food store. But almost no people.

She needed to fill up the car, so stopped by a Shell station and parted with NOK 832. She felt a little peckish too, so went inside. A thin, bald man came out of a back room with two cardboard boxes, which he placed on the floor behind the counter. His face was lop-sided, as if one half was paralysed. His left eye and corner of his mouth drooped a little.

Emma averted her gaze. There was nothing tempting in the way of hot food, but she ended up asking for a hot dog anyway.

The man nodded and took the payment.

'Do you live around here?' Emma asked, putting the bank card back in her purse.

'Born and raised,' replied the man, as he pulled out a hot-dog bun.

Emma smiled and introduced herself. 'I work for news.no,' she added. 'I am investigating a possible Norwegian connection to a German prisoner currently on the run. There are a number of leads suggesting he may have been here in the village once. A long time ago.'

'Walter, yes,' the man answered immediately, opening the pre-cut bun with a pinch, then wrapping it in thin paper. 'Bit of an odd one. Find out anything yet?'

He fished out a barbecue sausage – wrinkly and with grill marks – and placed it in the bun. In front of him he had an assortment of top-pings in various aluminium trays – prawn and potato salad, crispy fried onions, pickles.

'Just ketchup and mustard, please.'

'You'll find those over there,' he said, pointing to a rack over against the wall with eight different bottles, as well as napkins. He handed her the hot dog.

There were questions she was dying to ask him, but she wanted to let him talk freely. Fortunately, there was no one else in the petrol station at that moment.

'I heard about it on the news,' he continued as Emma strode over to the bottles. 'It's hectic here in the summer, but not many people come at this time of year, so I've got a bit of time to kill, and I watch the news.'

Emma found herself wondering what had happened to his face. She noticed a scar too, just below the cheekbone.

'But Walter, yes,' he said. 'It's been a long time since he was here. Now, let me think, when could that have been?' He looked up to the left, but did not seem to arrive at any conclusion.

'But you still remember him?' Emma asked, taking a bite of the hot dog. The sausage was far too hot, so she had to wait a few seconds before she could chew it.

'Oh yes,' the man responded. 'A lot of strange things happened that summer.'

'Strange?' she mumbled, the food still waiting in her mouth. 'What kind of strange things?'

He shrugged, 'I had a summer job that year. Here, actually, so it must have been in 2004. That was the summer I started working, so I wasn't spending much time with the others.'

'The others?' Emma asked, and finally swallowed.

'My friends,' he said, putting the lids back on the hot dog toppings in front of him. 'Who I went to school with, hung out with. We'd spend most of our time down at the campsite. We'd swim, mess about.'

'But you remember Walter Kroos from that summer?'

He nodded and glanced quickly at a screen behind him, showing some horse race. At the bottom was a long rolling line of numbers and strange horse names.

'I didn't have any problems with Walter. I remember him as being a fairly quiet guy. Shy. And then he was German, of course, which came with its own problems.'

'How'd you mean?'

'It was the language barrier mainly,' he said, picking up an empty wrapper from behind the counter and throwing it in the bin. 'Mostly we all spoke Norwegian. But Walter hung out with us anyway.'

'And not everyone liked that?'

He hesitated a moment before answering.

'We'd all grown up together, y'know, pretty close-knit. And then suddenly *he* appeared. From Deutschland.'

Emma smiled a little at the word choice.

'It is utterly insane that he wound up becoming a murderer.'

'Sorry,' she said, a thought hitting her, 'but could I get your name?'

'Trygve,' he said, smiling again. 'Trygve Klepp.'

Emma was annoyed at herself for having neglected to bring her notebook in with her from the car, but Trygve Klepp was an easy name to remember.

'You said a lot of strange things happened that summer. Could you be a little more specific?'

'Well ... ' Klepp shrugged, as if regretting what he had said. 'I didn't mean anything in particular, really. As I said, we hung around a lot, were rowdy, got up to no good. You know – teenagers.'

Emma paused for a moment, before asking the next question.

'You said there are a lot of people here in the summer?'

'Oh yeah,' Klepp said, as if it was something he was proud of. 'Lots of foreigners.'

'Right, but you've managed to remember Walter Kroos's name after all this time – and among so many people?'

Klepp seemed a little uncomfortable.

'He must have made quite an impression?' Emma continued when he didn't answer.

'Nah, I mean, I guess.' He shrugged again. 'You should really talk to Rita about this. Rita Alvberg. She had more to do with Walter than me. She's in Osen right now, I think. She stopped by the station a few days ago. Her mother died last week.'

Emma tried to memorise that name as well.

'You don't have any photos, by any chance, from that summer? Of Walter Kroos?'

Klepp shook his head. 'People take photos of everything these days,' he said. 'I don't think anyone had a camera phone back then.'

He thought a little.

'Rita had a camera, actually,' he eventually said. 'She preferred to have her own photo taken, mind, but you can ask her.'

Emma thanked him for the tip.

'You probably know Jarl Inge Ree too then, I'd imagine?'

Klepp lifted a hand up to his face, scratched his scarred cheek.

'Everyone knows who Jarl Inge is,' he said slowly. 'He doesn't live here anymore.'

'No, I know. He's in prison.'

'Where he belongs.' There was a sudden bitterness in his voice as he said this. He continued, more cautious now: 'But don't tell anyone I said that.'

'I won't,' Emma said, scrutinising him afresh, trying not to stare. Klepp had something of the vulnerable about him. Maybe something sad too, she wasn't sure.

'Is there anyone else in the village who might be able to tell me anything about Walter?'

'Samantha Kasin,' Klepp answered – quickly, too.

'Samantha?' Emma repeated, surprised.

'Yeah, they spent some time together that summer,' Klepp replied. 'She introduced us to him.'

Again, he looked like he regretted what he'd said.

'I really shouldn't be saying all this,' he continued. 'It's not up to me. But talk to Rita. And Samantha. Maybe they can tell you more.'

17

Samantha calmly pushed the roller across the wall, but there was too much paint on it. It dripped onto the newspapers she had spread out on the floor.

'Wonderwall' was the name of the paint she'd chosen. She wasn't sure if the name was meant ironically or not, but it was supposed to be 'enduringly beautiful'. The wall did at least look better than it did before. She needed to see some colour.

Samantha ran the roller over the wall a few more times, putting a little less on it the next time she bent down to top it up. She kept rolling, up and down, up and down. Although her arm and shoulder were beginning to ache, there was something meditative about the repetitive work. It didn't require brain power – on the contrary, she could let her mind wander. To the jetty.

The water.

Samantha closed her eyes and saw a much younger version of herself plunging naked into the water, letting herself drift until she lost momentum and slowly returned to the surface. The cold water didn't bother her. A few more strokes, then she turned and blinked the water out of her eyes so she could clearly see the jetty.

And *him*.

Samantha opened her eyes again. Her skin had bristled.

She shook away the bad memories and continued to paint.

Then heard a sound from out in reception.

It struck her that she should have put up a sign saying that the campsite was closed for the day. There was no traffic to speak of at this time of year. She removed her work gloves and looked up at the woman who had entered the shop with a smile. It was the journalist from earlier.

'Six hundred and ninety kroner, was it?' she asked.

Samantha stared at her. 'Uh, yes.'

'I can't bear the thought of driving back to Oslo today. Do you have any cabins available?'

Samantha blinked. 'If there's one thing I've got, it's cabins,' she said. 'You've saved the day,' she added with a smile. 'Now maybe I can buy another can of paint.'

The journalist laughed.

'Any preference?' Samantha asked. 'All the cabins are pretty much the same.'

'If it were possible to get one by the water, that'd be great.'

Samantha smiled. 'That's what everyone asks for.'

She led the journalist back into the reception area and registered her on the computer system: *Emma Ramm, Falbes Gate, Oslo.*

'Do you need bedding and towels, Emma?'

'Please.'

'Then that'll be another hundred kroner.'

'That's fine.'

After she'd signed the papers and paid, Samantha gave her the key to cabin K–1634.

'Don't ask me why we have such an odd numbering system for the cabins here,' she said. 'It's not like we have one thousand, seven hundred cabins.'

Emma Ramm smiled and shook her head.

'Do you mind if I ask you something?' she began.

'Sure,' Samantha replied.

'Do you know Rita Alvberg?'

'Rita? Yes.'

Samantha clicked away on the computer, typed what she needed into the campsite administration software and opened a binder on the counter. She then punched two holes into the document with the journalist's contact details on it, and slotted it into the binder.

'Rita and I spent a lot of time together, growing up. But we drifted apart, like so many do when you get older.'

'I thought I'd take a walk over to see her after I've settled in. She's apparently home at the moment, after her mother passed away.'

Samantha frowned. 'I had heard that Harriet died, but not that Rita was home. But that's not so surprising I guess, given we're no longer in touch. And it's only natural that she would need to come back, to see to everything now her mother's no longer with us.'

'Do you know where she lives?'

'Sure, just drive straight over the bridge,' Samantha pointed out of the window, 'and then it's the third house on the right. It's a nice house. Blue. You'll see it from the road. It'll only take five or so minutes.'

'Great, thank you.'

Emma Ramm turned to leave.

Samantha couldn't help herself: 'Who was it who told you to talk to Rita?'

The journalist stopped in the exit, her hand on the door handle.

'A guy over at the petrol station,' she said. 'He remembered who Walter Kroos was, pretty well actually – he was here in the summer of 2004. He thought that Rita would be able to tell me more about him. Seemed that something or other happened back then.'

Samantha felt the colour drain from her face.

'So hopefully she'll remember what that was,' Ramm continued with a smile and waved the key in the air as if to say bye. 'Not everyone remembers that far back though.'

Samantha swallowed and tried to say something but couldn't.

Ramm stepped out the door: 'Have a nice day, Samantha. See you later, hopefully.'

18

Otto Myran greeted Blix with the same gentle smile as last time, and a friendly nod towards the nearest vacant chair.

Jakobsen followed Blix in, and took what appeared to be his permanent place, leaning against the radiator and the barred window. Blix had just taken his seat when Jarl Inge Ree was brought in. He sent Blix a scrutinising look and shuffled over to the empty chair.

Blix sat leaning forward and staring straight ahead, his elbows resting on his thighs. Ree sat down, folding his hands one over the other on his lap. Sighed demonstratively.

'Gentlemen,' Otto Myran began. 'It's nice to see you both again.'

Neither Blix nor Ree answered.

Myran adjusted his glasses a little and said: 'How have you been since we all last saw each other?'

Blix stared at the pattern on the floor. Ree shifted a little in his chair. Jakobsen drew a quick breath in through his nose, coughed.

'I want a PlayStation for Christmas,' Ree said at once, letting his eyes wander over the others in the room, awaiting a response. 'Well that's what we're talking about today, is it not?'

He scoffed when he got no reply.

'We can,' Myran replied. 'That's a good suggestion, actually. It's not long until Christmas. So you like the PlayStation then, Jarl Inge?'

'Get to fuck.'

Myran laughed, short and strained.

Blix rubbed his hands together and said: 'You've got a great vocabulary, Ree. Real varied and eloquent.'

'Kiss my ass.'

Ree's facial muscles tightened. Jakobsen removed his thumbs from his waistband, ready to intervene. Ree remained seated.

'Gentlemen,' the social worker said, starting again. 'I want us to continue where we left off last time. By asking each other questions. It can be about anything, as I said. Today, I think we can say absolutely everything is on the table. No restrictions.' He smiled slyly at them, as if he had done them a favour. 'But be respectful,' he added. 'It is still possible to ask personal, intimate questions, but politely. Who wants to go first?'

Neither Blix nor Ree said anything.

Ree looked over at Blix, who again rubbed his hands together slowly, as if he had all the time in the world and not a single worry.

The social worker leant forward and addressed Ree: 'Isn't there anything you'd like to ask Blix? Anything at all? Something simple?'

A long moment of silence.

'I want to know who the hottie is – the woman who came out of the visitors' room during one of your visits. Is she your daughter or something? No, wait, she can't be,' Ree corrected himself, laughing savagely. 'You don't have a daughter ... anymore.'

Myran seemed disturbed, but Blix didn't let the comment get to him.

'Emma,' he replied after a few seconds. 'Her name is Emma. She works at news.no. We go way back.'

'What does that mean?'

Blix thought over what the smartest answer would be.

'I ... shot and killed her father when she was a kid.'

'Are you fucking with me?'

'No.'

Blix noticed that he suddenly had Ree's full attention.

'What happened?'

Blix quickly rubbed his chin. It crackled as his palm passed over the burgeoning beard.

'Her father,' he began, 'was a scumbag. A drunk who killed Emma's mother in a fit of rage because she wanted to leave him, take the kids with her.'

Blix paused, feeling himself bristle a bit, an inner resistance to actually put it into words.

'I was new to the job,' he continued, regardless. 'When we got there, my colleague wanted us to wait for backup. But one of the neighbours said she'd heard a gunshot, so I feared the worst.' Blix paused again. He could feel himself growing warmer.

'And then?' Ree urged him.

Blix turned to face him and sighed heavily. Waited a long moment.

'I decided to go in. My colleague remained outside. I found Emma's mother in a pool of blood on the kitchen floor. Her father was standing in the living room with a gun aimed at Emma's head. Said he was going to shoot her if I didn't leave them alone.' Blix started talking faster. 'So it ... ended up with me shooting him in the forehead.'

Ree stared at him. 'You just gunned him down?'

'Not straight away,' Blix replied. 'I tried to talk him out of it, but it was clear he wasn't making an empty threat.'

Blix remembered every moment of what happened next. How Emma's father had toppled backward, the sound of his body crashing through the coffee table and slamming onto the floor. The smell of gunpowder filling the room. The smell of blood, brains. The startled look on Emma's face, her scream. How Blix had rushed towards her and lifted her up, carried her outside. Past her dead mother on the kitchen floor. The tiny body that cried and shook against his.

'It was her or him,' Blix finished quietly. 'It was the only option.'

Ree sat there, head tilted, gaping at him. 'What happened to your coward of a colleague?'

'Gard Fosse?' Blix shrugged. 'He was promoted, eventually, became my boss.'

'Sounds like a prick,' Ree responded.

'That's about right, yeah,' Blix nodded.

The corner of Ree's mouth curled up ever so slightly. Myran leant forward a little. He seemed more worried about how the conversation had developed than pleased that a dialogue had actually happened at all.

'But that was a long time ago,' Ree added.

'1999,' Blix confirmed.

'And you and the chick became best pals then, or what?'

'We met again years later, in connection with a case she was working on,' he said. 'We kept in touch after that.'

'Even though you made her an orphan.'

'Emma's always seen it as my doing her a favour.'

'You saved her life,' Myran interjected.

Blix didn't comment.

There was a long pause.

'I was just talking to her, actually,' he said at last. 'She called. She's ... in your hometown. In Osen.'

A slight muscle twitch, and Ree raised his right eyebrow.

'Why?' he asked.

'She's writing about Walter Kroos.'

Ree pursed his lips. Myran looked from one to the other.

'You've probably seen on the news that he's on the run?' Blix continued.

Ree didn't say anything, but Blix could tell that his mind was racing.

'Emma's spoken to a friend of yours,' he continued. 'Walter Kroos stayed at her campsite years ago, it would seem, on a summer holiday. She must've had an awful lot to do with him.'

Ree looked at him sharply. 'Samantha?' he began. 'Why ... what do you...?' He stopped himself. 'So...' Again he had to search for the words.

Then it was as if something dawned on him. 'Is *that* why we're here, doing this?' Ree exploded, jumping to his feet. 'This bullshit?' He waved his hand about wildly.

Jakobsen took a step forward, but remained passive.

'Is that what this is really about?' Ree continued, his voice raised. 'You want us to talk, but about Walter, is that it?'

Myran looked at Blix, as if pleading for him to help find the words, calm him down.

'What does any of that have to do with me?' Ree continued, shouting now.

Blix thought of the ripped-up pieces of paper found in Walter Kroos's toilet bowl back in his prison cell in Germany, but didn't mention it.

Ree pointed at Myran. 'You said this was a priority project, from the management or whatever.' His finger trembled. 'When I've only got three days left in this joint. Cut the bullshit.' Small drops of saliva sprayed from his mouth. 'We might have an hour and twenty-five minutes left on the clock, but you can bet your ass that'll be without me. Try and stop me.'

Ree walked towards the door. Jakobsen blocked his way.

'I'm out of here,' Ree said. 'Now.'

With his gaze, the officer conferred with Myran. The social worker just nodded.

The session was over.

19

Emma called to update Anita Grønvold on what she'd found out so far.

'I've ended up renting a cabin here,' she said, looking up at an aerial photo hanging on the wall in front of her. Hers was in the middle of a long line of cabins stretching towards an expansive area of forest. 'The woman who runs the campsite lied about not knowing who Walter Kroos was. She said she'd never heard of him, even though she was the one who introduced him to her group of friends back in 2004. She turned paler than a corpse when I said I knew that Walter had been here that year.'

Anita wanted the details. Emma told her everything she knew as she studied the picture on the wall. Right below the cabins was Osensjøen – the lake that fed into a river and flowed further down the valley. The photo had been taken as a red bus drove over the bridge that connected the centre of Osen to the more scattered settlement on the other side of the river. Emma searched for the blue house belonging to Rita Alvberg's mother, but was unable to locate it.

'Did you confront her about the lie?' her news.no boss asked.

'I was going to,' Emma replied, 'but I thought I'd get a little more information first. Something happened that summer. I don't know what role Walter Kroos played in it, or whether it has any connection with him escaping now, but I do know that he made quite an impression here in the village.'

The centre of the village didn't seem to consist of much other than the one, long street that ran down the middle. Between that and Osensjøen was a residential area made up of around fifty houses. From above, they looked like tiny pieces from a Monopoly game. Through the thick forest that encircled the village, various roads wound outwards like thin, grey veins. One of them led towards a larger, square area that looked like it had been carved out of the forest. A lumber mill, probably, Emma decided.

'Odd thing to lie about,' Anita added.

'Yeah, that's what I thought.'

The campsite itself reminded Emma of a large letter D, where the long row of cabins formed the straight line. Samantha's reception and kiosk, as well as the communal facilities, were located at the far end, curving round at the tip of the arc.

'If you're able to find some photos of Walter Kroos from back then, that would be great.'

'I'm working on it.'

It was still daylight outside, but for no more than another hour. A cool wind swept over the campsite. Emma hadn't packed anything for an overnight stay. She'd at least need a toothbrush and some toothpaste, and maybe even a change of clothes.

As she drove out of the campsite again, she saw that the lights were on in two other cabins. Rubber boots and rain gear were hung out to dry on the outside of one of them. In the other: no signs of life. There was also no car parked outside.

Emma followed Samantha's directions, out of the centre of Osen and over the small, narrow bridge that spanned a stretch of river, which raced down into the valley. It was powerful, and easy to imagine that if someone ended up in the water, the outcome would be fatal.

She pulled over in front of the third house on the right – one that certainly stood out among the others in the area, blue as it was. The paint was peeling off in places. The window frames had been white, once. Now they were tinged brown from dirt. But it was a large house with an expansive garden, and in an idyllic location. It was a short way to the river, but the dense undergrowth made the water inaccessible.

A dark-grey Nissan Leaf was parked outside, with the power cord connected to a wall socket. There was another car parked in the carport – a small Volkswagen. Emma guessed that the electric car was Rita's, while the car in the port must have belonged to her late mother.

There were lights on in the house, but unlike the houses next door, no smoke rose from the chimney.

Emma walked up the steps to the front door and rang the bell. She hadn't managed to find much out about Rita Alvberg, aside from the fact that she worked at a pre-school in Stovner, a little north-east of Oslo. Emma had discovered nothing to indicate that she was married or had children of her own.

Emma tried the bell again. The roar of the river did its part to muffle every other sound, but Emma still couldn't hear anything from inside. The door remained closed.

She typed in the electric car's licence number and sent it to an SMS service she subscribed to. The answer took mere seconds: the car was registered to Rita Alvberg. There was a mobile number with the same name, which Emma also tried, but it went straight to voicemail.

It was a nice area, Emma thought. Maybe Rita was just out for a walk. She drove back into the village centre, bought what she needed at the shop and headed back to the Alvberg house. There were still no signs of life, but she did spot a man outside in the neighbouring garden, leaning on a rake. An older guy, wearing a hat and an old-fashioned all-weather jacket.

Emma waved.

The man did not return the gesture, but simply said: 'Arvid was also here, earlier today.'

Emma squinted at the man and took a few steps closer. 'Arvid?'

'Arvid Borvik. The sheriff. He walked around here. Asked if we'd seen anything of Rita.'

'Did he now?'

The man in the neighbouring garden neither answered, nodded nor shook his head. 'Asked when we'd last seen her,' he said.

'And when was that?'

A sceptical expression crossed his face.

'Sorry,' Emma said, and introduced herself. 'I just wanted to talk to Rita about something.' She decided not to mention Walter Kroos.

'It doesn't look like she's home though,' she added. 'When did you last see her?'

'Yesterday,' he said after a moment's thought. 'Late in the day. Looked like she was going for a walk.'

'But you didn't see when she got back?'

He shook his head. 'I was up at the lumber mill yesterday evening. I don't really pay attention to much.'

Emma smiled and thanked the man, before walking back to her car. Something had made the police pay a visit though. They didn't do home visits unless someone had expressed some concern. Rita's home in Oslo had presumably been checked before they tried her mother's house.

She got behind the wheel. She had the name and number for the pre-school Rita Alvberg worked in saved in the notes on her phone. Emma started the car and called them, hooking the phone up to the hands-free system. A man answered. Children's voices could be heard in the background.

She introduced herself and asked for Rita.

'She ... isn't at work today,' the man said.

'Do you know where I can get hold of her?'

There was a bit of a delay on the line.

'No,' he said eventually. 'But I know her mother died recently. She's taken some time off. She was supposed to be back at work again this week, but...'

Emma put the car in gear. 'Have you been trying to get hold of her as well?'

In the background, a child started screaming. The man turned his attention to the child, told them to calm down and that they would be going for another walk tomorrow.

'Uh, I know the manager has been ringing around a bit,' he said to Emma, 'but ... to tell you the truth, we've no idea where Rita is.'

Again, a short pause.

'There must be a good explanation for why she hasn't turned up,' the man continued. 'I'm sure she'll be back in tomorrow.'

Emma thanked him and hung up. Before driving away, she glanced in the mirror, unsure of what to make of the fact that no one knew where Rita Alvberg was.

20

Walter was used to making time pass. In prison, that was pretty much all he did – busied himself without thinking too much about the clock. There was always someone telling him what time it was anyway, where he should be, what he should be doing.

On the shelf above the fireplace were a couple of comics, alongside a small collection of mismatched books. Everything was in Norwegian, probably left behind by previous guests. He pulled out one of the comics and flipped through it, but didn't manage to decipher much of anything from the speech bubbles.

His father had ordered him to read when they'd stayed here. Half an hour every day. Walter thought back to the day after the campfire, when he sat outside the cabin in a rusty camping chair, reading a book in the shadow of the cabin's overhanging roof. The air was still: full of a quiet, oppressive heat. And he hadn't been out there for more than a few minutes when Samantha suddenly appeared before him.

'Hello,' she said, with a smile so wide that the skin on his arms immediately began to tingle.

Samantha was barefoot, and all she was wearing was a bikini and a thin, floaty and almost transparent singlet that barely reached her thighs. On her head was a straw hat with flowers. And underneath that, sunglasses with dark-yellow, almost heart-shaped lenses. It was impossible not to stare at her, brown and beautiful as she was.

'What're you reading?' she asked, taking a few airy dance steps closer to him. Walter quickly looked down at the book and closed it.

'Nothing interesting,' he said sheepishly. 'Just some ... school stuff.'

'*School stuff?*' She rolled her eyes and laughed at the same time. 'You're doing school work now? Aren't you on holiday?'

'Yeah but...'

Walter didn't know how to respond. And in the next moment, his father emerged from the cabin, his reddish-brown belly bulging out over his dark-blue swimming shorts. He stopped dead when he saw

Samantha. Taking off his black *Terminator* sunglasses, he shot a quick, surprised look at Walter, before returning his eyes to Samantha.

'*Mein Gott*,' he said, hitching up his shorts.

Walter didn't like how his father's gaze slid up and down her body before he put his sunglasses back on.

'You have to speak English,' Walter told him, in English, and a little more grumpily than he had intended. 'Samantha doesn't speak German.'

'Who is this beautiful girl?'

Walter turned a bright red, all the way up to his forehead. He hated that his father used such a word to describe her. He didn't have time to say anything – Samantha took the initiative and introduced herself. She walked right up to his father and offered him her hand. Curtsied a little, even.

'Mmm,' his father said, continuing to stare at her. 'My name is Kurt.' There was an awful silkiness to his voice.

Walter stood up. 'Come on,' he said to Samantha, who was still smiling and being her usual friendly self. Walter put the book down on the chair.

'And where do you think you're going?' His father's words were directed at Walter. The softness in his voice had evaporated.

'Just for a walk.'

'Have you finished reading?'

'Uh, yeah.'

'So that's a no,' his father corrected him.

'I can finish reading later.'

'Oh you can, can you?'

'Yes,' Walter retorted. 'I can.'

There was something about Samantha's presence that emboldened Walter somewhat.

'Come on,' he repeated to Samantha. 'Let's go.'

'It was nice meeting you,' Samantha said, turning back to Walter's father. Who didn't respond.

Walter took a step away, expecting at any moment for his father to shout or come charging after him and pull him back by the scruff of his neck. But that didn't happen. The further away from the cabin they got, the stronger Walter felt. He had managed to talk back to his father and get away with it.

Samantha steered them in the direction of the water and the jetty again, without them having talked about going swimming. Walter felt lighter, taller. Whenever he was near Samantha, it was as if he entered a secret, closed room where nothing else existed.

'Is he always like that?' she asked after a while.

'What do you mean?'

'So strict?' Samantha elaborated.

Walter thought for a moment – he didn't know how else to answer than 'yes', but still he couldn't bring himself to say the word.

'Fathers,' Samantha said – as if that explained everything. And maybe it did.

When they arrived at the jetty, they sat down with their legs dangling over the edge.

Samantha asked, 'Why do you have to do homework now, in the middle of your holiday?'

Walter never really talked about anything difficult or embarrassing. Not with teachers nor with the counsellors at school, not even with his friends – the few he had, anyway. But with Samantha, it felt like he could say anything.

'I'm dyslexic.'

He looked out over the lake, which rippled at that very moment, as if it had goosebumps. It was the first time he had said that out loud. At home they treated it as an illness they should never talk about. But it was there all the time, in everything Walter did, in everything he tried to achieve. The letters hopping about the page, shuffling along the line, making him feel small, stupid, making the others think and believe the same. He knew that's what they all thought.

'Do you know what that is?'

Samantha nodded.

'My father thinks that if I read enough, I'll learn to recognise what order the letters should come in. Reading is like everything else in life, he says. If you want to be good at it, you have to practise. It sounds simple. But it's not. Not for me.'

Samantha's forehead had formed into a series of thoughtful creases. She took his hand and squeezed it gently. Feeling her fingers against his made him gasp.

'What's wrong?' she asked.

'It...' He smiled, unsure of what to say or do. But again, it was as if Samantha gave him courage. 'I'm not really used to girls ... being like you.'

His heart beat faster, he could feel it pounding underneath his T-shirt.

'You mean ... girls ... who touch you.'

The question saddened him for a second, but he nodded anyway.

'Then ... you're probably not used to this either.'

Samantha sat closer, closer, closer. And then she pressed her lips to his.

She tasted of something sweet.

He had seen her put something on her lips before, a little round tub that she would dip her pinkie into.

Strawberry.

Yes, strawberries, that was what she tasted of.

Walter didn't know what to do. He just followed her lead – their lips moved slowly. Then he felt her hand against his cheek too, surprisingly cold on such a hot day as this, but he enjoyed feeling it there, the same way he enjoyed closing his eyes, allowing the moment to fill him up, the moment that stretched out into seconds, maybe just two or three, but they were the best, most beautiful seconds of his life.

She stopped, and pushed herself away from him a little. Smiled.

'Your cheeks are red,' she said.

Walter swallowed and leant forward a little. He didn't want her to see what had happened in his trousers. She laughed, which made Walter start laughing too.

'Now you can say that you've *kissed* a girl too,' she added.

It made him a little sad again – he had hoped that wasn't the only reason she'd done it, just so he would have something to tell his friends when he got home.

'How was it?' she asked.

'Um, good,' he said, and immediately regretted it.

Samantha started to laugh. God, how he loved to hear her laugh. 'It was *good*?' She rolled her eyes. 'Well now I'm really disappointed.'

'It was more than just good,' he said, feeling his cheeks glow.

'It was ... really good?' She grimaced, teasing him, and laughed again.

Walter grabbed her hand. As soon as he did, her face transformed, and a more serious expression took over. As if something happened to her too, at the exact moment he slowly leant against her.

And he saw what he wanted to see in her eyes.

It was not sympathy or pity. She wanted it, too. And when he kissed her, she drew a short breath in quickly through her nose. Then she kissed him back – hard.

He had no memory of where the time went after that, not until Samantha suddenly got up and said she had to go home.

'I have to practise,' she said. 'It'll be on TV tomorrow evening. *Live,* this time.'

She pulled the singlet down so that it covered her bum and rearranged the straw hat a touch so it fit better.

'It's the semi-finals,' she added. 'So there's a lot at stake.'

Walter got to his feet and asked: 'Are you nervous?'

Samantha lifted her shoulders high and took a deep breath in. 'A little,' she said, exhaling hard. Then she shook her head. 'I'm really nervous, actually.' She laughed. 'All of Norway will be watching.'

'What're you going to sing?' Walter asked, straightening his T-shirt a little as well.

She looked at him and said '"I Will Always Love You."'

Walter knew it was far too early to be saying such things, but it still felt like she was telling him.

'The one by...' he swallowed '...what's her name ... Whitney something?'

'Whitney Houston,' Samantha said. 'Dolly Parton actually wrote it.

The best song in the world. But it is unbelievably difficult to sing. Especially at the end.'

There was no TV in the cabin, but Walter knew he had to watch it somehow.

'You can do it. I know you can,' he said.

Samantha smiled, but he didn't think she seemed very convinced.

'Walk back with me?' she asked.

'Of course.'

There were more people on the beach now than when they had arrived. Samantha waved to those she knew. Several shouted over to her, wished her luck. She didn't seem embarrassed or ashamed to be there, next to him. They were walking close to each other, but still not as close as he would like them to be. Some of these people might have seen them kiss. It didn't seem to worry her. And why should it?

On the way back, Samantha told him how the singing competition was going – everything that happened behind the cameras, what the other artists were like; how the TV people had been at her house and had interviewed her parents, even her uncle. She had a large cheerleading squad who would make posters and show up at the studio where the competition was going to be. She was happy and grateful for the support, but her father kept telling her that she mustn't let it go to her head. That she mustn't get carried away.

Walter didn't interrupt her, he loved listening to her talk, the energy in her voice, the amount of commitment and excitement about everything that was going to happen next – things she didn't even know anything about yet, but which she had obviously dreamed of. What if she won the whole thing? What would happen then?

Walter tried not to think too far ahead. Right now, he just wanted to enjoy this sweet, unfamiliar, rushing feeling in his body, for as long as he could.

'Right then,' she said, stopping at a fork in the path, one way continuing over towards the campsite, the other towards the road. 'I have to go home and change. What are you going to do now?'

'I ... don't know,' he said. 'I guess I'll...'

'Read?' she suggested.

He wouldn't be able to concentrate. Not after everything that had just happened. But his father would be furious.

'I don't know what's going on tonight,' she added. 'I'll need to practise a bit now and … then my uncle and cousin are still staying at ours. I might be able to sneak away for a bit, but I can't be sure. Dad always goes on about how important family is and blah, blah, blah.' She rolled her eyes. 'Now more than ever,' she continued. 'What with everything that's going on. And my uncle and Fred are going home tomorrow.'

Walter nodded. 'I'll look out for you,' he said.

'I think it'd be better if *I* looked out for *you*,' she said.

Walter didn't understand what she meant by that, but said 'okay' regardless.

'If I can't make it tonight, maybe we could meet down at the jetty tomorrow morning, say, ten o'clock?'

Walter lit up. 'Of course,' he said. 'I'd love to.'

＊

Walter remembered how he had hoped she would kiss him again, but she didn't. Not then, nor later.

She just walked away.

And that's when everything went wrong.

21

The bathtub was full. Samantha stood in front of the mirror and massaged her wrist as she clenched and unclenched her hand. She still had one coat left to do. The streak of dried paint in her fringe was going to be difficult to wash out.

She took her wine glass back into the kitchen and filled it from the box on the counter. Maybe that would stop her trembling hands.

Her phone screen lit up. Two unread messages: one from her mother who had had dinner on the beach and was wondering what Samantha had been up to. Her mother had also attached a picture, presumably taken by a waiter. Palm trees and blue sea. In the background, the sun was setting behind a cluster of rocks, stretching out to sea.

Samantha put off answering it, just sipped her wine and read the next message.

Markus wanted to know if she was going out tonight. Samantha shook her head to herself – she was too tired, couldn't bear the thought of talking to anyone. She'd talked enough today, especially with the journalist turning up, asking questions about Walter.

She took the glass and her phone into the bathroom. The steam from the bath had settled on the bathroom mirror. Samantha turned off the tap and did a few quick online searches.

Emma Ramm had covered several high-profile cases in recent years. She had also written a book.

'Wow,' Samantha said out loud.

She clicked onto the front page of news.no and was greeted by a picture of Walter. It hit her so suddenly and unexpectedly that she felt her chest tighten.

The headline: 'German Murderer May Be in Norway'.

Samantha caught her breath and had to look away. Her free hand stretched out for her wine glass. She drank and swallowed hard before picking up the phone again. The picture of Walter had been taken on the day he was arrested. He stared into the camera with a completely blank expression.

Samantha closed her eyes and breathed in slowly through her nose.

That summer when...

It was the worst day of her life, that day she took Walter down to the jetty. And they had kissed. God. She hadn't planned for that to happen.

Samantha opened her eyes again and blinked a few times. She could see them, her friends, who she'd bumped into on the road back home, after she and Walter had gone their separate ways. Their expressions made it clear that something was wrong.

'Where have *you* been?' Rita had asked.

'Me?'

Samantha stopped in front of her best friend, Jarl Inge, and Markus. Jarl Inge's arms were crossed tight over his chest.

'We stopped by your house,' Rita continued. There was a fierceness to her voice. 'Your mother didn't know where you were either.'

'Yeah, I didn't tell her where I was. I didn't realise I was obliged to report my whereabouts.'

'That's not what we mean,' Markus said. 'We were just ... wondering where you were.'

'You usually say something,' Jarl Inge interjected. 'If there are plans.'

'I was just ... down by the lake. On the jetty.'

'The jetty?' Rita couldn't seem to understand why Samantha had been there of all places.

'Yes, I was with ... Walter.'

'With *Walter?*' Again, there was a trace of disbelief in Rita's voice. 'What exactly is that all about, anyway?'

'Huh?'

'The German,' Rita continued. 'The German kid.'

Samantha frowned. 'What do you mean?'

'He's gross. Haven't you seen the way he looks at you?'

Samantha thought about what had just happened on the jetty.

'It's not just you either, by the way,' Rita continued, pushing her breasts forward a little to demonstrate. It took a few seconds for Samantha to understand what her friend was saying.

'Damn Nazi punks,' Jarl Inge spat. 'I mean, Rammstein? What the fuck even is that?'

Samantha knew that Jarl Inge was in love with her, and that he had been for a long time. Markus too, for that matter.

'There's something wrong with that guy,' Rita continued.

'Wrong?'

'Yeah, wrong.' Rita didn't elaborate.

Samantha was so surprised by this cross-examination that she was unable to say anything.

'But by all means,' Rita said with a sigh. 'We're not going to stop you.' And then she walked straight past her.

The others followed, Markus at the back. He gave her a quick glance as they passed, but said nothing.

'Where are you going?' Samantha asked, more subdued than usual.

'Didn't know we were obliged to report our whereabouts,' Rita replied. 'But the kiosk or something. I don't know. *Sieg heil.*'

✳

Samantha put her phone down on the sink, took her clothes off and dipped her foot in the water. It was too hot. She stood and waited until it became a little more bearable, then lowered her body into the tub. The heat stung her skin. She felt it in her heart too. And she still felt it in her hands – they would not stop shaking.

She hadn't sung particularly well when they practised that day, hadn't been able to keep her focus or really immerse herself in the words.

She shuddered.

No.

She couldn't bear to go there. Into her thoughts. *Those* thoughts.

Some memories were simply too painful to relive.

22

Emma stood by the window with her phone in her hand. Darkness had fallen, and the moon was rising above the edge of the forest on the other side of the water.

She still hadn't managed to get through to Rita Alvberg.

There was no sheriff's office in Osen anymore. The nearest police station was Elverum, about forty miles away. When Emma dialled the number, she was immediately greeted by a voice on their answer phone, reciting their opening hours. She was then transferred to the operations centre. When she asked, the young woman denied that there was any active missing-persons case in the area.

'Where does this person live?' the operator asked.

'In Oslo,' Emma answered, 'but she's from Osen. Her car is parked outside her childhood home.'

'In any case, it'll be Oslo that would have to initiate a missing-persons case,' she was told. 'You'll need to contact them. Regardless, I cannot provide information on any case we may be assisting with.'

Emma thought it sounded unnecessarily bureaucratic, but didn't comment. Besides, the woman on the other end had indirectly given her the confirmation she was looking for.

'Would it be possible to speak to Arvid Borvik?' she asked.

'Let me just check the rota,' the operator replied.

She could hear the clacking of the keyboard.

'One moment please, I'll transfer you.'

The call rang out, and she was not redirected back to the operations centre. She hung up and pulled her laptop over.

Several hits came up for Arvid Borvik. Some of them were articles about the local sheriff's office closing, and how the officers there had been transferred to the police station in Elverum. There were articles in connection with Borvik's fiftieth birthday, including an in-depth interview with the local newspaper, in which it emerged that he had worked in Osen since 2001. He was not from the area, but had fallen in love with a woman who worked in a clothes shop in the village. After that, he had stayed.

It was seven o'clock.

Emma needed to do something. Talk to people.

She threw on her jacket and locked the cabin. The temperature had dropped a few degrees since she was last outside. She decided to leave the car where it was and walk towards the centre of the village. She had spotted a pub on her route earlier that day. It was Friday evening, so if she was going to meet any of Osen's locals, she reasoned, it would surely be there.

The pub, which was simply called Pøbben, was not particularly big – just the one room, with a long, wide bar along one wall, with several people sitting side by side, every place taken. Off to the side, three guys were throwing darts at a dart board. One of them leant against a pool table. The pub smelled of food and stale alcohol, as if it hadn't been thoroughly cleaned since the previous weekend.

No one was sitting alone. People were drinking and chatting. As soon as Emma stepped inside, it was as if all conversation in the room paused for a moment. She felt all eyes on her – a stranger in a village where everyone knew everyone else. She had hoped that Samantha Kasin or Trygve Klepp would be there, but saw neither.

On a narrow stage in the corner of the room, where there was no space for anything other than a chair and a mic stand, was a man sitting on said chair, singing and playing the guitar. She had entered halfway through 'Wanted Dead or Alive', and Emma concluded that he hadn't put Bon Jovi's song to shame. A poster on the wall said that the guitarist's name was Markus Hadeland.

She ordered a beer and found an empty table. Sipped the beer slowly as she looked around. The guitarist received polite applause between each song. He had no problem taking requests from the audience, songs he took on board without a second thought and played without having to even look down at the neck of his guitar, or consult an iPad for lyrics. Emma allowed herself to be impressed.

When Markus Hadeland took a break, she walked over to the bar again and stood next to him. Ordered a glass of red wine this time. She felt a pang of hunger, but nothing on the traditional pub menu tempted her.

'Do you have any Guns N' Roses in your repertoire?'

Hadeland seemed surprised by the question. 'Guns N' Roses,' he repeated, as if he needed to think twice. 'I can play a fair few of their songs, but not that many are appropriate for this crowd. Other than maybe "Knockin' on Heaven's Door".'

'And that's not really even a Guns N' Roses song either.'

'No,' he said, laughing a little nervously, as if he thought it strange to be spoken to, or corrected. 'You're right about that.'

Emma liked him. On stage, he was confident and in his element. As soon as he put the guitar down, he became awkward, unsure, and didn't keep his eyes on anything, or anyone, for long.

'I'm Emma,' she said. 'From Oslo. But I'm staying here for a few days, I think.'

He extended his hand in return and introduced himself. 'Markus. From Osen. Staying here for the rest of my life, probably.'

Which made her laugh.

'You're good.'

'Um, thanks. Thank you very much.'

'Are you a musician?'

'That could be debated,' he said, flirting with her now. 'But I play a bit now and then. Here, mainly. Sometimes I make the trip over to some of the neighbouring villages. I haven't scared the pants off them yet, obviously.'

'You should record an album,' a man a little further down the bar said.

'Ah, well, I don't know about that,' Hadeland said, smiling.

Emma scrutinised him. His hairline indicated clear signs of a hair transplant.

He cleared his throat and said: 'Could I perhaps get you...'

In the next moment, Emma's wine glass was placed in front of her.

He stopped and smiled. 'Your next glass, then, maybe.'

Emma smiled but didn't answer.

'So what ... um, why are you *here* on a Friday night?'

'For the music, of course.'

Which made him laugh. He nodded briefly to the bartender who, without having to ask, started seeing to Hadeland's order. It only took a few seconds before a beer landed in front of him.

'I'm here because of Walter Kroos,' Emma admitted.

Hadeland was about to take a sip from his pint glass when he paused for a moment, long enough for Emma to realise that he knew who she was talking about. Hadeland finally took a sip. Emma watched him as he swallowed. Again his eyes sought something indeterminate.

'I'm a journalist,' she continued when he didn't say anything. 'I work at news.no. I'm trying to find someone here in Osen who can tell me a little about Walter Kroos. I know he was here one summer quite a few years ago. The summer of 2004, if I'm not mistaken.'

Markus Hadeland pushed himself away from the bar a little, took another sip.

'I heard he was on the run,' he said at last, but it didn't seem like he had caught wind of the latest developments.

Emma told him about the piece she had published on the case. Markus Hadeland just stood there, pint glass in one hand, as she spoke.

'Do the police think he's on his way here then?' he asked. The thought seemed to make him anxious.

Emma shrugged. 'They don't know.'

'But that's why *you're* here.' He started tapping his index finger on the bar.

'Correct.'

Hadeland said nothing.

'I spoke to Samantha about him,' Emma continued.

Hadeland's gaze quickly returned to Emma. 'What did she say?'

'Nothing.'

'Nothing?'

'Nothing. Trygve Klepp thought I should talk to Rita Alvberg, but she's...' Emma stopped herself, not wanting to speculate on what could have happened to her. 'You seem surprised,' she said instead.

'What's that?'

'You seem surprised that Samantha didn't say anything about Walter Kroos.'

He hesitated. Took another sip and looked around the room.

'What went on that summer?' Emma pressed. 'Did something happen between Samantha and Walter?'

Hadeland put down the glass and wiped his mouth. 'I've got to go,' he said with a nod towards the stage. 'It was nice talking to you.'

Emma remained at the bar. On stage, Hadeland sat down and started tuning his guitar, seemingly back in his own world. He glanced quickly at Emma, and there was a seriousness in his eyes, but also something pained, something vulnerable.

'It's no surprise that he doesn't want to talk about Samantha,' the man who had been standing on the other side of Hadeland said, addressing Emma. 'They were married for a few years,' the man continued – stout with a full moustache and bushy black hair. 'Two or three years, maybe? I don't remember.'

The man, who Emma estimated was in his mid-fifties, took out a packet of Petterøes 3 tobacco and a filter, and began to lay out the contents into a paper with what seemed like familiar movements. Emma glanced towards the stage again, where Hadeland looked to be deep in his own thoughts.

'He probably never quite got over it,' the man added, letting his tongue slide over the edge of the paper.

Emma wondered why the marriage hadn't worked out, but there could be a thousand reasons, unrelated to anything she was looking into.

'Tom Erik,' said the man, extending his hand towards her.

Emma took it hesitantly, momentarily unsure of how clean his fingers were.

'Emma,' she said, smiling.

'I heard,' Tom Erik replied, the cigarette now hanging from his bottom lip.

'Do *you* know anything about Walter Kroos?' Emma asked, as it seemed he had caught most of the brief conversation she had just shared with Markus Hadeland.

'I only know what everyone else knows,' he said, opening his mouth just wide enough to get the words out. He then removed the cigarette from his mouth and held it between two fingers.

'And what does everyone else know?'

On stage, Hadeland struck a chord on the guitar. The chatter in the room immediately died down to a respectful hum. Tom Erik turned a little in his seat, so that he was almost facing Emma. He leant in a little closer and said:

'That his father was a rapist.'

23

The small TV at the foot of the bed was on. Some American film. A man was being chased through a warehouse. Blix wasn't paying attention. He lay on his bed reading a book, but there was company in the images moving across the screen.

The book was one of those thick classics he had never managed to finish. He had just reached the end of a chapter, but had not taken in anything he'd read.

He sat up, straightened the pillow under his back a little. His right shoulder ached. The pain spread up his neck and into the back of his head.

He had grown accustomed to it.

The pain came and went, but it was never completely gone. It seemed as if it simply relocated itself around his body. Sometimes he felt it in his leg, other times in his hips or back. The pain in his shoulder often came in the evening.

He had fallen almost ten metres, straight onto the concrete floor. Emma had been there. He had held her gaze as he fell, but his only other memories were of the sounds of everything that happened afterwards. How Delta had stormed in. The footsteps, storming closer; shouting, gunshots. The reverberation between the walls when the guns went off. Then the liberating thought that it was all over and that he had fulfilled his promise – to take down the person responsible for Iselin's death. After that, the darkness had set in.

He felt no remorse for shooting the man who took her life. Almost the opposite, in fact. He would have regretted it had he not.

He returned to the top of the page and read a few sentences before glazing over again. It wasn't the pain or the thought of what had happened that disturbed his concentration, it was Jarl Inge Ree.

Three quick turns of a key suddenly came from the other side of the cell door, making him put the book down. The officer outside didn't ask to come in, just pulled the door open.

Jakobsen.

'Medicine,' he said, holding out a white plastic cup.

Blix stood up. The movement caused the pain in his shoulder to radiate down his arm. On top of that, the fight with Ree had made his muscles stiff. He staggered over to the door.

Three pills rattled in the bottom of the plastic cup. Blix chucked them in his mouth, filled the cup with some water from the tap, and drank.

Jakobsen nodded, satisfied, backed out of the cell and turned the lock.

On the screen, an American actor jumped from one rooftop to another. Blix crumpled up the cup and chucked it into the bin. Left the book where it was. Instead, he sat down at his desk, pulled open the drawer and took out a notepad and pencil.

He opened the pad to the first blank page. The pencil was sharp, completely unused. Out of habit, he tried the tip against his fingertip before lowering it to the paper and writing: *J I R*.

Jarl Inge Ree.

Then he drew a circle around the letters, and made a connecting line to a new circle, in which he wrote: *W K*.

Walter Kroos.

He looked from one bubble to the other. Apart from them, the page was empty. Without a computer or phone, he felt helpless. He had no records to get information from, no one to call. He had nowhere else to look for information other than Jarl Inge Ree.

He drew an extra ring around his initials.

He had another name he could add, actually: Samantha Kasin.

He wrote *S K* and connected her to Ree. If Blix had been out, working the case, that's where he would have started.

He jotted down one more name, at the very top corner of the sheet: *Emma*.

If he could rely on anyone, it was her. If there was information in Osen, she'd be the one to find it.

The pain in his shoulder was just starting to ease, at the same time, his evening lethargy started to settle over him. He straightened up a little in his chair and sat there, staring down at the paper. Wrote over the *W* and *K* again. Made them thicker.

It was rare for anyone to escape from a prison in Norway. In Germany too, for that matter. There was a running story in the wing about a convicted Albanian robber who got out by hiding under rubble and other debris on an open-bed truck, but that was fifteen years ago. No one had seen him since. Rumours were that he later had plastic surgery to change his face and was running a narcotics network from Tirana. But while the inmates spoke about that story, Blix had never heard any of them talk about their own escape plans.

For him escaping was utterly unthinkable. Naturally, they all yearned to be out there, in the open, but it would take something else entirely to pull off what Walter Kroos had done. Blix had nothing on the outside to motivate him though. So for Kroos, there had to have been something. He had to have some unfinished business beyond the prison walls – something in Norway. A thought that had grown with every day and eventually turned into an all-consuming obsession. A goal in life that everything else revolved around.

Blix put the end of the pencil between his teeth. A couple of ideas floated by. The intense longing to reunite with someone, or to have the opportunity to say a final goodbye – to a dying relative, maybe, or a former lover. The desire to finish something unfinished or to seize the opportunity to do something they had already started. None of the theories he visited felt good enough for him to write down.

He drummed the pencil against his teeth before placing the tip against the paper again. This was what he was good at. Thinking and formulating theories. And the only thing he could imagine that could adequately fuel Walter Kroos's escapade was hatred and an intense desire for revenge.

24

The man beside Emma was still sucking on his unlit cigarette. On stage, Markus Hadeland struck the first chords of a Creedence song.

'What happened?' she asked over the music. 'Who was it that Walter Kroos's father raped?'

The man grimaced, as if it was an inappropriate question.

'I don't know the details,' he said. 'And I wasn't there myself, of course.' He smiled wryly at his own joke. 'And I didn't hear about it until quite a while afterwards either.'

The man named Tom Erik stepped down from the bar stool. Clearly the nicotine cravings couldn't be denied any longer. The music and sound level also made it difficult to continue the conversation. Emma considered going outside with him, but didn't want to be too insistent.

'I could do with getting your full name,' she said instead. 'In case I need to quote you on anything.'

'Well, you can't do that anyway,' he said, stopping. 'But you can have my name.'

He took out his wallet and fished out a business card. 'In case you need some ... wood someday,' he added. The sheepish smile emphasised the poorly concealed allusion.

It came as such a surprise to Emma that she was unable to say anything. She nevertheless accepted the card and swallowed as she read the name written there.

Tom Erik Ree
Warehouse foreman
Osen Lumber Mill

'Ree,' she cleared her throat. 'Would you be related to Jarl Inge?'
He nodded.
'Jarl Inge is my son. D'you know him?'

There was nothing to indicate that he was embarrassed that his son was incarcerated.

'Not personally, but I know who he is,' Emma answered.

'You look like his kind of woman,' Tom Erik Ree continued as he let his gaze slide up and down her body.

Emma bristled at the remark, and thought she would get great pleasure from kicking him where it would hurt the most, but he just turned and walked away.

Emma stood with her back to the bar. Samantha Kasin or Rita Alvberg, she thought. Those were the only names she had, the only people she knew who Walter Kroos had had any contact with. If Walter's father had assaulted Samantha, that might explain why she wouldn't admit to knowing who Walter was. You don't talk to strangers about that kind of thing.

Emma looked over to the door with a sense of restlessness. She hoped that Tom Erik Ree would return, but also dreaded the thought of him coming back in. Two songs later, and he still hadn't reappeared, so she took one last sip from her wine glass and set it down. As she made her way out of the pub, Markus Hadeland started a new song that made her stop in her tracks and smile at the stage. The chords of 'Knockin' on Heaven's Door' were unmistakable. Markus sent her a confident smile as he began to sing. Emma sent him a quick wave goodbye and went out.

Tom Erik Ree was not there.

There were a few cars parked up outside, but Ree wasn't in any of them. He must have gone home, she concluded.

Emma considered going back in, but it had been a long day, and she was tired. Hungry too, so she walked further into the centre to see if she could find something to eat, preferably something other than a hot dog.

From the centre of the village, she could see the end of Osensjøen and the river below. And she realised that she could also see Rita Alvberg's childhood home on the other side of the river. There was light on in one of the windows, but it was impossible to tell if anyone was home.

Emma was about to move on when the headlights of a car some distance away made her pause. The car slowed down and drove into the driveway of the Alvberg house. Maybe it was Rita, Emma thought, and stayed to see if any more lights turned on inside. They didn't. But the car didn't turn around either, nor did it drive off again.

Emma stood there for a few seconds, mulling it over, then started making her way down towards the bridge. Walking briskly, she would be on the other side within seven to eight minutes.

The wind howled as she crossed the bridge, the chill passing straight through her. Below, the river roared.

A Volkswagen Passat was parked in the yard next to Rita Alvberg's electric car. A broad-shouldered, burly-looking man was doing something by the front door. The crunching of Emma's footsteps on the gravel made him turn around.

'Hi,' Emma said first, and introduced herself as a journalist from news.no.

The man at the door didn't say who he was, but Emma recognised him from the photos in the local newspaper.

'Arvid Borvik, right?' she asked.

The policeman neither nodded nor shook his head. 'Can I help you with something?'

He had that hostility in his voice that many police officers have upon meeting journalists

'I tried to call you today, a few times,' Emma responded.

Borvik remained silent.

Emma gestured towards the house behind him. 'It was about Rita Alvberg,' she continued. 'I've been trying to get hold of her – I understand that you'd been here too.'

Borvik came down the small staircase with heavy steps, still without saying anything. His stomach pushed against his shirt buttons. Over his shirt, he was wearing a tired, black leather jacket. Behind him, Emma could see that he had put a police seal over the lock on the door.

'Have you been in?' she asked.

Borvik nodded. 'She's not there,' he replied. 'No one has heard from her since Tuesday. I don't know much more than that. She's been reported missing to the police in Oslo. We'll start a search at daybreak.'

Emma looked around. 'Where, exactly?' she asked.

'In the immediate vicinity,' Borvik replied. 'Where she was last seen,' he added and made a movement with his head in the direction of Osensjøen and the surrounding forest. 'The paths criss-cross all over the place in there. The terrain can be pretty difficult in places, especially along the water's edge.'

Tomorrow, Emma thought. That meant she didn't have much time before the other journalists would show up.

Borvik opened his car door. Emma took a step towards him and crossed her arms over her chest to show that she was freezing.

'Are you driving back over the bridge?'

Borvik sent her a sceptical look.

'It wouldn't be possible to get a lift, would it?' she asked. 'I'm staying at the campsite.'

Borvik hesitated, as if trying to come up with an excuse not to take a passenger, but he clearly couldn't think of one.

'Get in,' he said.

'Thank you,' Emma said. 'I appreciate it.'

She jumped in and fastened her seat belt. The car rocked a little when Borvik climbed behind the wheel. In the footwell, she battled for space with empty cardboard cups, a newspaper, pebbles and dry leaves.

Emma thanked him again.

There was nothing to suggest that Borvik was interested in small talk. Slowly and silently he manoeuvred the car back onto the road and switched on the high beams.

'You're probably wondering what I'm doing here,' she started.

When Borvik didn't answer, she said it was about Walter Kroos.

'Have you been notified about him?' she asked.

'We are aware that he has escaped,' Borvik confirmed.

'Is that information that was sent out to all of the police districts, or just yours, given that Walter Kroos was here in 2004?'

The question seemed to make Borvik uncertain of how to answer. Finally he said: 'Not sure.'

'Did you have anything to do with him back then?'

'No.'

'I have information that his father raped a girl here that summer,' Emma continued. 'Do you know anything about that?'

Borvik moved his hand over to the gear stick. There was a sound as his wedding ring came into contact with the hard leather. A few seconds passed.

'No.'

'So the rape wasn't reported then?'

'Not to my knowledge,' he replied.

Hm, Emma thought.

'Do you know Samantha Kasin?'

'I know who she is. I knew her father well.'

'Kenneth.'

'Kenneth, yes. He died a few years ago.'

'Yes, I heard about that. Cancer, if I'm not mistaken?'

Borvik didn't answer.

'What's she like, would you say?'

'Samantha?' Borvik thought for a moment. 'Like everyone else.'

He switched off his high beams and put his foot on the accelerator as they crossed the bridge. It only took a few seconds, then they were on the other side.

The campsite was only a minute or two away.

'Have the police in Oslo made contact about Jarl Inge Ree as well?'

Borvik opened his mouth as if to say something, but stopped.

'Why would they?' he finally responded.

Emma stared out of the windscreen as she thought how to answer.

'He'll be released from prison in a few days.'

'As he has been before,' Borvik said. 'We don't usually take any special precautions when that happens.'

Emma thought that was an interesting choice of words.

Borvik slowed down and stopped at the entrance to the campsite.

'Thanks for the ride,' she said and unhooked her seat belt. 'Will you be participating in the search tomorrow?'

He nodded.

Emma was about to step out of the car, but stopped.

'What do you think happened to her?' she asked.

Borvik breathed in heavily. 'The Oslo police are investigating,' he replied. 'We just carry out orders at their request.'

Emma hesitated a little longer before getting out. 'Could something criminal have happened to her?' she asked.

'There is nothing to suggest that,' Borvik replied. 'She was here to clear the house out after her mother died. That can bring up a lot ... memories, thoughts...'

It had also crossed Emma's mind that this could, of course, be a voluntary disappearance.

'Thanks again – I'll probably see you around tomorrow then,' she said and finally got out.

The policeman just stared ahead in silence.

Emma closed the door.

Back in the cabin, she sent a text message to Anita Grønvold and told her what she would be sending over in the next half-hour.

Anita called a few seconds later: 'So Rita Alvberg disappears just a few days after Walter Kroos escapes?'

'That does seem to be the case,' Emma replied.

'Did they know each other?' Anita asked.

'They met when Kroos was on holiday here in 2004,' Emma answered.

'Write about that, and connect it to the fact that he might be on his way to Norway.'

Emma heard Anita light a cigarette.

'A little speculative, perhaps,' Anita added, 'but it wouldn't be incorrect.'

Emma opened her laptop screen.

'And one more thing,' Anita said before hanging up. 'Be careful.'

Emma glanced out of the window, into the darkness outside. It occurred to her that Walter Kroos could already be in Osen.

Emma began to write. It also dawned on her that she hadn't been able to buy herself anything to eat. Her stomach rumbled. But she couldn't bear to go out again.

As she finished typing up the introduction, a sound just outside her cabin made her stop and look up.

Wood creaking.

As if someone had stepped on one of the loose planks out on the decking.

She held her breath and listened. Pushing herself up from her chair, she walked over to the door, unsure if she had locked it. It had no peephole, nor any windows to the side.

It was quiet outside.

And the door, she noted, was locked.

Slowly and carefully she walked to the nearest window. The light from inside made it difficult to see out, so she turned everything off and tried again.

A faint glimmer of light lay over the campsite. In a day or two there would be a full moon.

She saw no one.

Heard no one.

But someone *had* been out there. Just outside her cabin.

That, she was sure of.

25

Curiosity had driven him out.

The woman who had passed his cabin earlier that day was clearly alone. Walter had wondered who she was, and what she was doing here.

He stood outside the entrance to the cabin. Turned his head in the direction of the campsite's kiosk – closed now, of course.

He thought of his father. Thought back to how he had looked at Samantha that summer day when she came to find him there. How quiet his father had been when Walter returned, ready to be scolded for running off like that, without finishing his reading. He had expected to receive some sort of punishment, a double reading penalty, but that didn't happen. Instead, his father just sat there on the sun-bleached lounger and drank, without saying a single word to either Walter or his mother.

It was often the case that his father disappeared into himself.

Walter thought it had something to do with his professional career in the military having been put on hold. While serving as an ISAF soldier in Afghanistan, his father had been shot in the shoulder. The injury reduced his mobility to such an extent that he was transferred to the reserves. In practice, they no longer had a use for him.

Walter wondered if perhaps his father missed life in the military. The cohesion of the unit, the camaraderie. The banter, the tension. The assignments. But there was no purpose for him anywhere anymore.

Or maybe he was just tired of *them*. Walter. His mother. Of life in general.

That night, Walter waited by the window of his room.

For the first time in a long time, he wasn't listening to music. He needed to be able to hear whether Samantha came by. He even considered going for a walk to look for her, but had no idea where she lived.

It was half past eleven when he heard his father start to raise his voice in the next room. He heard his mother trying to calm him down, without success. His father's fist smashed into the table before he stomped across the floor. The front door slammed shut. What they were arguing about this time, Walter couldn't figure out, nor did he bother leaving his room to ask his mother.

He wondered what Samantha was doing.

He didn't like that she hadn't shown up, even though he knew it wasn't certain that she would be able to get out of the house. Still, it bothered him. He missed her. Needed to see her.

He had never known anything like it.

At some point he must have fallen asleep, because he was suddenly woken by his parents arguing again outside in the living room.

'Leave me alone!' His father's voice. Angry.

A chair scraped against the floor. The unmistakable sound of a beer can being opened. His mother saying something that Walter couldn't quite hear, then his father answering:

'Stop asking me, woman!'

A little later, Walter could hear the tell-tale signs of his mother crying – she had gone to bed.

Walter only realised when he got up the next morning that his father had collapsed on the sofa instead of joining her in bed. One of his father's legs was hanging off the edge of the sofa with his foot on the floor. On the table next to it were several empty beer cans. On the floor, bloody, crumpled paper towels.

Apart from his father's snoring, the cabin was silent. His mother, Walter assumed, was still asleep. He didn't want to be there, so he left. Ten o'clock was quite a while away yet, so he headed down to the beach to meet her there.

Ten o'clock came and went, but no Samantha.

Then ten past. Then half past. As it approached quarter to eleven, Walter got up and started to make his way back to the campsite. A strange sense of unease rose through his body.

Jarl Inge Ree was sitting outside the kiosk, flipping through a magazine. It was already boiling hot out.

'Have you seen Samantha?' Walter asked – first in German, then in English.

Jarl Inge looked up and waited for a few seconds, before shaking his head and saying: 'But I have a message for you. From her.'

The knot in his stomach tightened.

'She ... can't see you anymore,' Jarl Inge told him. 'She doesn't want to see you anymore.'

Walter just stared at him. 'Why?'

'Why? You can ask your father why.'

'My dad? What do you mean?'

When Jarl Inge didn't answer, Walter took a few steps closer.

'Where is she?'

'Dunno.'

'Is she home?'

'I think it's best if you just leave her alone now. For everyone's sake.'

Walter didn't understand a single thing he was saying.

'Why? What happened?'

Jarl Inge rose from the bench. He pushed his shoulders back and made himself as tall and wide as he could.

'I said, ask your father.'

Walter took a few steps around Jarl Inge and entered the kiosk. A girl he hadn't seen there before was standing behind the cash register. Walter asked if she had seen Samantha.

The girl shook her head.

'What about her father, is he here?'

'I ... I don't know where he is.'

Walter's face was red hot. 'Where do they live?'

The girl hesitated before giving him the address. Walter made her write it down and asked her to explain the way. In shaky English, she tried to give him directions. It wasn't far.

Jarl Inge was gone when Walter came out. He quickly made his way off the campsite. He couldn't wrap his head around what had happened. Had he done something?

Walter left the main road and ran towards a residential area. Passed a playground where a mother and a small child were playing on one of the swings. He checked the street names and consulted the note he had brought from the kiosk.

There.

The name on the mail box at the entrance to a white-painted house left no doubt that Walter had come to the right place. There were no cars outside. Walter went to the door and rang the bell. No one came to answer it. He knocked too. Yelled, several times, and pressed the bell again.

No movement from within.

He made his way around to the back of the house, out onto a sun-scorched lawn, past a dirty charcoal grill. Peeked in through the windows.

There was no one there.

But then he noticed that one of the windows was open. A bedroom, perhaps.

Walter stepped closer. Stopped, listened.

Sounds.

Movements ... a duvet?

'Samantha?' he asked.

The rustling stopped.

'Samantha, please,' Walter begged. 'I just met Jarl Inge over at the kiosk. What is going on?'

It had occurred to him that it could be Samantha's mother lying there, until he heard a weak voice coming from the other side of the window.

'Walter...' It was Samantha. 'Please,' she said. 'Please don't ... don't come here again.'

'What ... what are you saying?'

She sniffed. 'Please, I'm begging you,' she said. 'Go ... please, go away.' She continued to sniff.

'I don't understand anything, Samantha. Jarl Inge said that...' Just breathing made his chest hurt. 'Can't you come out here, so we can ... talk about it?'

Samantha didn't answer.

Walter didn't know what else to say. He tried to make himself as tall as he could, but he couldn't see through the crack in the window.

'Please, Walter,' Samantha said when she realised he was still outside. 'Please, just go,' she cried, 'I can't take it...'

※

Now, Walter wiped his shoes on the doormat and stepped into his cabin. Thought about what Jarl Inge had said to him outside the kiosk back then.

Ask your father why.

But Walter hadn't asked him when he returned to his family's cabin that day.

It was almost a whole year before he eventually did, but he had never received an answer.

26

Something was different on the wing. There was a different atmosphere. The shift had occurred yesterday evening, after dinner. And it had only become more apparent at breakfast.

Blix sat at the end of the table as usual with his bowl. He wasn't the only one who felt that something was in the air. Everyone seemed more tense. The other inmates' eyes flickered around the room, the conversations more subdued.

All because of Valdemar Hjorth.

He had entered the wing with an irrational kind of superiority, a natural force and authority that had changed the dynamic among the inmates.

Blix leant forward against the table and watched Valdemar Hjorth as he came from the kitchen with three boiled eggs on a plate and a large glass of milk. He walked in the same way he had yesterday upon entering the wing, radiating confidence with his swaying gait.

He gestured with his plate to indicate where he wanted to sit. The little Dutchman sitting opposite Blix shuffled a little to the side to make room. Valdemar Hjorth sat down a little way away and made a remark about the selection of breakfast items. His voice sounded as if it came from somewhere deep inside the chest, reverberating outward. There was nothing about the man, who was a few seats away from Blix now, that resembled the same man who had once broken down in tears in the interrogation room. He obviously felt he had to prove himself somehow. At some point, he would probably go for Blix.

The prison officers had also sensed that something might be going on, or at least Nyberget had. He always seemed to disappear whenever a fight broke out. Now he had retired to the guardhouse, leaving the common area to Kathrin. She had sat down on the sofa and was restlessly leafing through some papers.

Jarl Inge Ree appeared at the entrance to the cell corridor and let his gaze drift over the table. For a moment it looked like he was going to turn around, but then he continued into the kitchen. After a short time he came out again with his usual stack of toast. Instead of sitting down at the long table, he took his food back to the cell with him.

Blix had finished eating. He got up to get himself a cup of coffee, but left his plate so that no one would take his place while he was gone. Normally he would take his coffee into the cell with him, but Ree's movements made him decide to stay out in the common area. He took a sip and leant forward to talk to the Polish man on the other side of the table.

'Have you spoken to the new guy?' he asked.

Grubben shook his head.

'Have you spoken to anyone about him?' Blix continued. 'Does anyone know him?'

Grubben lifted his head from his plate and looked around.

'The baker serve time with 'im before,' he said in his broken Norwegian, referring to a northerner convicted on a narcotics charge, currently sat a few seats down from Hjorth.

Blix let his gaze linger on the Pole, as a sign that he wanted to hear more.

'In Skien,' was all Grubben added.

Blix sipped his coffee. Valdemar Hjorth finished eating and went into the kitchen with a glass and a plate. As soon as he finished, Blix got up, went into the kitchen with his own dishes and followed the route Hjorth had taken, out into the cell corridor. Voices reached him from cell number six – Jarl Inge Ree's cell. An angry exchange of words behind the closed metal door.

Ree's voice was growing more intense. Higher. Blix hadn't heard him like that before.

'It wasn't me!'

Blix didn't catch what was said next, but recognised Valdemar Hjorth's voice. Deep and threatening.

The little Dutchman came slapping down the corridor in his rubber sandals. Stopped momentarily at the sound of Ree cursing loudly on the other side of the door.

The Dutchman curved past Blix and rushed into his own cell. The sounds now coming from inside Ree's indicated that the argument had turned physical. Someone was slammed against the wall with such force that the inspection hatch in the door rattled. Things cascaded to the floor.

Blix opened the door.

Jarl Inge Ree was the one pushed up against the wall. Valdemar Hjorth was standing in front of him with a pair of tweezers. The two claws were rammed into each of Ree's nostrils. A thick stream of blood was already flowing out of one.

Valdemar Hjorth turned to Blix. Hatred and anger burned in his eyes. 'Out!' he commanded.

Blix cast a quick glance in the direction of the guardhouse.

Ree tried to say something, but Hjorth's arm was pressing into his throat. He tried to wriggle free, but got nowhere. There was something decisive about Hjorth's look as he slowly squeezed the tweezers together. His face was flushed. Ree gurgled and kicked his legs.

Blix strode towards them.

If he tried to tear Hjorth free, he risked dragging Ree's nose with him. Instead, Blix clenched his fist and gave Hjorth a short, sharp punch to the kidneys to make him let go. Hjorth moaned, but the blow didn't have much of an affect.

Blix struck again, swinging his fist into Hjorth's temple. The blow threw Hjorth off balance, enough for Ree to slide free.

Hjorth roared and went after Blix with his hand still clasped around the tweezers. Blix dodged the first blow and parried the second. The third hit his chin and swung him half around.

Ree staggered to the bed and sat with his face buried in his hands. Blood ran between his fingers.

Hjorth threw himself at Blix, sending him into the wall. Together they collapsed to the floor. Blix got hold of Hjorth's hair, forced his head back and clawed at him, but without sufficient force. They rolled around on the floor of the cramped cell. Punches and kicks filling the room. Blix got the full blow of an elbow to the ear. The pain paralysed him for a moment, enough for Hjorth to land two more punches. One came into contact with the side of his jaw.

Yelling could be heard from the corridor. Blix spat out a mouthful of blood and caught sight of a uniform in the crowd that had gathered outside. The fight continued. Blix lashed out with a kick, powerful enough to throw off the man now crushing him. He crawled up, put a knee on his neck, grabbed one arm and twisted it behind his back, pushing it up until he felt something give, snap.

Hjorth screamed in pain.

Blood dripped from Blix's own mouth and nose, onto Hjorth's back. From the hallway, two officers forced their way into the cell and lifted him away. Hjorth tried to kick out at him, but the officers overpowered him and he was pulled away.

Ree slowly got up from the bed. His nose seemed intact, but blood was still leaking from it. He glanced quickly at Blix and lowered his gaze.

27

The room was cold, sterile. Blix hadn't been in this one before.

Jarl Inge Ree hurled a ball of bloody paper towels in an arc across the room; it landed square in the bin.

'The doctor's on her way,' Nyberget told them, sitting down in a chair across from the two men. 'She won't be long, but she'll need to see him first.'

He nodded towards the door to the emergency room where Valdemar Hjorth was waiting with two officers.

Blix opened his mouth and moved his jaw from side to side. He was bruised, but everything felt as it should.

'I'm not sure she needs to see me,' he said.

'Not up to you,' Nyberget replied shortly.

Ree stretched his legs out and leant all the way back in his chair.

Nothing happened for a few minutes.

Blix broke the silence: 'What was that all about?'

Ree wiped his nose on the back of his hand and pulled his legs back in, underneath the chair. 'A misunderstanding,' he replied.

'A pretty serious one,' Blix argued.

Ree didn't respond. Blix thought through the options. Drugs and money troubles were the root cause of most conflicts.

The hands on the large clock above the door were approaching half-nine. Ree changed his sitting position again.

'Maybe I could get some paracetamol or something, while we wait?' he said. 'It hurts like a bitch.'

Nyberget studied him, then stood up. 'I'll have a look,' he said and went into the next room.

Blix drank from a glass of water he had put on the linoleum floor in front of him.

'Walter Kroos is in Norway,' he said, leaning forward to set the glass down.

Ree turned in his chair. He clicked his tongue. 'What do you mean?' he asked.

'I mean what I said,' Blix replied. 'Walter Kroos is in Norway.'

'How do you know?'

Blix just sent him a look by way of a response.

'They haven't caught him yet then?' Ree asked.

'Not that I'm aware,' Blix replied.

'When did he get here?'

'Wednesday.'

'And you found out...'

Blix didn't answer. He leant towards Ree, but kept his eyes fixed on the door, through which Nyberget could enter at any moment.

'What's your history with him?' Blix asked in a low voice.

'We have no history,' Ree retorted.

Blix fixed his gaze on him. The least Ree could do after what had happened was answer his questions.

'You have *something*,' Blix corrected him. 'So how do you know him?'

Ree hesitated.

He exhaled heavily through his open mouth, as if gearing up to answer him. 'He was in Osen once,' he said. 'At the campsite, as your friend's already found out.'

Blix leant forward a little more, waiting for him to continue.

'He was on holiday with his parents,' Ree said. 'That was the summer Samantha stopped singing.'

'What do you mean?'

Ree began to tap his feet and look around the room, as if he didn't know where to start, or if he should even say anything at all.

'Walter's father raped her,' he said, finally.

'What?'

Thoughts raced through Blix's head. He couldn't get it all to add up. If Walter's father raped a Norwegian girl, his name would have been in the Norwegian police registers. Walter's too, probably. Gard Fosse would know about it.

'Are you sure?' he asked.

'Of course I'm fucking sure,' Ree barked. 'Do you think I'd just make something like that up?'

'Sorry,' Blix said.

'He assaulted her while she was cleaning the kiosk,' Ree continued. 'Afterwards ... she was devastated. Had to withdraw from the *Hit of the Summer* final and everything. It ruined her career.'

Blix nodded. He had achieved something of the same rapport he had experienced so many times in the interrogation room. When a suspect finally opened up and chose to cooperate.

'Was it reported?' he asked.

Ree shook his head. 'Don't think so,' he replied. 'The Kroos family ran back to Germany with their tails between their legs. Fast as they could.'

'But he still could've been reported? Why wasn't he?'

Ree touched his nose. It had started bleeding again.

'Damn it,' he said.

He crossed the room to pull out some more paper towels and glared at Blix.

'You know why,' he said. 'There's no point. Most sexual assault cases aren't reported. The police don't do anything about them anyway.'

Blix waited until Ree had dried his nose

'She was your girlfriend?' he guessed.

Ree came back across the room to his chair. 'Yeah, or ... not back then,' he replied. 'Only afterwards. Someone had to take care of her, but it was difficult to get a relationship to work after something like that.'

He sat back down.

'We were on and off,' he continued. 'Breaking up, getting back to-gether. She got married to another guy from the village, a musician, but it didn't last long. Samantha and I are back together now. It's kind of always been the two of us.'

Blix said nothing, waited for Ree to say more.

'She'll be picking me up when I get out on Monday. I don't know what'll happen after that, but ... I won't be living in Oslo, that's for sure. I'll probably stay with her to begin with.'

Ree studied the paper towel before holding it up to his nose again.

'What do you think Walter Kroos is doing in Norway?' Blix asked.

The door opened before Ree could answer. Nyberget was back. He scrutinised them, as if it would reveal whether they had done anything while he was out of the room.

'Here,' he said, placing a plastic cup on the counter by the sink.

Ree stood up and studied the pills at the bottom of the cup before tossing them into his mouth and swallowing them with tap water.

'You can come in,' Nyberget said, pointing to Blix.

'Now?' he asked.

'They're taking Hjorth to the get an x-ray,' he said. 'Doctor seems to think his arm's broken.'

A noise resembling laughter escaped from Ree.

'Up you get,' Nyberget said, nodding to Blix. 'You've got visitors waiting for you after this.'

28

Emma slowly opened her eyes and reached for her phone. A message from Irene was waiting for her. Her sister wanted to know where Emma was, and if she could perhaps look after Martine tonight?

Emma sighed. She hated disappointing them. But the police were starting their search for Rita Alvberg today. She couldn't go home.

Emma answered and checked her watch. Just after eight.

Her stomach growled.

She stood up and pulled open the curtains. The clouds stretched across the sky in various layers, but they were drifting away quickly, as a group. Emma threw on her clothes, thinking she would find breakfast somewhere, but as soon as she went out, her eyes were drawn to two marked police cars driving onto the campsite. They parked by the outdoor stage, where a small group of people had already gathered. Several of them were wearing Red Cross uniforms and carrying equipment, but there was also a group of volunteers.

Emma walked towards them. By the time she arrived, the police officers had started to remove various items from the cars. Arvid Borvik handed out instructions. Emma recognised several people she had seen in the pub the night before, and smiled when she saw that Markus Hadeland was one of them.

She walked over and said hello.

'Hi,' Hadeland replied, a little shy.

'Thanks for the nice evening last night.'

'Uh, likewise. Too bad you had to leave so early.'

'I'd had a long day,' Emma said. 'I was tired.'

They stood looking at each other for a few seconds.

'You're helping the search for Rita today then?' she asked.

Markus nodded. 'We were a couple once, years ago,' he said. 'But it's been a long time since she's lived here.'

'What do you think happened?'

'I ... don't know,' he said, kicking at a patch of dirt. 'She lost her mother a short time ago. But ... I'm not sure.'

Emma took out her phone and snapped a couple of pictures of Borvik, who was still organising the search teams. There was little doubt that this was where they would be setting up the command centre.

'It's kind of you to come along and look,' she said.

'It's nothing,' he said, placing his hands in his trouser pockets. 'We Oseners have to look out for each other. And I know every nook and cranny of this place.' He smiled.

Arvid Borvik was marshalling the crowd and giving out instructions. One group was to search along both sides of Osensjøen, while another was to focus on the paths and surrounding forest. The last group was to explore the area from the mouth of the river towards Rita Alvberg's childhood home.

'Pay particular attention to the undersides of both the small and larger precipices,' Borvik announced. 'She may have fallen and not been able to climb up. She may have also tried to cover herself to keep warm, if she thought that no one was coming to help.'

The severity of what he said seemed to have an effect on those present. Everyone seemed worried.

In the next moment, Emma's phone vibrated. An unknown mobile number. As Borvik continued to speak, she pulled away from the others a little and answered.

'Hi, it's Blix.'

'Good God,' Emma exclaimed. 'This early on a Saturday morning?'

'Yeah well ... I've been up for a while. I was wondering how it went. In Osen, that is.'

Emma smiled. 'Does that mean you've decided to help?'

There was silence for a few moments. Outside the kiosk, Emma caught sight of Samantha Kasin throwing a rubbish bag into a large refuse bin on the side of the building.

'Jarl Inge and I, we ... I think we may have built up enough of a rapport,' he finally answered. 'I mean, I still don't know if I'll be able to get anything out of him, but I can try.'

'Excellent,' Emma replied.

'We'll see. I don't really know what I can do, but the more information you can feed me from the outside, the better. Have you spoken any more to Samantha?'

'Not yet,' Emma replied.

'Walter's father raped her,' Blix said. 'In the summer of 2004.'

Emma moved the phone to her other ear. 'How...' she began. 'Did Jarl Inge Ree tell you that?'

'We spoke about it,' Blix confirmed.

'I met Jarl Inge's father in the pub yesterday,' Emma informed him. 'He said the same, but not who did it.'

Emma looked around. The search crews were on their way out, the groups dispersing in different directions.

'Something else is going on here as well,' she said 'A woman has been reported missing. A childhood friend of Samantha who was here to clean out her mother's house after she died.'

She told him what she knew about Rita Alvberg, and about the search operation that was under way.

'Walter Kroos is in Norway,' Blix said.

Emma frowned.

'Are you sure?' she asked. 'Have you spoken to Fosse?'

'Yes, and I've seen the photos,' Blix replied. 'They have recordings from the CCTV at Oslo Central Station. He arrived by train on Wednesday.'

'What are your thoughts?' Emma asked. 'Do you think Walter Kroos might have something to do with the disappearance?'

'I'm not sure,' Blix replied. 'You'll have to ask the local police up there.'

Emma glanced over at Borvik, felt her news fingers starting to twitch.

'I've been given unlimited call time,' Blix continued, 'but I can't hang around the phone all day. I'll try to call again later today. You can call this number whenever you want, but it may take some time to get through to me.'

'Sure.'

'Good luck,' Blix added. 'And be careful.'

The space around the stage began to empty. New volunteers kept arriving and were sent out to search. It struck her that maybe she should help; but that wasn't why she was here. The person she really wanted to find was Walter Kroos. And if he *was* actually in Osen already – where would he hide?

29

Her wrist ached; the pain radiated up through her arm. Samantha moved the paint roller over to her left hand. She no longer cared how it looked – she just wanted to finish.

A car drove past outside. It sounded like a larger vehicle. She took a few steps back and squinted. A minibus from the Red Cross.

Arvid Borvik had called her the night before to ask if they could use the campsite as a command centre. Markus had also texted her and told her that Rita was missing. There was a notice on the Osen community Facebook page, asking people to participate in today's search operation. He'd asked if she wanted to help.

Samantha felt a sharp pang in her chest. Her childhood best friend was missing, and here she was, painting a damn wall.

She closed her eyes, thinking back to the day after the rape, when she found Rita waiting outside her front door. Samantha had started crying immediately. Rita said nothing, just stared at her with those big, glossy eyes and followed her into the living room.

They had sat down on the couch. Rita took one of Samantha's hands and held it, squeezing it gently. With the other, she stroked Samantha, up and down her arm, shoulder, occasionally her leg.

'Is there anything I can do?' Rita finally asked, her voice soft, caring.

Samantha shook her head. Wiped away the tears. Her lips were so dry – she hadn't had anything to drink since last night. Hadn't eaten anything either.

'Where ... where are your parents?' Rita asked.

'The campsite, I think.' Her voice cracked. 'Dad, he...'

Samantha was unable to continue. Couldn't bear thinking about her father right now. She felt she had to go to the bathroom, but just the thought of undressing and wiping herself afterwards made her legs tense up.

Again she felt his hands on her.

That hard, clammy grip.

His strong fists.

His breathing, the sounds he made.

'Shouldn't they have taken you to A&E or something?' Rita asked.

Samantha just shook her head.

'I'll go with you,' Rita told her.

'No, it's...'

They just sat in silence together. It was a long time before one of them said anything.

'What ... are you going to do about tonight? About *Hit of the Summer*?' Rita asked tentatively.

Hit of the Summer.

God, she hadn't thought about the competition at all. There were only a few hours left before she had to leave for Oslo.

Samantha started crying again.

Her dream...

This was supposed to define the rest of her life. This was how she was meant to find fame. She was supposed to sing and perform all over Norway. The whole world, even.

'I can't go now,' Samantha sniffed. 'I can't do it.'

'I'll go with you,' Rita told her. 'I'll help you.'

Samantha shook her head as the tears flowed.

'How can I possibly sing now?'

Rita said nothing for a long time, just let Samantha gather her thoughts.

'You are so strong,' she said. 'The strongest person I know.'

Samantha dried her wet cheeks.

'And it'll just be three minutes, maybe four. Then it'll be over. Four minutes, Samantha, where all you have to do is do what you do best.'

Her father had downplayed everything and told her to pull herself together, as if what had happened was somehow something she had planned. In any case, he wasn't going to drive her to Oslo. She would just have to take the bus, as he had told her she would last week. After she had started to do well in the competition, he had pushed her to do more and more work at the campsite. Empty the bins, wash the floor. 'You're not a superstar yet,' he had said. 'You have to stay grounded.'

Now, Samantha opened her eyes and blinked a few times, staring at the floor, the globs of paint all over it. She thought of Rita, who had put her in the shower that day. Who had put on her clothes, her make-up, who had accompanied her to Oslo. She had been with her every moment of that horrendous day.

In Oslo, they were met by a TV crew who wanted to film her the entire time. Rita would have none of that.

'Samantha's going to need as much peace and quiet as she can get,' she said.

The person in charge had objected, saying the artists had signed a contract that said they had to be available for the TV cameras at all times, 'except when they're in the bathroom'.

'Not happening,' Rita had barked at him, with an authority Samantha had never heard before. 'Not today. And if that doesn't work for you, then we'll go home. Right now.'

The man had given up.

Then, before she had to go out for the sound check, Rita had helped her warm up her vocal cords. She more or less dragged the notes out of her. When it was almost time to go on stage, Rita took her aside and said:

'I know you're nervous. I know you're in pain and that you have a lot going on in your head right now. But ... listen to the music. When it starts. Think about the words you're going to sing and what they mean, and then close your eyes. Think of someone you love,' Rita continued. 'Think about ... your grandmother. Think of Amalie. Good, sweet Amalie who always brought us juice and waffles when we played outside her house. Think about her. And close your eyes.'

Samantha was about to burst into tears, but she nodded.

The programme coordinator beckoned her over with a hand.

The time had come.

Samantha lifted her shoulders high and slowly lowered them. Rita was right. It would be over soon. She didn't have to say anything beforehand. The presenter just had to introduce her, then the rest was up to her.

Four steps up, and she was backstage. In the dark. She kept tripping over the cables. A hand pulled her to the place where she was supposed to stand, behind a screen that would be raised. There wasn't going to be anyone else on stage but her. No dancers. The musicians would be behind her. Samantha just needed to focus on herself.

She turned her gaze towards Rita, who was standing just off stage with eyes that said: *You can do this. You can do this.*

'And now ladies and gentlemen…'

The presenter's voice.

'…an extraordinary talent – Samantha Kasin, the star from Osen, the girl with the contagious smile and a big, big heart.'

Dry ice was released from two machines on either side of her. Samantha couldn't calm her racing heart. And as the presenter asked the audience to welcome her on stage, and the wall in front of her swiftly flew up into the rafters, Samantha lifted the microphone to her mouth and closed her eyes.

'*If I…*

… should stay…'

There was still applause when she opened her eyes. A bright light blinded her. And behind that light – an indefinable darkness. She closed her eyes and continued, grateful that it would be just her for the first thirty seconds. She could decide the pace herself.

'*So I'll go, but I know…*'

She couldn't hear how she sounded, but it couldn't possibly be good – she had no strength, and her vocal cords trembled. Singing solo made all the flaws, all the nervousness, only more apparent. She regretted choosing that particular song.

Think of Grandma.

Think of Grandma.

'*I'll think of you every step of… the way…*'

Walter popped into her mind.

Walter's father.

Rita. Jarl Inge. Markus. Trygve.

Grandma, she thought.

Grandma, Christmas Eve. The whole family around the table. Mum.
Dad. Uncle Abel. Fred.

Nothing would ever be the same.

'And I...'

Samantha's voice cracked, she heard it herself, and in the next second
the beautiful strings of the entire orchestra began right behind her – just
listen to the music, listen to the music. It caught in her throat – it was
just so beautiful, so sad. She tried to continue singing:

'... will always...'

'...love you...'

It was as if her knees gave way, she collapsed, and she couldn't hold
back the tears, all while the music continued behind her – stopping was
not an option, she forced herself back up, onto her feet, and squeezed
her eyelids shut, even harder, she had to – had to – finish.

Samantha cried through the whole song, she sobbed more than she
sang, and when it was over, everyone in the audience stood up and ap-
plauded as she ran off the stage. She couldn't be there, couldn't bear the
thought of being interviewed afterwards and hearing the verdict from
the judges, looking out into the audience and seeing all the people,
thinking of all the hundreds of thousands of people who were sitting at
home seeing her standing there, making a fool of herself.

Backstage, Samantha fell straight into Rita's arms. How long they just
stood there and cried, she had no idea, but during the first commercial
break the presenter came up to them and cried too.

'Damn,' she said. 'You were amazing! I am in awe over how you em-
bodied the song.'

Samantha knew it wasn't true, she hadn't been amazing, but she
couldn't bring herself to say anything.

'She was singing for her grandmother,' Rita answered on her behalf.
'Amalie, who died when Samantha was ... eleven.'

She had actually been twelve, but that didn't matter.

The host wiped the tears from her cheeks. And when she went on
stage again afterwards, she told the viewers about Amalie, about how it
all been too much for poor Samantha, who would be unable to go on

stage with the other artists later that night. Instead, Samantha just sat in the dressing room and cried, together with Rita. Nevertheless, the sympathy votes abounded, enough for her to advance to the final.

Rita organised their escape from the studio, making sure they could get out of there without the journalists seeing them, out to Jarl Inge and his father, who had come from Osen to pick them up. They drove home in silence, with Samantha in the back seat next to Rita. She had only one wish – to hide from everything and everyone. But it was impossible to keep the TV cameras and journalists away from Osen in the days that followed. They called and called, over and over again, throughout the day. Going outside was out of the question. Samantha just barricaded herself in her bedroom.

The pressure to say something, to explain, to tell them about Amalie, about herself, her expectations for the final – all conveyed to her via her mother – was suffocating. She too had urged Samantha to pull herself together and move on: 'This is your chance,' she'd said.

It was all too much.

She'd sunk deeper and deeper into the darkness, couldn't eat, couldn't drink. In the end, her mother had to call up TV2 to tell them that Samantha was too ill to take part in the final.

And that was that.

She hadn't been able to pull herself together.

Her dream had shattered.

It took a few weeks before the media stopped hounding her, but the competition had its winner, and although both managers and producers contacted her later, wanting to explore the possibility of a collaboration, Samantha couldn't bear the thought of ever holding a microphone again. She was barely managing to go from one day to the next. Jarl Inge helped her take her tablets, which calmed her down, made everything a little easier. For a while they helped her let go of the restlessness and anxiety, the painful memories.

Rita and Markus were around her all the time as well. Trygve too, occasionally. They kept her entertained, helped keep her mind on something else.

Eventually, everyone forgot what had happened.

Everyone except Samantha.

Why had she stayed here for all these years since?

Why hadn't she just left? Gone somewhere else?

The answer was simple: it was too painful. She hadn't been able to break free of what had happened, not really. She hadn't felt strong enough. Although it had occurred in Osen, this was where her life was. This was where she belonged. After her father died, it had also been up to her to take care of the campsite, the little heart of the village that meant so much to so many.

But it was time to finally deal with the pain head on. To move on. She was going to paint a thick, wide line under the past. She was going to finish what she had started.

Outside, through the window, the remaining search crews were moving off. Markus met her gaze and raised a hand. Samantha didn't wave back.

30

The lawyer's eyes darted up from his wristwatch as Blix was led into the visiting room. He seemed annoyed, but his face changed when he saw Blix.

'What happened?'

Blix sat down, but didn't want to talk about it until they were alone. 'Sorry to keep you waiting,' was all he said. 'I had to make a phone call.'

When the murder charge had been brought against him, Blix had asked that Einar Harnes be appointed as his defence counsel. They had met a few times during a number of large, often controversial, cases, and Harnes had always been thorough – he was not the type of lawyer to stand outside, talking to the press, playing up to the cameras with grandiose words. He saved those for the courtroom.

The door closed behind the officer. Harnes repeated his question.

This time Blix answered: 'I ended up in the middle of something involving two inmates with some unfinished business on the outside.'

'I take it the doctor's had a look at you?'

'That's why I'm late,' Blix nodded. 'Nothing really. Some cuts and bruises. It'll feel worse tomorrow.'

'This shouldn't be happening,' Harnes noted. 'Is there something you want me to pursue?'

'Not yet,' Blix replied. 'I think I may have broken one of their arms, but it's unlikely to have any consequences. They'll be transferring him to another wing, I think.'

'I can ask for the incident report so you can be sure your role is portrayed correctly. It may impact your future assessments.'

'If that's your advice, then by all means,' Blix replied.

The lawyer nodded and jotted something down in his notes.

'Have you been notified?' he asked.

'About what?'

'The answer to your application,' Harnes said.

Blix shook his head, communication on the inside was always slow.

'Your day release has been granted,' Harnes informed him, and presented a copy of the reply. 'Unescorted.'

It would be a year on Monday since Iselin was killed. Blix had applied for a day's leave to visit the grave with her mother.

'I spoke to Merete before coming here today,' Harnes continued. 'She'll pick you up at eleven. You must be back before five. You can have a dinner together, or whatever you choose, as well.'

'Thank you,' Blix said. 'I'll call her later.'

Harnes pulled a folder from his bag. 'We need to talk about the appeal too,' he said.

'Can it wait?' Blix asked, gesturing to the plasters on his face.

He hadn't managed to get through to Fosse yet, and wanted to make sure he knew what Walter Kroos's father had done when he was last in Norway.

His lawyer hesitated.

'Let me just quickly tell you about something that may prove quite important for us,' he said.

'What's that?'

'I've been working with a Swedish expert who my colleagues in Stockholm have used with great success,' Harnes explained. 'He's currently building a digital 3D model of the crime scene to visualise what exactly happened. Where you were standing, Emma's position, Timo Polmar's movements.'

Blix felt a jolt pass through his body at the mention of the man who had killed Iselin.

There was no doubt in his mind about what he had done in the seconds afterwards. The crime-scene investigation had been thorough: reconstruction and digital calculations of distance, height difference and timings had all been carried out. The question in court had instead been about what he had thought when he pulled the trigger. Thoughts Blix had trouble recalling. His decision was made in a fraction of a second, with no room for any kind of deliberation.

During the trial, however, he had grown comfortable with the version

Harnes had devised. That his course of action was justified because Timo Polmar could not be allowed the opportunity to harm Emma as well. The lawyer argued that when Polmar turned his back on Blix, it was to go towards Emma. In such a scenario, they described it as acting in self-defence, and Blix, therefore, should not be punished.

The judges had reviewed the case differently. Four bullets to the back was an overreaction. He had been handed twelve years.

'Do you think it'll make a difference?' he asked.

'You and Emma were the only ones there,' the lawyer replied. 'So the court made a decision based on your testimonies alone. We still need to make them see what actually happened. We have the opportunity to do that now.'

Blix was not so sure that the outcome would be any different from last time. In the media and the courtroom, a picture had been painted of him as a trigger-happy cop. Timo Polmar was the third man he had shot and killed during a career spanning just over twenty years.

His lawyer went through a few more points about the upcoming trial. Blix had to concentrate to keep up, but had no objections to the strategy.

It was Nyberget who came to collect him when the visit was over. The swelling around his temple throbbed, and he could feel a severe headache building up.

'I need to make a phone call,' he said once he was back on the wing. 'To Gard Fosse, Oslo police,' Blix added. 'The number is on my call list.'

Nyberget looked at him disapprovingly, but nodded. Clearly bound to agree with the new phone privileges Blix had been given.

Five minutes later he returned with the secure phone the prisoners were sometimes allowed to use and closed the door behind him.

Fosse was already on the line.

'Sorry,' he said. 'I was busy when you called earlier. Have you got anything?'

Blix sat on the edge of the bed.

'Have you sent anyone to Osen?' he asked.

'Nicolai Wibe is on his way up there right now,' Fosse answered.

'Walter Kroos's father raped a girl at the campsite in Osen the last time he was in Norway', Blix explained. 'Samantha Kasin. Who is now Jarl Inge Ree's girlfriend.'

Fosse was silent for a moment.

'So we have at least one connection between Ree and Kroos,' Fosse finally commented. 'But what does the note the German police found in his cell mean?'

'Does it have to mean anything?' Blix responded, picturing the mind map he'd drawn the night before. 'He may have just written down the names of the people he met that summer. If it does mean something, it could refer to something he may be planning on doing before Jarl Inge Ree gets out. Ree intends to return to Osen.'

The line crackled as Gard Fosse cleared his throat.

'There is another situation unfolding up there,' Fosse began. 'A missing woman.'

Blix stood up again and took a few steps over to the desk. Emma had told him about this, but he wanted to hear about it from Fosse.

'Rita Alvberg, thirty-two years old,' Fosse continued. 'Originally from Osen, living in Oslo, but the last sighting of her was in her hometown. A major search operation is now under way.'

'Anything to indicate that Walter Kroos has something to do with it?'

'There is nothing to suggest that anything criminal has happened,' Fosse replied. 'But the last time anyone saw her was on Wednesday. The same day Walter entered the country.'

'Have you made this public yet?'

'An hour ago,' Fosse replied, dropping his voice slightly, a rather biting tone to it now. 'Emma Ramm managed to publish something about it before we gave the go-ahead.'

'Have you alerted Samantha Kasin?' Blix asked. 'Spoken to her at all?'

'She's probably already aware,' Fosse said. 'But I'll get Wibe to establish contact.'

'What about the phone in Ree's cell?' Blix continued. 'Have you looked into that?'

'We've got hold of the carrier and obtained its historical data traffic,' Fosse said. 'Only nightly calls. In addition to the two saved numbers, he has also been in contact with a number registered to the Osen campsite.'

Blix nodded. He still remembered the number.

'Both the saved numbers are criminal acquaintances of his,' Fosse added. 'The analysts believe it was used to control narcotics traffic from his cell, but we're following up on that.'

'What will you do when he gets out on Monday?'

'We have a reconnaissance team on stand-by,' he answered, and it seemed to Blix like Fosse didn't want to share any more information with him. 'Hopefully Walter Kroos will be caught by then.'

They ended the call. Blix sat down, poked the tip of the pencil, and lowered it to the page to add Rita Alvberg's name to the mind map.

At the top, he wrote *2004* with large, circular movements.

The answers can always be found in the past.

31

The news that Walter Kroos had been seen in the country, combined with the fact that a woman was missing from the very place he last visited in Norway, sent the rest of the media into a frenzy. Emma noted with satisfaction that her competitors continued to quote news.no, but she knew that wouldn't last – they would soon descend on Osen.

For now, she had three major advantages: it was Saturday, which meant that the country's newsrooms didn't necessarily have access to their regular crime reporters, but instead had to send inexperienced free-lancers or weekend substitutes. Secondly, Emma had been in Osen for a while; and lastly, she had also acquired sources that could turn out to be valuable. If Rita Alvberg was found, for example, she had an agreement with Markus Hadeland that he would text her right away.

Around three o'clock that afternoon, when Emma had briefly retreated back to the cabin to eat some crispbreads and cream cheese, a message from him popped up:

They're going to start searching the lake.

Emma threw on her jacket and headed down to the water. More press had arrived, including a TV crew from NRK.

Arvid Borvik was standing a short distance away with some of the search groups, watching as the divers got ready. There were three of them in all – two set out from the shore, while the third slid down into the black, cold water from the far end of the jetty. Emma took a couple of photos on her phone. Borvik was busy talking to someone. As soon as he was free, she had to try to get a comment from him.

Markus was there too, keeping to himself a bit, a few feet from the others. She went over to him and thanked him for keeping her updated.

'What happened to you?' she asked, nodding towards his feet. She could hear gurgling coming from his hiking boots.

'It's a bit boggy in some places, along the water,' he said with a smile. 'I, uh, fell in.' He shook his head. 'Rookie mistake,' he added.

'You should get home,' she said. 'Get a change of clothes.'

'I will. I just ... want to see what happens here first.'

'It may take some time.'

'I know. I ... want to keep an eye on things.'

They stood and observed what was happening. The thought that there could be a dead body out there made Emma shudder.

'I spoke to Jarl Inge's father briefly yesterday,' she said. 'He told me that you and Samantha Kasin were married once?' She said it as a question.

'Yes,' he said. 'I ... suppose we were.' Markus looked down. 'But we weren't meant to be, not us. So...' He trailed off, tried to smile.

'How long were you married? If I you don't mind me asking?'

He leant his head over to his left shoulder, then over to his right. His neck cracked.

'Two years, seven months,' he answered. 'We were both passionate about music, but it was pretty unsuccessful from the start. She and Jarl Inge were on-again-off-again for years, and I think she got tired of it, so ... I tried to pick up the pieces, you could say. But that didn't go particularly well either.'

Again a melancholy veil clouded over his gaze.

'There's a lot I could say about it,' he continued, 'but I'm not sure I really want to.'

'I can understand that,' Emma replied.

'Samantha struggled a lot with anxiety and...' He stopped himself, as if suddenly realising that he had, in fact, said a little too much after all.

'Are you referring to the rape?'

He waited a moment, before slowly nodding.

'I heard it was one of the summer visitors,' said Emma. 'A German.'

Markus seemed to hesitate.

'Is that not the case?'

He stayed silent.

'There were some rumours about that, yes,' he started. 'But it wasn't a tourist.'

Emma frowned.

'Then who was it?'

Markus clenched and released his hand.

'Doesn't matter. He's dead now anyway.'

He stared across the water.

'Dead?'

'Yeah...'

He didn't continue.

'You're right, I think I should be getting home, change my clothes,' he said, smiling apologetically. 'Starting to get cold.'

32

The smell of fresh baked goods wafted down the hall. The northerner in cell eight had almost completed an apprenticeship at a baker's in Arendal when he was caught with seven kilograms of amphetamines. He had finished his course while incarcerated. Every Saturday he would bake a cake or some kind of pastry.

This time it was cinnamon rolls with almond flakes and powdered sugar icing. The baking trays were left out on the kitchen counter for the other inmates. It was just a matter of helping yourself. The whole arrangement was a joint venture, with everyone chipping in a few kroner from their daily allowances.

'Three each,' the northerner told them.

Grubben stepped aside a little and let Blix help himself first.

He thought he could sense a change in the air, after what had happened earlier in the day – a shift in how the other inmates viewed him.

'Grand,' he said to the northerner, popping two of the buns on a cardboard plate. 'Thank you.'

He licked his fingers clean of powdered sugar and went out into the cell corridor, heading down to number six. The door was half open. Jarl Inge Ree was lying on his bed, his nose bandaged up. Blix knocked on the doorframe, but didn't go inside.

'Here,' he said, holding the plate out for Ree.

Jarl Inge Ree frowned at him.

'You don't have to do that,' he said with a sigh.

'I guess you didn't smell it,' Blix said, gesturing to his nose with the plate.

Ree smiled faintly. He sat up and grabbed one of the rolls. Blix took the other.

'Rita Alvberg is missing,' he said and took a bite.

Ree stopped chewing. 'What?'

Blix repeated what he knew.

'You know her?' Blix concluded.

'Of course. Christ,' Ree answered. 'I've known her my whole life.'

He sat with the cinnamon roll in his hand and picked pieces off it with his fingers.

'What do you think happened?' Blix asked.

Ree took another a bite of the roll. 'How am I supposed to know that?' he snapped.

'The police believe she may have disappeared voluntarily,' said Blix.

'Nah, not Rita,' Ree said. 'She's not like that.'

Blix didn't say anything.

'Have they located him, Walter Kroos?' Ree asked.

'Not that I know of,' Blix replied.

'They've connected the dots though? Rita disappearing at the same time Walter Kroos arrives in Norway?'

'They're aware of that, yes,' Blix said. 'Can you think of any reason why he would want to harm her?'

Ree looked away, swallowed as he thought.

'No,' he said finally, but then seemed to think of something: 'Is Arvid Borvik involved?'

'I've heard the name mentioned,' Blix nodded.

Ree stood up. 'I wouldn't trust that bastard,' he said. 'Completely useless. The only thing he can do is confiscate modified mopeds and catch illegal anglers. Punish people for lighting campfires in the summer.'

'Did Rita and Walter Kroos know each other?' Blix enquired.

'Yeah, she met him that summer,' Ree replied, lifting one of his hands to his face. 'But Walter only had eyes for Samantha.'

He stood with the half-eaten cinnamon roll in his hand and turned abruptly to Blix.

'Has anyone spoken to her? Samantha?' he asked.

'Have you?' Blix asked.

'Not since Thursday,' Ree replied. 'But I didn't know about any of this then. Someone should tell her.'

He threw the rest of the roll away, but missed the bin.

'Is Jakobsen working today?' he asked. 'I don't have any more call time.'

'No, it's Kathrin,' answered Blix. 'I'm sure it'll be fine.'

Ree disappeared out of his cell.

Blix took an overview of the cell. Nothing seemed any different from when he had searched it before. He walked down the corridor to his own cell and sat down at the desk. He was starting to get a better idea of everyone involved, but was still far from understanding what it was all about.

33

Walter peered out through a gap in the curtains. He was ready to run if any of the police officers approached the cabin. But they all stayed over by the outdoor stage – people dressed as if they were going hiking. And people decked out with Red Cross equipment also arrived. They were then divided into groups and sent out into the forest. With so many police at the campsite, Walter had to stay indoors.

Which gave him plenty of time to think.

He kept going back to the day they had had to leave Osen, how he had sat in the back seat, staring out of the window. He had not understood why they had to go home several days earlier than originally planned. Although, he was also happy about it – he didn't know what had come over Samantha, and why she wanted nothing more to do with him. There was no indication that his father was going to explain the sudden decision either – he simply sat in the front seat, a tight grip on the steering wheel. His hands still covered in wounds.

After they got home, and for the next few days, his father continued to rage around the house, slamming doors. Every question, even if it was just to see if he wanted something to eat, was met with fury. Walter stayed as far away as possible, did his homework and eat in his room listening to music. But he couldn't stop thinking about Samantha, and about what Jarl Inge had said.

She ... can't see you anymore. She doesn't want to see you anymore.
Why? You can ask your father why.

His father, who had returned that evening with bloody knuckles.

Walter had to try and find out what had happened. But his father was more unapproachable than ever. Walter didn't dare ask. Instead, he wrote Samantha a letter, to ask *her*. In the library, he found a holiday guide for Norway in which the campsite in Osen was listed. He sent the letter there.

Winter came and went without him getting a response.

Spring too.

It wasn't until June, when the summer holidays were approaching again, that a letter addressed to him appeared in the post. At first he didn't even consider the possibility that it could be from Samantha – he had given up on hearing anything from her – but when he tore open the envelope and saw the large, round girl's handwriting, he struggled to breathe.

It was not a long letter.

She began by apologising for not answering him until now, and for not being able to see him on the day they left. She also thanked him for not pressuring her, and said she was sorry that she hadn't been able to tell him what had happened.

She wrote:

I still can't, but please, Walter, if you had any thoughts of returning this summer: don't. Not now, not later. Please, I can't do it.

Walter had had to read the sentences several times over to understand their meaning. When the conclusion hit him, he had been close to throwing up.

Something had happened between Samantha and his father.

That would explain everything.

His father's bloody knuckles; *you can ask your father why*. How his parents had argued. Samantha not coming out to see him, who didn't want to see him ever again. Their sudden departure the next day, his father's horrendous mood in the weeks after they got home.

One evening, his father was busy doing something outside in his shed, and Walter ventured in. It smelled of sawdust and alcohol. His father was sanding the handle of a butter knife.

'What do *you* want?' he barked.

The anger in his voice made Walter nervous.

'I just wanted ... to see what you were up to,' Walter said.

'What I'm *up to*?' his father spat back. 'Jesus Christ.' He shook his head.

Walter wondered if he should come back another time, but remained where he was.

His father continued sanding. Continued drinking.

'Are you just going to stand there?' he grumbled. 'Don't you have anything better to do?'

'Dad,' Walter began. 'What ... what actually happened in Norway?'

'What are you on about?'

'Last summer,' Walter elaborated. 'At the campsite. We came home early.'

The grinding, back and forth against the wood, stopped.

'You were injured,' Walter continued. 'Your right hand.'

His father looked down at his own hand. The wounds had healed long ago, but it was as if he could still see them.

'And you argued with Mum.'

His father snorted. Averted his gaze and muttered something Walter couldn't hear.

'Did it have something to do with Samantha?'

His father froze.

His reaction was good enough for Walter. The final confirmation.

'What did you do, Dad? What happened?'

His father returned to sanding the butter knife.

But Walter wasn't finished. 'The last night we were there, you went out,' he said. 'And you didn't come back until late, and then you argued with Mum—'

'Go inside.'

Walter sighed. 'Dad, please, I know something happened that night. Why did we suddenly have to go?'

'Did you not hear what I said?'

'Did you not hear what I asked you?'

His father's gaze flew up to meet Walter's. A fire raged in his eyes.

'You go inside right now,' his father snarled between gritted teeth. 'And never talk to me about—'

'I saw how you looked at her,' Walter persisted. Tears were pricking his eyes. 'And you saw that Samantha and I had ... something good, together, and you probably didn't like that, did you?'

'Walter, I swear...' He raised the butter knife at him. His hand was white with sawdust.

'For once, something good happened in my life,' Walter maintained, not even sure where the words were coming from you, 'and you had to ruin it. Of *course* you had to ruin it!'

His father stood up so abruptly that his chair was flung backward and crashed to the ground. He needed a moment to find his balance, but in the next, without Walter even seeing it coming, he hit him. Walter was thrown backwards and crushed against the wall. His entire face felt as if it was paralysed.

He slowly sank to the floor. His father towered over him. Clenched fist trembling. Seconds later, blood started trickling from Walter's nose.

'You should be grateful,' his father said with a snort. 'That little tease would never have wanted you. Not really.'

Then he stalked out of the shed.

And they never spoke of it again.

34

I need you to wash the floor today.

Samantha wiped the smudge of fresh paint off her hand as she thought back to her father's words that night. How things could have been so different if she had just refused.

It had already gone ten o'clock.

They had been sitting around a plastic table at the back of the kiosk, mainly because it was a short distance to all the drinks her father kept in the back room, but also because her mother wanted them out of the house so she could go to bed early. Things always got late and rowdy when her father and uncle got together.

Uncle Abel wanted to know everything about the singing competition. What the presenter and the other TV stars were really like. Cousin Fred said nothing, just stared ahead and drank his squash.

'I need you to wash the floor today.'

Samantha stared at her father in disbelief.

'No ifs and buts,' her father continued. 'I worked from eight to eight today. What have *you* done?'

Samantha was going to say that she had been preparing for the show for the following day, in the hopes of advancing to the finals and changing her life – not just hers, but maybe all of theirs. But she hadn't had the courage to say that.

'Your mother has a bad back,' her father went on. 'You know that. You can help out a bit. You're not a superstar yet. And the floor is dirty.'

'But *right now,* Dad?'

'Of course. When else are you going to do it? Tomorrow? You always sleep in late, you won't have time tomorrow.'

That wasn't true – she never stayed in bed later than nine o'clock, but her father seemed to be the only person who didn't understand that teenagers need a lot of sleep.

'Good on you, Kenneth,' Uncle Abel said, a crooked smile on his face. 'It's important to keep the youth of today grounded.'

'Or on that dirty floor, at least.'

They both laughed.

'You can give 'er a hand, right?' Uncle Abel said, patting his son on the shoulder. Fred continued to stare straight ahead with his slightly too-big eyes.

'Isn't my kiosk,' he said, sounding like he was six rather than twenty-one. Samantha had never quite understood what was wrong with Fred, but she hadn't asked either.

The family usually got together a couple of times a year, once in the summer and then sometime between Christmas and New Year. It usually ended with the brothers getting shit-faced, and Fred sitting in the TV room watching cartoons. Samantha always had to 'take care of him'.

Play cards with him or something.

But it wasn't exactly possible to do anything with Fred. Everything would just turn weird or uncomfortable. He didn't know how to talk to other people. Only answered questions, never asked any himself. And when he did say something, it was usually things she didn't understand.

Reluctantly, she sighed and stood up. Went back into the kiosk and found the bucket and a mop. She wasn't going to bother doing it thoroughly. Just enough so the worst of the stains was gone, and for the kiosk to smell of cleaning fluid.

The air was warm and close.

Samantha opened the front door a crack to encourage a draft and some fresh air. She took off her thin hoodie and started in the innermost part of the shop. She sighed when she saw that a bag of flour had fallen off the shelf and onto the floor. There had been a hole in it. It was surrounded by a white layer of powder.

She sent an angry thought to her father, and headed into the back room to get a dustpan and broom. Swept it up. Only when she lifted the torn flour bag from the floor did she realise that she should have done that first.

Samantha groaned, threw the flour into the nearest bin, and swept it all up once more.

She was finally able to splash some of the soapy water onto the floor.

With heavy, slow movements, she let the mop slide over the surface. She couldn't put into words how much she hated washing floors.

The bell rang above the front door.

Samantha rolled her eyes and shouted into the front of the kiosk: 'We're closed.'

No response.

She continued washing the floor. When she stopped to wipe the sweat from her forehead, she heard footsteps in the room.

'We're closed,' she repeated, louder this time. 'I'm just cleaning up in here.'

No answer this time either.

She put down the mop and walked around the nearest shelf. But there was no one there.

'Hello?' she called.

Complete silence.

She shrugged and went back to the bucket. Bent down to wet the cleaning rag. In the next moment – a footstep, right behind her. She turned quickly.

'Oh,' she said, and smiled. 'It's *you*. God, you scared me.'

She suddenly felt the need to cover up. And then realised he was standing on the part of the floor she'd already cleaned. He'd leave footprints.

'What's up?' she asked.

He said nothing.

'Do you need something?'

He didn't answer that either.

'No? Okay...' she said. 'I just need to finish up in here.'

Samantha grabbed the rag and squeezed out a few more drops. She was about to reach over for the mop resting against the shelf of canned goods when she felt a tight, hard grip around her wrist.

'What are you doing?' she said.

Suddenly his face was right up against hers. He tried to kiss her, but she managed to squirm away. But the next moment he grabbed her with his other hand as well and pushed her up against the shelves, so that several of the items fell to the floor.

'Stop,' she insisted, before shouting again. 'Stop it!'

It didn't help.

He was strong.

Much stronger than her – she was unable to wriggle free. And when he brought his hand suddenly and violently to her crotch, the horror overwhelmed her. His eyes shone with aggressive desire. She tried to cry out again, but he just lay one hand over her mouth – hard.

He pushed her to the floor.

Then he was on top of her. Used his legs to push hers apart.

This is not happening, she said to herself. Dear God, this is not happening. He let go of her face for a moment so he could yank down his shorts, long enough for her to scream, but in the next moment his hand was on her face again, clenched this time, and he hit her, so hard her head thudded against the floor. A sharp pain spread down her neck, and it was like she couldn't feel her own face.

But she still tried everything in her power to push him away.

Nothing worked.

He tried to pull down her bikini bottoms.

She grabbed hold of them, determined not to let go. But when he pulled her hand away, parts of her bikini followed, the flimsy fabric falling apart in her hands, and suddenly she was exposed. With his lower body right on top of her. And as he penetrated her with a furious grunt, the doorbell rang.

＊

Samantha had never got rid of that bell.

It jingled right now as she stepped outside and closed the door behind her. It was good to feel the cold air on her face. Being in a room with fresh paint for that many hours had made her dizzy, even if she'd kept one of the windows wide open.

She looked around.

The police had not yet packed up for the day, but what she had to do could not wait.

She looked up and took a deep breath in.

Then set course for cabin K–1492.

35

The lead diver stood on the jetty with his goggles and earpads pushed up on his head. Arvid Borvik had gone over to convey a message. It looked like the lead diver then passed on the information to the two divers below the surface.

Emma was usually quite adept at reading people's lips, or at least getting the gist of what was being said, but Arvid Borvik had so much snus pushed under his upper lip that made it impossible to work out what he was saying.

According to a local history website, Osensjøen had been formed by snow and ice filling a natural basin left behind by a melting glacier. At its deepest point, it reached eighteen metres, but it was a large lake, and the middle was quite a distance from the shore.

The divers had been working in shifts for an hour and a half. The air bubbles rose steadily to the surface. The water had darkened as the afternoon light gradually faded.

The diving leader must have received a message through his earpiece. He adjusted his goggles and seemed to spring into action. Borvik, whose body language was normally drowsy looking and plodding, also seemed to waken up, and turned to give a brief message through the police radio.

Emma took another photo. The journalists around her also began to move. They hurried down towards the jetty, but were told to keep their distance.

The lead diver was giving instructions via the underwater communications. One diver came ashore empty-handed, while the lead diver swam out to the third to assist.

Emma looked around. The press turn-out would not have been so great if this had been a normal search operation. None of the journalists spoke to each other as they waited. One of the youngest reporters seemed nervous, almost queasy.

A diver broke the surface, with the other coming up not long after. The sound of cameras clicking on the other side of the jetty filled the air. Emma squinted. It looked like one of the divers had brought something with him to the jetty. Too small to be a body, she decided.

The object was lifted up. A shoulder bag, with straps and silver fittings. Borvik squatted down to inspect the object. He gingerly poked around inside it and discussed something with another policeman who had arrived, then he stood up.

The divers received a message and headed for land.

With slow steps, Borvik approached Emma and the other journalists. 'What did you find?' one of them asked.

It looked like Borvik was considering whether or not it was something he should share with the journalists.

'A fishing bag,' he answered after a moment's pause. 'Looks like it's been down there a while, full of old hooks and rusty fishing gear.'

He straightened his back, and continued, his voice taking on a rehearsed, authoritative air:

'We are ending the underwater search for today, but will commence again with the addition of sonar tomorrow,' he explained. 'The search parties in the immediate vicinity are on their way back. We will continue tomorrow.'

He gave them a short nod, as if he didn't intend to say anything more, but this announcement triggered an avalanche of questions. Everyone took the same angle. A VG journalist spoke the loudest: 'Any news about Walter Kroos?' he asked.

Borvik hesitated.

'I am here to head a search operation,' he said. 'I cannot answer about other police matters.'

The journalists didn't give up, and instead just asked the same questions various other ways. Borvik manoeuvred his way through them, as if he were swimming in unknown waters, but he did manage to avoid saying anything that implied the police suspected that Walter Kroos was behind the disappearance.

Emma offered a question: 'Have any stolen vehicles been found in the area?'

Borvik frowned and quickly glanced down at his wristwatch. 'As I said: I am here in connection with a search operation and cannot answer on other matters.'

Another journalist understood where Emma had been going with her question.

'What about public transport?' she asked. 'Have you spoken to bus drivers, have they seen Rita Alvberg? Or Walter Kroos?'

'There is nothing to indicate that Rita Alvberg has left Osen,' Borvik replied. 'That was all. Thank you.'

The questions continued, but Borvik turned his back on them. When he had gone, the group of journalists quickly disbanded. Emma headed back to her cabin and updated the article she had left open on her laptop. With a changed title and revised preamble, it would appear new. When the job was done, she sat down with her phone and typed out a message to Markus Hadeland:

Hey. Hope your foot are dry now. ☺ Can I just ask you a question real quick? Who were you referring to when you said that the person who raped Samantha was now dead?

The message was sent with a *swoosh*. A few seconds later *Read 18:23* appeared below the message. But he didn't answer. Emma leant back into the sofa and mulled it over.

There was only one person in Samantha Kasin's inner circle who she knew was no longer alive. Her father.

But was that not a steep assumption to make?

Nevertheless, Emma sat up and entered her father's full name – Kenneth Kasin – into a search engine. Added 'death' as a search term too, and the first hit that came up was a link to a page in the local newspaper that talked about the campsite owner's passing. In the article, he was described as a pillar of the local community, a proud drinker of Osendøl beer and a hard worker to whom no one could compare.

The journalist who had written the column was called Siri Jespersen. A year later, she had returned to the campsite and written an update about how things were going since he had passed. The article stated that the campsite had gone through a transition phase; Kenneth's brother

Abel managing the business from his law office in Oslo, while the widow was seeing to the day-to-day operations. Samantha was not mentioned.

Abel Kasin referred to his brother's death as yet another tragic event that had affected the campsite and the small family. What other tragedies he was referring to were not mentioned, perhaps because everyone already knew what he meant.

Emma hadn't heard of Abel Kasin before, so she decided to look him up as well. Fifty-four, a lawyer, resident of Skjetten, just north of Oslo. Divorced. He worked primarily in business law.

Emma switched back to the original newspaper article. Siri Jespersen was pictured between the headline and the introduction, with an email address and a mobile number listed just below the small portrait. Emma called her.

Siri Jespersen answered within the first few rings, answering by saying just her first name. Emma introduced herself.

'Am I interrupting anything? I'm aware it's a Saturday night.'

'Not at all,' Siri Jespersen replied. 'It's fine – I actually saw you around Osen today. I'm in the office writing it up myself.'

'Then I won't keep you long,' Emma said. 'I'm just trying to get an overview of Osen as a village. The people here. What happened here in the past. What's going on now. To get a better picture of what kind of place it is.'

There was silence for a few seconds.

'Well,' Siri Jespersen finally said. 'I'm not from Osen myself, but the newsroom is divided in such a way that I usually end up covering the smaller events over there. People mostly live off the forest and the river. Forestry and hydropower – two cornerstones of Norwegian industry. Where would we be as a society without them?'

Emma played along. 'There aren't that many well-known people from around here, I've noticed,' she began. 'Except for Samantha Kasin, if you could call her that.'

'Yes…' Jespersen did not continue immediately. Then: 'Yes. I guess she is still kind of a local celebrity, in a way.'

'It's a shame she didn't pursue performing.'

'True.'

'And then she lost her father as well.'

'Correct.'

Jespersen clearly had nothing more to say about that.

'Have there been ... any murders or accidents of note here?' Emma asked. 'Any suspicious deaths, that kind of thing?'

Again, a pause on the line. Then:

'Murder? Not that I know of. Accidents – we had one fatality on the record four or five years ago. An employee at the mill who ended up trapped behind some pallets. Suspicious deaths – don't think so, not in my time anyway.'

Emma had started doodling on the notepad in front of her.

'You wrote a column about Kenneth Kasin's death, I saw.'

'Sure, I might've done.'

'You interviewed Abel, his brother, who said that there were no end to the tragedies their family had had to endure. Do you remember?'

It seemed that Jespersen had to think about it.

'Uhhh, I think so?' she said.

'That's what it says in your article.'

'Then he must have said it,' Jespersen said with a laugh.

'So, from that, it seems like there may have been a number of tragedies in the family?' Emma said it as a question.

'Yes, sure, they've had their fair share of struggles.'

Emma wondered if it was Samantha's rape that the reporter was thinking of, but didn't want to ask the question directly.

'Abel lost his son, quite a few years ago', Siri Jespersen continued.

'His son?'

'Yes, he drowned,' the journalist said. 'In Osensjøen.'

Emma stood up and walked over to the window, looked out over the dark water.

'Did you write about that as well?' she asked.

'Oh, no – that was a long time before I started here, but I remember it happening. He was a little backward, Abel's son.'

'Do you remember his name?'

'Fred,' Siri Jespersen answered. 'Same as my grandfather.'

Fred, Emma repeated to herself and sat back down in front of her laptop.

'How old was he?'

'In his twenties? I think.'

Emma typed the name into a search engine and looked it up.

'Have you heard any more news on Walter Kroos?' she heard Siri Jespersen ask on the other end of the line.

Emma studied the information that had come up on the screen.

'No,' she replied a little absently. 'It seems that all traces of him come to a dead end outside Oslo Central Station. Have you heard anything?'

'No,' Jespersen replied. 'I actually tried to call Karina Kasin, but couldn't get hold of her.'

Emma had also tried getting in touch with Samantha's mother.

'I won't keep you,' she said. 'Thank you for your help. I'm sure we'll see each other around.'

She hung up and opened the top news article about a drowning accident in Osen on 22nd August 2007. The victim was not named, but the age matched that of Fred Kasin.

Arvid Borvik was pictured and interviewed in the article. He would not speculate on what might have happened, but added that they were going to investigate the matter as per routine.

Emma sat back and tried to gather her thoughts. All she could conclude was that something wasn't quite right.

36

Just act like it's nothing. Pretend like it's totally normal.

Samantha had repeated the same words to herself over and over while she was painting. At least the renovation project was giving her something to focus on, a distraction when everything else was so unsettling.

The evening round of the campsite was another routine that to anyone watching would look completely normal. Her father had walked it every night. He'd even prevented a fire once. Some Italians had put their campfire ashes into a cardboard box. It had smouldered and caught alight on the decking. Another time, he had caught two boys breaking into one of the caravans at the far end of the campsite.

Samantha wasn't quite as vigilant when she did her inspection rounds. She only really bothered every third day, maybe even less often now that it wasn't holiday season. She had never come across anything amiss, anyway.

There was no indication that anyone was in K–1492. No lights, no rubbish in the bins outside, no fishing equipment or other gear.

Samantha looked around.

Three women came walking down the road from Osensjøen. She didn't see who they were, but it didn't matter – their backs were to her.

Samantha took a step up onto the deck. It was damp after the wet autumn. As she took a few steps closer to the front door, the soles of her shoes creaked on the old wooden surface. A guest would have heard her approach.

She stopped in front of the door.

Took a slow, deep breath in through her nose and closed her eyes for a few seconds. When she opened them again, she briefly considered turning around and coming back later. Her right hand, still sore from all the painting, made the decision for her: she turned the handle and pulled on the door.

It was locked.

She knocked. No movement from inside. She knocked once more

and pulled the door handle again. Again, she turned round to check her surroundings. No one had seen that she was here, or what she was doing.

And then, a brief glimpse of movement behind the curtain.

But she saw no one.

Samantha was about to knock once more when the handle slowly turned. In the next second, the door opened a fraction, then was cautiously pushed open for her.

In front of her: a tall man with short hair and a beard.

He was wearing military-green all-weather trousers and a plain black T-shirt. His arms were hairy and thin. Dark hair stuck out from the neck of his shirt.

The years had settled on Walter's forehead.

The wrinkles were deep.

The same around his eyes. A face that seemed marked by everything he had done and been through. Everything he had carried with him.

'Hi,' she said.

'Hi,' he said back.

She smiled – a faint smile.

'I ... wasn't sure if you ... had made it here,' she said. The right words were even more difficult to find in English. 'I haven't dared come over until now,' she added.

She had cast many glances over to K–1492 in the last few days, but hadn't seen a single sign that he was there.

'But you found the key, I see.'

Walter nodded. He craned his neck and peered behind her, out over the campsite.

'If you let me in, we won't have to worry about anyone seeing us.'

Walter apologised and opened the door fully. She stepped in and slid off her shoes. Walter stood there watching her, as if he didn't quite know what to say or do.

Neither did Samantha.

It didn't feel right to hug. She wasn't a hugger. Not anymore. Before, it had been the natural thing to do when meeting an old acquaintance, but she hadn't seen Walter in seventeen years. A lot had happened in that time.

Walter swallowed a few times. Didn't take his eyes off her.

His beard gave his face character.

In Samantha's mind, Walter had always been sixteen. Smooth skin, thin, quiet. There was no doubt that he was still taciturn, and it didn't look like he'd put much effort into being any other way. The T-shirt hung loosely from his shoulders. Other than that, he hadn't really changed that much.

He was just older.

She wondered what *he* thought about seeing her again after so many years. Samantha knew he had been head over heels in love with her. Did he still like what he saw? She hadn't taken quite as good care of herself as she should have, but people did still turn to look at her when she walked past. And someone always flirted with her in the pub.

They sat down at the kitchen table.

The duvet was rolled up at the end of the sofa that Walter had clearly been sleeping on. A cane chair was placed next to it, acting as a bedside table. There was a paperback book on it.

No one forced him to read anymore. And yet he did anyway.

'How are you?' she asked.

'Fine,' he said.

With that, it suddenly became very difficult to think of what else to say.

'I made the master bed up for you,' she tried, with a nod towards the nearest room.

'It's better here,' he replied, glancing over at the sofa. 'More room.'

She nodded.

'You ... got out all right then?'

'Yeah, it went ... exactly as planned. Good plan. Good suggestion.'

'And it was fine getting out of the country too?'

'Yes.'

Silence settled over the table.

'What are you doing here?' he asked. 'Now, I mean. It's a little early.'

'The police know you're here,' she said.

The look on his face made her hold up her hands and say: 'No, I mean ... I don't mean *here*. But in Norway.'

He visibly relaxed.

'You've been in the Norwegian media – they're saying you're a wanted man. And a journalist is here too, asking about you. She knows you were here in 2004.'

He seemed contemplative again.

'You can't stay,' Samantha said. 'It's too risky. Far too much police presence, and ... journalists. It's one thing that they're looking for you, but ... they're looking for Rita now too. Rita Alvberg. You may remember her?'

He nodded.

'She's missing.'

It didn't seem to concern him all that much.

'So, um, we need to hide you better,' she said. 'I ... you ... can come to my house. It's safer there. And my mother is in Spain right now, so it's perfect, really. I should have had you come to my house straight away, actually...'

He said nothing.

Samantha stood up. 'I've got to go now,' she said. 'But come to my house tonight, after everyone's gone to bed. When there's no traffic on the roads.'

'When would that be?' Walter asked.

'Eleven, maybe. Half-eleven.'

He nodded.

'I'll be there.'

37

Several of the former inmates had etched their names into the cell wall.
One was deeper than the others:
Roy Bolt, 1997.
Blix studied it every night.

Roy Bolt had probably been lying in bed just as he was now, and had
used a screw or some other sharp object to scratch his name into the
wall, his head resting on the pillow. The wall had been painted over many
times since 1983, but never plastered.

Blix had no idea who Roy Bolt was. None of the officers in his wing
were old enough to remember either. The baker had said that the last
person who'd lived in the cell before Blix was a scammer from Skien.
Blix remembered him from the news.

Jarle Mogen.

He had started a company that used currency trading to lure investors
with promises of preposterous returns. It had worked like a pyramid
scheme. Money from new investors covered payments to those who had
previously joined the company and wanted to cash in their investments.
The payouts were success stories that attracted new stakeholders. Often
the money taken out at the bottom was reinvested at a higher step in
the pyramid. In reality, there was no value creation, and the entire en-
terprise collapsed. It was said that Jarle Mogen had more than a billion
kroner sitting somewhere in foreign currency. On the day he was released, he reportedly travelled straight to Brazil.

Blix could hear the sound coming from the TV in the neighbouring
cell. He flicked through the channels on his own until he found the same
programme, so the sound was synchronised. It was an old American
comedy that looked like it had just started.

As a result, he didn't hear the footsteps coming down the hallway,
only that one of the officers suddenly knocked and opened the inspection hatch.

Blix sat up. The floor was cold.

'Phone for you,' the officer on the other side of the door said, passing him the cordless handset through the hatch. 'I'll come and get it in half an hour,' the officer added.

It was an auxiliary device; you couldn't actually make calls from it. The display showed that the call had already lasted well over a minute.

'Blix speaking,' he said – the same way he had always answered when his work phone rang.

'It's me.' Emma's voice.

Blix sat down at the desk.

'Anything new?' he asked.

'No, not really,' she replied.

Blix listened as she told him about the search operation.

'Why are you calling?' he asked when she finished. 'You said there wasn't *really* anything new – what have you found out, then?'

Emma hesitated, as if thinking through how to word the next part.

'Did I tell you about Markus Hadeland?' she asked.

'No. Who's that?'

'Samantha's ex-husband. I met him in the pub yesterday and then again today. He was helping with the search.'

Blix jotted down the name.

'I asked him about the rape,' Emma continued. 'He didn't seem like he wanted to talk about it, but what he did say was that it *wasn't* a tourist who did it.'

'Then who was it?' Blix asked.

'Whoever it was is apparently dead now,' she continued. 'But Markus didn't want to say any more about it. I got the feeling that it was someone from the village.'

'You'll have to talk to him again,' Blix said.

'Agreed, but currently he's not responding to my messages,' Emma said.

He heard her drink something before she continued.

'There was also a boy my age who died here a few years ago, drowned in the lake – Osensjøen. He was Samantha's cousin and had some sort of intellectual disability.'

'What was his name?' Blix asked.

'Fred Kasin,' Emma replied. 'His father is a lawyer, works in commercial law mainly. Abel Kasin. He apparently helped out with the running of the campsite right after his brother died, but not anymore.'

Blix noted that down too.

'Have you spoken any more with Fosse?' Emma asked, changing the subject.

'A few hours ago,' Blix replied. 'He's dispatched one of the investigators to Osen.'

'Who?'

'Nicolai Wibe.'

He could hear Emma typing something on her laptop. Presumably Oslo police sending an investigator to Osen would be news in a case that was otherwise silent.

'I've not seen him around,' she said.

Blix wondered if he should mention that his day release had been approved to visit to Iselin's grave, but decided not to.

'There is a way you can find out,' he said.

Emma didn't follow.

'Find out what?'

'Find out more about the rape,' Blix added. 'You need to talk to Samantha again. She's the one who'll be able to tell you.'

She seemed reluctant to do so.

'I'll try Markus Hadeland again first,' she said. 'He'll probably be playing at the pub again tonight.'

They were about to end the conversation.

'Wait, have you got your laptop there?' Blix asked abruptly.

'Yes?'

'Can you look up a name for me?' he asked. 'Roy Bolt.'

He heard her fingers typing away on the keyboard again.

'Who is he?' she asked.

'I thought you could tell me,' Blix replied. 'Any hits?'

'Convicted murderer, it says.'

Blix listened as she read aloud.

'Killed his girlfriend with an axe somewhere in Telemark in 1994,' she summarised. 'Then chopped her head off afterwards and tried feeding it to the pigs on his parents' farm. An absolute psycho then, to answer your question.'

'I see,' Blix nodded.

'The last online article is from 1997,' Emma continued. 'It says he was found dead in his cell. Does he have something to do with the case?'

'Ah, no,' Blix replied. 'It was just a name that came up – something else. Forget I asked.'

38

Her head itched beneath the wig.

Emma usually showered daily, even when she hadn't exercised. Admittedly, she hadn't been in Osen for more than a day and a half, but she longed to feel warm water on her body. She felt dirty and gross, and she was going out later after all.

Emma grabbed the towel Samantha Kasin had given her the day before, as well as the shower gel she had luckily thought to buy while at the shop, just in case, and stepped out into the dark, cold evening, heading for the communal facilities. She didn't like the idea of showering where so many strangers had showered before her. All the promises in the world about how spotless and squeaky clean it was didn't take away from that fact. Exactly why it bothered her, she wasn't sure.

The ground crunched beneath her shoes, broadcasting her every step. The two occupied cabins that had been illuminated a few hours prior now lay in darkness. Still, it felt like someone was watching her.

The wind blew in from the north. She could hear it pummelling the trees nearby. The darkness of the forest had a peculiar mystique about it. The pitch-black, the unknown, that space that could be concealing anything. And now especially, while people were looking for a missing person in there ... A cold shiver ran through Emma.

She felt exposed, perhaps even more so because she couldn't see anyone else. And she was on her way to the communal facilities, which were probably also devoid of people.

But there was no question of turning around and going back to the cabin. There was defeat in letting fear get the better of her. She was a grown woman, damn it. She was strong, and if anyone wanted to try her, then—

She span round.

She'd heard the sound of a motorcycle accelerating suddenly and violently not so far away. The silence that followed, the whipping of the wind, settled back around her quickly. But there was no one around. Or so she thought, anyway.

Fortunately, the communal facilities had outside lights, which made the surroundings a little less ominous. There were also lights on in the reception and kiosk. Both were closed. Emma turned once more to look around before letting herself into the facilities and quickly closing the door behind her. It locked automatically.

There was a kitchen inside, with a fridge and freezer, as well as a laundry room with several washing machines and tumble dryers. Next to the central area was a TV room, but no one was in there. Although – she started second-guessing herself – was there someone? She whisper-shouted a half-hearted 'hello?', which felt ridiculous, and which didn't get a response.

Emma found a shower cubicle she could lock and turned on the water. She undressed and placed her clothes on a wooden bench along with the towel. As she stood under the stream of water, she sent an envious thought to her journalist colleagues who had travelled to Elverum to spend the night there. They were probably enjoying a nutritious dinner right now, had had a much more glamourous shower, and were generally feeling much fresher, while she was standing alone here in a hideous community shower block in godforsaken Osen.

It was a bit surreal being back at work, Emma thought, closing her eyes. To be *in it* – in the middle of something, thinking about a case, of people to talk to, of leads to follow. Once she started, she couldn't just switch off or slow down. Working had always been a curse. It drained all her time, her energy. Perhaps that was why she had railed so much against the thought of continuing in this job, this profession. It always came first, took precedence over everything else. Family, friends.

A partner?

It was Saturday night.

People were going out to enjoy themselves, find themselves a date, someone to spend their life with, or even just the night. But not Emma – she was working. Again. She was kind of going out, but it wasn't exactly for enjoyment or pleasure.

Emma quickly dried herself off and got dressed again. Half-ran back to the cabin, where she found out via a quick internet search that the pub in Osen closed at one o'clock. She had three and a quarter hours to get something worthwhile out of the evening.

Before leaving, Emma sent Samantha Kasin a quick text, asking if she would be at Pøbben tonight, or whether she would be going later and fancied a glass or two of wine? When Emma left the cabin a little before eleven, she was yet to receive an answer.

On her way out of the campsite, she felt an urgent desire for chewing gum, and made a hasty decision to swing by the petrol station. It wasn't a long detour, just a couple hundred metres towards the other end of the high street.

As she approached the entrance, the doors slid open automatically. A man threw a hot dog wrapper into the nearest bin.

Emma tilted her head, trying to see his face.

'Wibe?' she asked.

The man turned to face her. Nicolai Wibe from the Oslo police. Blix's former colleague.

He took a bite of the hot dog in lieu of responding.

'I assume you're here for work?' Emma continued.

Wibe took his time chewing.

'For a short while,' he replied. 'I imagine you are too, so you'll have to talk to someone else.'

'But you are here because of Walter Kroos?' Emma asked.

Wibe took another bite of the sausage and walked past her, towards his car.

'The local police are dealing with the media,' he said over his shoulder, with food still in his mouth.

Emma remained in the same spot, watching him until he had driven away, before turning and going inside.

The man with the scarred face was on shift. He didn't look up when Emma entered. She grabbed the few items she needed and went up to pay.

Trygve Klepp looked up as she approached.

'Well, well, well, if it isn't the journalist?'

There was a hint of teasing in the last word, as if *journalist* was a ridiculous job title.

'Hi,' Emma said, glad he recognised her.

'Still here then?'

'Indeed,' she said. 'You too?'

That made him laugh.

'Not got too many choices in that regard, you know. Bills to pay.'

He tried to wink, but the paralysis on one side of his face made it look a little odd.

'How's it going? Found Walter yet?'

Again, there was a glimmer of a challenge in the way he asked. The question posed with a hint of a smile, as if he didn't think she'd be able to.

'Not yet,' she said. 'But I have a feeling he's here.'

'Do you now?'

He pulled Emma's items over and scanned them through.

'That everything?'

'Yes thanks.'

Klepp tapped away on the cash register then signalled that the machine was ready to accept her card.

'Jarl Inge Ree is due to be released soon,' she said, tapping her card against the machine, which approved it with a little beep.

Klepp briefly ran his hand over his cheek. 'Receipt?'

'No thanks.' She put the items in her bag. 'How do you feel about that?' she asked.

'About what?'

'About Jarl Inge Ree being released. I believe he's planning on settling back in the village, or so I've heard. Last time I was in here, you said he belonged behind bars.'

'Did I?'

'Yes.'

Klepp busied himself with something behind the counter.

'You even told me not to quote you on that,' Emma continued.

'Oh, God, really?'

Emma could tell that he was more uncomfortable than he was surprised by his own words.

'I didn't mean much by it,' he said. 'But it's no secret here in the village that Jarl Inge has always been an utter asshole.'

'In what way?' Emma asked, even though she knew Ree's criminal past and present.

Klepp took a deep breath in and sighed. 'And you won't write anything about this?'

'Not if you don't want me to.'

He planted his hands firmly on the counter in front of him, so that the muscles in his upper arms tensed.

'I've known Jarl Inge my entire life,' Klepp began. 'I think there was even a time when we were best friends. Or at least *I* saw *him* as that. But that didn't stop him from doing this to me.' He pointed to his face.

'What happened?' Emma asked. 'If you don't mind me asking?'

'To be honest, I don't remember,' he replied, smiling.

A lie, Emma thought, but she didn't want to push him on it.

'Typical Jarl Inge, though,' Klepp continued regardless. 'When something in his head clicked, it clicked. Didn't matter who it was about or who got in his way.'

He waited a moment before continuing.

'He slammed my face into a coffee table.'

Emma grimaced.

'And he'd smashed a beer bottle first,' Klepp went on. 'On the same table. And skin mixed with broken glass...' He shook his head. 'Bad combination,' he finished.

'So I've heard,' Emma said. 'And how long ago was that?'

He looked up to the left as he thought. 'A little over ten years, maybe?'

'Did you report it?'

'You don't report Jarl Inge Ree,' he scoffed. 'Not here in the village, anyway.'

'Why not?'

Klepp smiled. 'It does more harm than good, so to speak.'

Emma thought she understood where he was coming from. In Osen, it seemed that people would rather sort things out themselves than involve the long arm of the law.

Klepp quickly checked something on his phone before returning his gaze to Emma.

'Heading to the pub then?' he asked, looking at her.

'What makes you think that?' she asked with a smile.

'The chewing gum and Fisherman's Friends you've just bought,' Klepp replied. 'The Saturday night usual.'

Emma laughed.

A little *ding* chimed behind her as the door opened. A new customer came in.

'Just a quick visit,' she replied. 'What about you?'

'I close up here at midnight,' Klepp replied. 'But maybe I'll swing by afterwards.'

'Do,' Emma said.

She wasn't done talking to him.

39

Walter went through the rooms in the cabin one last time to check that he had everything. He hadn't brought much, just a few items from his cell, as well as a backpack and some money from home. He hadn't had time to pick up anything else.

In Norway, he had grabbed a tied-up bag of discarded clothes left beside a recycling bin. Almost all of the clothes were still in the bag, with the exception of the black and slightly oversized T-shirt he was wearing.

Maybe he should scrub down the surfaces, he thought. Remove any fingerprints. On the other hand – it was bound to become known at some point that he had been here, so what did it really matter?

Walter collected what rubbish he had in a bin bag and tied it up. Locked the cabin and went out into the bitterly cold night. The sky was clear and full of stars. To his right, the glistening moonlight on the surface of the lake. His footsteps over the turf sounded like thunder in the otherwise silent surroundings. His legs felt strangely weak, powerless. Presumably because he was going to Samantha's house.

He would *stay there*. Hide there.

Over the years he had imagined what her house looked like, what it smelled like. What things she surrounded herself with. What habits she had.

Question after question, year after year.

Walter threw the bag of rubbish into a bin and checked around him as he approached the highway. He didn't like the fact he was so visible there, beneath the streetlamps, but he had no other choice. Fortunately, it wasn't far and there were no cars nearby.

He had only walked a few metres on the pavement when the sound of shoes against asphalt not far behind him made Walter jump and turn his head ever so slightly. In a brief, sideways glance, he caught sight of a woman in a red jacket. Walter had only seen one other person with similar clothing in Osen: the woman staying at the campsite.

He increased his speed, careful not to turn and check behind him, even though he wanted to. Only seventy, maybe eighty metres more, then he could take a different route, leave the pavement.

Had she got closer?

He adjusted his cadence even more and headed off onto the path between the pavement and the housing estate. For a quick moment, he couldn't resist the temptation to glance back. It did seem as if she'd caught up with him.

He turned into another side street, disappeared round the side of a house and slipped into a garden, where he crouched down behind a child's playhouse and listened.

After a few more minutes, he crept over to the street again and looked out.

He was alone.

Walter dropped his shoulders and allowed himself to breathe. He waited a few moments longer before continuing down the path. Stayed in the shadows until he arrived at the house Samantha lived in.

She saw him through the kitchen window as he stepped into the driveway. Within seconds, she was at the front door, holding it open for him. Walter smiled.

She had changed since seeing him earlier that day. Now she was wearing light-blue jeans and a white top.

'Come in,' she whispered. 'Hurry.'

He glanced at the neighbouring house before walking past her and inside. She closed the door behind him. Walter put down his backpack. Took his jacket off and hung it up. His shoes wreaked. He hoped Samantha didn't notice.

'Did anyone see you?' she asked.

'That woman staying at the campsite,' Walter told her. 'She was walking behind me on the road. Fifty metres or so. She must have seen me, but I don't think she recognised me.'

Samantha crossed her arms and stared at him.

'She didn't follow me,' Walter insisted.

'Are you sure?'

He nodded.

'She's the reporter I told you about,' Samantha said. 'The one enquiring about you.'

Walter didn't know how to respond.

'I don't like this,' she said. 'And I don't like her being here.'

'Neither do I.'

They moved down the hallway.

'Stay away from the windows,' Samantha warned him. 'I have nosy neighbours.'

Walter couldn't remember the last time he was in someone else's home. It was a situation he was uncomfortable with. He felt like an intruder. He had no idea how he should behave.

'Can I get you anything?' she asked. 'A beer or something?'

'I'll have whatever you're having,' he said.

'I don't want anything.'

He turned his palms upwards. 'Well in that case.'

She smiled. It was good to see her smile again.

'Shall we ... sit in the living room?'

Walter followed her. Samantha grabbed the remote and turned off the TV. It immediately felt stuffy, quiet.

He placed his hands on the couch. Moved them to his thighs, quickly scratched his right cheek. His beard crackled. Samantha pulled her legs up on the couch and rested one elbow on the armrest.

'I've made up the spare room for you,' she said. 'The towels are on the bed. I imagine you'll be wanting to take a shower.'

Walter wondered what it would be like showering in freedom again. At Samantha's house.

'I've found you some more clothes as well,' she continued. 'They were my father's. They might be a little big.'

'Thank you,' Walter said. 'I appreciate it.'

She threw a quick glance over at his backpack.

'What do you have with you?'

'I didn't have anything in my cell,' he began. 'Not of value anyway. But I brought the letters.'

'The letters?'

'From you,' he said, smiling, a little embarrassed. 'I couldn't leave them there. Otherwise the police would've got here before I did.'

'You ... kept them?'

'From the very first one you sent,' Walter answered. 'In the summer of 2005. When you asked us not to come back.'

Samantha nodded slowly.

'But I don't have *that* one here,' Walter added, motioning with his head towards the bag. 'That one's in my bedroom back home.'

She put her left hand on her knee and with her right, squeezed the muscles in her forearm.

'You've really kept all of them?'

'Yes.'

'Can I have a look?'

The seriousness in her eyes made him get up and get his backpack. After he sat down again, he took out all the envelopes.

He had tied a string around them. Some had started to fade, become discoloured. A couple of the envelopes also showed signs that he was going through a bad time when he opened them.

The first appeared on an autumn day in 2011.

Samantha had heard about what had happened, and the sentence he had received. She thought it was an awful thing to read, but at the same time, had held out a hand to him. She had a feeling that maybe not many people knew him, not really. It was a strange thing to claim, she wrote, having only been with him for a few summer days back when they were still teenagers. But she still felt that she knew who he was. That she understood him. So, if he needed a friend, she would gladly be one. She presumed that he didn't have that many.

She had been right about that too.

His first instinct had been: no. Don't let her into your life again. You're facing a long prison sentence. It'll only make everything hurt that much more, being back in touch with a childhood crush. The brief fling that summer had only left him with wounds and painful memories.

He put the letter away, but didn't throw it away. Periodically, he would take it out again and read it. Samantha's offer was like a boomerang that always came back.

And then, one day, he sat down with some paper and a pencil. It took the entire evening just to write one draft of the first paragraph. The next day, he threw his attempt in the bin. What could he share about his life behind bars that she would be at all interested in?

Little, he soon found out.

But he thanked her for writing to him. It was well received, and a nice thought. He wrote a little about what his days were like. How everything repeated itself. And who would have thought that he would end up working in the prison library?

She had answered him the following week. After that, they continued to exchange letters. For Walter it had been something to look forward to. There hadn't been much to look forward to in B-39 of Billwerder Prison.

Walter handed her the stack of envelopes. Samantha untied them.

'Wow,' she said. 'Did I really write so many?'

He didn't answer.

'I didn't keep yours,' she admitted. 'Sorry.'

Her nails were painted dark red. Walter noticed a white dot on one of them. Paint, presumably.

'Are they sorted by year as well?' she asked.

'Yes.'

Samantha studied her own handwriting on the outside of the envelope, took out the contents. It was just one A4 page.

Walter remembered almost verbatim what she had written:

Dear Walter,

Thank you for answering me. It means a lot. Just know that you can write to me at any time. I will always answer.

It is good to hear that you have found yourself more or less settled. Do you have someone who can visit you? Are you getting enough fresh air? How is the food? Have you made any friends in there?

Here in Osen, everything is pretty much the same. My mother's rheumatism is getting worse and worse, and she can't help out much at the campsite anymore, apart from telling us what to do and what not to do. I can't help but roll my eyes even as I write this. And my father complains just as much as always, and yells at everything and everyone.

I still spend a lot of time with Jarl Inge and Rita, who you may remember? And Markus, of course. The one with the guitar. Markus is a bit tiresome, in a quiet, observant kind of way. It's difficult to explain. But he still plays the guitar and always asks me to sing with him. Sometimes I give in, usually when I've had a few too many drinks, but I can't bear to do it properly. From the heart, as it were. There is too much pain in my soul, I think, after everything that happened with the competition. I'm sure I'll tell you about it, one day.

Something awful happened here too. Fred, my cousin, drowned. He was swimming in the lake, but got into some trouble or something, I think, and sank to the bottom. Jarl Inge was there when it happened. My parents were beside themselves. It's sad, of course. My uncle is having a difficult time at the moment. But life goes on, right? You just have to try to forget. It doesn't help to dwell on the past too much.

I hope you are keeping well, Walter.

Tell me more about how you are doing. Anything.

Sending you a hug,
Samantha

She put the letter down. Several, thoughtful creases had appeared on her face.

'That feels like an eternity ago,' she said.

It hadn't taken Walter as long to answer the next time. Or the time after that. Eventually they started to trust each other. Their letters became more familiar.

'Maybe we should burn these,' she said, looking up at him. She had just skimmed through the last letter. 'Just in case.'

Walter thought about it. He didn't like the idea of getting rid of them. It was one thing to remember the content, word for word, but there was a kind of comfort in them, their physicality, in having them in his hand.

They became more concrete then, not just something he could recall from his memories.

'We don't need to do that right now,' she said, as if she had read his mind.

'Have you heard anything from Jarl Inge lately?' Walter asked.

'I spoke to him today, actually.'

'How was he?'

'He's heard that you escaped,' she replied. 'And that Rita is missing.'

'What did he say about it?'

'He wondered where I'd heard what had happened. I told him what I could.'

Samantha yawned.

'Are you tired?' he asked.

'A little.'

She sent him a gentle smile. 'It's been an intense few days,' she added. 'A lot to think about.'

Walter couldn't think of anything to say.

'Maybe we should go to bed,' she suggested. 'You must be tired too.'

He actually couldn't remember the last time he was more awake. Sitting here, in the same room as Samantha, after all these years...

It felt like a dream. And he didn't want to wake up.

Samantha had been his first crush. His only one, to be perfectly honest. He had to concede to himself, he was still in love with her. Now perhaps more than ever, without really being able to explain why.

40

Two cars with aggressively large tyres were parked up side by side in the pub car park. The dirty rear and side windows made it impossible to judge whether anyone was sitting inside either of them. Three women were standing outside the front door, smoking. As Emma got closer, they stopped chatting and turned their attention to her.

'Hello,' Emma said, but got no response.

Through the door, she could hear the hum of laughter and conversation, accompanied by a song over the sound system that Emma recognised but couldn't quite place. As she entered, the noise inside the pub died down slightly, as if her sudden presence was something everyone had to witness. The first to meet her gaze was Tom Erik Ree. He was standing in the exact same place as last time, a pint of beer on the bar in front of him. It looked like he'd come straight from work, as he was still wearing his workwear and a cap that said *Osen Lumber Mill*. Ree's eyes bored into hers, a look Emma interpreted as loathing.

Markus Hadeland, on the other hand, beamed when he caught sight of her. He took his pint glass off the bar and came over to meet her at the door.

'*Today*, you have no choice,' he began. 'I'm treating you to a drink this time. What can I get you?'

Emma thought about it. The selection of wine wasn't the best she'd ever seen.

'I'll have a bottled beer, if they've got any. Thanks. Something light, preferably.'

Markus seemed to like that she was a little picky. He guided her over to the bar. Emma had to squeeze past Tom Erik Ree, who didn't make room for her. Hesitantly, she nodded to some of the others lined up at the bar. She saw several faces she recognised from the search crews. Maybe they'd come out tonight to talk about what might have happened to Rita Alvberg. Or maybe they just wanted to forget that she was missing.

After a few attempts to get the bartender's attention, Markus managed to order Emma a beer. A moment later, a bottle of Sol was placed in front of her. A wedge of lime had been pushed into the neck. Emma poked the piece of fruit all the way down into the beer and lifted the bottle to her mouth.

'Thank you,' she said.

'Cheers,' Markus said, taking a swig from his own.

'You're not playing tonight then?' she asked.

'No,' he said, shaking his head. 'I thought I'd give them a bit of a break.'

Emma laughed.

For a while they stood side by side in comfortable silence. Markus glanced at her every now and then, and smiled. He seemed more relaxed today, she thought. Not quite so shy. It made her wonder if he had been at the pub for a while already. His eyelids looked a little heavy.

Emma leant a little closer and asked: 'What do you do when you're not playing the classics for the locals?'

'Oh,' he said, smiling – his breath smelled of alcohol. 'I work as a music teacher at a couple of schools in the area. It doesn't exactly constitute a full-time position, so I try to do some private lessons here and there. Sometimes I pitch in on some album recordings and stuff like that too, but that's mostly for fun, really. There's no money in it.'

An old song by Depeche Mode blared out of the loudspeakers. Tom Erik Rec gave her another intense glare, as if he had more right to be there than she did. Emma just stared back until he found something else to focus on.

'Fred Kasin,' she said after a while, looking up at Markus. 'Samantha's cousin. Was he the one who raped her?'

Markus, who was in the process of lifting the glass to his mouth, stopped. He paused before taking a sip.

'You said that whoever it was, was dead now,' Emma continued when he didn't answer. 'And that it wasn't Walter Kroos's father. And Fred Kasin...'

Markus looked around quickly.

'Is that not something we should talk about in the pub?' Emma asked. 'Or at all?'

He smiled apologetically. 'Not here, at least,' he said.

'No?'

'No, there's...' He lowered his voice.

Emma moved a little closer. 'Too many eyes and ears here, perhaps?'

He smiled, nodded his head ever so slightly. 'Something like that.'

Emma decided to leave it at that. For now, at least. She had got the answer she was looking for, the confirmation.

'He drowned, I read,' she continued. 'A few years after.'

Markus's neck had turned a flaming red. 'Tragic,' he said simply, and drained the rest of the glass. 'Can I get you another?'

'I'm not done with this one, but thanks.'

Markus turned to the bar, waiting for the bartender's attention again. Emma regretted being so direct. Felt she'd gone too far this time.

Markus stood with his back to her for a while, before he disappeared off to the toilet. Emma pulled out her phone, mostly for the sake of the company. When a bar stool became available, she sat down and continued to check her social media and various online newspapers. *NRK* had released information that Rita Alvberg had been in her hometown more than usual over the last year and a half, in connection with her mother's illness. Her friends ruled out any struggle with suicidal thoughts being the reason for her disappearance. 'Someone is responsible,' the newspaper had concluded, the alleged criminal nature of the disappearance already made clear in the headline.

When she looked up again, Markus was deep in conversation with someone else. Trygve Klepp eventually appeared, but he headed straight to the pool table with some friends. This was a waste of time, Emma decided, resolving to head back to the cabin and make a better plan for how to tackle tomorrow.

She dreaded the walk back in the dark.

A little earlier, she had thought that Markus might've walked her home, but she couldn't even see him now. She would just have to suck it up. She began to weave her way through the crowd of people standing between her and the door, when she suddenly she felt a strong hand around her left upper arm.

'What do you think you're doing?'

Tom Erik Ree pulled her aside, a little away from the people mingling in the centre of the pub. His grip was surprisingly firm. The night before he had seemed almost warm, welcoming, but now there was an air of hostility to him. She was about to pull her arm out of his grasp, when he let go and said:

'I hear you've been sticking your nose where it doesn't belong, asking questions 'bout Jarl Inge.'

Emma looked around. No one seemed to be eavesdropping, or paying any attention to them.

'Digging up the past,' Ree added.

Emma swallowed, trying to compose herself. 'Uh, yes,' she said. 'That is what journalists tend to do.'

'Pack it in,' he growled, his eyes boring into hers. 'It's already ruined his life, all the bullshit you journalists have written about him. The disrespect, the distain you've exposed him to...' He grimaced and shook his head.

Emma cleared her throat and said: 'It is the job of the press to—'

'Spare me the righteous-press bullshit, I've heard it a hundred times before.'

Contempt radiated from Ree's face. He edged a little closer.

'The past is the past,' he continued. 'Jarl Inge will be released on Monday, and he intends to start anew, lead a better life.'

'Does he now?'

'Yes,' Tom Erik Ree spat. 'He does.'

I'll believe it when I see it, Emma wanted to say, but didn't.

'And he has family here. Friends.'

'Clearly. I've heard all about how he treats his friends.'

A fire raged in Ree's eyes. 'He has a girlfriend now, here, in the village,' he said, shoving his index finger in her face. 'Don't fuck this up for them.'

Emma straightened her jacket a little and said: 'I understand that we have a slightly different perception of law and justice, right and wrong.'

'Go home,' Tom Erik Ree said in a trembling voice. 'Leave us all alone.'

'You know,' Emma began, taking a tiny step closer. 'Macho bullshit like this. Intimidation tactics and veiled threats and phrases like "the past is the past" and "leave us all alone"? They're the kind of things someone says when they have something to hide. And do you know what that does, to someone like me?'

Ree didn't answer.

'I think actually I'd quite like to stay a few more days,' she continued. 'So I can ask more questions and knock on more doors.'

Ree returned her gaze but said nothing.

'I've even got Arvid Borvik's number,' she added, waving her phone in front of him. 'And if it becomes necessary I'll—'

Tom Erik Ree belted out a laugh. 'Oooh yes, now I'm really scared,' he said, his voice dripping with sarcasm. 'Have a safe trip home,' he continued, a wry smile on his face. 'To your cabin. You should remember to lock the door – plenty of dangerous people round these parts.'

41

Blix cracked the top of the egg, scraped the contents out onto a slice of toast and sprinkled some salt on top. He ate slowly, drinking a sip of milk after every other bite.

Jarl Inge Ree came to breakfast late. He seemed tired, as if he'd had a bad night's sleep. His skin was pale with dark bags under his eyes. The bandage over his nose was askew. He strode into the kitchen and returned after a while with his usual stack of toast. There was plenty of room around the long table, but Ree planted himself across from Blix.

'Any news?' he asked and began spreading a thick layer of fish paste over the top slice of toast.

'Nothing,' Blix replied.

Ree looked around, as if to make sure no one was sitting close enough to overhear their conversation.

'Have you spoken to anyone?' he asked in a low voice.

'I spoke to Emma Ramm last night,' Blix replied. 'She's still in Osen. They are continuing the search for Rita today.'

Ree began to butter another slice of toast, without having eaten the first.

'What about the police?' he asked. 'Do they know any more about Walter Kroos?'

'I haven't heard from them,' Blix replied. 'Not since our conversation yesterday.'

The little Dutchman came and sat down with them. Ree began to eat. The chewing caused the tape on his bandage to loosen on one side. He dropped the slice of toast onto the plate, cursed and pressed the bandage back into place. It came off again just as quickly.

'Fuck's SAKE,' he said again, louder this time.

'It'll be sorted within a few weeks,' Blix said.

Ree grabbed the butter knife, as if he needed something to hold on to. 'My nose hurts like a bitch,' he snapped.

The outburst of rage made the Dutchman chuckle, although he probably didn't understand much of what was being said.

Ree turned to him. 'What the hell are you laughing at?' he asked.

'Nothing,' replied the Dutchman. 'Sorry.'

The room went quiet. The other inmates watched in silence, anticipating what would happen next.

'Is something funny?' Jarl Inge Ree asked the man.

Before the Dutchman could answer, Ree had grabbed the back of his head and smashed his face into the plate. His fork bounced over to Blix's side of the table. The Dutchman pushed himself up from the table and jumped to his feet. Red jam slid off his face and onto his T-shirt.

Ree was just as quick onto his feet, ready to go.

Blix stood up, picking up his plate and glass of milk and taking a few steps away. He couldn't risk anything that jeopardised his day release tomorrow.

Grubben was suddenly there, standing between Ree and the Dutchman.

'Hey, boss,' he said, right in front of Ree's face. 'Relax. You're getting out tomorrow. Don't ruin it.'

Jakobsen arrived, stopping a few metres away. 'What's going on?' he asked, one hand on his radio, ready to call for reinforcements.

Jarl Inge Ree turned to him. 'Nothing,' he replied. 'Just a misunderstanding.'

'No problem,' the Dutchman added.

Jakobsen scrutinised the situation and looked around at the rest of the table, before ending on Blix.

'It's fine,' Blix said.

Jakobsen stayed a little longer.

'Clean up after yourselves,' he said.

'I've got it,' Grubben said, picking up a knocked-over glass.

Jakobsen went back to the guardhouse.

Blix emptied the rest of the milk and took the glass and plate to the kitchen. He then returned to his cell and lay down on his newly made bed.

It wasn't long before there was a knock on the cell door.

Blix sat up with a grimace. The pain in the shoulder had set in already. He would have to ask for his pain medication early.

'Yes?' he shouted.

Jarl Inge Ree entered, and stood a few paces inside. 'Will you let me know?' he asked. 'As soon as you hear something?'

'I'll keep you updated,' Blix promised.

Ree stood there, hesitating. 'Maybe you could call now, and see if there's any news?'

'I can't call unless I've got something new to tell them,' Blix said, standing his ground. 'The only reason I could call now is if you had anything more to say about Walter Kroos.'

Some of Ree's temper returned. 'I told you,' he said. 'I don't know shit. Nothing more than what I've already said.'

Blix paused a moment, then said: 'The police think you might know something.'

'Why would they?' Ree spat. 'I haven't spoken to the guy in seventeen years.'

'Well, he certainly remembers you,' Blix said. 'The German prison officers found your name on a note in his cell.'

Ree stared at him, opened and closed his mouth for a moment, and then took a few more steps into the room.

'What the hell is that supposed to mean?' he asked. 'What kind of note?'

Blix shrugged. 'I don't know any more than that.'

Ree cursed again.

It had been almost been a day since Blix last spoke to Fosse. He was also curious as to whether there had been any more developments.

'I can try calling,' he said, getting up from the bed.

'I'll wait here,' Ree said without asking if Blix minded. Blix went to the guardhouse. Jakobsen scowled at him.

'I need to make a phone call,' Blix said. 'To Gard Fosse.'

Jakobsen reluctantly got up, pulled out a folder and dialled the number listed there.

'Hold the line, you have an incoming call from Alexander Blix,' he said when the call went through. He transferred the call to a handset and gave it to Blix.

Blix took it with him into the phone booth, so he could talk to Fosse undisturbed.

Fosse got his question in first: 'Anything new?'

'Not really,' Blix replied. 'Nothing other than Jarl Inge Ree getting very stressed and insisting that I ask whether you've caught Walter Kroos yet.'

'And how do you interpret that?' Fosse asked.

'Not sure,' Blix replied. 'He maintains that he's told me everything he knows, but I'm not sure I believe him.' He heard footsteps walk past. 'So you haven't caught him then?'

'We carried out a search operation in a hostel outside Horten yesterday,' Fosse began, 'on the basis of what we considered solid information. But it turned out to be a German landscape architect. We've had a little over a hundred tips come in. People have reportedly seen him from down south in Kristiansand up to Hammerfest in the north. You know how it is. We do know that a Salvation Army soldier spoke to him outside Oslo Central Station on the day he arrived. She had explained how to get to the nearest currency exchange. Where he then exchanged nearly nine thousand kroner. After that, we have nothing.'

'What about the missing woman?' Blix asked. 'Rita Alvberg.'

'Still missing,' Fosse confirmed.

Blix had more questions, about Samantha Kasin and the rape, but didn't get a chance to ask.

'I'm getting another call,' Fosse told him. 'I need to take it – I'll call you this afternoon.'

The line cut off, replaced by a long beeping signal. Blix handed the phone back to Jakobsen and returned to his cell. Ree was sitting in the chair in front of the desk.

Blix summarised the little he had learned. Ree sighed and stared at the floor. After a while he lifted his head and fixed his gaze on a picture of Iselin.

'That's my daughter,' Blix explained.

Ree said nothing, but remained seated, as if waiting for Blix to tell him about her. Jarl Inge Ree was not a man he would usually share anything about Iselin with.

'She had just turned twenty-three,' he went on, nevertheless, taking a seat on the edge of his bed.

If he spoke openly about Iselin, there was a possibility that Ree may be equally as open about Samantha.

'Of those twenty-three years, I got maybe one year with her,' he continued. 'There was always something or other. Overtime. Other people's needs, other priorities. Her mother and I divorced when she was little. Iselin stayed with her. It wasn't until a few years ago that we had a proper relationship.'

He reached for his pillow and put it behind his back.

'She'd not long started at the police college when she died,' he continued, crossing one leg over the other. Suddenly struggling to keep the tears back.

'Sounds ... horrendous,' Ree said. 'I don't know if I'd be able to manage, having a photo of her up on the wall.'

Blix sat up and cleared his voice. 'People say that ... we have to move on, keep living. But it's hard. Taking it one day at a time is hard.'

Neither of them said anything for a while.

'What are you going to do when you get out?' Blix asked.

Ree looked at the floor again, sitting there in thought.

'I'll take it one day at a time,' he said, standing up.

42

After a restless night, Samantha eventually got to sleep in the early hours of the morning, but the thought of everything that had happened, and everything ahead of them, made her get up long before daybreak. Now, two and a half hours later, the fatigue was starting to set in, but it was too late to go back to bed.

She heard the occasional noise coming from the guest room. A slow, steady snoring through the walls.

Walter Kroos.

A German killer on the run.

Samantha had to shake her head when she thought about it. That a more or less random summer encounter so many years ago could have such major consequences. But that was life. The choices you make, the consequences you just can't foresee, which may then result in so many other, unintended consequences. Something bad happens, you step off the path for a moment, and then you find another path, and another – maybe this one's better, maybe it's worse.

Everything in her life had changed after she met Walter. It wasn't his fault. It was just bad timing. It happens.

Samantha didn't want to think too much right now. Of course she knew the consequences of what she had done and what they were going to do together, but she couldn't dwell on that for too long. If she did, she might begin to regret her actions, get nervous – and scared – and she didn't have time for that.

The phone rang.

Samantha didn't dare pick up. Her mother had called the day before too, and sent several text messages. She had heard about the search for Rita. *It's so awful*, her mother had written. *So soon after Harriet passed away*. Samantha had played along, but couldn't bring herself to call her back.

The slow breathing from the guest room ceased.

A few minutes later, she heard Walter's feet meet the floor. He still took some time before opening the door and walking into the kitchen, careful not to get too close to the window.

'Good morning,' he said.

'Hi.' She smiled.

It was nice to see him, here, at home.

'Did you sleep well?' she asked, even though she knew the answer.

'God,' he said, smiling, his face still tired from such a heavy sleep. 'I slept so well.'

'That'd be the mattress,' Samantha said. 'I've heard it's good.'

Walter laughed and sat down.

'Can I get you a coffee? I've got some here.'

'Please, I'd love some.' He was about to get up.

'You sit,' she said, pushing her own chair back. 'Milk, sugar?'

'No, thank you.'

She poured the coffee into a plain yellow cup and sat back down. Her own coffee was getting cold, but she couldn't be bothered getting up again to refill it.

'You didn't change into any of Dad's clothes then?' she asked. 'I put them out ready for you on the chair in there.'

'Oh,' he said. 'I ... forgot to try them on.'

Walter took a sip of his coffee and wrapped both hands around the cup as if to warm them.

'Good coffee,' he said. 'Much better than what I'm used to.'

It made her smile, but at the same time, made her sad. With any luck, she would have him here for a few more days. It was silly to hope for any more. But she already knew she was going to miss him.

'Did you keep all of your father's clothes?' Walter asked.

'Yes...' Samantha looked down. 'Well, no, not all, of course, but ... a lot of them.'

She leant her head over to her left shoulder, then to her right.

'It was Mum who wanted to keep them.'

'They weren't as important to you?'

'Me?' Samantha shook her head. 'We already had pictures of him everywhere in here, so I didn't understand why we absolutely had to keep someone's old clothes.'

But she understood now.

She had realised that yesterday, when she brought down the box of clothes from the attic, to check if she needed to wash or air them out at all before Walter could use them. Suddenly, her father had become tangible to her again, triggered by his smell, which still lingered in his clothes.

She had pictured him then, in her mind; heard his voice, his laugh, how he would always hum. She had seen him at the campsite, in the kiosk, always busy with something or other. She had seen him in the living room, one leg propped up on the back of the sofa while he was waiting for dinner. And then she had watched him gradually wither away, becoming a thinner, paler and increasingly ragged version of himself, a man who would do anything to avoid death.

When it finally happened, eight months later than any of them expected, Samantha had been more relieved than sorry. She was glad that he was no longer in pain, but she had not felt any sadness or loss, not until last night.

She had hated him so intensely.

So deeply, so completely.

'But you...' She cleared her throat – it was suddenly hard to swallow. 'I imagine you probably didn't keep anything?'

Walter slowly took a sip from his coffee cup. 'No, we did. Some things – some butter knives, I think.'

'Butter knives?'

'Yeah...' He fixed his gaze on the tabletop. 'Dad had a thing for butter knives. He made them himself.'

Samantha nodded slowly. 'Did you ever talk to your mother about ... what you did?'

'Not really,' Walter replied. 'It took a few years before she came to visit me. She...'

His jaw muscles tightened. His gaze darkened, as if he had disappeared back in time, into his thoughts.

'Mark Twain once said that you should never tell the truth to those who don't deserve it.'

'What do you mean?' Samantha asked.

'Mum knew what had happened,' Walter said. 'That night, with Dad and you. But she never said anything to me. I asked, but she never said a thing,' he repeated. 'I clearly didn't deserve the truth.'

He clenched one of his fists and kept his gaze locked on the tabletop.

'Maybe she was trying to protect you,' Samantha suggested. 'Protect me?'

Walter raised his voice. 'There was nothing to protect me from. The fact that something had happened to you – I already knew that. I would have been able to handle the truth, what you told me later. But...'

He looked away, as if he couldn't bring himself to finish the sentence. Samantha wasn't sure if he was more angry or more disappointed. He took a while before trying again.

'Everything that happened with my father could have been avoided if only she had...' Again he stopped himself.

'Was that why you...?' Samantha didn't finish the question.

Walter's breathing had become laboured. 'She tried to stop me,' he replied. 'When I got home. She wouldn't let me borrow the car, wouldn't lend me the money. She said she would call the police if I didn't leave, if I didn't turn myself in and go straight back to Billwerder. I ... it...'

He looked down again. Shook his head.

'I didn't mean for it to happen,' he said. 'It wasn't something I had thought about or planned, like with Dad. It just happened.'

Samantha wanted to reach across the table, but didn't. She could see that he was processing what he had done.

To give him a little more time, she stood up and poured the rest of her cold coffee into the sink. Put the cup in the dishwasher. The inside rattled as she closed it.

She thought of the painful conversation they had had about Walter's father, when Walter had had access to a phone in his cell. The shock that had forced him to hang up, only to call back a little later. He had demanded she tell him everything.

Samantha had repeated that it wasn't, in fact, Walter's father who had raped her, but that he had heard her scream and entered the kiosk. He had torn the assailant off her and knocked him to the ground.

The truth must have been hard for Walter to take. The fact that his mother had never been willing to share the truth with him either. He had believed that his own father had raped the girl he was in love with. The rage had turned him into a killer. It had defined his life.

Communication, she thought. It was incredible how much dishonesty and concealment could destroy a life.

'Thank you,' she said now. 'For being so honest with me.'

Walter said nothing.

'Why do you think *I* deserve the truth?' she asked.

The question seemed to make him uncomfortable. 'I'm not sure. Maybe because you are straight forward and honest yourself?'

Samantha opened the fridge. She had pretty much told Walter everything there was to tell.

'Are you hungry?' she asked.

'A little.'

She took out a pack of sliced ham and rummaged around for the loaf of bread she had bought two days ago.

A noise outside made her straighten up and look towards the kitchen window. The sound of gravel crunching beneath tyres. A car parking up. The engine cutting out.

Samantha rushed to the window and opened the curtain a fraction.

'Shit,' she gasped. 'You have to hide. The police are here.'

43

The road sliced through a section of tall pine forest. Emma smiled to herself. It felt good to be behind the wheel again, on the road. She felt a strange relief, to have put Osen behind her, even if only for a few hours.

Fred Kasin's mother hadn't wanted to say much over the phone, but had agreed to meet her.

Emma drove into a town centre that must have been built at a time when brick buildings with hipped roofs were fashionable. She parked on the high street, Storgata, close to an off-licence. It was a nice morning in Elverum. The cafes had just opened. Emma found their agreed meeting place – a little spot that offered home-baked products and traditional jam, made the 'old-fashioned way'.

It was a pleasant venue. High ceilings and a cosy, warm atmosphere. Sissel Salvesen was already sitting at one of the tables when Emma entered. She was in her mid-fifties with a full face of make-up and smile lines. Her hair was cut short and pitch-black, with the exception of a few strands in her fringe, which were red. Hanging over the back of the chair was a handbag from a famous designer in the same shade of red.

When Emma approached, Salvesen was holding her phone with both hands, her arms extended far out in front of her, and peering at it through her glasses, which sat a little lower than the bridge of her nose. Squinting, she tapped out a message with her index finger. Her nails were unnaturally long and painted in the same, shiny red. She seemed irritated about something.

Emma stepped forward and introduced herself.

'Oh, hello.'

'Is this a bad time?' Emma asked, glancing down at the woman's phone.

'Oh, no, no,' Sissel Salvesen said with a laugh. 'It's just one of those mobile games that I've got hooked on. Driving me nuts.' She put the phone down. 'I'll have played them all soon.'

Emma smiled and sat down.

After the initial introductory small talk was over and they both had coffee and a raisin bun in front of them, Emma began:

'Thank you for agreeing to talk to me about the Kasin family, and your son. As I said on the phone, I don't have anything in particular to ask you about, I'm just trying to get a better understanding of what happened to the family. And you were of course a part of it for many years.'

Sissel Salvesen nodded slowly.

'I don't have children myself,' Emma continued, 'so I have no way of knowing what it's like to ... lose one.'

Salvesen lowered her gaze, put her hands around the coffee cup as if she needed it to hold on to it.

'I was glad when you called, actually,' she said. 'And sad. It's nice to get a chance to talk about Fred. It keeps the memories alive; keeps *him* alive, in a way. But it hurts, of course. It's the kind of thing you never quite get over. But I'm doing okay now.' Salvesen tried to smile. 'Things are okay.'

Emma waited a moment.

'Please, tell me about your son,' Emma encouraged her.

Sissel Salvesen smiled. 'Fred,' she sighed. 'He was born in Fredrikstad, but that's not why we called him Fred. He was named after my grandfather. Abel wanted him to be called Günther, after one of *his* ancestors, but my grandfather had died the month before he was born. So Fred it was.'

She went on to talk about his early childhood, growing up, going to school, and about the lack of provisions and understanding around his special needs. She didn't say what it was that Fred had had, but Emma got the impression that it was a case of congenital brain damage.

'It was a shock, of course. When he died. So ... sudden, and cruel. You spend so long just trying to understand the fact that it has happened, dealing with all the grief and pain that entails, and then you just have to ... try to carry on with your life. But a part of you is always there, in the past. In all the questions you can't help but ask yourself – if you could have done something differently. What if you had been there yourself that day, what if you had been at the lake with him? What if Fred had stayed home? What if his father and I had not been separated at the time?' She shook her head.

Emma shuffled in her seat slightly. 'Can you tell me a little bit about what did happen?'

Salvesen took a sip of her coffee. 'I'm not quite sure what you want to know, but...'

'Whatever you feel like sharing with me,' Emma suggested.

Salvesen let her index finger slide down the edge of the cup. 'The water that day – it was cold,' she began. 'I don't actually know why he went in, why he decided to go swimming – it wasn't the time of year for it. But he did. Fred was kind of like a small child, impulsive, and he wasn't a particularly strong swimmer.'

'Was he alone when it happened?'

'No, there were a few people there. His cousin and her boyfriend – Jarl Inge Ree.'

Emma looked at her. 'Samantha was there too?'

Salvesen nodded. 'They were the ones who called the police, her and Jarl Inge.'

'Were they in the lake too?'

'No. Or, well, Samantha was. And Jarl Inge eventually was, when he saw Fred going under. That's when he jumped in and tried to save him.'

'And where was Samantha, when it happened?'

'I don't know exactly where. But she tried to save him too, but ... it was too late.'

Salvesen looked down at the table again. Emma tore off a chunk of the raisin bun and chewed slowly.

'Did the police investigate the accident?'

'They went down there,' Salvesen sighed, 'but there wasn't much of an investigation, no. And Borvik never does any more than he has to.'

'Arvid Borvik?' Emma asked. 'Is he not a good policeman?'

'I don't know if you can call a man like that *the police*.'

Emma frowned. 'How do you mean?'

Salvesen was about to continue, but hesitated, composed herself.

'Borvik always takes the path of least resistance. I'm not the only one who thinks that.'

Emma pulled at the bun again, removing another piece, but waited a few moments before putting it in her mouth.

'Before the accident,' she said, swallowing the mouthful. 'What was the relationship between Samantha and Fred like?'

The question made Salvesen suddenly look up at her. 'Why do you ask?'

'I was just wondering, that's all.'

'Fred was ... a special boy with special needs. But no one was that interested in helping out, you know, with looking after him, other than those closest to him. And by that I actually mean just Abel and me.'

The sudden ferocity in Salvesen's voice made Emma drop the subject.

'And how has your contact with the Kasin family been, with everything that has happened?' she asked instead.

'As good as non-existent,' Salvesen said. 'Those people...' She shook her head. 'We had a fairly good relationship for a while. I felt that I was welcomed into the family, when I first met Abel. But then they more or less all went a bit crazy.'

'Crazy?' Emma asked. 'How so?'

Salvesen paused.

'I shouldn't say any more about that.'

Emma tried to wait it out, hoping her interviewee would break the silence, but Salvesen did not continue.

She took a sip of her coffee.

'You shouldn't dwell too much on the past,' she said finally. 'You've got to move forward somehow. Not get tied up in the past.'

'I understand that you don't want to go into too much detail...' Emma started.

'Correct. And, no offence, but I don't really know you.'

'Sure, I can understand that,' Emma said. 'And strictly speaking, it's none of my business either. I'm just very curious. It feels like an awful lot has happened to the Kasin family that nobody really wants to talk about.'

Salvesen looked straight at Emma. 'Have you tried talking to Abel about this?'

'I hadn't got that far yet.'

'Well, you can save yourself the trouble – he's not going to say anything. What about Karina – Samantha's mother?'

'Her I have tried calling, but she doesn't answer.'

Salvesen nodded slowly, as if the lack of response didn't surprise her.

'And Samantha, she...' But Emma held back. She didn't want to say anything about having caught Samantha in a lie about her relationship with Walter Kroos – it didn't feel relevant. Or was it, actually?

Sissel Salvesen put her empty coffee cup down and said: 'I'm afraid it'll be up to one of them to shed some light on the dark history of the Kasin family. I've already said far too much.'

44

Blix pulled his jacket a little higher up his neck. He should have worn a jumper. The temperature had dropped every day this past week. Outside the curved wall of the prison, the deciduous trees had turned yellow.

He used the hour in the open air to move his body, walking round and round the periphery. One lap was a hundred and eighty-three steps. He generally managed to get in about forty laps in an hour. The first week, he had done a series of calculations in his head as he walked. Multiplied the length of his stride with the number of steps, compared that to his normal walking speed and made an estimate of how long a lap was. No matter what these calculations came to, he had come to the conclusion that he must walk about 5.5 kilometres every day.

He always walked alone. Most did. He hadn't expected to make any friends during his sentence, but had, before coming to prison, believed that there was a strong community and unity among the inmates. There wasn't. No one trusted each other here.

One thing they all had in common, as they walked around during their hour outside, was that they always walked anti-clockwise. As a silent protest against the norm, they always headed out to the right side of the yard first and turned left to start the lap. Upstream.

He heard footsteps behind him and glanced over his shoulder.

Jarl Inge Ree limped towards him until he was right beside him.

'What happens when they catch him?' he asked, shoving his hands into his jacket pockets.

'Walter Kroos, you mean?'

'Yeah.'

Blix shrugged. 'It depends,' he replied.

'On what?'

'There are a few formalities to see to first,' Blix began. 'Then he should be transferred over to a German prison, but if he doesn't agree to the extradition, his case would have to be dealt with in the Norwegian court.'

'What, like, a trial? To send a murderer back to where he came from?'

The gravel crunched beneath their shoes.

'Not a trial like the one you're thinking of,' Blix said. 'But the prosecutors in Germany would send a formal request for extradition. And then a Norwegian judge has to go through it, to make sure that the order is legally binding and that the other conditions are fulfilled. Germany isn't ever a problem though. But we don't extradite people to countries where they risk facing the death penalty, for instance.'

Their strides were different lengths and were out of step. Ree shortened his stride so they were in sync.

'So that's it?' he asked. 'They just send him off straight away, when it's all done?'

'Only if he's not suspected of committing crimes in Norway,' he replied. 'The Norwegian police don't release anyone who they believe is involved in Norwegian criminal cases.'

'What do you mean?' Ree asked.

'He's been on the run in Norway, right?' Blix started. 'So he may have committed crimes here. Did something to get money, for example.'

A crow landed on the path in front of them. It hopped along the ground briefly before taking off again.

'And we still don't know what's happened to Rita Alvberg,' Blix added.

'So will they question him when they catch him?' Ree asked.

'Ah, well, I would, if I were leading the investigation,' Blix answered.

Ree spat on the grass. 'And then shit gets brought up again,' he said.

'It would be natural for them to ask him about Rita, in any case,' Blix said. 'They met each other last time Walter Kroos was in Norway. They may have come across each other again.'

'What about Samantha?' Ree asked. 'Will they be talking to her too?'

'They probably already have,' Blix replied.

They walked another half a lap in silence before Ree cut away and sat down on one of the picnic benches. Blix continued, now nearing lap twenty-three. He went three more rounds before Ree got up and started hitting a punching bag.

45

Samantha had just one thought on her mind: get rid of them as quick as possible; don't let them set foot inside. She hadn't noticed the police car in time to clear the breakfast table – the food, glasses and plates that would indicate that she had, or very recently had, a guest. Enough evidence that the question might arise. She couldn't take that chance.

She opened the door and went out onto the steps. Looked down at Arvid Borvik, who was standing with a man she had not seen before.

'Hello Samantha,' Borvik said. 'This is Nicolai Wibe from the Oslo police.'

He nodded. She met his gaze. There was a trace of distrust in his eyes.

'Wibe is assisting us in the investigation into Rita Alvberg's disappearance,' Borvik continued. 'And is here as a representative for an active police operation in the capital.'

Samantha swallowed.

'Can we come in?'

She kept a firm grip on the doorknob. 'I'm in a hurry, actually, I've got to head straight to work. What can I help you with?'

Borvik and Wibe exchanged a quick glance.

'You may have seen the news that Walter Kroos has escaped from a prison in Germany,' said Borvik. 'You remember Walter?' The policeman tucked his thumbs into his belt, his fingers flat on his hips. 'From the summer of 2004?' he added.

Samantha held his gaze. 'I remember Walter, yes.'

The other policeman took a step forward. 'Has Kroos contacted you at all?' he asked.

'No.'

'What about in the last few years – have you had any contact with him?'

She shook her head.

Borvik gave his sidekick a nod, as if to say that he would take over.

'Walter Kroos is in Norway,' Borvik began. 'We don't know where exactly, or what his plans are, but we've come here to ... warn you.'

'Warn me?'

'Yes, in case...' Borvik didn't seem to know how to finish the sentence.

'Then consider me warned,' she said. 'Was that all? I've got a really busy day ahead...'

'Just a couple more questions,' Borvik said. 'When did you last see Rita Alvberg?'

A car drove past behind them, heading out of the village. Samantha followed it with her eyes as she thought back.

'Sometime last autumn I think, last year,' she said. 'I bumped into her at the pub. She was home for a few days, what with her mother being ill.'

Borvik nodded and pulled his thumbs out from his belt. 'We're continuing the search for her today.'

'Well, good luck, I hope you find her.'

'You wouldn't know about anywhere she may have gone, or liked to go – or if there's anyone she may have fallen out with, do you?'

Samantha snorted. 'It's been years since Rita and I were close enough to know of each other's daily whereabouts.'

'So the answer would be no?' the other policeman interjected.

'I have no idea if she was in any kind of trouble, no. When we were young, she spent a lot of time down at the jetty, but I understand that you've already looked there.'

'We have,' Borvik said. 'You ... haven't been out looking for her yourself?'

'Believe it or not,' Samantha said, 'the police aren't the only ones with jobs to do.'

'You've been renovating, I noticed.'

'Well observed, Arvid. You really don't miss a thing, do you?'

The policeman didn't rise to the sarcasm.

'Right then,' he said instead. 'We won't keep you any longer. You'll let us know if you see or hear from Walter Kroos?'

'You'll be the first person I call.'

'Thanks, we'll be seeing you.'

Samantha pulled the door open and closed it behind her. Leant against it and squeezed her eyes shut. Waited until she heard them get in the car and drive off before she allowed herself to open them again.

Walter was waiting for her in the hallway leading to the bedrooms.

'How did it go?'

'Fine,' she replied brusquely. 'Nothing to worry about.'

'What did they want?'

'Just asking about Rita,' she sighed. 'If she had any enemies or what have you.' She rolled her eyes.

Walter remained standing on the same spot. 'Is it safe to come out?' he asked.

'No more or less than it was ten minutes ago,' she said.

Walter took a few steps closer. All of the colour seemed to have drained from his face.

It's time to tell him the rest, Samantha thought.

And she knew exactly where to start: Arvid Borvik.

46

Samantha lay on the cold, wet floor. She couldn't move. She heard voices. Walter's father shouting something. A mixture of German and English. Uncle Abel's voice too, but lower. His lawyer voice.

Suddenly, Rita was there too.

She squatted down and grabbed one of Samantha's hands. Helped her up, into her father's office. Rita looked around and grabbed a blanket, which Samantha clung on to, even though she wasn't cold. She couldn't, wouldn't, sit down. It hurt too much.

She stared at the window. The reflection from the ceiling light meant she couldn't see anything but the walls of her father's office and Rita's back.

'Do not shower or wash yourself,' Rita said, 'Don't go to the toilet either, if you can help it.'

Samantha didn't understand what she meant, but she was glad her friend was there. Glad to hear a kind, familiar voice. Through a gap in the door, they could hear dark, bass tones. Men, discussing something. She couldn't hear what they were talking about.

After a while, Samantha's father came to them in his office.

'You need to go now,' He was talking to Rita. 'And do not say a word about this to anyone,' he added. 'We will sort this out within the family.'

Rita nodded hesitantly and pushed herself away from the table.

'I'll come see you tomorrow,' she told Samantha. 'Call me anytime, if you need anything – anything at all.'

Samantha couldn't bring herself to speak. Couldn't do anything but take one breath at a time. She wanted her mother. Hadn't they called her?

'Come,' her father said.

He hadn't said a single word to her until now. Hadn't asked what had happened, or if she was okay.

Samantha bristled – she didn't want to go out there again. Fred could still be out there. But she couldn't stay in the office forever.

Her father led her out the back of the kiosk. Fortunately, she saw nothing of Fred. At that same moment, a car parked up nearby.

Samantha recognised it. It belonged to the village policeman, Arvid Borvik – a good friend of her father.

She was relieved to see him there.

That meant Fred would be taken care of. Locked away.

Uncle Abel spoke to the policeman first. They shook hands. Abel put a hand on his shoulder and directed him to a spot out of earshot. They stood there for a few minutes, and Samantha couldn't hear what they were talking about. She could only see them out of the corner of her eye.

Her father walked over to them. He also shook Borvik's hand. After a brief conversation, all three approached her.

'Where's Mum?' Samantha asked.

'Samantha, dear,' Uncle Abel began. His voice one of pity. 'We know you've been through something dreadful this evening. That should never have happened, we know that. I am terribly sorry. I don't know what happened or what ... came over him.'

Samantha couldn't look directly at him as he spoke. But there was something about his voice that scared her.

'Fred, he can ... He sometimes just does things and doesn't realise the consequences. He doesn't know the difference between right and wrong. He doesn't have the same inhibitions we normal people have. Today, unfortunately, you were in the firing line.'

A stabbing pain shot up from her abdomen and settled in her stomach.

'She barely had any clothes on,' her father said in a low voice, mostly addressing Borvik. 'Basically just a skirt and bra.'

Samantha glared at him. Her gaze then moved over to Uncle Abel, then to Borvik. The policeman just stared back, no trace of warmth in his eyes. Was he not here to arrest Fred? Shouldn't she be taken to the hospital? Shouldn't someone be taking some samples from her?

'It is best for the ... family,' Uncle Abel said, still addressing her, 'if we kept this ... terrible event, this accident, in the family.'

Samantha couldn't hold back the sobs.

Accident.

'And as Borvik here has already said – it won't do any good if we report this,' Abel went on. 'We all know what happened, and I promise you I will do something about it. But Fred isn't criminally sane. He's just a big kid. There's simply no point in making this a police matter. All it'll do is cause a whole lot of fuss, and it'll only develop into a fight where there'll be no winners, only one big loser.' He waited a little, before he finished: 'Think of the family.'

Samantha hadn't processed or understood everything they had said, but it sounded like they weren't going to do anything about it.

Uncle Abel turned to Samantha's father. 'I'll have a word with the German tomorrow, make sure he doesn't say anything.'

'Tell him he can get a full refund for the entire stay,' her father suggested. 'If they leave immediately.'

Samantha closed her eyes and thought about Walter. She'd never see him again. But now, she didn't want to either. Now, she wasn't sure how she was going to manage anything at all.

✳

They were sitting at the kitchen table again. Samantha's hands were clasped around a cup of tea. Walter's glass of water was empty.

The body's memory of what happened was indelible. She could still summon every single emotion she felt that night. Anger, despair, pain. The feeling of being let down by those closest to you. Hatred – toward Fred. Toward Borvik, when she realised that he wasn't going to do his job.

In her letters and phone calls, she had told Walter what had happened when his father intervened, but never what happened afterwards.

'Who called the police?' Walter asked.

'Rita.'

Samantha took another sip. Her tea had gone cold.

'We need to figure out what to do about that journalist,' she said. 'She knows that I lied about knowing you, and she's been running around asking lots of questions about Fred and Jarl Inge.'

'That's not good,' Walter said.

'No. And that's not our only problem.' She sighed deeply. 'There is something else I need to tell you.'

47

There was more to get out of Markus Hadeland, Emma thought as she turned off the road and onto the campsite. The police and Red Cross were still stationed around the outdoor stage. The divers' car was also there, but their efforts didn't seem to have yielded any results.

She parked up in front of the cabin. Markus Hadeland had been happy to see her in the pub the night before, but as soon as she mentioned Fred, he'd clammed up like an oyster. And then avoided her completely.

She sent him a message, asking if it'd be possible for them to meet sometime the same day.

I'm helping look for Rita, he answered quickly.

Emma decided to push him a little:

I just had an interesting chat with Fred's mother. Looks like all of the village secrets are about to come to the surface.

It was a claim with somewhat dubious veracity, but it wasn't far from the truth – they certainly could be. Emma added that they could perhaps meet somewhere where there weren't so many prying eyes and ears. By the time Markus answered, Emma had had time to eat a light lunch and open an email from a reader who commented on how sexy her byline photo was.

Can you come to my house tonight at seven? Come on foot.

'Huh,' Emma said out loud.

Perhaps Markus didn't want anyone to see that she was there? That in itself was strange. Maybe a little disturbing too. Emma nonetheless confirmed that she would be happy to.

Tonight at seven o'clock.

Meaning that she would have to stay an extra night.

She searched for Samantha Kasin's number and called it. She didn't pick up. Emma could see, however, that her car was parked next to the reception building. Emma threw on her jacket and put on her shoes.

It was a cool autumn day, but no wind to speak of.

Samantha looked up from behind the counter as Emma entered. The light from the computer screen gave her face a white glow.

'Hey,' Emma said, smiling.

She hadn't seen Samantha in glasses before. They suited her. Emma hadn't so much as had the thought by the time Samantha removed them. She laid them on the counter, beside the computer mouse.

'What can I do for you today?' she asked. The wrinkles on her forehead seemed deeper.

'I was wondering if I could stay here a little longer?' Emma asked. 'One more night, for the time being, I think.'

'I'll just have to check,' Samantha said. 'As fully booked as we are at the moment.' She winked at her.

Emma laughed.

'Stay as long as you want,' Samantha told her 'I'm just glad there's someone here.'

'Should I pay by the night or ... how do you want to do this?'

'We can just settle up when you're ready to go,' Samantha said. 'Not a problem.'

'Brilliant.'

Emma turned to leave, but stopped, changing her mind.

'Samantha, I ... spoke to Sissel Salvesen earlier today.'

Samantha looked up at her.

'We talked about her son. Your cousin Fred.'

Samantha said nothing, just stared.

'He drowned in Osensjøen in 2007. You were there. You and Jarl Inge.'

Still, silence from Samantha.

'But the incident wasn't investigated, if I understood her correctly?'

Samantha sighed. 'Will you be writing about that too?'

'Not necessarily.'

'I thought you were here to write about Walter?'

'I am. Or am trying to, at least. But something happened the summer Walter Kroos was here that I'm trying to understand the extent of, and whether that has anything to do with why he came back to Norway.'

Again, Samantha remained silent.

'I know what happened to you that summer.'

The muscles in Samantha's face tightened.

'It is ... alleged here in the village that it was Walter's father who raped you. But there are other things that indicate that this was not the case.'

'Things,' Samantha said disdainfully. 'What *things*?'

Emma didn't like having to remind Samantha of such a terrible time in her life. That was the absolute worst part of this job, having to dig into people's private lives, things she really had nothing to do with.

'I can't disclose my sources,' she said.

Samantha looked resigned as she shook her head. Stared into Emma's face with fury in her eyes. But then, it was as if her gaze softened.

'Are you wearing good shoes?' she asked.

'Uh...'

'Can we go for a walk? I've been inside all day and I could do with some fresh air.'

'Uh, yes. Yes we can.'

Samantha stood up and pulled a shell jacket from the back of her chair. She bent over the computer and clicked a few times until the screen light disappeared. With another swift movement, she grabbed the keys lying on the table.

Emma went out first.

'It's always easier to talk when you're walking,' Samantha said with a smile. 'Or that's certainly been my experience.'

Emma didn't quite know how to interpret Samantha's surprising change of mood.

They moved away from the reception building, towards the cabins.

'Where do you fancy walking?' Emma asked.

'The forest is always a good starting point,' Samantha stated.

'Aren't they looking for Rita Alvberg in there?'

'Yeah, but ... we won't go where *they* are looking.'

'Okay ... show the way.'

They hadn't gone more than a few metres when Samantha said: 'I ... owe you an apology. When you first arrived in the village, I told you that I didn't know who Walter Kroos was. That ... was a lie. Of course I know who Walter is. And I'm sure you've known for a while that I did, in fact, know.'

Emma replied with an affirmative nod.

'The question came as a surprise to me. And ... at that moment, I didn't really want to get into how exactly I knew him.'

She shook her head slightly, seemed to be searching for the right words.

'The summer of 2004,' she continued. 'That's when he was here. We got on well, Walter and I. Spent a fair amount of time together. I don't know where it would've taken us. Probably nowhere but ... it didn't matter, everything was destroyed that night I was ... raped inside the kiosk.'

She looked at Emma.

'It was Fred, who raped me.'

Samantha lifted her shoulders up high and exhaled hard.

'Your cousin,' Emma said, even though she actually knew the answer.

Samantha nodded. 'But because Fred was who he was, it was hushed up by the family. Apparently the easiest way to deal with it,' she said. 'Fred didn't have barriers, you see, like ordinary people. He didn't understand right from wrong. He just took what he wanted, whether it was chocolate from the kiosk or ... something else, The family was just trying to protect him, so I believe, by not getting Borvik to take it any further.'

'Borvik?' Emma asked.

'Yes, Borvik,' Samantha repeated contemptuously. 'He was there, that night. Anyway, it wasn't *my* decision not to punish Fred. But I didn't have much say in it at all. In retrospect, maybe it was the right thing to do. Fred probably would never have been convicted anyway, and it would have just led to a lot of gossip in a small place like this. And elsewhere, I imagine, given ... I was quite well known at the time.'

She pointed to a path that led into the forest.

'But precisely because this happened in such a small place, it didn't take long before *everyone* knew that something had happened. Trygve Klepp had seen Walter's father at the kiosk, so a rumour quickly spread that he was the one who raped me. It ... was an easier story to sell, as cynical as that may seem. Walter and his family left Osen the next day, and then that was it, they were gone. It was easier to blame someone who was no longer there and couldn't retaliate.'

'I understand,' Emma said, mostly just to say something.

The undergrowth on either side of the path had been trampled by the search teams passing through the area. Samantha continued to talk about how the village embraced her to an even greater extent than before, as the trauma of the rape and everything afterwards put an end to her singing career. She got away with a lot, because of who she was. This led her to push the boundaries of what was actually acceptable. She drank a lot, tried all kinds of drugs.

'Nobody stopped me,' she said. 'No one dared speak out about me either.'

'Not even your parents?' Emma asked.

'My parents,' Samantha said, scornfully. 'I guess they pretended not to notice. Or quite literally looked the other way. They didn't know how to deal with any of what happened, I think. There are no easy options though,' she said, as if to excuse them. 'When something like that happens, especially within a family. And my mother wasn't well anyway, and then my father got sick not long after, and that was enough to contend with.'

Without Emma noticing, they seemed to have found themselves in the deepest, thickest part of the forest. Samantha walked ahead of her on the narrow path. It widened in some places, and she would wait, so that Emma could walk beside her. In between, Samantha would point out certain plants and tell her what they were called, and where it was possible to find cloudberries and other edible plants.

As she spoke, Emma would occasionally hear the sound of twigs snapping, not too far away. The search parties, Emma thought. Had to be them. Or an animal.

'Do many people know what really happened?' Emma asked.

Samantha shook her head. 'Just a few. Rita, for instance. She was there that night and helped me.'

'What about Markus?'

Samantha let out a short laugh. 'We were married for a few years,' she replied. 'So I had to tell him. Jarl Inge knows too, of course. We were on and off for years.'

Emma had a sudden thought, and discreetly patted her jacket pocket to check that her phone was there. It wasn't. As a rule, her phone was the first and last thing she checked she had with her whenever she went out. But she'd only planned on nipping to reception. She hadn't thought about her phone after that.

'I imagine it wasn't easy being around your cousin or uncle after that?' Emma asked.

'No,' Samantha said. 'But we didn't have that much to do with them anyway. We would usually see them once or twice a year, but after that summer, it was a long time before they came back. Well, actually, Uncle Abel would often come by if there was something or other he had to help Dad with – legal stuff to do with the running of the campsite – but if I knew he was coming, I'd always just go to see Rita or one of my other friends. I wanted nothing to do with him.'

'But then Fred was here, in the summer of 2007,' Emma noted. 'Three years later. The year he—'

'Correct,' Samantha interrupted. 'He was.' She exhaled hard again. 'That was ... unfortunate.'

'What do you mean?'

Samantha looked as if she were trying to figure out how to word the next part.

'I knew they were coming, so I went to stay with Jarl Inge. We were together at the time. *Again*,' she quickly added, with a small smile. 'And we went down to the jetty, as we always did.'

The path split in two, on either side of a small cluster of trees. Samantha took to the right, Emma the left. When they met again on the other side, Samantha continued:

'I've always been a swimmer. Not when it's *too* cold, like everyone seems to be doing these days, but I'll be in that lake as soon as early spring arrives, and usually won't stop until well into the autumn. I'm used to it. I like it.'

She pushed away a branch sticking out over the path, and held it aside until Emma had also passed.

'And since we were down by the lake, and it was quite warm and the weather was nice, I took my clothes off and jumped in. And by that I mean *all* my clothes. It was just me and Jarl Inge. No one nearby. Or so we thought.'

They began to walk up a small hill. Samantha was breathing heavily.

'What I didn't know,' she said, 'was that, before they came, Uncle Abel had instructed Fred to apologise to me. But since I wasn't there, he sent Fred out to find me. Eventually Fred came down to the jetty. He had been there with us a few times before, so he knew where it was and knew I often spent time there.'

She shook her head. 'So, I'm sure you can imagine, there I was, in the water, completely naked, and then suddenly there's Fred, standing on the jetty. It wouldn't have exactly been appropriate to get out with him there.'

Emma nodded.

'But then he just stood there and said he wanted to talk to me. I obviously wasn't interested in that, but he refused to turn around and go back. He had been told in no uncertain terms that he had to talk to me, and he seemed laser-focused on doing it. Once he got his head around something, he was unstoppable. But I was still in the water, and it was getting cold. Then, before I knew it, he'd taken a step off the edge of the jetty, and was in the water. And then he swam – right for me.'

Emma could see it all unfolding in her head.

'And I ... I just swam out even further, because I didn't want him anywhere near me, didn't want him to reach me. I had no clothes on. God knows what he would do if he saw me naked. But then he started struggling. He was thrashing about a lot, splashing and splashing, and his breathing was all weird and heavy. I didn't understand what was going on until I heard Jarl Inge shout something from the shore, waving his arms wildly. By then I was quite far away. Which is when Jarl Inge jumped in too. Fully dressed.'

Samantha had to take a break.

'But Fred had already drowned,' she continued. 'After a while, when I realised that it was serious, I swam closer. Jarl Inge dived and dived, but kept coming up back up without Fred. The water is, as you may have seen, quite murky. So, in the end ... we had to give up.'

Samantha's cheeks were glowing hot.

'We called the police, of course, and they arrived after twenty minutes or so. In the meantime, I had swum ashore and put my clothes back on. Jarl Inge, poor thing, was sitting there, soaking wet. They didn't find Fred until the next day. He had floated up to the surface, a long way from where he had disappeared.'

They came to an area dense with trees. Moss covered the forest floor.

'This is a nice area to forage for mushrooms, by the way,' Samantha told her. 'Lots of chanterelles.'

Emma followed Samantha's index finger with her eyes, but wasn't really that interested in mushrooms. She thought of Abel Kasin, who had made his own son jump to his death. Thought of the guilt that must plague him to this day. She could understand why Sissel Salvesen said he would never speak to Emma about it.

She followed Samantha, and was thinking so carefully through all she had said, she forgot to pay attention to where she was putting her feet. She stepped on a slippery tree root, and the ligaments and muscles of her right leg gave way. Emma yelled as a sharp pain shot through her ankle. She was close to falling to her knees, but pushed up on the other leg and managed to regain her balance. The pain made her skin prickle all the way up to her neck.

'You okay?' Samantha asked.

Emma could already feel her ankle swelling inside her shoe.

'Bloody hell,' she said, gritting her teeth. 'That hurt.'

She leant forward and held her breath as the first waves of pain washed over her. Slowly pushed herself up.

'All good,' she said, as she gingerly tried to put her foot down on the ground. A new wave of pain hit her. 'All good,' she repeated, mostly to convince herself.

Emma was glad she wasn't alone. The criss-crossing paths had been disorienting, and she wasn't sure if she'd have been able to find her way out by herself. Not without her phone.

They waited for a few minutes while the pain subsided somewhat. Samantha stood beside her, a hand on Emma's shoulder.

'It'll be further if we turn back,' she said. 'This way,' she pointed to the path ahead of them, 'and we'll be back home in half an hour. Is that alright? Can you walk that far?'

'I'll *have* to walk that far,' Emma said, trying to smile.

Slowly, step by step, they continued. It hurt terribly, but she took small steps and was careful to put as little weight as possible on her right foot. Samantha kept turning around and checking that everything was okay.

Emma needed to think about something other than the pain.

'But your uncle sent Fred out *alone* to look for you?' she said.

Samantha nodded and rolled her eyes.

'He didn't think that might be rather frightening for you? Didn't think that maybe Fred should have an adult with him?'

'My uncle might be a good lawyer,' Samantha said. 'But he doesn't know people. And he later said that "Fred had improved" ... whatever that meant.'

They walked a little further. Emma limping.

'Why are you telling me all this?' she asked.

A few moments passed before Samantha answered.

'So you know what happened,' she said. 'You're a journalist. You talk to people. People who actually know absolutely nothing about anything and just go off village rumours. And soon enough, everything's wrong.'

Emma was dragging her foot behind her now.

'I'm trying to think of a reason why Walter would break out of prison then,' Emma said. 'And come to Norway. These rumours about his father surely couldn't have reached him all the way in Germany. And even if they had, that's barely a strong enough motive to break out.'

Samantha shrugged. 'He had to go somewhere,' she stated. 'Maybe he just really liked Norway.'

They walked a little further.

'It can't have been easy for you to talk about this,' Emma said.

Samantha stopped and turned to her. 'None of this is *easy*,' she said. 'Moving forward when the scars run so deep. Staying here, the stigma. But I do the best I can.'

'I think you're incredible,' Emma said. 'Taking over the campsite. Renovating it. And then all this, with Walter Kroos escaping, your past being dug up again, thanks to the likes of me.'

Samantha smiled again. 'You have a job to do. But I'm sure you understand that I don't want you to write anything about this.'

'Of course.'

It had started to get cold when they eventually came out onto a dirt road. It made walking a little easier. Emma really had no idea where they were.

They rounded a bend. On the road ahead of them, a man stepped out from the edge of the forest. He stood there and watched them. She had a feeling she had seen him before.

48

Sundays were always long. After lunch, Blix became restless, as he was when there were too many unsolved matters in an ongoing investigation. He had had the same feeling during his first days in prison. The thought of something happening outside the walls, beyond his control, had made every day unsettled.

He tried to read a little, but couldn't concentrate. Instead, he slid his feet into his sandals and headed out into the corridor. The sounds of the TV blared from the common room. A football game.

The door to cell six was ajar. Blix walked over to it. There was a cardboard box in the middle of the floor. Jarl Inge Ree had already put a few things inside.

'Started packing?' Blix commented.

Ree looked up from the bed. 'Most of it'll fit in there,' he replied and nodded towards the box. 'The clothes'll go in the bin.'

Blix looked towards the drawer where the phone was hidden.

'Give them to Grubben,' he said. 'You're about the same size.'

Ree shrugged.

Blix leant his shoulder against the doorframe. 'How many times have you been to prison?'

'Five.'

'What's the longest time you've served?'

'This time. It'll be five hundred and seventeen days tomorrow.'

Blix hadn't thought about his own sentence in terms of days. In any case, it was far too early to start counting down.

'Any news?' Ree asked.

Blix shook his head. 'I tried to call Emma Ramm half an hour ago. She didn't answer, but will probably call back.'

The pictures that had been on Ree's cell wall had been taken down. They were now on the desk.

'Can I look?' Blix asked.

He didn't wait for an answer, just walked up to the desk. Picked up one of the pictures.

'Is this you?' he asked, turning it so Ree could see.

'Me and Samantha,' Ree confirmed, getting up from the bed. 'At the campsite.'

Blix picked up another photo. 'Who's that, standing at the back, in the brown trousers?'

Ree squinted at the picture. 'Fred,' he answered. 'Samantha's cousin.'

Blix studied the picture more closely. 'Was there something wrong with him?'

'I guess he had a screw or two loose, yeah.'

'Had, you say?'

'Yes, he's dead now.'

Blix waited a moment but had to send Jarl Inge a questioning look to get him to elaborate.

'He drowned in Osensjøen,' Ree continued. 'I don't know what happened, really. Probably got a cramp or something.'

Ree stepped forward and started to tidy up the other photos.

'How did Samantha take it?'

'Well, they're a small family,' Ree answered. 'And she has no siblings, and Fred was her only cousin.'

He took the last picture out of Blix's hands and put it in an envelope with the others.

'I think she tries to think as little about the past as possible,' he continued, dropping the envelope into the moving box. 'Same as me. It is what it is. You just have to make the best out of life.'

'The past always catches up with you in the end,' Blix said in an attempt to lead the conversation to something.

Ree didn't answer, just stared at him before turning and taking a stack of comic books off the shelf.

'Do you want them?' he asked. 'I'm trying to take as little as possible with me when I leave this place.'

'I'm good, thanks,' Blix said.

'I guess there's no point in giving them to Grubben.'

Blix smiled. 'Don't say that.'

49

The man stood right in the middle of the path ahead, as if he had no intention of letting them pass. Samantha took a couple of steps forward but Emma was holding her back; she needed someone to lean on.

It was Lars Einar Løvdal. He had a basket of mushrooms in one hand. The other he used to adjust his glasses, then his cap.

'Hi,' Samantha said. 'You're here.'

It was rarely fruitful to talk to Løvdal about anything other than fertiliser, the weather or mushrooms. He was one of Osen's eccentrics – a former farmer and widower who rarely, if ever, smiled or said anything nice. If you asked him about mushrooms, however, you'd get a whole thesis.

'So are you,' he said bluntly, and looked over at Emma.

Samantha introduced them.

'Lars Einar lives in the house next to Harriet Alvberg's. Rita's mother.'

'I think we might have met the other night,' Emma said. 'Nice to see you again.'

'What happened to you?' His tone almost seemed to suggest he thought Emma's injury was blameworthy. But that was just how he spoke to people.

Emma took a wobbly step to the side and explained how the injury had occurred.

'But it's fine,' she added. 'It's not *that* far back. I think. I hope.'

She tried to smile, but the humour just bounced off of Løvdal.

'You're not out looking for your neighbour then?' Samantha commented, nodding towards the basket of mushrooms.

Løvdal shook his head and said: 'There's no point.'

'What do you mean?'

'Rita's not in here,' he said, with a jerk of his head at the forest.

'What makes you think that?' Emma asked.

He snorted. 'Common sense. They've been using dogs and heat-seeking devices, and God knows what else, in here for two days now. She's not here.'

Emma hobbled a step closer. 'So what do you think happened?'

Løvdal took off his cap and quickly scratched his almost entirely bald head. The movement made him look down his nose at her.

'Ach, I wouldn't want to speculate,' he said and slapped the cap back on his head. 'Not out loud anyway. We've all done it in our heads, I'm sure.'

'You think she's dead.'

'Don't you? *Both of you?*'

Samantha felt the knot in her stomach tighten.

'But you don't think she's here in the forest, then?' Emma asked.

'I just said that,' he said, irritated. 'But she's not the type of person to hang herself and dangle from a ceiling lamp somewhere either. So...'

Emma examined Løvdal with a curious gaze.

'We should probably be getting back,' Samantha said. 'Get some ice on your ankle.'

'Sure...'

'Good luck with the foraging,' Samantha said.

'It's a miserable year for mushrooms,' Løvdal scoffed.

Samantha and Emma moved on.

When Løvdal was out of sight, Samantha said: 'He's always been weird. He's lived alone now for about fifteen years, I think. I don't think people should be alone for that long. It makes you ... strange. You get used to doing whatever *you* want. You've got no one around to correct you.'

They were finally out of the forest.

'You don't have any ice in your cabin, do you?'

'I don't think so,' Emma said.

'Okay, well, you go in, I'll be back in a few minutes.'

Emma hobbled over to the cabin.

Samantha checked her phone and hurried to the kiosk. Almost half-one already. It had been an unproductive day. Or, actually, she thought, maybe it hadn't.

She let herself into the kiosk, walked through the cold room and into the back room. She took a bag of ice cubes from the freezer section of a fridge. She also brought a pack of freezer bags and a clean tea towel from the kitchen. She was soon back outside again.

In the cabin, Emma had slumped onto the sofa with her foot raised on a chair. She had also removed her sock – her ankle was red and swollen.

'That doesn't look good,' Samantha said, squatting down in front of her.

'It's not that bad,' Emma said, forcing a stiff smile.

Samantha squeezed some ice cubes into one of the freezer bags and tied it shut. Wrapped it in the tea towel. Emma gasped in pain as Samantha placed the ice pack directly onto her ankle.

'I didn't have any other compresses,' she said. 'This is the best I've got. Leave it on for twenty minutes. Any longer than that and you could get frostbite. Take at least a ten-minute break before applying the ice again, and continue doing that three to four more times throughout the day. Preferably tomorrow too.'

Emma looked up at her. 'Thank you.'

'It's the least I could do. After all, I was the one who dragged you out into the forest.' She laughed. 'Right then. I should be getting back. Rest up.'

'Thanks. Before you go, you wouldn't mind doing me one quick favour?'

'Of course.'

'Could you just hand me my laptop and phone?'

She pointed to the living-room table, where Samantha spotted both devices.

'At least then I can do something productive while I sit here like an old cripple.'

✳

Samantha took the fastest route home – diagonally across the field of the oldest caravans and onto the road. Approaching the house, she couldn't see any sign of Walter through the windows, but he quickly appeared from the bedroom once she was inside.

'Did something happen?' he asked.

Samantha exhaled hard, relieved to be home. 'The journalist popped up,' she replied. 'I ended up having a long talk with her.'

She told him all about their walk.

'I don't think she'll be a problem anymore,' she concluded.

Walter didn't seem convinced.

'And what did you get up to while I was out?'

Walter explained how he had mostly been lying in the bedroom staring up at the ceiling. And that he had been thinking.

'What were you thinking about?'

'You and ... everything.'

'What do you mean?'

'How painful and difficult it must have been for you, all these years. And how similar we really are, you and me.'

She took a few steps closer. Felt a deep sense of gratitude that he was here, with her.

Walter was right.

They *were* the same.

Equally lost, equally enraged.

She took his left hand and held it, squeezed it. He had rough fingers. The palm was scratched and scarred.

She let her index finger follow the lifeline on his hand.

'Hm,' she said.

'What is it?'

'Have you ever had your palms read?' she asked.

Which made him laugh. 'No.'

'You have an M in the palm of your hand.'

'An M?'

'Look.'

With her index finger, she traced over his hand, showing him how the three different grooves in his palm formed a distinct M. She did not look up at him as she explained.

'Those who have an M in the palm of their hand,' she said, 'so the head, heart, and life lines form an M' – she redrew the letter – 'they're very special. They have unique talents, and they are very intuitive. You ... are good at reading people.'

She looked up at him.

'That doesn't exactly sound like me,' he said.

It was suddenly as if sixteen-year-old Walter was standing in front of her again. The boy whose family had never told him to believe in himself. Never told him that he was special. It hurt to think about it.

She made the same motion over his palm a third time.

'You're creative too,' she said. 'You ... come up with solutions for problems.'

'Okay, well *that* definitely doesn't sound like me.'

They both laughed.

Her phone vibrated in her back pocket. She pulled it out.

'Speak of the devil,' she muttered, holding up the phone for Walter.

'Who is it?' he asked.

'Jarl Inge.'

50

Blix went back to the guardhouse with the phone. Emma had a special ability to convey information in a short and concise manner. Probably something she got from working in journalism, which was essentially about getting as much information as possible into the smallest word count.

Yet, he hadn't got answers to all his questions. If he had spoken to Samantha Kasin, he would have asked more. There was something striking about the fact that the man who had raped her then drowned in front of her eyes three years later. It was coincidences like this that awoke what could be called a 'gut feeling'. They were what he had been looking for. Irregularities. Things that didn't seem entirely rational.

He held the phone out to Jakobsen. 'Now I need to call Gard Fosse,' he said.

Jakobsen made it look like it was some huge sacrifice to connect the line.

'I was just heading out,' Fosse said when he finally picked up on the other end.

Blix took the phone into the nearest cubicle. 'Any updates?' he asked. 'About Rita Alvberg or Walter Kroos?'

'The short answer is no', Fosse said.

Blix refrained from asking for the long answer.

'It wasn't Walter Kroos's father who raped Samantha in 2004,' Blix began. 'I was misinformed. It was her cousin.'

'So why did Jarl Inge Ree tell you that it was the father?'

'The family wanted to cover it up and probably found no reason to correct the rumours,' Blix said. 'But there's something else, potentially related, I think you should check.'

'And what's that?'

'The rapist drowned three years later, while swimming with Samantha Kasin.'

There was a brief moment of silence before Fosse asked for the cousin's name.

'Where do you think this will lead us?' he asked next.

'I don't know yet,' Blix replied. 'But according to Emma—'

'You got this from Emma Ramm?' Fosse interrupted.

'Yes, but she got it directly from Samantha Kasin,' Blix replied. 'According to her, Jarl Inge Ree was there when Fred Kasin drowned. But he didn't mention that when he told me that her cousin had died.'

'I understand,' Fosse replied. 'But what does this have to do with Walter Kroos? He was back home in Germany by then.'

'I just want you to look into it,' Blix said. 'It wasn't that long ago – there should be an electronic copy of the case file.'

'Fine,' Fosse replied. 'I'll see what I can do.'

'If anything does come up, I'll need to hear back about it by tomorrow morning,' Blix continued. 'Ree will be released at eleven.'

'I know,' Fosse replied without offering any further assurance.

Blix ended the call, went back to the guardhouse and handed over the phone.

'Just one thing,' Jakobsen said, putting the phone back in its place. 'I don't know what you're up to or what's going on, but I understand enough that it's something to do with Jarl Inge Ree.'

Blix didn't respond.

'Whatever it is, stay away from him until lock-up tonight. Not everyone deals with the thought of being released that well. Ree got into a fight with Grubben in the kitchen an hour ago. You and Ree have been at each other's throats before, and I don't want any trouble.'

'Understood,' Blix replied with a nod.

Jakobsen leant back in his chair and swivelled it round to face the TV screen. Blix turned and walked along the corridor to cell six.

Jarl Inge Ree had not made any progress with his packing. He was lying on the bed staring at the TV. Some day-time quiz programme.

'They've searched for Rita in the water, along the river and throughout the forest,' Blix said. 'To no avail.'

'What does that mean?' Ree asked, sitting up.

'If I were the investigator, I would seriously start to consider whether she had been the victim of some crime,' Blix replied. 'But she could simply have been overlooked, especially if she *is* in the water. Freshwater is always difficult. Mud and poor visibility.'

'What about Walter Kroos?'

'Nothing.'

Blix sat down at the desk. He had intended to confront Ree with the information that it was not Walter's father who had raped Samantha, but chose not to. Instead, he wanted to test Ree in a different way.

'What are the currents like, in the water up there?' he asked.

Ree didn't seem to understand what he meant.

'I was just thinking about when Samantha's cousin drowned,' Blix continued. 'Was he found far away from where he disappeared?'

Ree blinked a few times, rapidly.

'I don't know where exactly they found him, but there's probably some sort of current, out toward the river.'

'Do you know where he went under?' Blix asked.

'Not far from the jetty.'

'Was that where you used to swim?'

'Yes.'

'Had he swum out far?'

Ree suddenly seemed irritated. He grabbed the remote control and changed the channel.

'Far enough,' he replied, staring at the TV.

'So you weren't there yourself?' Blix asked.

Ree changed the TV channel again. 'No one could have helped him anyway.'

Blix considered pressing him further, but without any documentation from the police case file, he had nothing but Emma's information to go off.

'Have you asked Grubben about the clothes?' he asked instead.

It didn't seem like Ree had caught the question. Blix asked again. Suddenly, Ree threw the remote control to the foot of the bed and jumped up.

'For fuck's *sake*,' he said.

Blix slowly got up from the chair and left it in the middle of the floor between them. Ree clenched his fists and opened them up again. A certain look had taken over his face, and there was something wild in his eyes that made Blix think of a trapped animal. Something indeterminate.

'Sorry,' Blix said before Ree could say anything more. 'Didn't mean to disturb you.'

He took a step back, towards the cell door.

'I'll leave you in peace.'

Ree seemed to have returned to his senses. He moved over to the closet instead and pulled out a pile of T-shirts.

Blix wanted to leave, but remained where he was.

'Is Samantha still picking you up tomorrow?' he asked mostly to smooth over the tense situation that had just arisen.

'Yep.'

Blix gave him a wry smile. 'What's the first thing you're going to do?'

Ree smiled back. 'After screwing the missus?'

Blix chuckled along to get him to continue.

'I don't have a checklist or anything,' Ree went on. 'Anyway, it's never how you think it's going to be, when you get out, but I'll probably have a beer or twelve. Samantha's invited some friends round, I think.'

He dropped back onto the bed and reached for the remote control. Blix slapped his hand lightly against the doorframe.

'See you at breakfast, then,' he said.

He didn't get a response.

51

Emma removed the ice pack and studied her swollen ankle. Her skin was red. The cooling had numbed the injury somewhat, but the pain was still noticeable.

Under normal circumstances, it wouldn't have taken her more than a quarter of an hour to walk to Markus Hadeland's house. She could drive, of course, and park nearby. But just working the pedals presented its own challenges.

Emma texted Markus and explained what had happened, asked if he wouldn't mind coming to her at the cabin instead. To her surprise, Markus answered straight away: *OK*.

After they had arranged for him to bring some food, it occurred to Emma that maybe she didn't really need to talk to him now, given what she had learned from Samantha that afternoon. But it'd be nice to have some company, if nothing else.

Markus turned up a little after seven. He had a rucksack and a carrier bag with him.

'I hope you like stroganoff,' he said, patting the backpack with one hand. 'And red wine,' he added with a smile, lifting the plastic bag in the air.

'That sounds perfect,' Emma said, laughing.

She let him in and closed the door.

'How are you doing?' he asked when he saw that she couldn't step on her foot properly.

'Better,' she replied. 'I think.'

'Where did it happen?'

'In the woods,' Emma answered. 'I was out walking with Samantha.'

Markus was about to take his shoes off when he stopped and looked up at her.

'You were out in the woods with Samantha?'

'Yes?'

Emma looked down at him. Markus continued to untie his shoelaces.

'You seem surprised,' she said.

'No, no,' he said. 'Or, a little, maybe. How did you get her on board with that?'

'It was her suggestion, actually.'

While Markus stepped out of his shoes, Emma explained how the walk had come about.

'Hm,' Markus responded, and hung up his jacket. He grabbed his backpack and the bag, and took a few steps inside.

'Where do you want this?'

'There's good,' Emma said, nodding towards the coffee table.

Markus walked past her.

'What did you "hm" for?' she asked.

'Huh?'

'It seems like you thought it odd that Samantha and I would go for a walk together.'

Markus pulled the bottle out and started fiddling about with a wine opener.

'No, it's just ... I don't think Samantha's ever gone for a walk with anyone in her entire life. At least she never did that with me.'

'She didn't?'

Markus didn't seem to want to elaborate. Emma fetched two glasses from the kitchen cupboard.

'It seemed like she knew the forest well,' she said, putting the glasses down on the table. Turned round to fetch the plates.

'It's not that – she's out there a lot, walks a lot, she just ... always goes by herself.'

Emma was back with the side plates. Markus struggled a little to get the cork out of the bottle, but managed it in the end. The gurgles that followed as he poured the wine always evoked a delicious, warm feeling of anticipation in Emma. He handed her the glass and raised his own.

'Cheers,' he said.

'Cheers. And thank you for all this,' she replied.

'My pleasure.'

They each took a sip. Markus studied the glass and its contents. He seemed satisfied. A soft, buttery wine from southern Spain.

'It should still be warm,' he said with a nod to his backpack.

'Ideal,' Emma said. 'I'm starving.'

He pulled out the dishes and bowls – four in all. Mashed potatoes, rice, salad, and a substantial casserole dish with steak, sauce and mushrooms.

'Wow,' Emma said. 'You shouldn't have.'

They sat down.

'I should have had some parsley too,' Markus admitted. 'And preferably some pickles and beetroot. But I didn't have a chance to go to the shop.'

'This is perfect.'

They served themselves and started to eat. It dawned on Emma just how hungry she was. It all tasted amazing. The wine too. She thanked him again.

'Do you like to cook?' she asked.

'No.' He laughed. 'But I like to eat good food.'

'That makes two of us. I mostly just make pancakes. And that's only when I have my niece visiting. She loves them.'

Emma took another bite. Markus did the same. He seemed to her like a solid guy. Someone who had perhaps grown up in the wrong place, among the wrong friends.

'Were you out looking for Rita again today?' she asked.

Markus finished chewing his mouthful.

'The divers have ended the search,' he said. 'And there aren't many more places left for us to look. Not here, in the immediate area, anyway. She could have disappeared somewhere else, of course. But then someone would have seen her. And her car's still parked in her mother's driveway.'

Emma took a small sip of wine.

'We ran into Rita's neighbour out in the woods today,' she said. 'He thinks she's been murdered.'

Markus didn't answer right away.

'If that's true, it'd be awful,' he finally said.

'You can't think of anyone she may have fallen out with? A scorned lover or ... someone with a grudge?'

Markus, who had the glass of wine in his hand when she asked, stopped and thought for a few moments. He finished his sip and shook his head.

They continued to eat.

'It was a nice walk.' Emma looked up at him. 'Earlier today,' she added. 'With Samantha. Even if the content of the conversation wasn't so pleasant.'

Markus stopped eating. Waited for Emma to continue.

'Samantha told me what happened.'

'With ... what?'

'With Fred,' she said. 'In the kiosk. In 2004.'

She didn't elaborate, just waited for Markus to comment. He took a large gulp of the wine and kept his grip on the stem. Swirled the contents round and round a few times.

'The last time we spoke about it, you said that she had struggled a lot with anxiety after everything that happened.'

'Yes...'

'You also said there was a lot you had to say about your divorce.'

She let the statement hang there. Last time she brought it up, he hadn't wanted to talk about it, but Emma hoped the situation was different now.

He put down his fork and wiped his mouth. A few long moments passed before he said:

'Samantha, she ... wasn't exactly easy to live with. All the anxiety, it took over, as did all the partying. I've always liked a good party – it wasn't that. But ... maybe not several times a week. Not after we got married. I thought that might calm her down a bit, but...'

Emma said nothing.

'For me, I ... it felt natural to think and talk about having kids someday but...' He looked down. 'She would get mad if I mentioned it. Said things like: "Do you really think I want to have children with you?" Like she thought I would be a bad father or had bad genes or something.'

'That's cruel,' Emma said.

Markus took another sip of the wine. He drank fast.

'The thing about Samantha is that ... I never felt like she really wanted to be with *me*. We had shared interests – music, really – but I was the sort of guy who she thought would look after her, not the guy she actually wanted to share her life with. I was a lifeline, almost. But she was completely off the rails, at times.'

He grabbed the fork again and pushed the food around his plate a little.

'That also applied to ... the more, uh, personal things. The intimacy. I was ... by no means ... the only guy in her life.'

He quickly raised his eyes to Emma and lowered them again.

'There were ... other men. Jarl Inge, of course; after all, he never really gave a shit that Samantha and I were married anyway. It was like he felt he owned her, almost, since he had been with her before. And Samantha, she ... just shrugged it off. Whatever, you know. It was just sex. If I wasn't happy about it then I could go.'

He made a waving motion toward the door with his hand. Took another bite and chewed slowly. Washed the food down with more wine. The glass was almost empty. He poured more for them both.

'Thank you,' Emma said quietly.

'Regardless...' He shrugged this time. 'It went as you might imagine. And I was actually kind of happy inside when it ended. Or relieved. It was tiring, living like that. Always kind of on my toes, wondering how she was and ... where she'd been.'

Emma understood what he meant.

'We became good friends again after a while, but you know, it's always there. Like a kind of ... disappointment, maybe? The fact that it didn't work out between us is my greatest failure in life, I think. I was not the medicine she needed.'

A silence lay between them for a few moments.

'Wow,' he said with a short laugh. 'I really know how to lighten the mood around a dinner table.'

'I asked,' Emma smiled.

They continued to eat.

After a while she said: 'Samantha told me what happened when Fred drowned too – in 2007.'

Again, Markus stopped chewing. 'Seriously?' he asked.

'Mhm.'

'What did she say?'

She retold the story.

When Emma had finished, Markus said:

'Hm.'

'There you go again.'

'What?'

'You "hm-ed".'

Markus sat up a little. 'No, I just...' He hesitated. 'It just ... strikes me as a bit odd.'

'How'd you mean?'

He took a deep breath. 'Well, first that she wants to go for a walk with you, and then that she wants to share the worst, most painful parts of her life. With *you*. No offence, but you are, after all, a stranger *and* a journalist. It took years before she would talk to me about it. And then I was the one who approached her about it.'

'Why would you want to talk to her about that?'

'Because ... I wondered what had happened.'

'All those years later?'

'Yes, I...' He ran a hand through his hair.

'She never told you herself?'

He shook his head. 'She just said that he'd drowned and there was nothing she could do.'

Emma sat up a little. 'But you still wanted to know more?'

A new expression had fallen over his face. 'Yeah. I thought there was something strange about the whole thing.'

'In what way?'

He took another sip from the wine glass. 'Well, first that she decided to go swimming that day. It wasn't exactly swimming weather. And secondly, that Fred...' He paused again. 'That he would jump in after her like that. He wasn't exactly a swimmer.'

'According to Samantha, he was determined to talk to her. To apologise.'

'Yeah, that's what Samantha told me too, that he was just "laser-focused". And sure, that bit makes complete sense. Fred was like that – if he had his mind set on something, then he would do it. But still...'

He let the sentence hang in the air between them. Then he raised his palms.

'I shouldn't be saying any of this to you. Speculating.'

'Why not?'

He sighed heavily.

'Because ... it's been years. Life has moved on. What role does any of it play now?'

52

The soap foamed between his fingers. Walter rubbed his hands a little more before rinsing them off. Samantha had hung up a separate towel for him, while the extra toothbrush stood in the glass beside hers.

He considered taking it out. His teeth were stained red from the wine. Lips dry, almost cracked. He wet a finger and rubbed them a little.

Maybe it could be like this, he thought. Life. An evening spent in front of the TV with a woman. Each enjoying a glass of red wine. If only his life had taken a different direction. If only he hadn't killed his father. He just had to accept his fate, though, try to make the best of what he had. Right now, he was savouring another evening of freedom with Samantha. He couldn't think of anything better.

She was sitting in exactly the same place when Walter returned – on the sofa, glass of wine in front of her. She had topped them both up.

Walter sat down.

The TV was on. Brian Johnson, the vocalist of AC/DC, was interviewing Mark Knopfler about his life, his career. Samantha held on to the wine glass but didn't drink from it. Just stared at the TV, seemingly uninterested.

'Are you nervous?' he asked.

'A little, maybe.' Her attempt to smile was unsuccessful.

'It'll be fine,' Walter assured her. 'It's a good plan.'

Samantha didn't seem convinced. 'So much could go wrong.'

Walter didn't know what to say to that.

'When are you leaving?' he asked.

'Around eight a.m., I think. You don't need to get up.'

He laughed. 'It's probably more a question as to whether I'll be going to go to bed at all.'

That made her smile, slightly. But properly, this time. She still seemed more worried than Walter had seen her before.

On the TV, Mark Knopfler played a few verses of a well-known song. The presenter nodded his head to the beat.

'You're not nervous?' she asked.

Walter thought about it.

'It's not something I do every day, of course,' he said. 'But no, I'm not nervous.'

'Because you've done it before?'

'I mean, I haven't done *that* before exactly.'

'No, sure ... but you know what I mean.'

'Like you said – there's always some risk involved.'

Samantha disappeared into her own thoughts again. Walter did the same. He thought about how dark it was outside. The night that lay before them. Maybe he should eat a little.

Suddenly she turned to him and said:

'How old were you when you were here? In 2004?'

Walter frowned. 'Sixteen.'

'You'd never ... kissed anyone, I remember. Before...'

Walter shook his head. Smiled at the memory.

'Have you kissed anyone else?' she asked.

'Yes, of course.'

'Have you really?'

Her gaze felt uncomfortably penetrating. Walter was getting hot.

'No,' he said. 'Not really.'

She didn't take her eyes off him. Instead of saying anything else, she grabbed his left hand.

'So ... you've never had sex with anyone either then, right?'

The question caught him off guard.

It was a topic they had talked about a lot in Billwerder. *What was her name, the first bird you fucked?* Walter had said Samantha. Told them about her, dreamed about her. Dreamed that what he told them was true.

He never went into detail to Sven, Patrick or the others, partly because he didn't know what to say. Nor did he want them to realise that he didn't know what he was talking about. Perhaps they had their suspicions. Who knew?

Samantha stroked his hand. The touch was enough for a warm tingle to rush through his body. Without him realising what was happening, she had climbed on top of him. Walter didn't know where to put his hands, or where to look. Her breasts were right in front of him.

She cupped his face in her hands and bent down.

Kissed him.

Soft, tender.

Just as she had done that summer so many years ago. It was like being back on the jetty. It was sunny and warm.

Walter's lips were dry, but she moistened them with the tip of her tongue as her breath became heavier, faster. She moved even closer to him and pressed herself harder against Walter's lower body. When she stopped kissing him, and instead moved her hands down to his belt buckle, he said:

'Okay.' And took a deep breath. 'Now I'm nervous.'

Samantha laughed. But she didn't stop.

53

Emma cast a dejected glance at all the mess on the kitchen counter, suddenly missing her own apartment. There, she had full control over everything, and know where things should go, where things *were*. Now she had to look for washing-up liquid and a brush, cloth and a tea towel. She had to think a little more than she liked to after a long day on the job.

It had been a nice evening – one which had, however, come to a rather awkward end. In addition to the delicious dinner, Markus had also brought instant coffee and cognac. Along with his alcohol intake, he had also grown more confident in himself and in what he wanted for dessert. At one point he asked Emma if she had someone waiting for her back home in Oslo. The anticipation in his eyes was unmistakable.

Emma could say, hand on her heart, that she did like him, just not in *that* way. Something she verbalised, to avoid any misunderstandings. And it wasn't long then before Markus got up and put the dishes back in his backpack, saying something about having some ungrateful, uninterested pupils to teach tomorrow morning. The way he said it made Emma think that the adjectives were meant just as much for her as they were for them.

Emma threw away the leftovers and washed up. She tied up the bin bag and put it by the door, until it occurred to her that she didn't want the cabin to stink of old food when she woke up in the morning. She could put it outside, on the decking, but then that'd attract all sorts of animals. The nearest bin wasn't that far away.

She went looking for it.

Her ankle was sore, but fortunately, her shoes were quite roomy. Emma hobbled over to them and tried to slide them on. She managed it, albeit not without pain, but the shoes actually offered some ankle support. Enough for her to put her jacket on and open the door.

Outside, she stopped and put the bin bag down. It was cold, so she pulled her jacket around her more tightly. The full moon illuminated the camping area, making it a little less ominous, so late into the evening.

Emma scanned her surroundings. Spotted a large bin under one of the nearest lampposts.

Slowly, and careful not to put too much weight on her injured foot, she started to limp her way over to it. Once there, she opened the lid and threw the bag in. The bin was almost completely empty, but it reeked. It was presumably not emptied that often, now the season was over. She let go of the lid so it fell back into place, turned and started to walk away; but then stopped after a few steps and hobbled back.

The sharp smell hit her again. She held her breath and looked down into bin. Underneath her own bin bag was a plastic bag with Lidl's unmistakable yellow-and-blue logo.

Lidl, she thought.

The German low-price supermarket chain that had tried to gain a foothold in Norway in the 2000s. There were no shops left in the country now – Rema 1000 had taken over all of Lidl's old premises. Emma knew that they had Lidl in both Denmark and Sweden, and the bag could of course have come from other Scandinavian guests that'd been here recently.

But it could also have been from German guests.

Or rather – one German.

She looked around. Felt the urge to open the bag, to see if she could find any other indication of who had thrown it in there. The smell was nauseating, and the bin was too deep for her to reach down for it anyway. She suddenly felt exposed, like someone was watching her, even though there wasn't another person in sight. The emptiness, the silence, made her shudder.

She closed the bin and hurried back to the cabin. As she entered and slowly eased off her shoes, she regretted having run off so quickly. Her ankle felt as if it was twice as swollen as it was before. The pain throbbed.

Emma hauled herself to her bag, which was hanging over the back of one of the dining-table chairs. She always had an emergency supply of painkillers with her. There were four tablets left in the pack. She popped two of them out of the strip and swallowed them with the dregs of the glass of water that she had left on the table. Maybe they'd help her sleep, she thought.

Three and a half hours later, she squinted at the mobile phone on the bedside table for the nth time.

03:06.

She sighed.

Her foot throbbed. Any position she moved into was painful and uncomfortable. She had tried putting a pillow under her ankle as well, so it didn't have to touch the bed, but that hadn't helped either. As for sleep, it didn't help that her mind was racing about everything Markus had told her about Samantha. And Fred.

There was one particular phrase that she kept coming back to.

Laser-focused.

Samantha had used the exact same wording to describe Fred to her as she had to Markus. And there were no other discrepancies in the story. It made Emma wonder if Samantha had planned what she was going to say. Practised it. The fact that even Markus, who knew her so well, hadn't been able to connect the dots in the Fred story only made Emma even more sure that something about it wasn't quite right.

She pushed the duvet aside, swung her legs out of the bed and put her feet on the cold floor. Standing up, she felt a new wave of pain travel up her leg from her ankle. She swallowed the last two tablets and wondered what time the shops opened.

Emma walked over to the window that faced out onto Lake Øsensjøen.

The light from the full moon varnished the water's surface and also draped it in a beautiful, shimmering veil. The water was still. Behind it: a dark forest and a small elevation in the terrain. The sight calmed her, made her breathing slower. She squinted.

Something moved down on the jetty.

Even with the moonlight it was impossible to see anything more than a silhouette.

Emma put her hands against the window, cupping them around her face to see better. It looked almost like someone was holding something, dragging it behind them. She hobbled into the bedroom and retrieved her phone. Opened the camera and tried to zoom in on the jetty, but the image was too grainy.

The person moved slowly. Stopped. Dropped something over the edge of the jetty. From this distance it was impossible to see what was really going on, but the timing itself was enough to make it suspicious. But it would take forever to get the police there at this time of night. And what could she really tell them? She had no idea what was going on out there.

It had been three days since she came to Osen.

Three days in which she had searched, dug and steadily got closer to a more complete picture of the wounds the inhabitants of the village carried, and of the delayed effects of those injuries, all somehow related to the summer that Walter Kroos and his family had been here. She was missing the last few pieces of the puzzle that would enable her to understand it, yet she felt she was closer than ever – she could feel it in her whole body. She wasn't sure that whatever was going on down at the beach had anything to do with Rita Alvberg, Walter Kroos or Samantha Kasin. But Emma had a strong desire to find out.

She put weight on her foot again.

Pain.

She had managed to walk earlier that evening. She could do it again. She could endure a little pain.

Emma threw on her jacket and slipped outside. Locked the door behind her. Double-checked that she had her phone with her this time. The pain tore through her ankle joint, but she neither stopped nor turned back.

Above her, the sky was full of stars. She was hit by a raw chill that seemed to emanate from the surrounding vegetation. Emma took short steps, careful where she placed her feet, in order not to make too much noise. She periodically stopped to listen for movement, but she heard none.

When the beach opened out in front of her, she stopped behind a tree thick enough to hide her completely. There was nobody there. Yet there was still something on the jetty. A bundle of some kind. Emma wondered whether the person had really left, but in the next moment, she heard a sound coming from the boathouse further down the beach. A boat came gliding out.

The water gurgled beneath the bow.

A man with a hood pulled up over his head sat with the oars in either hand, bending forward, then stretching out with each pull. He manoeuvred the boat out towards the middle of the lake, twisting his upper body round as if to navigate. Rowed a few times with just the left oar, so that the boat turned back towards the jetty.

Emma took out her phone and disabled the keypad lock. Used her jacket to hide the light of the screen. Swiped up to open the camera and started recording, making sure the flash was turned off. The video would be grainy, but so be it. She aimed the camera at the movements out on the water.

The movements were jerky, slow. He splashed and splashed with the oars. At last the boat arrived at the jetty. The man shipped the oars then grabbed the edge of the jetty. Pulled the boat closer, so that it eventually lay parallel. He stood up unsteadily. Waited a few seconds until he found his balance, then put one foot onto the deck.

The movement caused the boat to rock. He kicked off with the other foot and got up. He barely managed to grab hold of the boat before it slid away. Slowly pulled it back in again.

Emma moved a little to get a better camera angle. She alternated between watching with her eyes what was going on, and looking at what she was able to zoom in on via her phone screen.

The man seemed to be struggling with the bundle. The boat slipped a little away from the jetty again. The man had to use a foot to hold the boat close. It threw him off balance again, but at last he managed to get the bundle, the tarpaulin, whatever it was, into the boat.

He pushed himself up onto his feet. Found his balance and looked around.

Emma retreated behind the tree, unsure if he had spotted her. He turned his attention back to what he had been doing. Turned the boat in the water so that the stern was pointing towards him. Then he set foot in the boat. He was about to kick off with the other, but didn't make proper contact – his foot slipped against the wet wood, and once again he lost his balance. For a frantic half-second he tried to compensate, but a trip into the water seemed unavoidable. He fell in at the same time as the boat slipped away.

It took a second for him to come back up. The man gasped for air, his hands struggling to remove the hood from his face. The boat slipped further and further away. He swam after it, but he couldn't catch up, the distance only widened. Eventually, he gave up. Emma could no longer see the boat in the darkness, but she continued filming. Hoping the moonlight would illuminate his face.

He turned and swam towards the jetty. His movements were slow, weighed down by his wet, heavy clothes. He was breathing hard and fast. With his arms on the edge of the jetty, he paused.

A fraction of a second later, he turned his head, and looked straight at Emma.

At the same time, the moonlight shone on his face and judging by his movements – sudden, quick, as if he couldn't get out of the water fast enough – Emma knew she had been exposed. She turned and ran.

Her injured foot made it impossible to run fast, the pain shooting through her ankle with each step, made worse by the fact it was uphill. Emma still had her phone in her hand. She called 112 at the same time as she tried to run, and was quickly connected to the nearest available police operator.

Without looking back, she tried to explain herself. Her breathing was laboured as she gasped for air. She stumbled over her words and had to start over.

'Hold the line,' the operator said when Emma had finished.

'I don't know if I can do that,' she wheezed. 'I need both hands.'

'Put the phone in your jacket pocket,' the woman told her. 'Just don't hang up.'

Emma did as she was told. As she ran, she turned her head, to see if she could spot anything of the man.

Nothing yet, but it felt like he was getting closer. That he had chased after her.

Emma hobbled as fast as she could, one step at a time. She expected to hear breathing behind her, footsteps, feel a pair of arms wrapping around her and forcing her to the ground. She tried to squeeze all the strength she had out of her body, suppress all pain. The lactic acid in her thighs was starting to burn when she finally saw the road open up, a hundred metres or so ahead.

She tried to imagine the tram in Oslo in front of her, that she had to catch up with it. Again she looked back. Her right foot came into contact with a large stone. Her foot twisted over and a jolt of pain shot through her big toe. But she still couldn't see him. Couldn't hear him.

Emma fumbled in her jacket pocket for the key to the cabin, but before she could get a proper grip on it, it slipped out of her pocket. In the darkness, she frantically looked around, but couldn't see it. She dropped to her knees and scoured the ground. Then she found it, and grabbing a handful of grass and gravel along with the key, she pushed herself up again. Leapt forward without looking back. She stomped, gasping, dizzy, the last few steps to the door. Her hands shook as she tried to unlock the door.

She eventually managed to keep them under control and slid the key into the lock.

Managed to turn it.

And then she was inside.

She was safe.

54

The first police car appeared twenty-three minutes later. The second one wasn't far behind. The emergency lights danced over the rooftops and painted the trampled grass of the campsite blue.

'You did great, Emma,' the 112 operator said on the other end of the line.

'I don't know about that,' she replied.

It had taken her several minutes to bring her heartbeat back down to normal. Hidden behind the curtains, she had kept an eye out over Osensjøen, but couldn't see any more of the man.

Emma opened the cabin door and made herself known to the police officers, four in total. A man about Emma's age seemed to be in charge.

'Lars Martin Lundaas,' he said. 'What can you tell us about what happened?'

Emma took a quick minute to recount the events of half an hour prior.

'I have a video of it,' she said. 'It was dark and I was fairly stressed, so I don't know what the quality's like. I haven't looked at it myself yet.'

'AirDrop it to me,' Lundaas requested. 'Then I can take it further if needs be.'

Emma pulled her phone out and found the recording in her photo gallery. Selected it and sent it off. It was a large file, so the transfer took a while.

'He might still be in there somewhere.' She made a gesture over towards the greenery between the campsite and the lake.

None of the young officers seemed to know what to do.

'Is that the way?' one of them said, pointing to the rocky dirt road that led down to the beach.

Emma nodded.

'Okay. Take one of the cars,' Lundaas said to the others. 'Search the area. Drive all the way down to the water and find out if you see can anything of the boat.'

'It *could* be Walter Kroos,' Emma said. The officers turned to face her. 'Just so you're aware.'

'Is there anything that suggests that to be the case?' Lundaas asked.

'Yes and no,' Emma began. 'We know he's in Norway, and that he has a strong connection to this particular place.' She waved a hand to indicate the general area. 'But he hasn't been seen here. Not yet, anyway.'

Again they thought about it.

'I'll call the operations manager,' said Lundaas. 'To request armament.' He stepped away.

Emma felt her news-story fingers itching. First, they needed some clarification about what was in the boat.

Lundaas was soon back.

'Alright,' he said. 'Permission granted.'

The other three headed toward the cars and unlocked the firearms trunks. Watching them take out guns and check them for ammunition made Emma shudder. She had been up close and personal with weapons before. Various episodes from her past forced her to blink rapidly, as if trying to will the bad memories away.

'Use channel two,' Lundaas told the officers. 'And keep me posted.'

※

The car rolled off slowly down the dirt road. The sound of stones crunching under the tyres.

It's too late, she thought. More than half an hour had passed since she called the police. The person in the water – whoever he was – had had plenty of time to get away. There were other ways to get away from the area, aside from up the road and past the campsite.

Emma looked down at her mobile phone, where the video recording was still open. She started it. Could hear her own shallow breathing. Her hand also shook, so it wasn't easy getting a good, clear picture of what was going on. The lack of light made it even more difficult. But the movements were unmistakable. A man rowing a boat. The boat gliding towards the jetty.

She let the video play through, from the man's clumsy fall into the water to him trying to get up. She paused the clip as the moonlight shone on his face. Emma zoomed in, but the picture was too blurry. The police certainly had the tools to produce something sharper, she thought. She would just have to wait.

It was 04:26 when they finally heard the crackle of the police radio.

'No sign of anyone by the water,' one of the officers said. *'But there's definitely a boat at rest out there.'*

'We're checking the boathouse,' came a voice from one of the other officers.

Not long after: *'There's another boat in here.'*

'Use it to get out on the water,' Lundaas suggested.

'Copy.'

Over the next fifteen minutes, even more police cars arrived in the area. Above them, the sky was still pitch-black.

Again, the radio crackled. The sound of oars hitting the water. Breathing, splashing.

'We're just a few metres away,' one of the officers informed them.

'Copy. Report continuously.'

Emma kept her cool, not wanting to remind them that she was still there.

'Looks like a sleeping bag,' they reported. *'It's tied up. With a chain, by the looks of it. And a weight. There's...'*

The rest of the message faded. Emma took a step closer.

Lundaas asked them to repeat the last message.

'There's something inside it.'

'See if you can tow the boat to shore,' Lundaas decided. 'Don't touch the sleeping bag. Wait until I can get the technicians out.'

'Copy.'

Lundaas sighed heavily and turned to Emma.

'We don't really need you here anymore,' he said. 'Not right now, at least. You'll be wanting to get to bed, I imagine?'

Emma smiled but shook her head. Sleep was out of the question. She was going down to the beach.

55

The two boats were resting side by side, having been pulled ashore. Emma could see the bundle lying in one. She tried to take a few pictures. From a distance and in the grey, early morning light, the results weren't particularly good, but they'd have to do.

The police officers didn't seem to appreciate her being there, but they didn't say anything. Not even when she took a few steps closer and openly snapped away on her phone camera. Emma realised that none of them were in a position to say anything officially. After she had taken the photos she needed, she sat down on a large rock that straddled the line between the sand and the grass and typed out a long message to Anita Grønvold.

Emma's boss at news.no was usually up early. The first instructions and alerts from her normally popped up a little after five o'clock.

'Send me a few lines about what happened,' she wrote. 'As detailed as possible. Your eyewitness account.'

Emma opened up a blank document on her mobile phone and jotted down a few rough notes. It was uncomfortable, putting into words what she had seen and experienced. Reliving the fear that had settled in her lungs, legs, chest, she now realised. In the moment, she had felt as if she were in a film. That she could die at any point. It was something she had felt a few too many times in her life. It made her wonder when exactly her luck would run out.

It wasn't until 06:30 that Arvid Borvik eventually appeared, driving down to the beach. Just behind him: two cars with crime scene technicians, who immediately began setting up a tent as close to the water's edge as possible. There were so many people around the boats that it was impossible for Emma to see what they were doing – if they were lifting the sleeping bag into the tent or examining it in the boat itself.

The sun started to rise in the east.

Minute by minute, the colours around her started to come to life. There was something morbid about the whole scene – the beautiful contrasting with the dramatic. Police tape was set up around the boathouse.

Shortly after seven o'clock, Borvik made his way over to the stone Emma was sitting on. His steps were heavy and slow.

'Good morning,' he said.

Emma stood up and said hello.

'You've had quite a night, I take it?'

'You could say that,' Emma replied.

'How are you?'

'Good,' she said, surprised by the thoughtfulness of the question. 'A little cold, but fine.'

'Autumn,' he said. 'You still get a glimmer of summer every now and then, but you can sure as hell feel the winter now.'

Emma didn't want to talk about the weather.

'Is it Rita Alvberg?' she asked, nodding towards the activity down by the water's edge.

'It's ... too early to conclude.'

'But it is a corpse?'

Borvik ran a hand over his growing beard. 'I can confirm that we have found a dead body,' he began, 'but it is currently too early to say anything about either the identity or how our investigation will proceed.'

'But there's no reason to deny that this is a murder investigation, right?' Emma said. 'A body wrapped in a sleeping bag, a chain wrapped around it, a weight ... it's an obvious attempt to dump it in the lake in the middle of the night, after you've finished the search for Rita Alvberg in the water...?'

Borvik didn't answer.

'Did you see any cars?' he asked instead.

Emma shook her head. She had thought the same thing. If it was Rita Alvberg, the body must have been kept somewhere before it was transported down to the jetty. But she hadn't seen a car there. It had been completely silent.

'Could it have been Walter Kroos?' she asked.

'What makes you think that?' Borvik asked.

It was more of a feeling than anything else.

'The sum of many things,' Emma answered, nevertheless.

'What things?' Borvik asked.

She was aware that she had probably given too much significance to the Lidl bag, but she told him about it anyway. It piqued Borvik's interest though and he asked her to point to which bin it was in.

'It's also not the first time that something has happened in Osensjøen, that's connected with Kroos,' Emma continued.

Borvik did not seem to understand what she was referring to.

'Fred Kasin,' she elaborated. 'Who drowned here in 2007.'

She pointed out towards the water. The lake had turned an even brighter blue in the last few minutes.

Borvik seemed to have developed a nervous twitch. 'Walter Kroos wasn't here then,' he said.

'But his father was blamed when Fred Kasin raped Samantha,' Emma pointed out. 'And neither the rape nor the drowning accident were investigated.'

Borvik stretched his neck out.

'There wasn't much to investigate,' he eventually said. 'It was obvious the boy drowned.'

'You didn't think it was a little odd that the person who drowned, did so in front of the girl he had raped?' Emma asked.

Borvik seemed uncomfortable

'Fred would probably be alive today if the case had been handled properly,' she said.

'What do you mean?'

'If he had been held accountable for what he did. Then his father wouldn't have sent him to the jetty to apologise to Samantha, three years later.'

'It was the family who wanted—'

'But you were called in,' Emma interrupted. 'You were there and could have started an investigation immediately, could you not? If you wanted to?'

Borvik looked down for a few moments. When he raised his chin to her again, his cheeks were red.

'I ... have to go back,' he said, gesturing over his shoulder with his thumb.

Emma wanted to tell him to do his job this time, but let it go.

56

It was drizzling. Enough to turn the usually pale concrete wall a darker grey than usual. The sky was hard to read, but the clouds looked like they may contain more rain. From his cell, Blix had a view to the north, but he could see that the dark clouds were coming from the south. It would be a wet day at the cemetery.

He walked out of his cell, into the kitchen and took a bowl of cereal with him into the common room. Ree had grabbed his usual toast, but hadn't touched it.

'Not hungry?' Blix asked, sitting down across from him.

He received no response.

Blix poured milk over his cereal. A drop of milk slid down the carton onto the table. He wiped it away with a napkin and turned to the TV as he heard the news start.

Two Poles were talking away at the end of the table, drowning out the newscaster, but Blix managed to hear snippets about a body being found in Osen, something about a murder investigation.

Ree shouted at the Poles to shut up.

Blix pushed his chair out, walked over to the TV and turned up the volume. A reporter and a camera crew were already by the lake in Osen. Reporting live. The image on the screen showed police activity down at the water's edge. A forensics tent and police tape. The reporter had few details to offer. During the night, a body had been found on board a rowing boat that had been drifting out on the water. The police had not given any information about the body's identity, but they did note that this was the very same lake where a search had been made for thirty-two-year-old Rita Alvberg, who had been missing for more than four days.

The reporter was asked a number of questions from the studio about what theories the police might have.

'Thus far, the police aren't providing any details,' the reporter said. 'However, in recent days there has been speculation across the media as to whether the German murderer Walter Kroos – who escaped from prison in his home country last week – may be here in the village. We know that he had contact with the missing woman when he holidayed here in 2004.'

The reporter wrapped up their segment and the programme returned to the studio for the other news of the day.

Blix turned the sound down and turned to face the table. Jarl Inge Ree had got up and was walking away. He kicked a chair, then grabbed the back of it and threw it across the room.

'Hey!'

Kathrin's voice was sharper than Blix had heard before. The young prison officer stood in front of Ree and blocked his way with a warning palm.

'Put it back and clear the table,' she commanded.

None of the other prisoners said a word.

Kathrin took hold of her hip holster, her hand resting over the alarm on her belt.

Ree stood there, towering over her, then turned, walked back to the chair and grabbed it by the leg. He lifted it up in one swift movement and took a few steps before slinging it around him. The chair hit Kathrin in the side. The petite prison officer let out a short cry of pain. Before she could act, Ree was on her. A kick hit her in the hip and sent her into the wall. Another kick made her sink to the ground. Ree grabbed the chair again, lifted it over his head, and brought it down.

Kathrin raised her arms to protect herself against the next blow. Blood streamed out of a cut on her forehead.

Blix was across the floor in one leap. He pulled Ree off her. Grubben and another inmate also helped. They pushed him in front of them, out of the room and into his cell before any of the other officers appeared. Ree resisted, wanting to push past them and out into the hallway again. Blix grabbed his arm, twisted it behind his back and pushed him up against the cell wall.

The other officers arrived. The sounds of boots stomping down the hallway and the crackling of radios. Blix was dragged out of the cramped cell and pushed across the corridor. In the distance, an alarm sounded.

He was pushed into his own cell. The door locked behind him. From there, he heard the entire wing being shut down. Prisoners shouting and protesting, metal doors slamming.

Blix sat down on the bed. It was seven minutes past eight. Merete was supposed to pick him up at eleven. He had no idea how long it might take before the wing would be opened again.

It grew quiet around him.

He turned on the TV. The next newscast was at half-eight.

Nothing new.

At ten to nine, the inspection hatch opened. Jakobsen peered in.

'Visitor,' he said.

Blix got up and turned off the TV. The hatch closed again, the key slid into the lock and the door opened.

'How's Kathrin doing?' Blix asked.

'She's okay,' Jakobsen answered. 'Under the circumstances.'

'What happens to Jarl Inge?'

'No idea,' Jakobsen said, and sent Blix ahead of him, down the tunnel and over to the visitation wing.

Gard Fosse was already in the room, waiting for him. One side of his jacket collar was folded inward, as if he'd been in a rush. Jakobsen repeated the usual instructions and left them alone.

'Rita Alvberg's body was found last night,' Fosse informed him. 'Murdered, wrapped in a sleeping bag.'

He told him how the body had been prepared, ready to be dumped in Lake Osensjøen, but that someone had surprised the perpetrator and he'd been scared away.

'It was Emma Ramm who surprised him,' Fosse added.

'Emma?' Blix asked. 'Is she okay?'

'She filmed everything,' Fosse continued. 'It'll soon be all over the news.'

'Have you spoken to her?' Blix asked.

'No, but I have seen the film. It's dark, grainy and blurred, but the technicians have cleaned up a sequence to identify the man.'

'And?'

'It was Walter Kroos.'

Blix sat back in his chair, trying to collect his thoughts.

'We have roadblocks set up to the north and south,' Fosse went on. 'It may be too late, but the local police officers seem to believe he is still in the village.'

Fosse was clearly stressed.

'Hostage negotiators are on standby,' he added. 'This could develop into the worst possible scenario.'

Blix recounted what he had seen on the news broadcast and Ree's subsequent outburst.

'I think he's afraid that something may happen to Samantha.'

'Wibe already visited her,' Fosse said. 'She has been warned. We've sent several of our own units up there as well, but the local police are leading the operation. I hope they know what they're doing.'

They sat for a while in silence.

'Have you got the case file?' Blix asked. 'The drowning incident?'

Fosse pulled a thin stack of papers with a green cover out of his bag.

'What do you expect to find?' he asked, placing the documents in front of Blix.

Blix didn't even open the folder to look at the contents. On the cover: the name of the investigator. The local sheriff – Arvid Borvik.

'Borvik was called when Samantha was raped in 2004,' he said and put his finger under the name. 'He never filed a report. Three years later, the rapist drowned in front of the victim.'

He opened the first page and let his gaze glide down the table of contents. In addition to Samantha Kasin, only one witness was questioned. Jarl Inge Ree.

'But how can that have any connection to this?' Fosse asked. 'To whatever's happening here with Rita Alvberg and Walter Kroos?'

Blix had no answer.

He could not grasp what this case was really about.

57

When Emma opened her eyes, she immediately recognised the unpleasant feeling of having slept too long. She reached over to the bedside table and checked the time on her phone.

'Shit,' she sighed to herself.

She had slept for almost three hours. Anita Grønvold had been trying to call her.

At some point in the wee hours of the morning, Emma had had to take a quick lie down. She had set her phone alarm to go off an hour later, but had no memory of turning it off.

Outside on the path, a police car drove slowly by.

She pulled out her mobile phone and quickly read the news. Fortunately, she hadn't missed anything important. The discovery of the body itself was still the lead item.

The reporter for *Dagbladet* had spoken to a few of the neighbours in the area, who said they were terrified. They also had photos of the roadblocks and uniformed police around the area. Just fluff, a column filler – typical when the media had nothing new to write about. Of course people were going to be scared when there was a killer on the loose.

Emma sat on the edge of the bed as she texted Anita and explained what had happened and that she would call in a little while. She then searched for the number to Blix's prison wing.

'You'll have to call back later,' a brusque employee cut her off.

'When?'

'No idea.'

'Can you pass on a message? Tell him to call me.' She heard a sigh on the other end. 'And say it's urgent,' she said before he could protest. 'That it's important.'

The man hung up without responding.

Emma wasn't sure if the message had been noted or not, but she didn't bother calling back to check. Instead, she got dressed and quickly ate three crispbreads. Her body screamed for coffee, but she'd figure that out once she was out of the cabin. She was pleased to note that it was easier to put her shoes on now. She had thought that the events of last night would have made the pain worse, but the swelling had actually gone down somewhat. It was also less painful to put her weight on the foot.

The campsite was now full of people. It looked as if every journalist covering the case had swarmed the lakeside. Emma noticed several people just hanging around and waiting. Siri Jespersen, who Emma had spoken to earlier in the week, was one of them.

Emma walked over and introduced herself.

'Hi, yes, of course,' Jespersen said. She had dressed well for the occasion: a fleece underneath a bright-orange shell jacket. Ready for a long day at work.

'I hear we have you to thank for all this.'

'Oh,' Emma said. 'Who said that?'

'Borvik had a short briefing here a little while ago. We asked who found the body, of course,' Jespersen said with a smile. 'A guest at the campsite? That couldn't be anyone else but you.'

Jespersen continued smiling at her. Emma saw no reason to deny it.

'Did Borvik say anything about when they'll be going public with the identity?' she asked.

Jespersen shook her head.

'But everyone's taking it for granted that it's Rita Alvberg. The question is who the suspect is.'

Emma wanted to say something about Walter Kroos, but held back.

Over the next few minutes, she allowed herself to be interviewed about what she had seen and experienced. Emma felt that she owed Siri Jespersen a good news report; after all, she was the one who, just a few days ago, had given her Fred's name. In any case, she didn't see Jespersen as a direct competitor to news.no.

'Did you get hold of Karina Kasin in the end?' Emma asked when Jespersen had finished.

'Samantha's mother? Yes. Took a few tries though.' She rolled her eyes.

'Did she have anything interesting to say about the family's internal affairs?'

'No, but she did confirm that Abel Kasin was out of the day-to-day running of the campsite. Ages ago, apparently.'

'Nothing else? Nothing about ... Samantha?'

'Nope.'

Emma pondered that for a moment.

'I heard some gossip about Jarl Inge Ree – just now, actually,' Jespersen continued. 'The boyfriend she was on and off again with for years, apparently. He's being released from prison today. There was talk about he and Samantha supposedly trying again or something, but ... the mother denied that.'

'She did?'

Jespersen nodded. 'That train has left the station, apparently. A good thing, as well, she said.'

Markus had said something completely different during dinner last night. Who, between Markus and Samantha's mother, had the best overview of Samantha's love life was impossible for Emma to judge. Nevertheless, it was an interesting piece of information, and she thanked Jespersen for it.

Even more police patrols had arrived at the campsite. A civilian car with an Oslo licence plate was parked up beside them. Emma thought nothing of it at first. But the search operation had primarily been a local job. The fact that investigators from Oslo had arrived meant that there must be talk of a larger operation.

Emma caught sight of Lars Martin Lundaas – the officer who'd had primary responsibility for the police operation last night. She walked up to him and said hello.

'Big turnout,' she said, glancing at all the police cars and officers.

'Yeah ... a high-profile case, I'm sure you're aware.'

'For the Oslo police as well?'

Lundaas busied himself, poking his bag of snus out from under his upper lip.

'Does this have anything to do with Walter Kroos?' Emma pushed.

He nudged a pine cone with the toe of his shoe.

'You've identified him on the video I took...' Emma half asked, half stated.

He gave an incomprehensible response.

'What was that?'

'I can't comment on the matter. You'll have to talk to Borvik.'

A little way away the number of uniformed police officers was now in double digits. Several of them had firearms attached to their belts. There was something determined, serious about them.

You're too late, she thought.

Whoever she had discovered at half-three last night would be well away by now.

'Has the victim been identified yet?' she asked.

Lundaas shook his head. 'Talk to Borvik,' he repeated.

Emma thought about what she could do next, what she could write. Rita Alvberg was dead. Murdered, obviously. It was only a matter of time before it would be made public. The other media outlets had written about her life, they had interviewed colleagues, friends from Oslo. But as far as Emma could gather, none of them had spoken to any of Rita's childhood friends.

Emma thought of Samantha again and turned her gaze towards the reception building. Samantha's car wasn't there. Not that odd, given everything going on. Maybe she was at home. Emma wanted to thank her for her help yesterday. It could be a great way to start a conversation about Rita, maybe even dig around a little more about Fred's death. Maybe, Emma thought, Samantha had a cup of coffee to offer as well. Even with her dodgy ankle, it wasn't too far to walk.

Emma considered calling Anita as she made her way over to Samantha's house, but decided against it. She had nothing new to report yet.

A cat disappeared around the back of the house as she walked up to Samantha's front door. Her car wasn't there. Some sounds reached her from the kitchen window, which stood ajar. The sound of plates being cleared away.

She walked up the steps and rang the doorbell. Took a few steps back. Leant a little to the side to look in through a gap between the kitchen curtains, but could only see a steel-grey fridge with various shopping lists and Post-it notes on it.

She waited about a minute before trying the bell again. She could hear it ringing through the hallway from out on the doorstep, but no one came to open the door.

'Hm,' Emma said under her breath, and took out her phone. Scrolling down her call list, she found Samantha's number and pressed the call option.

It rang.

And rang. And rang. But Samantha didn't answer. Nor could Emma hear the phone ringing from inside the house.

Emma walked back down the steps, took a few more strides away. Turned and looked up at the windows. All of the curtains at the front of the house were drawn. Emma couldn't be sure, but she didn't think all of them had been like that when she first got there.

She went back to the steps. Tilted her head slightly, as if to try and hear better. There was definitely someone inside. The sound of a floorboard creaking.

She peeked in through the gap between the kitchen curtains again.

A face stared back at her.

58

His shirt hung looser around the neck. Blix tightened it with his tie and put on his jacket. It was the same suit he had worn during the trial. He had retrieved it along with a shirt from the personal belongings storeroom the day before. He'd ironed the shirt and tried the suit on. He'd had to make another hole in his belt as well.

The wounds from the fork Ree had drilled into his cheek had made shaving difficult, but he was satisfied. Only a small patch of stubble covered the bruise. He checked the mirror one last time and fixed his hair quickly before taking his coat off the hanger and heading out into the corridor. The wing was back in normal operation. He was the only one there. The other inmates were in class or at work.

The door to cell six was open. Blix poked his head in. The room was empty.

He walked over to the guardhouse. Jakobsen turned his chair towards him, let his gaze slide over his clothes and nodded.

'I'll escort you out.'

He stood up and grabbed a Post-it note from off the desk.

'Message for you,' he said, holding it out for him to take. 'It got a bit hectic here...'

Blix took it. Emma had called, wanted him to call her back.

The words 'urgent' and 'important' had been jotted down, with 'important' underlined.

'Could I try calling now?' Blix asked.

Jakobsen looked up at the clock.

'It'll only take a few minutes,' Blix added. 'It'll be a good while before I can call again.'

Jakobsen dropped back into the chair and dialled Emma's number for him. He sat and waited for a minute before hanging up.

'No answer,' he stated and prepared to leave.

Blix folded up the note and put it in his pocket.

'What's happening with Ree?' he asked.

'He's in a waiting cell.'

'So he's still being released?'

'Yes,' Jakobsen answered. 'But he'll get another sentence for what he did. You might be called in as a witness.' He pulled out a key ring and shook his head. 'So idiotic, the same day you're being released. Good thing for us is that he won't be coming back *here* anyway. Not as long as Kathrin works here.'

They walked silently down the tunnel and across to the other side of the prison. At the door to the exit he was handed over to an older officer he hadn't seen before.

The officer looked up from a computer screen and measured him with his gaze.

'Blimey,' he commented. 'Are you getting married?'

'Not today,' Blix replied.

The man's eyes returned to the screen. 'Day release until five o'clock,' he said. 'First time?'

Blix nodded, and could feel the anticipation of getting out. Out of the building, anyhow.

'You are aware that if you don't return by the end of your curfew, it will result in reactions from the prison management,' the officer continued. 'Anything from a written reprimand and loss of access to any other applications for day release, to loss of unemployment benefits or other benefits.'

Blix confirmed he was.

'Gross infringement of the conditions may be reported to the police and result in an additional penalty of up to three months,' the officer added before turning around in his chair. 'Let's go.'

A minute later Blix was standing on the other side of the gate. It had started to rain. The raindrops hit him in the face. He drew in a deep breath of air, had thought perhaps that it would be different, outside the walls.

It wasn't.

He pulled on his coat and scouted the car park for Merete. His gaze stopped on an older, red Volvo. There was a woman behind the wheel.

Samantha Kasin.

Her hair was a little different, but he recognised her from the pictures on the wall in Ree's cell. There was only one other car parked up – a family. The undercover police had to wait elsewhere.

Blix hadn't been waiting for more than a couple of minutes before Merete swerved into the car park and stopped in front of him. Blix got in and quickly closed the door behind him.

'Sorry I'm late,' she said.

'You're not late at all.'

She leant over to him and gave him a short, stiff hug.

'You're injured,' she said, tapping a finger against her own cheek.

'You should have seen the other guy,' he smiled, and blinked quickly. 'It's nothing though,' he added. 'Nothing to talk about anyway.'

He glanced into the back seat at a large bouquet of red roses. Blix felt a pang of pain in his chest.

'They're beautiful,' he commented.

Merete put the car into gear and pulled out of the car park.

'It'll be weird, being there,' he said.

'I guess you didn't get to see the tombstone,' she said. 'It turned out nice.'

An alarm went off.

'Seat belt,' Merete reminded him.

Blix fastened himself in, then leant forward and squinted up at the sky. A plane was heading south.

'I thought we could go back to mine afterwards,' Merete suggested. 'Have something to eat. That way you can see my flat as well. We have time for that.'

'I'd love to,' Blix replied.

They drove for a while without speaking. Blix and Merete had been divorced for almost twenty years. They didn't have much to talk about. The fact that they were going to visit their daughter's grave made the atmosphere even heavier.

'Who was it that hurt you?' she asked as they joined the motorway towards Oslo.

'He won't be there when I get back,' Blix replied.

'Because of what he did to you?'

Blix shook his head. 'He'd served his time,' he replied. 'Was going to be released today anyway.'

He hesitated a moment, then began to tell Merete about Jarl Inge Ree. Mostly to have something to talk about. By the time they arrived at the cemetery, he had told her everything.

'Sounds like he didn't want to leave,' Merete said.

'What do you mean?' Blix asked.

'Don't you get additional punishment or put in solitary confinement for doing something like that?' she asked. 'It almost sounds like he was hoping he wouldn't be released.'

Blix explained how the prison had no option to hold him once his sentence was over, but it did make him think.

Merete was right.

Jarl Inge Ree had been afraid of being released.

59

Samantha had no record of how many times she had visited Jarl Inge in prison. It was a long drive, so he understood that she couldn't come down that often. The summer months were also the high season for the campsite – a time when it was impossible for her to leave Osen. She was busy dawn to dusk.

Visiting someone shut away from society was always an odd experience. Being checked over with a metal detector and x-ray machine on the way in. Having to leave your belongings – your watch, keys, phone – at the door. She'd also had the narcotics dogs sniffing her in places where they had no business sniffing her. And there were rules for everything: how many newspapers or magazines she could bring him; items that she brought him had to be inspected and given the go-ahead before the visit even started. And she was never allowed to give them to him herself. She wasn't allowed to give him money. If she wanted a drink or chocolate, there were vending machines inside. And if they wanted more intimate time together, then they'd have to plan for that as well. The sheets and towels were always ready when they entered the visitors' room. They probably had the exact same set-up in a women's prison.

Samantha shuddered.

There was another car in the parking lot. In the back seat, she could see two children who appeared to be around eight to ten years old. On the driver's side, the mother sat with her hands on the steering wheel. She seemed tired, pale. Maybe she had taken the kids out of school for the day.

Samantha looked down at the time on the dashboard.

Jarl Inge was late, as always.

She thought about how long she had known him. It felt like a lifetime. She had no memory of a life without him. He had been her first real boyfriend. They had argued like cats and dogs a few times, but had always found their way back to each other. She had believed that he would always support her. Help her. Be there for her.

Her thoughts drifted back to that day in September when she found out that Uncle Abel and Fred were planning on coming to Osen. Samantha's father wanted her to be there to welcome them when they arrived, as if to put on a whole show that everything was okay, that it had all been forgotten. Water under the bridge. Samantha had stormed out of the house and run all the way to Jarl Inge's house, who had suggested that they go down to the lake. They could just stay there until Abel and Fred had gone home.

They had sat at the end of the jetty, Samantha with her head resting in Jarl Inge's lap. He ran one hand over her hair as they talked about everyone but Fred. But Fred was in every conversation, in every thought, in every breath.

She suddenly pushed herself out of Jarl Inge's lap and stood up.

'What are you doing?' he asked.

Samantha started to undress. Jarl Inge smiled crookedly and looked around.

'Isn't it a little—'

'I'm going for a swim,' she said. 'Coming?'

She stood naked before him. His gaze quickly glanced up and down her, falling on her breasts, her exposed crotch, but primarily, it was wonder she saw on his face, not desire.

'You're going swimming ... now?'

'Yes, I need to cool off a bit.'

'It's too cold for me,' he said. 'And we don't have any towels with us either.'

Samantha shrugged, turned around and jumped in. The water was colder than the last time she had been down at the lake, but it felt pleasant against her glowing cheeks. She quickly got used to it. She disappeared beneath the surface and took a few long strokes out into the water, away from the jetty.

The lake was, as always, dark and murky. She often thought about just diving in and floating down, down, down, until she reached the bottom. And never coming up again.

Behind her, Jarl Inge shouted something about not swimming too far out. But she just kept going. Enjoyed feeling how the water covered her body, all of it. There was nothing between her skin and the water. She was naked and free. The sound of the water moving, rippling, calmed her.

She flipped onto her back, floated there.

Her chest popped up over the surface of the water. The sky above her was white and blue, the occasional speck of grey. If there was wind in the air, she didn't feel it.

She heard voices.

Out of the corner of her eye, she caught sight of some movement on the jetty.

She pulled her limbs in and turned, blinking rapidly.

Felt a sharp pain stab her between her ribs.

Suddenly struggled to breathe.

On the jetty, next to Jarl Inge, stood Fred.

He just stood there.

It looked like Jarl Inge was saying something to him, but Samantha couldn't hear what. Fred just stared out over the water. At her.

This is not happening, she thought.

This can't be happening.

She couldn't go back to the shore while he was there. Not naked. There was no knowing what could happen, even if Jarl Inge was there.

Where was Uncle Abel? Had Fred come down here alone? She was too far from shore to see.

Fred shouted something she couldn't hear. He repeated the same words over and over. She took one stroke forward and let her body glide closer to the jetty. He waved, as if beckoning her to come closer. To him.

Like hell, she said to herself. The mere fact that he was there infuriated her.

'I have to talk to you!' he shouted in his slightly mumbled way.

About what? she thought to ask, but Samantha refused to engage in any kind of dialogue with him. She just wanted him to leave. Why wasn't Jarl Inge saying anything? Chasing him away?

Again, Fred shouted.

Samantha didn't know what to do. It was getting cold. There was no indication that Fred intended to leave until he had spoken to her.

'I have nothing to say to you,' she yelled.

'I need to talk to you,' he repeated, as if he hadn't heard what she had said. Samantha started to tremble.

'Just go away!'

Her lips had begun to quiver. Her skin prickled. She would have to get out soon.

'I'm not talking to you,' she said. 'Never.'

Samantha watched as Jarl Inge said something to Fred, but she couldn't hear what exactly. It was quiet again, up on the jetty. Fred continued to stare at her with his huge, round eyes.

But, in the next moment, he had taken a step off the edge of the deck. And was suddenly in the water. With his shoes and clothes on.

'Oh my God,' she whispered.

He managed to get his head above water. Coughed, coughed again. Thrashed around, his clothes weighing him down. Nonetheless, he came towards her, slowly, even as the water splashed in his face. He waved and splashed his arms. Samantha turned slightly and swam backward. The distance increased. Fred threw his arms around, like a four-year-old who had never been in the water before and didn't know what to do.

And then his whole head went under.

He came back up again. Spat, swallowed, spluttered. Couldn't seem to make any headway.

From the jetty, she heard Jarl Inge shout: 'He needs help!'

Fred spluttered.

Samantha could see the desperation in his eyes. Despair, horror. But it did nothing to her. She had hated him every single day for three years. Had wanted him to experience pain too. To be scared.

Fred's head disappeared below the water again. Where he stayed for a few seconds, before his hands came flailing back up. He gasped, loudly.

'Samantha!' Jarl Inge roared.

She swam a little closer.

He's going to drown, she thought. She moved closer again. For a few seconds he managed to stay above the surface, but then slid under once more. One second turned into two. Three. Four.

He broke the surface of the water with a loud gasp. Thrashed around even worse than before. He locked eyes with her and tried to say something, but his mouth was full of water. Only gurgling sounds came out. She knew this was a dangerous situation. People who were about to drown often panicked and grabbed the first and best thing that could help them. She could be pulled under. And held there. She remembered all too well how strong his hands were.

Still, she swam a fraction closer.

Took care to keep a good enough distance from his flailing arms. From the pier, Jarl Inge shouted again: 'Do something!'

Samantha didn't answer. Just stared into Fred's pleading eyes. Watched his helpless movements. He was weaker. An apathetic veil had clouded over his eyes. He had less and less strength in his arms, but he continued to wave them. Attempts to give his body any buoyancy were futile.

His head slipped under.

'Samantha!' Jarl Inge's desperate yell.

She heard a splash. Saw him swimming towards them.

Fred's head was still under water, but his hands were above the surface. Samantha swam over to him now. But instead of grabbing his hands to lift him up, she pushed them down.

There was still life and some strength left in him.

He clung to her hands and pulled her towards him, trying to pull himself up. But Samantha fought back. It was as if his fingers, recognising them – feeling their grip, their strength, their intensity, their will – forced out of her a primal scream she hadn't known she harboured. The cry gave her strength, and she pushed him down, and down, and down, until she, too, slipped beneath the surface, and continued to push him further down. She kicked him off her and pushed, pushed, pushed ... until Fred let go.

Samantha waited for a few seconds, before slowly letting herself float back up to the surface. Where she found herself looking at Jarl Inge, who had only just got to them. 'Where is he? Where is he?!'

Samantha said nothing.

She just felt a strange peace wash over her soul. She didn't even notice that she was breathing. No longer felt the imprint of his fingers against her own. The effort had not affected her. She wasn't tired. On the contrary.

Jarl Inge dived beneath the surface. Kicked violently and swam down.

Samantha just stared straight ahead, barely registering the movements in the water, only just hearing the bubbles rising from the depths. She didn't move. Just treaded water, calmly.

Jarl Inge drew a deep breath in as he broke the surface. He huffed and puffed, splashed and swallowed.

'Shit,' he spat, taking a deep breath in again. And returned beneath the surface. It didn't take as long for him to come back up this time.

Alone.

Samantha continued treading water, slowly, silently. She wasn't cold anymore. She lowered herself so that the bottom half of her face was below the water, her lips resting just above it. She breathed slowly, in and out, watched as her breath formed small ripples.

When Jarl Inge came up for the third time without Fred, he gasped and, looking at her, said: 'Samantha – what the fuck did you do?'

*

Jarl Inge knew what she had done that day.

He had helped cover up what had happened. But it had come at a price. Jarl Inge had had a hold over her, a kind of power, in all the years afterwards. But that, Samantha thought, would come to an end soon. She just didn't understand why he hadn't come out of the gate yet. It was already half-eleven. She hadn't got the date wrong, had she?

Her phone rang.

Its sound and vibration in the cup holder made her flinch. The number on the display made Samantha sit up a little too.

It was Emma Ramm.

Samantha thought about the text she had received from Markus last night. He had had dinner with Emma Ramm at the cabin. The honesty in the way he expressed himself suggested that alcohol was involved. As always, the more Markus drank, the more reckless he became.

I think maybe I said a little too much about you and your cousin and stuff, he wrote. *Sorry.*

Before she left that morning, Samantha had sent a text back, wondering what the hell he had actually said. *Forget I said anything,* he had replied, obviously sober, meek, and cautious again. *I didn't say anything wrong, anyway.*

On the way to Ullersmo Prison, Samantha had called him several times, without getting an answer.

Classic Markus. Always one to back away when things got uncomfortable.

Samantha glanced at the phone again.

Let it ring out.

60

It only took Emma a moment to realise who was standing on the other side of the window. And in that moment, the face disappeared from the gap between the curtains.

Quick, heavy footsteps from inside made her rush down the steps and take a long leap out onto the gravel. As she landed, another sharp pain shot into her ankle.

The door behind her opened.

Emma tried to limp away, but didn't have the chance to get very far. Walter barrelled into her. His strength and speed hurling them both forward.

Emma's knees hit the gravel first, then the rest of her body. Her phone slipped out of her hands. The right side of her face slammed down against the hard, sharp stones. And then Walter was on top of her.

The adrenaline overrode the pain.

Emma tried to fight back. She screamed – a cry that came from somewhere deep in her chest. She didn't recognise her own voice.

Walter's response was to pick her up. Emma tried to wriggle free, but he was too strong. He grasped hold of her from behind and held a hand over her mouth. His long arms made it impossible for Emma to move hers. She wanted to bite him, but her jaws wouldn't budge. Step by step he dragged her backward towards the house. Emma kicked her legs, ramming her heels into him, but it didn't slow him down.

Walter backed up the steps again, into the hallway. Didn't stop until they were in the kitchen. There, he forced her onto her stomach and placed a knee between her shoulder blades. Pressed her face into the floor. In a cold, calm voice he spoke to her in English:

'I'll kill you if you scream.'

Only then, did she feel the pain from hitting the gravel. A burning sensation rippled out across one knee. She could feel that she was bleeding. Walter held her to the floor a little longer, then pushed himself up and removed his knee from Emma's back. Replaced it with a heavy foot, holding her in place while he rummaged in one of the nearest drawers. He found what he was looking for then gathered her hands behind her back. Emma felt the glue from a roll of tape stick to her skin. Her hands were bound together. It became impossible to move them.

Again he lifted her up and held her by the neck, hard.

For the first time, Emma looked into Walter's eyes. Blue, cool. There was neither aggression nor anger in them. He pushed her out of the kitchen, into the living room. Placed her on the couch. With her face pressed into the couch cushions, he pulled off her shoes. She screamed as his bare hands pushed against her injured ankle. Walter thrust her head down and told her to shut up.

Another snap from the roll of tape. He then clamped her legs closed and taped them together too.

Suddenly, his face was close to Emma's ear again. His breath smelled bitter.

'If you shout or so much as make a noise,' he whispered, 'I'll tape your mouth shut too.'

It was difficult to get enough oxygen into her lungs. The fear had settled in her chest. Her heart thundered. Her cheeks were red hot. It felt like the muscle on the back of her thigh was going to cramp up. Walter went back outside. Only to return a few seconds later with Emma's phone. With a few simple movements, he took out the SIM card and snapped it in two. Dropped the pieces in a glass of water on the living-room table. Only now did she hear that the exertions of the last few minutes had tired him out too. He needed a few moments to collect himself. He stood there, motionless, for a long time, as if thinking over what to do.

Emma tried to come to grips with what had happened. How could Walter be here, at Samantha's? She hoped someone had seen the fight out on the gravel or heard her scream. There were a lot of police in Osen right now.

Emma tried to twist around so she could see him better. She eventually managed it, although it left her in an uncomfortable position.

Walter Kroos had less hair than in the outdated pictures she had seen of him, but he still had some of that boyish look about him. But that just made him all the more frightening. Unpredictable.

She shifted her gaze to the drying rack beside him. A pair of twisted woollen socks hung out to dry, as well as a pair of trousers, a T-shirt and a black hoodie.

Emma swallowed.

It *was* Walter she had seen last night.

A man who had killed two people.

She corrected herself.

Three, counting Rita Alvberg.

61

The tombstone was simpler than he had imagined. A grey, granite slab with a polished front, the letters in black lacquer: *In loving memory*.

Blix had let Merete choose everything. After, the thought had occurred to him that the text should have been placed so that there was room for his name there too, when the time came. Unlike Merete, he didn't envision himself finding someone else to share the rest of his life with. If he could fit in here too, then neither he nor Iselin would have to be alone.

Merete placed the flowers in a grave vase and pressed it into the ground. Blix bent down and swept some of the yellow autumn leaves from the red heather bushes. When he stood up, Merete put her arm around him. He leant against her.

The tears flowed.

'I came here every single day at first,' she said, before her voice cracked.

Blix swallowed.

He had dreaded this day. Had been afraid of how he would react. Of the grief, the longing, the loss, drilling into him even harder as he stood there looking down at his own daughter's name on a tombstone. He had been afraid that he would completely collapse and not be able to get up again.

Iselin was dead.

Gone.

Forever.

Blix stifled a hiccup.

He missed hearing her voice. Her laughter. Knowing that he could just pick up the phone and call her, or she could call him. The joy he always felt when he saw her name on the screen. They never spoke for long on the phone. Neither of them liked it. There were short conversations. Short questions. Never long answers.

He missed hearing what she had been up to, what she was going to do. Who she had met, what she had learned at the police college. What plans she had, what dreams. It was incomprehensible that he would never again get to hear her answers.

The sorrow was mixed with anger. A burning, intense rage against the man who had taken Iselin from them. But the overwhelming feeling that reared its head again now as he stood in front of his daughter's grave for the first time was the loathing Blix had for himself.

He hadn't been able to save her.

That's what he had told her, ever since she was little.

That he would always look after her. Take care of her.

That had been his real job.

The most important job of all.

But he had failed.

He would never be able to forgive himself for that.

The rain had drenched them both. Merete shivered. Blix didn't want to be the one to suggest they go. He shifted his weight from one foot to the other, loosening his arm around Merete a little.

'Do you want some time alone?' she asked. 'I can come back another day.'

He shook his head.

Merete turned first. Blix had trouble getting his legs to obey. She had to support him the first few steps back to the car.

62

Samantha wondered if she should go up to the gate and ring the intercom again, when it finally slid open. Jarl Inge looked from side to side before he spotted the car, and then her. Samantha felt her chest tighten.

Jarl Inge rubbed a hand over his mouth and nose. He was carrying a large bag over his shoulder and had a small cardboard box under his arm. Usually, he swayed from side to side as he walked, as if to tell everyone just how tough and dangerous he was. But now, his shoulders were rounded, his posture forward. He had his eyes fixed on the ground in front of him, as if he didn't want anyone else in the car park to see him.

Samantha shuddered.

Opened the door and got out. The occasional drop of rain hit her. She waved and went to meet him. Put on a cautious smile. Jarl Inge continued towards her with his gaze fixed on the ground. Even from a distance, Samantha could see that he had a bandage over his nose. Only when he was halfway across the car park, did he nod a hello.

They met with a brief hug.

'Finally,' she said, pushing herself away from him. 'You're out. Congratulations.'

Jarl Inge didn't respond to that. Instead, he said: 'Have you heard?'

'Heard what?'

He wiped a few drops of rain from his face. 'Rita,' he said. 'They've found her.' His eyes darted around.

'They don't know if it's her yet,' Samantha said.

'They do,' he said. 'They just won't say. Who the hell else could it be?'

Samantha said nothing.

'Let's go,' he continued, hauling the bag back onto his shoulder. 'Give us the car keys,' he added, holding out his hand.

'No.'

Jarl Inge looked at her sceptically. 'No?'

'In case you've forgotten,' Samantha began. 'You don't have a licence. You get out and the first thing you do is drive home? Are you thick?'

He sighed heavily and said: 'Whatever. Let's just go.'

They walked towards the car.

'Thank you for coming to pick me up,' Samantha said sarcastically. 'It's good to see you too.'

He didn't respond, just threw his things into the back seat, opened the passenger-side door and climbed in. Samantha got in and started the car. Put it into gear and drove out onto the road.

'Where's my phone?' he asked. There was an aggressive edge to the question.

'Your phone?'

'Yeah, you said you were going to buy me a phone. Where is it?'

'It's ... at home,' she said after thinking about it. 'I ... didn't think to bring it.'

Jarl Inge sighed. Shook his head.

Samantha took the exit for the motorway, then glanced back over her shoulder, at his belongings in the back seat.

'I thought you had a phone?' she said.

He made an exasperated gesture with his hands. 'Are you stupid? I couldn't bring that out with me, could I? I gave it to Grubben.'

Samantha pursed her lips. Merged into the motorway traffic and drove just over the speed limit. The windscreen wipers swept in an arc at regular intervals. If the traffic didn't hold them up, they would be home in an hour and a half.

63

The wrought-iron gate slid noiselessly back into place. Blix turned and took one last look at the graveyard. Wondered how long it would be until he would be back. If it would be easier then.

They got into the car.

The moisture in the air had created a layer of condensation on the inside of windscreen. Merete started the engine and turned the air con on full blast.

Blix leant back, his head against the headrest. Listened to the hiss of the air con. The steam was gone within a few seconds. He wiped his eyes with his fingers and stared blankly ahead.

Merete started driving.

Blix knew that his destructive thoughts would lead to nothing good. He tried to drive them away just as he did in bed in his cell at night. Redirect them onto something else.

In the last few days, Jarl Inge Ree had been that focus.

Blix sat in thought for a little longer before turning to Merete.

'Could I borrow your phone?' he asked.

Merete glanced down at her phone, resting in the centre console.

'Why? Who are you calling?' she asked.

'Gard Fosse,' Blix replied. 'I just need to give him a quick message.'

Merete didn't answer, just pursed her lips. He looked down. Should have waited before he started talking about something else. Gained a little more distance between this and the visit to the cemetery.

'I think you're right,' he said to explain. 'That Jarl Inge Ree was afraid of being released today.'

He picked up the phone and had to ask for the code to unlock it.

'I think his number is still saved,' she said. 'From way back when.'

There was a bitterness to her voice that he recognised from when they were married. An undertone that suggested she disliked what he was doing.

Blix found the number. Fosse replied, short, dismissive.

'It's me,' Blix said, explaining where he was calling from. 'I don't think Walter Kroos's escape has anything to do with him having a plan *with* Jarl Inge Ree. I think Kroos wanted to be in Norway when Jarl Inge was released.'

Fosse didn't seem to understand.

'I think it might be about revenge,' Blix continued. 'Ree is afraid of Walter Kroos, because he knows he'll be next, after Rita Alvberg.'

Fosse didn't seem convinced. 'That is obviously one possibility,' he said.

'Where is Ree now?' Blix asked.

The answer did not come immediately:

'We don't know.'

'Have you lost sight of them?' Blix asked.

'We had to reprioritise,' Fosse replied. 'The discovery of the body last night and the video recording of Walter Kroos changed our assumptions somewhat.'

Blix laid his head back on the headrest and stared up at the car roof. 'So you've got no intelligence on him?' he asked.

No answer.

'Samantha Kasin picked him up from the prison today,' Blix said. 'They are on their way back to Osen. They could be in danger, both of them.'

'It is a possibility,' Fosse responded. 'But there's never been a greater police presence in Osen than there is now. If Walter Kroos isn't already miles away by now, and still intends to try something, *today,* then he's even dumber than he looks.'

Realising that he was getting nowhere, Blix ended the call.

Merete approached the Majorstua junction. They would soon be at her flat.

'I need to call Emma as well,' Blix said.

Merete said nothing. Emma's number was also saved in her contact list. This time, it went straight to voicemail. Blix stared at the phone in his hands. Wondered if he should try to get hold of Arvid Borvik.

'I've made a chicken casserole,' Merete told him. 'The one with curry that Iselin liked so much.'

Blix mumbled a reply.

'And I baked an almond cake yesterday. With the yellow cream you like.'

Blix started typing out a text to send to Emma, explaining that he was the one who had tried to call.

It was *urgent*. It had been *important*.

He didn't like that he couldn't get a hold of her. But to believe that something had happened was perhaps stretching it a bit far. Fosse was right – there were police all over the village. Still, he couldn't quite shake that ominous, nagging feeling in his stomach. The one he had relied on in all his years as a police officer.

He continued staring down at the phone screen as they drove on. Hoping that Emma would call back. He opened the internet app and searched for news.no. It had been a while since the cases with Emma's byline on them had been updated. A quick scan of the competitors' online newspapers showed that they were publishing a lot more up-to-date information than her last article.

That was unlike Emma.

She had set the agenda for the news coming out of Osen ever since she had arrived.

Emma had been trying to get to the bottom of what had happened when Fred Kasin died, he thought. She would continue to pursue the matter until she reached her goal, he was sure.

And yet she didn't call.

Blix thought it through. It was about 200 or so kilometres to Osen. So about two to three hours by car, depending on the traffic. He should be able to make it up to Osen and back before his curfew was over.

Merete pulled into the garage.

Blix turned to her.

'I am so sorry to do this but ... can I borrow your car?'

Merete manoeuvred the car into a vacant space.

Her lips tightened again. 'You want to borrow the car ... now?'

'I have to check something,' he said. 'It may take some time.'

'How long?'

Blix would not say what or where he was going.

'It could be important,' he said instead.

Merete sighed, seemed as if she were about to say something, but stopped herself. Instead, she shook her head dejectedly before slamming both hands on the steering wheel and swinging open the door. In one swift movement, she dragged her purse from the back seat with her and got out.

She left the keys in the ignition. The car sat idle. She leant in and snatched the phone out of his hands.

'I should have known you hadn't changed,' she said, her voice trembling. 'And today of all days.'

'Merete...'

'Fuck you, Alexander.'

64

They drove toward Minnesund Bridge. In the field on the right, a flock of crows sat around a pool of water.

'So, how does it feel?' Samantha asked.

'How does what feel?'

'Being out again.'

He continued to stare out of the window. Shrugged. 'S'alright.'

He started to bite one of his fingernails. One of his legs was shaking restlessly.

'Did you bring any food?' he asked.

'No.'

'I haven't eaten today.'

'Why not?'

He spat out the tip of the nail. Didn't say anything.

'We can always stop at a petrol station or something if you're hungry.'

Jarl Inge remained silent.

Samantha's phone rang. The sudden vibration made him flinch.

'Who is it?' he asked, looking at her accusingly. Samantha turned her phone round in the cup holder of the centre console so she could see the display.

'Just Mum.'

He snorted.

'I'm sure she's happy I'm out again.'

Samantha had spoken to her a few days ago. Her mother had wanted to know what would happen when Jarl Inge got out.

Then and there, Samantha had said that the relationship was over, a statement she had regretted afterwards. She knew her mother would call and make sure she hadn't gone to pick him up. Once a mother hen, always a mother hen.

'Is there a party tonight?' Jarl Inge asked.

'I ... thought it could just be the two of us tonight,' she said.

He looked over at her, eyebrows raised. 'Are you messing with me?'

'No...?'

'No, we should get the whole gang together,' he said. 'Markus. Trygve. Gitte. Bønna.'

'Okay, but...'

'Or do you just want me to sit at home and watch some talk show with you?'

'Don't you think it'd be inappropriate if we celebrated today?' she asked. 'The same day Rita's body was found?'

Jarl Inge didn't have a response.

'But by all means,' Samantha scoffed, 'I can just drive you up to your father's or something. Then you can get shit-faced or whatever there.'

They passed the exit towards Strandlykkja.

'How are things there?' he asked.

'Where?'

'Home.'

'Other than the fact there are police everywhere, it's the same as before. I'm almost done with renovating the kiosk though.'

It didn't seem to interest him.

'It must've been Walter who killed her,' he said after a while.

'Why do you think that?'

'Because he escaped and came to Norway, obviously?' Jarl Inge said. 'And he's killed people before.'

'But why would he kill Rita?'

Jarl Inge seemed lost for words.

'Why the hell haven't they caught him yet?' he eventually spat out.

Samantha shrugged. 'How should I know?'

She thought about the evening and the night she and Walter had spent together. How strange, but nice, it had been to be so close to him after so many years. She had guided him through it. Shown him what to do. Saw how his embarrassment gradually gave way to reassurance. Happiness. Pleasure. The foreignness to the pleasure too, which he eventually embraced, wholly and completely.

She had grown even more fond of him then.

Felt an affinity with him that she couldn't quite explain, one which turned to sadness. Soon it would be over. She had no illusions that Walter would be able to stay on the run forever.

'Rita,' she began, and immediately felt the knot tighten in her stomach. 'She came to me one day last autumn, I can't remember exactly when. Her mother was ill, so she was home quite often. It was nice to see her again, of course. It had been a long time since I'd seen her.'

Jarl Inge continued to stare out the window.

'It's strange,' she began. 'When you meet people again who you've known all your life, but there's been a gap of a few years without any contact. With some, it's as if not even a second has passed; you're back on the exact same frequency. While with others, it's just impossible to go back to what you once were.' Her finger tightened around the steering wheel. 'It was like that with Rita.'

Jarl Inge turned his head towards her, but said nothing.

'I realised that there was something she wanted to talk to me about. That something was on her mind, was bothering her.'

Samantha waited a moment, before continuing:

'She ... wanted to talk about what happened that night. When Fred ... raped me.' Her knuckles turned white. 'I'd never really thought about the fact that Rita was suddenly there that night. I mean, she'd known that I had to spend time that night with Uncle Abel and Fred, and that I couldn't come out. But everyone always just hung out at the campsite anyway ... so it wasn't that unusual that ... she was there, so ... I assumed that she was just nearby when it happened.' Samantha swallowed, her throat now dry. 'She told me that she had ... been mad at me. That she hadn't liked Walter. Or that I was hanging out with him so much. You didn't like that either, I remember. You were a little jealous.'

He snorted. 'I was *not*. I didn't give a shit about Walter.'

'Whatever,' Samantha said. 'I was in the kiosk, cleaning up. I guess Fred had gone to ... take a piss or something, I don't know. Regardless, Rita bumped into him outside the kiosk.'

Samantha pulled into the left lane and overtook a yellow Opel Corsa. Knew instinctively that Jarl Inge was staring at her.

'And Rita, she...'

Samantha quickly glanced down at the speedometer: 132 kilometres per hour. She took her foot off the accelerator slightly.

'She thought it would be a good idea to ... "mess around" with Fred, to use her own words. To mess around with *me*. Like, to punish me for ... everything that happened with Walter. Because I chose him over you for a few days.'

She caught up to a black Porsche.

'So she told Fred that ... that I was an "easy fuck". That it was just a matter of trying. That I *wanted* it. Not only that, but she told him I liked him too. Fred, I mean.'

'Samantha...'

'"Don't you want to fuck her?"' She imitated Rita's voice. And continued: '"I know she's horny for you."'

Samantha shook her head.

'And inside the kiosk, it was free game, she told him. No one would see a thing.'

She flicked up the indicator and accelerated past the Porsche. Jarl Inge grabbed the handle above the side window.

'And *you* know what happened after that,' Samantha said, continuing to accelerate past three more cars. 'And of course, with everything that followed, Rita had the world's worst conscience. So she came and took care of me. Helped me the next day, when we had to go to Oslo for that godforsaken singing competition. You know, she was really the absolute best friend you could've asked for that day.'

Samantha eased off on the accelerator again. 'At least I thought so.'

They drove on in silence for a while.

'Rita had struggled with a guilty conscience about that for years,' she continued. 'When she came to me that day, she needed to get it off her chest. Came to me for forgiveness, I think, so life would be a little easier for her.'

She still felt his gaze fixed on her.

'It was just a joke, she said. She didn't think he would actually do it. Or would be able to do it, even. She hardly knew him.'

A car behind her flashed its headlights at her. It dawned on Samantha that she had been in the left lane for a while.

She swerved into the right-hand lane.

'What...' Jarl Inge cleared his throat. 'What did you say to her?'

'To Rita? I told her to go to hell. Everything that went to shit in my life started that night. And then to find out, many, many years later, that it was my best friend who practically pushed my rapist into the kiosk that night.' She narrowed her eyes. 'You think you know someone...'

She turned her head towards Jarl Inge now.

Felt how her chest tightened too.

'Oh, and Rita told me one more thing,' she said, her voice quivering. 'That she wasn't alone that night. Talking to Fred. *You* were there too. And, in fact, it was your idea. You put the words in her mouth. You even gave Fred a pat on the shoulder before he walked in. Wished him luck.'

Jarl Inge tried to say something, but Samantha cut him off.

'And you've kept this to yourself all these years, never thought to say a single fucking thing to me. Well, thank you very much. Thank you *both* for ruining my life.'

65

Emma was half sitting, half lying on the sofa, her hands tied behind her back.

'Where's Samantha?' she asked. Her voice trembled. She tried to calm her breathing.

Walter Kroos didn't answer her. Maybe he had hurt Samantha too, Emma thought. But she hadn't heard any other sounds coming from inside the house. And she hadn't seen Samantha's car outside either.

'It was you I saw last night,' she said.

It didn't feel as dangerous throwing out the accusations in English.

'It was you trying to dump Rita Alvberg's body in the water. Those are the clothes you were wearing,' she stated, nodding towards the drying rack.

Even now Walter would not communicate. He just walked back and forth in front of her, lost in his own thoughts. His forehead glistened with sweat. This was definitely not part of the plan, she thought, whatever the plan was.

Emma twisted, tried to place her body in a slightly more comfortable position. Her trousers were ripped just below her left knee. It still stung. The right side of her face also felt numb.

'What are you doing here?' Emma asked – her breath coming out in short, sharp gasps with each word.

Again, Walter didn't answer. He sat down in an armchair, but quickly stood up again. Walked over to the window and peered out between the curtains. There was something at-home about his movements.

Emma let her gaze drift around. On the table were two wine glasses, stained red around the rims. She glanced over at Walter again. His clothes were hanging to dry in the living room.

He was no intruder here – he was a guest.

And Samantha wasn't a victim, she was an accomplice.

They must have hatched a plan together before he escaped. They must have been in contact.

Emma was sure Blix was trying to call her. Maybe Anita too. The more time that went by without them getting through to her, the more worried they would become. Therein lay a kind of hope. But she hadn't told anyone that she was going to see Samantha. She'd come here on a whim. Unless someone had seen her heading down here, no one would know where she was.

The realisation made her breathing increase again. Shallow. Fast. Her thoughts raced as she desperately tried to find rational theories to all this.

Rita Alvberg was dead, killed after Walter escaped. Half of the village had come together to try and find her. Only when the water had been searched had Walter tried to dump Rita's body in there – several days after she had been reported missing.

Where had she been in the meantime?

Here?

From the house to the beach was a long way to carry a corpse, so it was unlikely that Walter would have carried Rita all that distance. Anyone could have seen him, even if it was the middle of the night. And he definitely hadn't been driving. Emma would have heard if a car passed by. So Rita must have been somewhere else in the days she was missing. Somewhere closer to the water.

Her eyes found the drying rack again. Looked properly at the hoodie hanging there.

Emma shuddered.

It said *Osen Campsite* on it.

66

Samantha looked away from the road for a brief moment. On the left lay Mjøsa – the lake as large, wide and beautiful as always. The rain had eased off now.

'That's not true,' Jarl Inge said beside her. 'I wasn't there that night.'

Samantha started to laugh. 'Why would Rita make up something like that?'

'To ... have someone else to blame.'

Samantha pressed her head back against the headrest and laughed demonstratively. 'You should've heard her,' she said. 'The night she came to my house. She wasn't messing around. She'd been to therapy, she told me, had been encouraged to apologise to me, lay all her cards on the table and what not. Maybe you should think about doing that,' she snarled. 'We've still got a while to go before we're home.'

Jarl Inge didn't answer.

'That night in Oslo,' said Samantha. 'When I more or less collapsed on stage in front of the whole fucking country. Rita told me she called you and told you to come and get me. You were both equally responsible for what happened, she said. And you brought your father with you, and there you were, in Oslo. Or do you deny that too?'

'No, but...'

'No, but what?'

'She...' He stopped himself. 'It was Rita who...'

When he didn't continue, unable to think of anything to say, she snorted and said:

'You've been a liar your whole life, Jarl Inge. You do it without even having to think about it.' She sighed. 'I kind of ended up being the same way myself. I've lied about Fred for, what, twenty years? Both about the rape and ... the rest of it. It's exhausting. I am so goddamn tired. Aren't you?'

Again he remained silent.

'But eventually I realised why *you* never told the truth about Fred.

You understood where my hatred came from and knew you were responsible for it. If the truth came out, everyone would know what you'd done.'

Samantha waited a moment before continuing:

'And, of course, you more than obliged when I needed help to forget. You got me everything I needed. Back then, at least. You thought you could make it all go away.'

Small drops of saliva hit the steering wheel as she spoke.

'Thanks for that as well, by the way,' she snapped. 'You turned me into a junkie. And it didn't even work. The pain never went away. You can't just put a plaster over a wound like that and think it'll heal by itself. Wounds leave scars that never go away. It's still as red and violent and deep as it ever was.'

It felt good to finally say this all out loud. She felt calmer. Lighter.

The silence hung between them.

After a while, he asked: 'What ... do you want me to say? Sorry? I didn't mean for that to happen?'

'I mean, that would have been a good place to start,' Samantha said. 'But it's too late for that now.'

'What do you mean?'

'If you don't understand that, then you're even dumber than I thought you were.'

Jarl Inge remained silent for a moment. Then said:

'But you've known about this now for, what, a year?'

'Something like that.'

'And you haven't said anything until now?'

Samantha stared at the road.

'You visited me?' he continued. 'You brought me things. Gifts. We even fucked in the visitors' room. You did all this,' he said, 'while you were actually furious?'

'Yes,' Samantha said. 'Correct.'

'That's just insane. Why?'

'*Why*? Because ... I needed time to think about how I wanted to handle it.'

'So you just covered it all up?'

'Yep.'

He shook his head. 'Well, you're a damn good actor, I'll give you that,' he said. 'Jesus.'

They passed the exit to Espa. Samantha usually stopped by the petrol station at this point to buy a chocolate-chip bun, but not today.

'What does all this mean, then?' he asked, still fuming. 'Have you figured out "how you want to handle it"?' He imitated her voice. 'Are you going to tell *me* to go to hell too? Is that what you've decided?'

Samantha smiled but didn't answer him.

A forest now lined either side of the road. The traffic flowed smoothly.

'You're not that torn up about the fact Rita's dead, are you?'

'No,' she answered him. 'Not at all.'

He twisted in his seat to face her. A seriousness, an uneasiness, had clouded his face. He studied her for a long time before saying:

'You know what happened to her, don't you?'

Samantha pursed her lips, moved her gaze to meet his. Then she answered:

'Yes.'

67

Regret and doubt set in as soon as he had pulled out of the garage. In fact, the same feeling grew with every kilometre he put between him and Merete. Leaving her like that felt like he was betraying Iselin too, as he had done so many times, back when they were a small family.

Glancing in the rearview mirror, Blix pulled into the left lane, bringing his speed up to just below the limit, to avoid attracting any kind of interest from the civilian traffic patrols.

The windscreen wipers worked furiously, sweeping in large arcs across the screen. Behind the forest to his left was the prison. He squinted over to see if he could still see Samantha Kasin's red Volvo there as he passed the exit, but only saw an old van parked up.

Time was an unpredictable factor when it came to the prison. She could still be standing outside the gate, waiting for Jarl Inge Ree, or they might as easily be close to Osen by now.

The car radio was on, but so low that he couldn't hear what was being said between the music and commercials. He turned it up to listen to the news. The missing person-turned-murder investigation and the intensified search for Walter Kroos were still the main story. The reporter at the scene was able to say that an operation was under way at a disused farm two miles north of Osen, but that the police were keeping their cards close to their chest.

The bulletin ended and he turned the radio off.

He wished he still had the phone.

In prison, it had taken time to adjust to not having the opportunity to contact others whenever he wanted to, or having access to the internet. Now he felt paralysed. If the police were in the process of arresting Walter Kroos, he would have to turn around and drive back.

The cars in front of him slowed down. It didn't take long before they were at a complete standstill. Blix merged as far over to the left as he could, to see what was going on further ahead.

He saw blue lights.

He cursed inwardly. There must have been an accident.

Slowly – far too slowly – they rolled closer.

Then they stopped again.

The car in front of him let ten, fifteen, twenty metres stretch between them and the car in front. Blix held his hand down on the horn. The woman in the driver's seat looked in her rearview mirror and gave him the finger.

Blix checked the petrol gauge. The hybrid car was already out of electric power. And the fuel needle had crept below half a tank.

He finally passed the scene of the accident. A Mazda had, somehow, managed to drive into the guard rail and had come to a stop on the hard shoulder, half of it poking out over the outside lane.

The traffic cleared, and Blix could finally hold his foot down on the accelerator.

A few minutes later, a red car appeared a few hundred metres in front of him. Blix glanced in the mirror and put a little more pressure on his right leg. He caught up with it, quickly ascertained that it was not a Volvo, but didn't slow down either.

The railway tracks ran parallel to the motorway. The airport train came up on the side of him and veered off towards Gardermoen. Blix continued north, not knowing what he was heading toward.

But it felt like he was running out of time.

68

The rain had collected at the sides of the road. Travelling so fast made the steering wheel jerk. Samantha stared at her hands, which were still shaking, just as they had been ever since that day last week when the bell out in the shop had suddenly rung.

She had been busy in the office.

Actually, the shop hadn't been open – she had just forgotten to lock it after nipping out to the bins with a few bags full of expired food. She got up quickly and went out into the shop. Stopped immediately when she saw who it was.

'Hi,' Rita said meekly. 'I ... saw your car, so I knew you had to be here.'

Samantha said nothing.

'Are you busy?' Rita asked. 'I was out for a walk and ... I thought I'd stop by.'

'What do you want?' Samantha asked.

The anger she had felt towards Rita over the last year had not diminished.

'You might have heard ... that my mum died?' Rita began.

Samantha nodded. 'Sad.'

She understood what Rita wanted. She was playing the sympathy and compassion card, hoping to improve the odds of them making up and being friends again.

'I didn't see you at the funeral?'

'That would be because I wasn't there,' Samantha said.

She had actually considered going. But when the day came, she couldn't bring herself to do it. Couldn't bear the thought of going up to Rita afterwards, as custom dictates.

Rita took a few cautious steps closer. Her cheeks were red. The soles of her shoes were muddy and made dirty footprints on the floor. Rita noticed.

'Oh, sorry,' she said. 'I ... there was no mat, by the door.'

Samantha didn't say anything.

'I've just been on a walk,' Rita continued. 'Through the forest.'

When Samantha didn't answer, Rita sighed and tried again:

'How long are you going to be mad at me?'

'I'm not mad at you.'

'You obviously are – you told me to go to hell the last time we saw each other, and now it's like you can barely even look at me.'

'I'm not mad at you,' Samantha repeated, looking up at Rita now. 'I am furious.'

They just stood there, staring at each other.

'You want me to forgive you, is that it?' Samantha continued. 'For what, exactly? For the fact that *you two* made a person with learning disabilities rape me? Because you tanked my singing career? Because you destroyed my entire life?'

'Markus told me that you're still with Jarl Inge,' Rita argued. 'You've clearly managed to forgive *him.*'

'Markus...' Samantha smiled to herself, shook her head. 'Markus talks a lot of nonsense.'

She turned and walked further into the kiosk. Heard Rita follow her. Samantha turned into the last aisle, and walked along the wall of shelving, stocked up with various canned goods. Stopped where she had put down the mop that time. Heard Rita coming up behind her.

All these years later, Samantha could still feel the clammy heat of the kiosk that night in 2004. Feel it on her skin. The scrubbing, the hot water against her hands, had only made her even sweatier.

'This is where it happened,' Samantha said, her tone sharper. 'This is where he tried to kiss me.' She turned around. 'And here's where he pushed me up against the food racks.'

With her arms straight, she pushed Rita into the kiosk shelves, as if to demonstrate exactly how it had happened that night. A few food cans and a couple of bottles of barbecue sauce fell to the floor. One smashed.

'And this is where he forced me onto the floor,' Samantha continued. 'You probably remember the skirt I was wearing that day.'

'Samantha...' Rita pushed herself away from the shelves.

'You can probably imagine what easy access he had,' Samantha continued, 'as he pressed down on top of me. Or you probably can *now* anyway. You didn't back then.'

Rita looked down.

There were four cartons of chopped tomatoes at her feet. She bent down to pick them up.

'Leave them,' Samantha said bluntly.

Rita still grabbed one of them.

'I said leave them!'

Samantha tore the carton out of her hands and squeezed it so hard that her knuckles turned white. She put it back on the shelf.

Left the other three on the floor.

'It was a mistake,' Rita begged, her voice unable to continue. She gathered herself and added. 'We were young, stupid ... We weren't thinking.'

'You weren't thinking.'

Samantha shook her head and bent down to pick up the smashed bottle.

'I ... I mean,' Rita went on. 'I've said sorry once before, and I'm saying it again now. I meant it with all my heart, and I do now too. But if you want me to grovel as well, you can forget it. It's been years since you were raped, Samantha, and it was only, like, five seconds. It's completely possible to show a little goodwill and realise that we did not intend for that to happen. It's possible to leave things in the past and move on. For the sake of old friendship, and for your own sake too. But if you don't want that, then that's fine by me. I've got better things to do with my life.'

Rita turned to leave.

Samantha followed. Barbecue sauce dripped from the glass bottle in her hand. Without hesitation, she swung her arm around and slammed it into Rita. The blow hit her in the temple. The bottom flew out of the end of the bottle. Rita spun around. She staggered into the food rack. Several more cans and glass jars fell to the floor.

Samantha lifted the broken bottle once more, and lunged forward in a stabbing motion, like the bottle was a sword. Rita gaped at her. The glass drilled into her throat and stayed there. She slowly sank to the floor with a frightened, tortured expression on her face.

✳

Samantha looked over at Jarl Inge.

He had turned pale. He just sat there, his mouth hanging open, staring at her aghast, as if he didn't know what to say.

'Stop the car,' he finally demanded, grabbing hold of the door handle.

Samantha ignored him.

'Let me out!'

'Why?'

'Jesus Christ, Samantha, you've killed two people!'

'You must've killed ten times that,' she responded. 'All those people you turned into drug addicts over the last fifteen or twenty years.'

'That's not the same.'

'Is it not?'

'I've not murdered anyone or held them under water until they ... they—'

'You literally put the syringes in their hands though.'

'It's a free world,' he retorted. 'What people do with their lives is up to them. You, on the other hand...'

He stopped himself. Let go of the door handle and looked away.

'Fuck me, you're even sicker in the head than I thought. You should've been locked up.'

Samantha slowed down and took the exit off the motorway, towards Elverum and Trysil.

Jarl Inge lifted himself up in his seat and wiped some sweat from his upper lip.

'Why are you telling me all this?' he asked.

'Because you're an accomplice,' she replied. 'And because you've kept your mouth shut before. And you're the only one I can trust.'

He glanced over at her. His lips parted, as if he were about to say something, but he stopped himself.

'No one else knows about any of this?' he asked a short while later.

The spray from the rear wheels of a lorry in front of them left a film of oily rainwater across the windshield. Samantha cranked up the speed of the windscreen wipers.

'No one,' she replied. 'Nobody's going to find out, either.'

Jarl Inge ran his hand over his mouth again. 'And what ... did you do with Rita after you ... at the kiosk...?'

'I dragged her into the freezer room,' Samantha said. 'Wrapped her up in an old sleeping bag. Then I cleaned up and washed all the surfaces. Waxed the floor. I'd been thinking about renovating the place for years, but I thought that was as good a time as ever to do it. Give the place a fresh lick of paint, give the kiosk a lift, you know? A new, fresh start.'

Jarl Inge groaned.

'You left her there then for ... how many days?'

'I didn't keep count.'

'But until last night at least?'

'Yep.'

'Jesus.'

They approached the turn-off to Løiten. Trees lined either side of the road.

'So the last thing you did before picking me up was try to dump Rita in the lake?'

Samantha shrugged.

'Everyone thinks it was Walter.'

Jarl Inge had always been easy to read. She could tell he was shocked and frightened, but also somewhat reassured. There was nothing to suggest that he suspected Walter of being in on any of this, or that he had any idea of what awaited him.

69

The woman on the sofa was younger than Walter had first thought. In her late twenties, maybe. She twisted round again. Met his gaze and threw new questions at him, interspersed with a few German words.

Walter stood up, grabbed one of the woollen socks from the drying rack and walked towards her. She realised what was coming, and turned away, clamping her mouth shut. He grabbed her jaw with one hand and forced her mouth open. Panic flashed in her eyes. He pushed the sock in until she vomited. As soon as he released his grip, she spat it out.

The roll of tape was on the table. He reached for it, forced the sock back into her mouth and taped over her lips. Most of the sock was hanging out of her mouth, underneath the tape. Dangling down over her chin. She screamed and protested behind the tape, but hardly any sound came out.

He pulled her off the couch by her legs and dragged her with him through the kitchen and down the stairs to the basement. She was whimpering behind him, and he heard how the back of her head hit the steps on the way down.

He dragged her into the far corner, into a small storeroom, furthest from the living room and the kitchen. He noticed a key in the lock of the door. He locked the door and took it out. Went back upstairs again.

The kitchen rug that had been in front of the basement door was all crumpled up. He flattened it out and stood there, listening. Heard no sounds from the floor below. Walter walked over to the counter and filled a glass with water. Drank, feeling his pulse slowing somewhat.

Water continued to drip from the tap. He turned it tighter and put the glass in the dishwasher. Checked that there were no other signs in the kitchen that there was a guest in the house, concluded that he was satisfied and went out into the living room.

The clothes were practically dry. He folded them – with military precision, as his father had taught him – as he thought about everything that had gone wrong during the night.

It had been his idea that *he* should move the body. He was on the run; it was only a matter of time before he would be caught. There was already speculation in the news that he was the one who had killed Rita, and if he did leave any traces behind that pointed towards him as the suspect, then it'd only help Samantha walk free.

He had never thought she would be capable of murder. Especially not like that, face to face, by her own hand. That was why he was here, why he had come, so she wouldn't be alone when Jarl Inge was let out. So she wouldn't have to do it alone this time ... they would be together, for the final step.

What had happened to Rita, however, was something else. An act of impulse. But Samantha had shown no sign of remorse. She had seemed cold and calm. The only problem they had run into was that Rita's disappearance had brought both the police and the media to the village, And then of course he had gone and messed up when trying to dump the body.

He collapsed the drying rack and carried it into the bathroom. Put the clothes away in one of the drawers under the sink.

He stopped and looked down the hallway again, at the door to the basement.

What would they do about the journalist?

Samantha would decide, Walter concluded.

She should be here soon.

70

The floor was cold and unforgiving. It couldn't be more than fifteen degrees in here. A cool box sat in her field of vision, just past it was a floor-to-ceiling cupboard. Emma spotted a mousetrap too, on the floor in the corner closest to her. The spring was still loaded.

Emma tried to relieve the pressure on her shoulder, hip and thigh, but quickly ended up back in the same position. The sock in her mouth tasted of old, wet wool. Every time she exerted herself, the lack of oxygen made her dizzy.

She looked up at the curtainless basement window, hoping to see someone out there. Someone who might notice her.

The minutes crept by. After a while, it was hard to stay focused. She had no idea how long she had been lying there. Any attempt to pry her hands free had been futile. The tape was too tight. She had tried to rub the tape around her ankles against the seam of her jeans, but she'd given up hope on that too.

She thought of Anita, and of Blix, who had both told her to be careful. But it was just something people said. Even if Walter Kroos was in Osen, she had never imagined that he would pose a danger to her. And certainly not in broad daylight.

She twisted round again, thinking of her sister. And of Martine, who was probably at school right now.

The thought of her niece made Emma roll onto her side. There, she had a better overview of the shelving attached to the wall. The shelves were full of canned goods, plant pots and Christmas decorations. She could try to break something. Use the shards to cut through the tape.

She wriggled closer. Centimetre by centimetre. The sweat trickled down her back, despite the temperature in the room. She had to pause, wait until she could breathe more calmly, before she edged further, taking a few small movements at a time. Once close enough to the shelves, she spotted a terracotta plant pot on the first shelf, and managed to heave her legs up beside it. With great effort she managed to kick the pot, which almost overturned.

She made another attempt.

This time, she succeeded – the pot fell on its side. With her feet, she then managed to nudge it all the way over the edge of the shelf until, finally, the pot fell to the concrete floor.

But it didn't break.

She inched closer to the shelves. There was another pot on the shelf above, but it was too far back on the shelf for her to reach it with her feet. Emma inwardly cursed as she breathed hard and fast, in and out through her nose. For a few moments she closed her eyes and concentrated on relaxing her body, bringing her heartrate down.

Footsteps moving around on the floor above made her open her eyes again and raise her upper body. The muscles in her stomach, throat and neck tightened. She managed to push over a cardboard box, but only some of its contents rolled out – a couple of old cables and an extension cord.

Emma slumped over.

There was nothing there to help her break free.

71

A dark spruce forest rose up on either side of the road. Tall tree trunks with an undergrowth of autumn-coloured heather. Blix caught one more news broadcast before he reached Osen. The police operation at the small, abandoned farm on the outskirts of the village hadn't resulted in anything. Otherwise, there was nothing new.

He had caught up with the traffic in front of him and was the fourth in a line of vehicles. The road offered few opportunities for overtaking. As it opened out, he noticed blue lights in the distance. A checkpoint. Traffic heading north was allowed to pass, but passed by slowly. All cars on their way out of the village were being stopped and checked by heavily armed police. The boot of a van was being searched as Blix drove past. A woman in the next car was ordered out to open the boot.

After another quarter of an hour behind the wheel, the landscape ahead came into view. The road ran along a river, and the settlement grew a little denser. Further on, the grey clouds were reflected in a body of water.

The campsite was signposted. Blix left the road. A large board welcomed him in Norwegian, German and English. It was already two o'clock. He only had an hour if he was going to make it back in time for the end of day release, but then he would have to leave Merete's car outside the prison.

The windows in the reception building were dark. Five to six people were standing under the eaves, sheltering from the rain. One of the men had a jacket with a logo from NRK News on the back.

Blix drove past and continued on into the camping area, passing rows of caravans before coming to an area of rental cabins.

He didn't know what kind of car Emma drove, but there was only one cabin with a car parked outside. A small, grey Audi. Blix parked up behind it and climbed out. He glanced inside the car as he passed. There was a water bottle and an energy bar on the passenger seat. Those could easily be Emma's.

He went up to the door and knocked. No response from inside. In the narrow crack between the door and the frame he could see that the door was locked. He tried the handle anyway before walking around the cabin and peering in through the windows. There was glass and a phone charger on the kitchen counter, and then two half-burnt candles and a laptop on the table in the living room.

He had left the engine running. He got behind the wheel again and drove back to the reception building. One of the cars, along with the NRK man, had gone. Blix parked where it had been, and got out.

'Hi there,' he said, glancing around among the journalists. 'I'm looking for a colleague of yours. Emma Ramm from news.no. She's not at her cabin.'

It didn't seem like any of the reporters recognised him. A young woman stepped forward.

'I spoke to her this morning,' she said.

Blix made up some lie about how he had left his phone on the roof of the car before driving off.

'It must be somewhere between Oslo and Osen,' he said with a wry smile. 'Could I borrow yours to call her?'

'Sure, I have her number here,' the woman in front of him obliged, finding it before holding out the phone.

Blix lifted the phone to his ear and turned away slightly. All he heard was a dialling tone. He double-checked the number on the display, and tried again, but didn't get through.

A police car drove slowly onto the campsite. Two officers looked out from either side. Blix turned his back to them.

'Straight to voicemail,' he said, handing the phone back. 'Thanks for letting me borrow it anyway.'

The woman smiled at him.

'Is it closed?' Blix asked, pointing at the door to the reception building.

'It's the low season,' the journalist replied.

'Do you know the area well?' Blix asked.

'Relatively,' the woman answered.

'Do you know where the owner lives?' he asked. 'Samantha Kasin?'

'Down by Osenløkka, I believe,' the journalist answered, nodding over in the direction she meant. 'I can find out though,' she added, making a phone call.

It wasn't long until she had the full address and gave him the directions.

Blix climbed in behind the wheel again. As he drove, he loosened his tie, yanked it off, and put it on the seat next to him.

72

The rain was back with full force.

Heavy droplets that made Samantha run across the gravel and fumble about for the house keys.

'Hurry up,' Jarl Inge said behind her. 'I'm getting soaked here.'

As she stepped into the hallway, he shoved her in from behind. Samantha turned and shot him an irritated look, before absent-mindedly taking off her shoes and hanging up her jacket.

In the living room, everything looked fine. The house was quiet.

'Christ, I need a beer,' Jarl Inge said, walking past her into the kitchen.

'Me too,' Samantha said.

Suddenly she noticed the sofa cushions were in disarray. She walked over and picked up the nearest one, shook it out a little and propped it back in the corner. Went to do the same with the next one, but ended up standing there, the cushion in her hands.

In the crack between two of the seat cushions were four small stones. There were a few new dark spots on the cushion cover too. Samantha brushed over them with her finger. The stains had sunk into the fabric and hadn't spread, but her instincts told her it was blood.

From the kitchen, she heard Jarl Inge grabbing a can of beer from the fridge and cracking it open.

Samantha turned the couch cushion over and looked around, trying to understand what Walter had been up to while she was gone. She spotted more gravel on the floor. She crouched down, picked it up and froze.

Under the sofa: a rogue trainer. Multicoloured with blue laces.

She bent over a little further, peered under the sofa.

And there was the other one.

She could feel her pulse beating in her temple. She recognised the shoes. Had seen them up close just a day or so ago, when she went for a walk with Emma Ramm.

There was some sand on the floor too. Almost like footprints.

Samantha followed them out into the hallway. Stopped at the entrance to the kitchen, where Jarl Inge pulled out a chair from the kitchen table. The legs scraped against the floor. He sat down and lifted the beer to his mouth.

'D'you have my phone somewhere?' he asked, stretching his hands up. He interlocked his fingers behind his head and pushed his shoulder blades back.

There was gravel on the kitchen floor too.

'Hellooo?' Jarl Inge tried again.

'Huh?'

'The phone you got me,' he said. 'You said you left it at home. I thought I'd call the guys. Let them know I'm out.'

Samantha walked into the room. 'I didn't buy you a phone, Jarl Inge.'

She grabbed the can of beer on the table in front of him, feeling the weight of it – he'd already had more than half the can. He just looked up at her with a puzzled look on his face.

'Did you seriously think I could afford it?' Samantha took a sip and shook the can a little. 'Thanks for getting a beer for me too, by the way.'

She continued past him to the fridge and took out another can. Opened it with a quick snap, put her hand in her trouser pocket and smuggled the little grey tablet into the mouth of the can. She heard the sound of the pill breaking through the foam, but still rotated the can a few times before placing it on the table in front of Jarl Inge.

'I'll get some food from the freezer to make dinner,' she said.

73

Walter was sitting on the carpeted floor in the hallway between the pantry and the basement toilet. He expected the journalist to do everything in her power to break free, so sitting here, it was easy to hear what was going on in the storeroom, and he could be there in a few seconds.

From the floor above he heard Samantha and Jarl Inge. Steps, walking around, the hum of small talk. Thus far, the tone seemed calm, civilised.

Walter had wondered what they would do once they got home. His first thought had been that Jarl Inge would want to have sex with her. He himself had mentioned this theory to Samantha too, earlier that morning, but she had just laughed.

'After everything I intend to tell him on the drive back, Jarl Inge probably won't be particularly keen to get me into bed.' She winked and added: 'If I know Jarl Inge, first thing he'll want to do is have a beer. And that works perfectly for us.'

Walter hoped it hadn't taken her too long to trick him into taking the pill. They'd have to come up with a plan for the journalist as well.

Footsteps moving across the kitchen floor. The door down to the basement opened.

He quickly got to his feet. From the lightness of the steps, he realised that it must be Samantha. He met her at the bottom of the stairs, where she brought an index finger up to her lips.

'What the hell is going on, Walter?' she whispered. 'Is Emma Ramm here?'

'I had no choice,' Walter whispered back. 'She came here, to the door and ... she saw me.'

Samantha shook her head. 'Where is she now?'

She bit her lower lip as Walter explained.

'Which means she realises that I...'

She stopped herself and thought for a few moments.

'We can't let her talk to anyone.'

They looked at each other for a few seconds. Walter understood what that meant.

'Take care of it,' she said. 'As quietly as you can. I'll let you know when you can come up. Should take about fifteen minutes.' Samantha turned to go back up, but stopped and looked back at him.

'Actually, I need you to go in there and get me some meat from the freezer,' she whispered.

Walter didn't understand.

'I told Jarl Inge that I was going to the freezer to get ingredients for dinner,' she explained and nodded towards the storeroom.

He went to the door and carefully unlocked it.

Emma Ramm looked up at him.

Held his gaze.

She had managed to get over to the shelves by the wall and to pull down some of the contents, but the tape was still intact round her hands, ankles and mouth.

He flipped open the freezer lid. It was almost empty. A couple of boxes of frozen pizza and a freezer bag of meatballs lay at the bottom. He pulled out the meatballs and closed the box. Cast another look at Emma, and left.

Samantha was waiting right outside. She took the bag and headed for the stairs.

Walter peered in at Emma.

As quietly as you can.

She was going to fight back. Inside the small storage room, things would easily topple over, smash. He pulled the door shut again and locked it. The best option, he reasoned, would be to wait until Jarl Inge had blacked out. Maybe they could do the same with her as with him – force a GHB tablet into her, and then wait for her to pass out too. Then he could just put her in the freezer. That had to be a comfortable way to die.

He sat back down on the floor again.

Waited.

Sounds from outside reached him. He stood up and stretched to look out of the basement window.

'Shit,' he whispered to himself.

A car had parked outside.

A man in a suit stepped out.

74

There was a leak from the gutter above the doorframe. Blix stood on the doorstep as the water from the gutter dripped onto the floor beside him. He rang the bell. He heard the sound of a clock ticking in the foyer just inside.

He rang the doorbell again and used the door knocker. It took some time before he saw any movement inside. The door finally opened and Samantha Kasin looked at him questioningly.

'I'm looking for Jarl Inge Ree,' Blix began. 'Is he here?'

Samantha seemed confused.

'I'm a friend of his,' Blix explained. 'And of Emma Ramm,' he added, turning slightly to look back out at weather. 'Can I come in?'

'It's ... not a good time,' Samantha said.

A voice came from further inside: 'Who is it?'

Samantha didn't get a chance to answer before Jarl Inge Ree had appeared behind her.

'Blix?' he asked. 'What the hell are you doing here? Did you escape?'

'I need to talk to you,' Blix replied. 'With both of you.'

'We only just got back—' Samantha began.

'This is Alexander Blix,' Ree said, gesturing in Blix's direction with the beer can in his hand. 'The policeman from the prison.'

Ree stifled a burp and pushed past Samantha, opening the door all the way. 'Come in,' he said.

Samantha still seemed reluctant, but stepped aside. Blix was aware that the soles of his shoes were wet and that they would leave marks on the floor, but he didn't want to take them off. An unwritten rule in the force dictated that one should never enter an unknown place barefoot.

They continued into the kitchen. Ree finished off his beer and set it down on the kitchen counter. Staggered over to the fridge to take out a new one. His steps were unsteady, as if he were walking across the deck of a moving boat.

'Want one?' he offered.

Blix shook his head and sat down at the table. 'I have to head back soon.'

Ree felt around in the air a little before managing to get hold of the back of the chair, and finally took a seat across from him. Samantha remained standing, leaning against the kitchen counter with her arms crossed in front of her chest.

The beer foamed over when Ree opened the new can. He gulped it down and wiped his top lip with the back of his hand.

'So what the hell are you doing here?' He slurred when he spoke, as if his mouth was dry. 'Weren't you going to a funeral or something?'

'It's about Walter Kroos,' Blix said. 'He's here in Osen. He was filmed last night, when he tried to dump Rita Alvberg's body in the lake.'

Ree narrowed his eyes slightly before glancing over at Samantha, then returned his gaze to Blix.

'What did you just say?' he asked.

Blix studied Ree. He must have had a lot to drink already. It seemed like he was having to put great effort into concentrating as he spoke.

'Walter Kroos is here in Osen,' Blix repeated.

Ree turned to Samantha again. 'Walter Kroos...' he slurred. 'But—'

'Who filmed him?' Samantha interrupted.

'Emma Ramm,' Blix answered. 'Which is partly why I'm here, actually. I'm worried about her. She's not picking up her phone.'

'But what does that have to do with us?' Samantha asked.

Ree's pupils had shrunk considerably, his eyelids heavy. The colour seemed to have disappeared from Samantha's face.

'Emma was covering Walter's escape and the murder of Rita Alvberg,' Blix continued, fixing his gaze on Ree. 'And I think he may be in Norway to come after you.'

It looked like Ree would fall asleep at any moment.

'That is just absolutely ridiculous,' Samantha scoffed.

Blix said nothing. Just scrutinised her.

'Emma came to visit you,' he said. 'She spoke to you about...'

Gravity pulled Ree's head down toward the table, but he woke up just before he crashed into it.

'Are you okay?' Blix asked.

'I ... don't quite feel right,' Ree replied.

75

Emma lay on her back with her legs up against the shelves. The freezer behind her whirred. Outside the basement window, the drainpipes from the roof gurgled. The noise made it difficult to pick up any other sounds or follow what was going on elsewhere in the house. But she thought she'd heard the doorbell.

She kicked the shelves as hard as she could, but couldn't muster up much power. But she didn't need a lot. Just enough to knock off something that would break, so she had a sharp tool to cut the tape with.

She kicked at the shelves again.

Something rattled up near the top. But the shelves were screwed to the wall. Emma couldn't get them to move enough. She tried a few more times but realised that her plan wouldn't work.

She sunk to the floor again, tried to breathe calmly in and out through her nose. Drive away the worst of her thoughts. She couldn't give up. Mustn't give up.

She moved her gaze back to the shelves.

Pushed herself up slightly.

At the very end of the bottom shelf she spotted a nail sticking up. It couldn't have been more than half a centimetre long. But it was enough, possibly, to create a tear in the tape, even just a small one.

Emma pushed herself, centimetre by centimetre, across the floor towards it. Every time she put any pressure on her right foot, a sharp pain shot through her ankle. Her clothes rubbed against the floor. Her sweater slid up towards her neck, exposing her lower back.

The surface was cold and rough, and it scraped against her skin.

But, finally, she reached the shelf.

She needed to pause again, get her breathing under control before raising her feet once more. She tried to position them so the tape was directly above the nail. From where she lay, it was difficult to see if she was successful. She just had to try, move her legs back and forth. She had no idea whether it was working or not.

Sweat ran down her forehead, only stopping when it reached the sock in her mouth. Again she felt dizzy. But she didn't stop this time, just continued to wiggle and rub and press her legs against shelf and the nail. She had to get out of there.

Until, suddenly, it felt like there was room between her ankles.

Enough room that she was able to push her legs apart even more. She repeated the movement, back and forth, back and forth. More and more she felt the tape give way.

And then her legs were free.

The freedom filled Emma with a newfound excitement. She could more easily position herself against the shelf now, to do the exact same with the tape around her hands. But with her back to the shelving unit, it was still just as difficult seeing exactly where the nail was. She just had to feel her way. Until ... there. She found it.

She stopped and listened.

Footsteps walking through the basement.

Walter Kroos was on his way.

Emma dug the tape down against the nail.

Harder, faster.

76

The refrigerator door had been left ajar. Samantha pushed it closed, but did not let Jarl Inge out of her sight.

'Is something wrong?' the policeman asked him.

Jarl Inge mumbled something incomprehensible. He groped around with his hands, as if searching for something to hold on to. One hand hit the beer can and knocked it over. With a lightning-quick movement, the policeman grabbed the can and put it back in its place, but that didn't stop the foam from flowing out onto the table.

Blix grabbed the napkin holder on the table, standing up as he did so. The chair hit the wall behind him. Jarl Inge had managed to get a grip on the table, but his upper body swayed.

'He needs some water,' Samantha said.

She turned to the upper cabinets. Turned on the tap at the same time and felt around in her pockets. The other tablet was still in there.

'Can I get you one too?' she asked.

'No thanks,' Blix replied, wiping the table.

She took out a glass and filled it. She held it out to Jarl Inge, who turned to her with narrowed eyes.

'You...?' he slurred. 'What the ... hell ... have you...?'

She pushed the glass into Jarl Inge's hands. He couldn't hold it. Samantha helped lift the glass to his lips, but he couldn't get them to make contact with the rim. The water she tried to pour into his mouth just ran down his chin and throat.

She put the glass down.

'I think we need to call a doctor,' Blix said, gathering up the soaked napkins. 'What has he had today?'

Jarl Inge tried to say something, but no words came out.

'I don't know,' Samantha said. 'He's never been like this before.'

She could feel that there was no strength left in him. She was having to hold him up.

'I don't have a phone,' the policeman said, looking at her expectantly.

Samantha didn't know how to answer him. Her heart was pounding hard against her chest.

'Help me get him over to the couch,' she said. 'He's going to fall.'

Blix came around the other side of the table. Samantha glanced back quickly at the kitchen knives, but there was no time to grab one. The policeman hauled Jarl Inge's arm up and over his shoulder, while Samantha moved over to the other side of the chair. Together they lifted him up.

'He seems intoxicated,' Blix said.

'Wouldn't surprise me,' Samantha said. 'But I haven't seen him drink anything other than beer today.'

They dragged Jarl Inge out of the kitchen. His feet scraped against the floor. Even though there were two of them, it was still an effort, pulling the deadweight of a body. Jarl Inge's breathing had grown laboured. They manoeuvred him over to one of the sofas. Blix laid Jarl Inge over on his side, then straightened up.

'He's completely out of it,' he commented. 'You need to call an ambulance.'

Samantha didn't know what to do.

'Just, stay here with him for a minute,' she said and hurried across the floor into the kitchen. She couldn't remember what she'd done with her phone. It wasn't on the counter, nor was it on the table. It hit her then that she had forgotten to bring it in from the car.

For a second she thought about going out and getting it. She wasn't actually going to call anyone, but the trip outside would buy her some time.

She was short of breath, could feel the panic begin to take hold. Maybe the best thing now, she thought, would be to take the car keys out with her, get in and drive off. Try and get as far away as possible.

Maybe she could get Walter to come up and help. Together they could—

Sounds reached her from the basement.

In the next moment, the policeman was suddenly behind her, standing in the kitchen doorway.

'What are you doing?' he asked. 'Why aren't you calling an ambulance?'

77

There.

The tape fell apart.

She was free.

Emma pushed herself up and tore off the remnants of the tape that were stuck around her wrist and to the sleeve of her jumper. She tried to find the end of the tape that was holding the sock in place in her mouth, but gave up immediately. Instead, she just grabbed the whole piece, ripped it clean off and spat out the sock.

With a gasp, she drew air deep into her lungs.

The door lock clicked. The handle moved downward.

Emma looked around quickly. Grabbed one of the plant pots she had tried to kick off one of the shelves.

In the next moment the door swung inward. Walter's face came into view. With all her might, she swung out her arm. With no time to aim, she didn't get good enough contact. Walter parried the blow and charged at her.

Emma struck once more.

The effort it took forced a roar out of her, but Walter was fast and strong – he stopped the blow and held the pot as he pushed her further back into the room, trampling over the box of wires, and not stopping until he had slammed Emma into the tall cupboard on the far side of the room. He rammed the pot in one sudden, powerful movement into the side of her face. She felt an awful crunching and splitting in her nose and cheek. The pain paralysed her.

Walter threw the pot away. It hit the lid of the freezer before smashing against the brick wall below the basement window.

He put one hand over her mouth and clamped the other around her neck. Pushed her higher up the cupboard door.

Emma kicked upward with her knee and hit him in the crotch. Walter crumpled and let go. It gave Emma enough room to move her arms, and enough time to gather all her strength and push him away – she forgot that she had an injured ankle and pushed off with her legs as well. Walter tripped over the box and fell backwards. Trying to regain his balance, he fumbled for something to grab hold of. His right hand made contact with the door, but not the handle. With his left, he swiped a row of canned goods off of the shelves, landing flat on his back with a groan.

Emma saw her chance.

She bent down and picked up a can. Blood poured out of her nose. She raised the can over her head and threw it at Walter with all the power she could muster. He dodged out of the way and crawled backward. Emma grabbed a basket of magazines and threw it at him. This time, she hit, but only Walter's outstretched hands.

Frantically, breathing wildly, Emma continued to throw whatever she could find – a plastic juice bottle, a serving plate, a saucepan. A bag of sugar burst as it hit the floor. Walter couldn't do anything other than protect himself from the random objects flying his way, but none of them did much damage.

Emma tried to kick him while he was still down, but Walter saw the move coming and caught her foot. Emma remained standing, hopping and wobbling on her other leg, while Walter pulled her towards him. Forced her down.

Within a second, the situation had flipped.

Walter was on top of her.

He broke through Emma's protective arms and again wrapped his hands around her neck. Emma tried to scream but no sound came out. She couldn't breathe.

She tried to squirm free, tear his hands away, but they were locked. Second by second she felt the pressure between her temples increase. The wildness in Walter's eyes made her realise that he wasn't going to stop until she stopped fighting. Before she stopped breathing.

Something was wrong.

Blix had guessed as much as soon as he set foot in the house. Now he could see it in Samantha Kasin's eyes.

Before he could say anything, he heard muffled noises coming from somewhere else in the building.

'Is someone else here?' he asked.

Samantha didn't answer.

'I can take care of Jarl Inge now,' she said. A brief smile flashed across her face. 'Thanks for your help.'

More sounds. Coming from the floor below. Something that sounded like a half-choked scream.

Blix looked at Samantha quizzically. 'What was that?'

She didn't answer, instead just retreated back towards the kitchen counter. Lowered her head, but held his gaze through the hair that had fallen over her face.

Blix walked out into the hallway, tried the nearest door. A staircase led down to the basement. In one fell swoop, Samantha had snatched a knife from the magnetic strip off the wall and lunged at him. Blix barely managed to jump aside. Samantha whirled around and waved the knife in front of her. Blix threw himself backward, into the living room. The next time she slashed at him, he grabbed her wrist and tried to wrench the knife loose.

Samantha threw her leg out in a kick that hit him in the groin. Blix bent double. She tore her arm free, screamed and lurched after him again. The knife caught his upper arm, slicing a deep gash in his bicep. Blix backed away, his hand holding the stinging wound.

Samantha took a swipe at him again, pushing Blix further backward. He came into contact with some furniture behind him, managed to skirt round it and get the armchair between him and Samantha.

'Walter!' she cried, turning her head slightly, calling over her shoulder for help.

Blix grabbed the armrests of the chair and pulled it towards him slightly, before launching himself against it and shoving it toward Samantha in one sudden movement. The impact was substantial, and it made her stagger back, waving her arms to keep her balance. Blix tipped the chair over and sent the back of it into her again. She let out a cry and fell. Tried to twist around to catch herself, but couldn't stop the trajectory of her fall. Her temple smacked against the edge of the table. Her body fell to the floor. Samantha lay motionless. Her hand slowly releasing its grip on the knife.

Blix took no time to see if she was okay. Instead, he dashed back into the hall and hurled himself down the stairs.

The door at the far end of the basement was open. The room was in disarray. Two people were on the floor fighting. Emma was losing, thrashing around with her arms, her legs splayed beneath the man on top of her – Walter Kroos. He pressed his full weight onto her, his hands clamped around her neck.

Blix was across the room in mere seconds, and kicked him, striking him in the hip. Walter toppled onto his side, but didn't let go. Instead, he dragged Emma with him so that she lay over him, her back to Blix like a shield.

He lifted his leg again and stamped the heel of his shoe into Walter's kneecap. A scream of pain filled the basement around them. Emma's movements grew weaker, limp. Blix grabbed her shoulders while kicking at Walter's face. With one more surge of effort, he pulled Emma into him. They tumbled backward and landed on their backs.

Emma gasped for air. Walter spat blood and heaved himself up, but could only manage to stand on one leg. Blix got up again and grabbed the nearest thing he could find: a kettle. He held it in his hand and swung it round with force. The bottom hit Walter's hand. With the next swinging strike, Blix aimed higher, at his head, but just missed him.

Walter backed away towards the tall cupboard. Suddenly he raised his hands above his head and shouted:

'*Halt!* Stop!'

Blix tightened his grip on the handle of the kettle, but remained where he was. Behind him, Emma spluttered, struggling to catch her breath. Her throat rasped as she tried to breathe.

Walter said something in German that Blix didn't understand.

'Get on the ground!' Blix demanded in English, pointing to the floor with his free hand. Walter dropped to his knees with his hands raised, then used one of them to support himself slightly as he lowered himself onto his stomach. Blix dropped the kettle and stepped forward, placing a knee on Walter's shoulders and pulling his hands behind his back.

Blix turned to Emma.

'Are you okay?'

She sat with her knees under her chest and a hand against her neck.

'Yes,' she answered, her voice croaky.

'I need something to restrain him with,' Blix said, looking around.

Emma pushed herself onto her feet.

'I can find the tape,' she said, leaning against the doorframe.

'No, stay down here,' Blix said sharply. 'Samantha's up there.'

He reached for some wires on the floor nearby. Used one of them to tie a knot around Walter's wrist.

Managed to tighten it. He secured his legs the same way.

'Where's your phone?' he asked when he had finished.

'Destroyed.' Emma cleared her throat. 'But what ... what...'

There was no time to explain. Blix grabbed her by the arm and led her out of the storage room. At the bottom of the stairs, he stopped to listen.

Sounds coming from outside.

'Stay here,' Blix told Emma, and ran up the stairs.

As he reached the first floor, the front door flew open. A man in a police uniform drew his gun when he saw Blix. Behind him, another officer did the same.

Blix held up his hands. The gash in his arm made him wince.

'It's Blix!' someone shouted.

A plainclothes officer with a police badge around his neck pushed his way forward.

Nicolai Wibe.

'I've restrained Walter Kroos,' Blix informed him, without lowering his hands. 'He's downstairs in the basement, third door on the right.'

He made a motion with his head as if to direct him, and took a step away from the door. The policemen advanced without holstering their weapons.

'Emma Ramm is also down there,' he called after them.

Movements from the living room made him turn to look. Samantha was standing now, propping herself up against the table. She was bleeding from a wound on the side of her head. She seemed confused.

'She's been hiding him here,' Blix said.

Two officers were ordered to see to her. Blix lowered his hands and warned them that Jarl Inge Ree was lying unconscious on the couch.

Wibe came up to him, seemingly unsure of what to say.

'You're bleeding,' he observed.

'It's nothing serious,' Blix replied.

A stocky, older officer seemed to be in command. He held out his hand and greeted Blix.

'Arvid Borvik,' he said. 'An ambulance is on its way.'

Behind them, Emma slowly made her way up from the basement. She stopped next to Blix. Put a hand on his shoulder.

'Gard Fosse called,' Wibe explained. 'He'd spoken to Merete.'

Blix nodded.

'He was worried you'd gotten yourself mixed up in something,' Wibe continued. 'The patrol found your car here.'

Blix was about to explain, but held back. He could see that Emma needed some fresh air. Together, they went out onto the front steps. A gust of wind whipped a sheet of cold rain at them.

Outside, the area was bathed in flashing blue lights. Among the police cars, space had been made for an ambulance. A woman in a red and fluorescent green jacket came running over to Emma with a blanket. She wrapped it around her shoulders and led her to the ambulance.

Emma sat in the back.

Blix checked his watch and worked out the timings in his head. If he left right away, he could make it back to the prison in time, he thought, sitting down next to her.

EPILOGUE

Despite the fact there was still well over an hour until the widely antici-
pated verdict, a large crowd had already gathered outside the entrance
to the courtroom when Emma arrived. The journalists formed an organised flock around her.

'What are your thoughts on Blix's chances of being acquitted?'

'Do you think the arrest of Walter Kroos and his Norwegian girlfriend may help the judges look at his case with more lenient eyes?'

'If Blix were to be acquitted, do you think he has a future as a police
officer?'

Emma stopped abruptly and announced to the crowd:

'I think I'll wait until the Court of Appeal has had its say, then I'll
have mine.'

Blix's lawyer Einar Harnes was waiting for her just inside the courthouse. He squeezed her hand softly and escorted her into a waiting
room. Blix stood up and smiled when he saw who it was.

They met with a hug that lasted a little longer than usual.

He smelled good.

He looked well too, Emma thought. Clean shaven, fresh haircut. The
new suit looked better on him. It was a tighter, more tailored fit – it
made him look younger.

They sat down.

'I'll be back in a bit,' Harnes told him. 'Just don't run away in the
meantime.'

Emma grinned, but as soon as the lawyer had closed the door behind
them, a heavy silence wrapped around them.

Blix grabbed the jug of water on the table and poured it into a plastic
cup for her. Picked up his own and spun it around and around a few
times; it was empty.

'How are you?' she asked.

'Good,' Blix answered at once. 'Or – as good as I can be, I think. I
don't really know.'

'You're nervous.'

'It'd be a lie to say otherwise.'

'You might be a free man by this afternoon.'

'True...'

If not, he would be driven back to Ullersmo. Back to his cell. To more days behind bars. More years spent alongside the men he'd told her about: Grubben, the little Dutchman, Jakobsen, Nyberget. Even for Emma, the thought was too painful for her to contemplate. What it must be like for Blix, she could only imagine.

'I got a letter from Jarl Inge Ree,' Blix told her.

Emma realised that he wanted to talk about something else.

'I didn't think he was the type to write letters?' she said.

'It wasn't that long,' Blix explained. 'He just wanted to say thank you, I think. Wrote that he would organise for a bottle of brandy or something to be smuggled in for me.'

Emma smiled. 'So, if this does go well, what are you going to do?' she asked, taking a sip of her water.

'I have no idea,' he replied. 'I haven't allowed myself to think that far ahead yet.'

'No idea at all?'

'None.'

They sat for a while in silence.

'What about you?' he eventually asked. 'Are you back at work full-time?'

Emma tensed and untensed her fingers a little. 'I, uh ... I've actually written my last article.'

Blix looked up at her. 'You've quit news.no?'

'I've quit journalism altogether.'

'Why—' Blix stopped.

'I can't go on like this,' Emma answered anyway. 'There have just been far too many close calls, far too many times. If I had hair, I'm sure it would've gone grey long ago.'

She pulled the wig back a little.

Blix smiled, but quickly turned serious again. 'Are you sure that's what you want?'

'No,' Emma admitted, with a smile. 'But I want to live. I want to start yoga and bake bread and ... go on a shopping spree in Sweden.'

'Get a husband and a house and kids, like everyone else?'

Emma thought for a moment. 'I don't think I'll ever be like everyone else.'

Blix leant back in his seat. 'So, what'll you do instead?'

She raised her palms. 'Become a bus driver, maybe.'

'A bus driver?'

Emma laughed at the surprised face in front of her.

'No, not literally. But ... something else, at least. I've had a few offers to write more books, but I don't know if I really want to do that either.'

Blix crossed one leg over the other. 'What did Anita Grønvold say about you quitting?'

'She thought I was joking at first,' Emma said, laughing again. 'But then, when she realised I wasn't, she seemed pretty shocked. And sad, I think.'

'I can understand that.'

'I'm welcome back anytime apparently, but I know that's not going to happen.'

Blix looked down at his fingers for a moment. Again, the air in the room felt dense

'How does it feel?' he asked, clearing his throat. 'Now you've made the decision.'

'Pretty good, actually. I immediately felt lighter.'

'Then you know it's the right one.'

'Sure. And it's kind of nice too, not really knowing what tomorrow will bring.'

'I can't really say I feel the same right now, Emma.'

'No, of course ... I understand. I'm sorry.'

They sat in silence again for a short while.

'But here we are,' Blix said. 'With neither of us knowing a single thing in this world. About anything.'

Emma smiled. 'That's something in and of itself,' she said. 'The fact we know that.'

'Ah, Socrates would be proud of us,' Blix joked.

She grinned.

On the wall, a digital clock flipped over by a digit.

Then another.

'Who or what was the last thing you wrote about then?' Blix asked.

'Arvid Borvik,' Emma responded. 'About the investigation and his suspension.'

'I've not been able to read the papers recently. How did he take it?'

'He still insists he hasn't done anything wrong.'

'Doing nothing can also be wrong,' Blix stated. 'Had he done what he was supposed to do when Samantha Kasin was raped all those years ago, then two people might still be alive today.'

Grey light streamed in through the window from a sky that threatened rain. Outside: the sound of car tyres rushing past the courthouse.

'Is Walter Kroos back in Germany yet?'

Emma shook her head. 'He's still in custody here, but is cooperating unreservedly, apparently. Samantha is currently under psychiatric evaluation. The impact of what happened that summer, in 2004, probably went much deeper than most noticed or were aware of. There's actually a fair chance that she will never be brought to justice.'

Voices and footsteps reached them, approaching from the hallway.

A woman called out for a man named Svein.

A while passed without either of them saying anything.

'Has Merete forgiven you?'

Blix looked down at his lap.

'For taking the car – yes. For everything else...' He didn't go on.

'She was supposed to be here today, I think,' he finally continued. 'But I don't know.'

Again, silence.

'Are you still hoping that you'll eventually find your way back to each other?'

Blix looked up at her and answered promptly: 'No.' Followed by a quick laugh.

'Are you sure?'

Blix squirmed. They had never talked about Merete, or at least, not beyond the factual and superficial. It was not in his nature to open up about things he found painful or difficult.

'I think at this point, I've probably disappointed her a few too many times,' he said at last, squeezing the plastic cup a little. It cracked.

Just before ten o'clock, there was a knock on the door. His lawyer, Einar Harnes, stepped inside.

'Right Alexander ... the judge is ready for you,' he said.

Blix took a deep breath. Needed a moment before pushing his chair back. And even when he did, and had tucked it back under the table, he didn't let go. His eyes were fixed on something indeterminate in front of him.

'Okay,' he said after a few seconds. 'Let's get this over with.'

ACKNOWLEDGEMENTS

(phone ringing)
(picking up)
Thomas: Hey Jørn.
Jørn: Hey. You got any scars?
(beat)
(beat)
Thomas: Hm?
Jørn: Scars, Thomas. Physical ones or ... you know. Mental ... things.
(beat)
Thomas: You're kidding, right?
Jørn: No.
Thomas: You want to know what kind of scars I have and where they are?
Jørn: Just if you'd like to share.
(beat)
(beat)
Thomas: I have a—
Jørn: I'm kidding.
(laughter)
(even longer laughter)
Jørn: Since *Stigma* is about scars and ... everything, I thought that ... you know.
Thomas: You're very funny.
Jørn: Thanks.
Thomas: I didn't mean it.
(beat)
(sigh)
Thomas: I have many scars.
Jørn: I don't want to know.
(beat)
(sigh)

Thomas: Did you actually want anything since you're calling?

Jørn: Yes. Tell me who you want to thank this time, now that our book is finished, so I can pass it along to West the Best.

Thomas: You mean West Camel. Our editor.

Jørn: Yes. He writes books as well. You should read them.

Thomas: Maybe I should thank him for *that*. For them.

Jørn: You should. They're good. He's a good editor too.

Thomas: I know.

(beat)

(sigh)

Jørn: He told us to keep it short this time.

Thomas: Did he now...

Jørn: Yes he did.

Thomas: Good thing you asked me about my scars, then

Jørn: I was kidding.

Thomas: No kidding.

Jørn: Hm?

Thomas: Never mind.

(beat)

(sigh)

Thomas: Okay, so here it goes. I want to thank Karen, our publisher, for ... well ... everything.

Jørn: That's a bit vague, no?

Thomas: Vague, but true. She's the one publishing us. That *is* everything.

Jørn: That *is* true. I second that.

Thomas: She has a last name too. Sullivan.

Jørn: I know.

Thomas: And a son named Cole, who helps us spread the word about what we're doing.

Jørn: All our words, actually.

Thomas: You're very funny, Jørn.

Jørn: Thanks.

Thomas: I didn't mean it.

(beat)

(sigh)

Jørn: Anyone else?

Thomas: You're leaving it all up to me as usual.

Jørn: I have my wife and kids to thank. And Theodor.

Thomas: I'm noticing that you're using the name of your dog, but not the name of your wife and kids.

Jørn: Well. They don't come running when I call.

Thomas: I wonder why. Maybe I should stop doing the same.

Jørn: Hm?

Thomas: Never mind.

(beat)

(sigh)

Thomas: I think I'd like to thank about twenty-five Hollywood composers. Maybe a few more.

Jørn: (...)

Jørn: (...)

Thomas: West told us to keep it short, so I'm not naming them.

Jørn: Okay.

Thomas: Same as you with your family.

Jørn: I don't have twenty-five kids, Thomas.

Thomas: Are you sure?

Jørn: Yes.

Thomas: Good to know.

(beat)

(sigh)

Thomas: I could name them, if you like.

Jørn: My kids?

Thomas: No, Jørn, the other ones. The composers.

Jørn: Ah. No thank you.

(beat)

(sigh)

Jørn: This is getting long.

Thomas: I know. West the Best will kill us.

Jørn: Maybe he will edit the hell out of this. I'm going to take my dog for a walk.

Thomas: Do *you* have any scars, Jørn?

Jørn: (...)

Jørn: (...)

Thomas: We're putting quite a few of them in book five as well. Maybe—

Jørn: No.

Thomas: No?

Jørn: No.

Thomas: (...)

Thomas: (...)

Thomas: Why do I get the feeling that no means yes.

Jørn: I don't know, Sherlock. I'm hanging up now.

Thomas: Okay, Scarface.

(beat)

(sigh)

Thomas: I have an idea for book six, by the way.

Jørn: Oh yeah?

Thomas: Yes. It's about scars, too.

Jørn: You're joking.

Thomas: Yes. Well, no. It's all about scars, isn't it. In some shape or form.

Jørn: True.

Thomas: I had chicken pox when I was a kid. Got a scar on my bum and everything.

Jørn: Please. Paint us a picture.

Thomas: I might.

Jørn: I hope book six isn't going to be about *that*.

Thomas: No, Jørn, it's not. Give my best to your nameless family.

(beat)

(sigh)

Jørn: They're called Beate, Sondre and Marte.

Thomas: I know, Jørn.